THE PRIMROSE MURDER SOCIETY

THE PRIMROSE MURDER SOCIETY

A NOVEL

STACY HACKNEY

WILLIAM MORROW
An Imprint of HarperCollins*Publishers*

Without limiting the exclusive rights of any author, contributor or the publisher of this publication, any unauthorized use of this publication to train generative artificial intelligence (AI) technologies is expressly prohibited. HarperCollins also exercise their rights under Article 4(3) of the Digital Single Market Directive 2019/790 and expressly reserve this publication from the text and data mining exception.

This is a work of fiction. Names, characters, places, and incidents are products of the author's imagination or are used fictitiously and are not to be construed as real. Any resemblance to actual events, locales, organizations, or persons, living or dead, is entirely coincidental.

THE PRIMROSE MURDER SOCIETY. Copyright © 2026 by Stacy Hackney. All rights reserved. No part of this book may be used or reproduced in any manner whatsoever without written permission except in the case of brief quotations embodied in critical articles and reviews. For information, address HarperCollins Publishers, 195 Broadway, New York, NY 10007. In Europe, HarperCollins Publishers, Macken House, 39/40 Mayor Street Upper, Dublin 1, D01 C9W8, Ireland.

HarperCollins books may be purchased for educational, business, or sales promotional use. For information, please email the Special Markets Department at SPsales@harpercollins.com.

hc.com

FIRST EDITION

Interior text design by Diahann Sturge-Campbell
Knife illustration © vladvm50/Stock.Adobe.com

Library of Congress Cataloging-in-Publication Data

Names: Hackney, Stacy author
Title: The primrose murder society : a novel / Stacy Hackney.
Description: First edition. | New York : William Morrow, 2026.
Identifiers: LCCN 2025016245 | ISBN 9780063466029 hardcover | ISBN 9780063466005 ebook
Subjects: LCGFT: Detective and mystery fiction | Novels
Classification: LCC PS3608.A2535 P75 2026 | DDC 813/.6—dc23/eng/20250502
LC record available at https://lccn.loc.gov/2025016245

ISBN 978-0-06-346602-9

Printed in the United States of America

26 27 28 29 30 LBC 5 4 3 2 1

For Roby

THE PRIMROSE MURDER SOCIETY

Chapter One

Lila Shaw's daughter did not look capable of hurting a ladybug, much less a teacher, despite the current accusations to the contrary. For one thing, Bea barely reached Lila's elbow. For another, her arms were the width of a crepe myrtle branch, delicate and decidedly unthreatening. Finally, there was the wash of tears varnishing Bea's big blue eyes. Lila's heart squeezed, and she reached across the narrow gap between their chairs to press her daughter's hand reassuringly. Bea glared up at her; a searing look of fury.

Then again, looks could be deceiving.

If Mrs. Givens, the head of school, noticed the interaction between Lila and Bea, she didn't comment. Instead she tented her hands on top of her desk. Her nails glowed a soft pink. Lila's nails were ragged these days, the biweekly manicures all but memories.

Mrs. Givens inhaled as if needing extra air before she began. "I realize Bea has experienced a rough few months with her father's troubles."

Troubles.

Yes, well, that was certainly one way to refer to the fact that the Justice Department had indicted Ryan on multiple counts of fraud after he fled the country to avoid arrest seven months ago.

"Unfortunately, this isn't the first time Bea has been in my office this year," Mrs. Givens continued.

It was more like the fifth time. Lila was entirely too familiar with the pale blue walls, the impressive bookshelves and gold-framed diplomas, and the cream brocade draperies framing the manicured front lawn of Meritt Academy. Yet the Shaws were a well-known and respected Eastern Virginia family, even with Ryan's scandal hovering in the background. They'd donated heavily to Meritt Academy for years. Lila herself was a former student. She could smooth this over, same as she had with the past four incidents.

"I understand your concerns, but I'm sure this is a misunderstanding. Bea didn't mean to throw a book. It probably slipped or—or she was joking around. She didn't intend to hurt anyone," Lila said, trying for a bright smile. Once upon a time, people had loved her smile.

Bea mumbled under her breath, and Lila curled up her toes. If Bea would only keep quiet and let Lila do the talking, but since when had her daughter ever done what Lila wanted? Bea's attire was proof of that. She wore an Atlanta Braves T-shirt that hung halfway down her legs and was marred in several places with unidentified brown stains. The shirt had belonged to Ryan, and Bea insisted on wearing it everywhere. At first, Lila had forbidden Bea from leaving the house in it, but had eventually given up when Bea refused to go to school without the shirt tucked into the navy uniform skort. After all the lawbreaking in their family, Lila figured it was best not to add truancy to the list.

"Did you have something to say, Bea?" Mrs. Givens asked.

"I think she said *I'm sorry*," Lila answered quickly before Bea could reply.

"No, I *said* that I did mean to throw the book, but I was trying to hit someone else," Bea said.

Lila's stomach roiled. Mrs. Givens blanched, looking shocked at Bea's remark.

"At this school, we don't throw books at anyone. Mrs. Rancer was bruised and scared by your behavior," Mrs. Givens said. "You owe her an apology."

Another child might blink, might cry, might drop her head in shame. Bea looked straight ahead and said, "I am sorry that Mrs. Rancer got in the way of the book."

Mrs. Givens sighed and studied Bea for several seconds. "Bea, will you wait outside for a moment with Mrs. Wainwright while I talk to your mother alone?"

Bea slipped out of the chair at once, clearly relieved that her part in this meeting was over. She didn't glance back at Lila in apology or fear. Bea merely opened the heavy wooden door of the office and let it shut slowly behind her.

"I'll talk to her. I'm sure there's an explanation for what happened, and she'll apologize properly to Mrs. Rancer," Lila said into the silence of the room.

"I'm afraid that isn't enough this time. This school doesn't condone violence in any form." Mrs. Givens looked down at the neatly stacked papers, adjusting one until the corners paralleled the desk. When she finally met Lila's gaze, her mouth turned down. "In fact, I don't believe Meritt Academy is the appropriate place for Bea at this time."

Lila sat back, the breath sluicing from her body. Meritt Academy was one of the only things they still had. Her in-laws had agreed to make the tuition payments after Ryan left. It was the most stable part of Bea's life, and now they were going to lose that too.

Lila leaned forward, aware of the tightness of her lips and the shaking in her voice. "Please, if you'll reconsider, take into account Bea's home life as you mentioned. I'm sure this will never happen again. I promise it won't. I'll deal with this at home, you can rest assured—"

"I'm sorry, Lila. I don't believe everything I read in the papers about Ryan, and I was more than willing to extend Bea a fair amount of grace to get through this difficult period in her life, especially since you and Ryan are both alumni. Unfortunately, her behavior is not improving. She's disruptive to the other children and now this. I know this isn't what you want to hear, but it's best for everyone. A new school might be what she needs to move forward."

"Is there anything I can do to change your mind?" Lila asked, sounding desperate.

"I'm sorry. There's not." Mrs. Givens stood, signaling the end of their meeting.

Lila rose on shaky legs, hearing the finality in Mrs. Givens's voice. She'd come in here expecting the worst—suspension, perhaps medical bills, certainly embarrassment—but she had not expected her daughter to be expelled from fourth grade. This was partially her fault. She should have disciplined Bea more after the prior problems. She'd tried. Of course she'd tried. There were television restrictions and lectures, most of which Bea ignored. It was hard for Lila to stand firm, especially when she knew Bea missed her father.

Mrs. Givens was still talking about how she saw no need to include the details of Bea's latest transgression in her transcript. She was calling the decision for Bea to leave Meritt Academy a mutual one, not an expulsion. This was a nod to the Shaw family. It was a kindness too, but Lila couldn't thank her then. Lila's mind raced with questions—*where would Bea go to school, what would other parents think, how could she possibly tell her mother-in-law, Patricia?*

Lila stumbled to the door and stepped into the waiting room. Mrs. Wainwright, the school secretary, wore a knowing look of pity on her face. Standing beside her was Amy Marshall, the current head of the Parents' Association. Lila's entire body wilted at the sight. She'd thought this day couldn't get any worse, but she was obviously wrong.

Amy's eyes widened in surprise and her eyebrows lifted a millimeter, which was as far as they could go with her regular Botox treatments. "My goodness, Lila. It's been ages."

Amy's gaze swept over Lila, taking in the sweatpants and old Clemson sweatshirt. Lila knew she looked awful. She should have changed before rushing up to the school but had only thought of getting to Bea and rectifying the situation, for all the good that plan had done. Amy, on the other hand, had taken her time preparing for her meeting. Lila recognized the deceptively casual Alix of Bohemia dress and Golden Goose tennis shoes, a combined cost of over fourteen hundred dollars. It was exactly the kind of outfit Lila would have worn to the school before Ryan left.

"Hi, Amy," Lila said and ducked her head to keep Amy from noticing that she hadn't put on mascara. She gestured for Bea to hop off the chair and scooped up her purple backpack. "We're in a bit of a rush."

"Am I still in trouble?" Bea piped up.

"We can talk about that later," Lila whispered.

"I can't believe a precious little girl like you would cause any trouble," Amy said in a high-pitched, cooing voice that Lila knew Bea would despise.

"I threw a book and hit my teacher," Bea said flatly before adding, "On purpose."

Amy straightened. Somehow her eyebrows raised another millimeter. She glanced at Mrs. Wainwright, who clucked beneath her breath. Lila edged toward the door, tugging Bea's shoulder. This entire situation was humiliating enough without Amy reporting back to every mama at Meritt Academy about her daughter's violent tendencies.

"It's been months since you came to book club," Amy said.

Lila flushed at this subtle attack. Amy and Lila both knew that Lila wasn't welcome at book club. Someone had removed Lila from the book club group text immediately after Ryan's indictment was made public.

"I've been busy," Lila said.

"Oh, us too, you wouldn't believe our schedule. We just got back from Turks and Caicos for spring break, and Caleb has a lacrosse tournament coming up this weekend. We've had to add a fourth day at the barn for Charlotte because she can't stand to be away from her horse, and I'm up here every other day planning the spring show. I'm about run off my feet." Amy smiled, a thin, tight expression that lacked all warmth.

"Well, good luck with everything," Lila said, bolting for the exit. Bea ducked under her arm.

Lila was only two steps into the hallway when Amy appeared, leaving the waiting room. "Lila, hold on a minute."

"Yes." Lila hesitated, wishing she had the courage to keep walking. Bea was already halfway down the hall, stopping at the water fountain.

Amy's face twisted into a scowl and she spoke in a low tone. "I thought you should know that everyone is still talking about you. You can deny it all you want, but the entire town knows you were involved in Ryan's fraud. You're not the brightest, but you stole a lot of money from a lot of people. Don't show up at the club or barre class or River Wine Night or anywhere. No one wants to see you."

Lila's vision narrowed to Amy's pursed lips painted fleshy pink like overcooked salmon. She could tell Amy had been saving up this speech for months, hoping to run into her.

"Do you have anything to say?" Amy hissed.

Lila's mouth opened but no sound emerged. She wanted to say she hadn't known about Ryan's scheme and if she had known, she would have stopped him. She wanted to say Ryan had deceived her too and left her behind with nothing. But the words were stuck, clogged in her throat.

"You're pathetic." Amy stomped back into the waiting room and slammed the door, the bang reverberating down the hall.

Lila's heart pounded and her ribs pulled tight. She backed away from the waiting room as if it was radioactive, staring at the wood grain of the door. After a moment, she hurried down the hall toward Bea.

"Is your friend mad at you?" Bea asked.

"She's not my friend," Lila said. "Come on, let's get out of here."

They walked to the parking lot in silence. Amy hadn't told Lila anything she didn't already believe. She'd gotten the angry emails from acquaintances, every committee she'd served on politely asked her to drop off, and no one invited Bea over for playdates. Her wider circle of friends had narrowed to Daphne and, though she still texted to check in, Lila hadn't seen her since Christmas. Ryan had left seven months ago, and she'd spent most of them hiding in her house. She'd *known* everyone in town hated her, but Amy's diatribe made it all the more real.

"Do I get to go home for the rest of the day?" Bea asked when they reached the car.

Lila closed her eyes, a wave of exhaustion breaking over her. "Bea, this isn't a holiday. Why would you throw a book at your teacher?"

"I already told you I didn't mean to hit Mrs. Rancer. I threw the book at Jackson who's a jerk and deserved it," Bea said, not looking at all remorseful. "And besides it was only a paperback. I wasn't trying to bludgeon him to death." Bea was obsessed with watching reruns of *Murder, She Wrote*, which had a lot of bludgeoning.

"Since we're going home, can you make mac and cheese for

lunch? But don't cook it in the microwave like last time. The cheese tasted gross," Bea continued.

Lila stared at her in disbelief. Bea was acting as if their conversation about Mrs. Rancer was over and done, as if her behavior only warranted a ten-second reprimand and she could now move on to criticizing Lila's cooking.

A guttural noise erupted from Lila's throat. "We're not talking about lunch right now! This is serious. You were expelled. That means you can't go back to Meritt Academy. *Ever*."

Bea froze. Her mouth gaped open, her eyes widened. A bolt of satisfaction surged through Lila. *There*. Bea finally understood the consequences of her behavior. Maybe now she would regret what she'd done and apologize to Lila for all the months of trouble.

Snapping her mouth shut, Bea tugged open the back door of their car. "Good. I hate Meritt Academy." She got in and slammed the door behind her.

Lila reached for the car door handle, her blood already pumping. This conversation was not over. Bea was about to get the biggest lecture of her life. Her cell phone buzzed from her pocket. She pulled it out and saw the name—Willingham, Bates & Carter—flash across her screen. Her stomach spasmed. This was the law firm representing Ryan. She pressed the green answer button and clenched the phone to her ear.

"Hello?"

"Yes, Lila, this is Gerald Partridge." Gerald cleared his throat. "I have some news. I'm afraid it's not particularly good."

Lila's legs turned to jelly. She leaned against the car, lightheaded. What now? *What else?* She glanced at Bea, who glared at her from behind the windshield.

"As you're aware, the government filed a motion to seize Mr. Shaw's property, which includes the house on Bluff Lane. I've done everything I could to fight it, but with Ryan having fled and the house in his name, we didn't have much of a defense. The judge is allowing the seizure," Gerald said.

"What does that mean for us?" Lila asked. She'd known this was a possibility. Gerald had warned her the government would try to seize their home as part of the case against Ryan, as *restitution*, he called it, but she hadn't believed it would really happen. After all, it was their home, where they lived, and Ryan wasn't even a part of that home anymore.

"It means you will have to vacate the house . . . by next week." Gerald cleared his throat again. "I'm sorry. I know it's sudden. I'll email you all the details and legal documents today, but you should start making immediate arrangements."

Lila dropped the phone; it clattered onto the pavement and went silent. The nausea hit her all at once. She bent over, gripping both hands on her knees. She reminded herself to breathe, to not vomit in the Meritt Academy parking lot.

She was losing the house. There was nowhere for her to go. Last week, she'd gotten fired from her customer service job because she'd had to take days off when Bea was sick. She had a rapidly dwindling bank account and couldn't afford to put a deposit on an apartment. Her in-laws had moved permanently to Palm Beach last year to avoid their son's scandal and made it clear that while they would pay for Ryan's defense and Bea's school, they expected Lila to pay for everything else.

If there was ever a question as to whether Lila Shaw had failed at life, the answer had become glaringly obvious. At thirty-five years old, she'd ended up homeless, in a failed marriage, with an empty bank account and a child who'd gotten kicked out of fourth grade. There was a horrible yawning pit in her stomach. She had never felt more alone in her life.

Sinking down onto the curb, she reached for her phone, noticing the screen was now cracked. There was only one option left. She scrolled through her contacts and clicked on one, listening to the phone ring before a voice came over the line. "Mama, we'll take the Primrose apartment."

Chapter Two

The Primrose did not look like a typical murder site. Stretching up five stories to a peaked roof and a circular tower, the building itself was clad in elegant rose-colored brick with large arched windows and cream stone trim. The circular slate driveway was lined with red azaleas and Mercedes sedans. The building looked safe and luxurious, a place where nothing bad could happen. Bea would never have to know about its dark past, and Lila herself had plenty of other problems. An unsolved murder from twenty years ago didn't even rank in the top fifty.

"It's pretty," Bea said, tipping up her pointed chin to stare at the top of the Primrose.

Lila exhaled at the unexpectedly positive comment. She had feared Bea would proclaim her hatred for the Primrose at first sight.

"This is a fun adventure. We're going to love living here. I know it," Lila said and squeezed her daughter's arm, injecting as much enthusiasm as she could into her voice. An adventure was not what she would call it if she was being honest. Desperation was probably a better description of their current life status.

"I do like it already." Bea beamed a rare smile. "Mostly because of the murder."

Lila swallowed, snared in her daughter's expectant gaze. "What . . . there's no . . . I mean, how do you—"

"Google," Bea said by way of explanation.

Of course. Google. Anyone who spent two minutes researching the Primrose would come across the story of Sophia Kent's unsolved murder. Lila really needed to put those parental controls on her laptop.

"Let's see what the inside looks like," Lila said, changing the subject. If she pretended like the murder never happened, maybe Bea would forget about it.

Lila picked up a suitcase in either hand. One was filled with photo albums and her grandma's candlesticks, the other with clothes. Bea pulled a single roller suitcase behind her. It was all they had left. Lila missed her Breville espresso machine (confiscated by the government) and Isabel Marant sandals (sold to pay the electric bill) and the currant rose–scented candles (broken by Bea in a fit of anger).

They made their way across the gray cobblestones. The cream awning over the front double doors announced the name in grand, black script—*The Primrose*. Lawrence Pfeifer, a noted Virginia architect, had designed the building back in the early 1900s as a luxury apartment hotel. Considered a historic landmark due to its aesthetic influence on the Richmond landscape, the Primrose was now an upscale condo building for adults over the age of fifty-five.

They stepped through the heavy wooden double doors into the lobby. Cream marble floors stretched out in either direction, and the ceiling was at least fifteen feet high with elaborate gingerbread trim. The walls were clad in a gold damask wallpaper, which shimmered above and below the large arched windows. An ornate chandelier dripped crystals and sent shards of rainbow lights flickering on the polished wood of a gilt-edged round table, topped with an impressive arrangement of fresh hydrangeas and peonies. Bea drew in a breath of delight, and Lila was suddenly hopeful that this was the right decision after all.

Two women and a man were seated on twin taupe velvet sofas facing each other in a small seating area off to the right of a grand piano. It was only one o'clock in the afternoon, but all three sipped large glasses filled with ice cubes and bronze liquid that was clearly alcohol. They were over the age of seventy-five and staring straight at Lila.

"She's not even wearing a crop top." One of the women slid on a pair of glasses that hung from a chain around her neck, sounding disappointed. She wore the odd combination of a sweater embroidered with cats and Alexander McQueen platform tennis shoes.

"I told you not every young person wears crop tops." The other older woman was taller with a gray bob that hit at her chin.

"But that's all I see on the TikTok," the cat-sweater woman protested. "That, and a lot of girls applying their makeup while they talk about who hurt their feelings."

"Men are allowed to get their feelings hurt too. I learned that from my granddaughter's therapist," the man said. "I meant to tell Florence that she hurt my feelings yesterday when she told us about the Faberleys' divorce."

"I was stating a fact. It has nothing to do with you," the woman with the gray bob said.

"Divorce is trigger-happy for me," the man said solemnly.

"I don't think you're using that term right," the woman with the gray bob said.

Lila stepped forward and called out, "Hello. We're looking for Susanna Moore."

Before the elderly trio could respond, a door swung open to Lila's left and a thirty-something woman in a severe black dress appeared in the doorway. "I'm Susanna Moore."

"Oh hi! There you are, appearing out of nowhere. Sorry we're a little late. This place is gorgeous," Lila enthused.

"One moment." Susanna disappeared back behind the door without explanation.

Meanwhile, the two women and man rose from the sofas as quickly as their canes and walkers would allow and scattered down the hall. No one spoke to Lila. She looked down at herself and brushed at her pilled pink sweater. Why was she surprised? She didn't look as if she belonged in this expensive building. Heck, she *didn't* belong. Everyone had probably vowed to steer clear of the new resident who was maybe a criminal, abandoned by her husband, and didn't wear crop tops. She thought of how her old tennis partner, Linley Moore, had pretended not to see Lila at the grocery store last week. She considered Patricia's deep sigh over the phone when Lila broke the news about Bea's expulsion—*good Lord, Lila, can't you do anything right?* Lila's face flushed. Her life was such an embarrassment. No wonder people avoided her.

The door swung open once again. Susanna's face was pale, and her expression was no-nonsense. "I expected you ten minutes ago."

Lila plastered on a smile. "I'm sorry. I left a message there was a big accident on the highway and—"

"I've had to push back my other obligation." Susanna's thin lips puckered up into a smaller, firmer line.

Several beats passed. Lila scrambled for something to say. Ten minutes wasn't that late, especially when she had driven over two hours in traffic from Norfolk. "You don't need to worry about us. We are good at finding our way. Just point us in the right direction, and we'll get out of your hair."

"But first can you tell me about the murder of Sophia Kent?" Bea asked. "I love murders."

"Excuse me?" Susanna said, sounding understandably horrified. Color bloomed on her cheeks in splotchy patches; red marbling on her pale skin.

"She's kidding. We had a long drive," Lila said quickly. As if a long drive was an explanation for a child loving *murders*.

"I am not kidding. I do love murders. I read all about Sophia's murder online, and I watched the *Dateline* episode," Bea said.

Susanna's face distorted and twisted into an angry mask. She looked accusingly at Lila. It was a look that said, *you are a terrible mother for letting your child love murders, what is wrong with you?* Honestly, sometimes Lila wondered the same thing herself.

"We can discuss this later," Lila placed her hand on Bea's shoulder and squeezed, warning her to stop talking.

Bea shook off Lila's hand. "I've never met anyone who knew a real murdered person except for Jake Fletcher in third grade who overheard his parents saying Uncle Frank was swimming with the fishes. Jake thought his uncle worked at an aquarium until I explained that *swimming with the fishes* meant he was murdered by the mob. Jake had only met Uncle Frank once, so he barely counts. Did you know Sophia?"

Susanna looked down her rather prominent nose at Bea, stopping at the ragged ends of the Atlanta Braves shirt. "This is a highly inappropriate conversation." She stared back at Lila. "My understanding is you are here for the sole purpose of cleaning out apartment 2B and preparing it for sale. As I'm sure you are aware, this building is intended for residents over fifty-five years of age. The Primrose Board made a rare exception for you and your daughter. Our residents are retired and expect a peaceful environment, and the board has given me the discretion to handle any problems pertaining to your tenancy. If your daughter becomes disruptive or creates any issues, I can evict you immediately." Susanna's gaze flitted down to Bea, who was openly scowling and looked like the very definition of an *issue*.

Lila swallowed down the bile rising in her throat. Her mama's latest boyfriend, Stanley Ranger, owned the apartment in the

Primrose. It had sat vacant for five years since his mother, Gloria, died. Mama had come up with this plan—Lila would live in the apartment, rent-free, and receive a small stipend from Stanley in exchange for cleaning it out. Lila hadn't wanted to rely on another of Mama's boyfriends but, once Bea got expelled and the government took their house, Lila didn't have a choice. She needed the Primrose for the next two months while she saved money and looked for a job. Her pulse kicked up, racing through the track of her arteries. They couldn't lose this place. They literally had nowhere else to go.

"I understand all your concerns. Every last one of them. You have absolutely nothing to worry about from us. Bea has no interest in bothering anyone unless they're a murder suspect, and then she'd interrogate them until they confessed." Lila laughed to show she was joking, but Susanna did not crack a smile.

"I'm going to assume you understand the gravity of this situation," Susanna said.

"We do. Yes," Lila said. Bea shrugged in response.

Susanna frowned, looking unconvinced. "I'll take you to the elevator."

"Did anyone ever die in the elevator?" Bea asked.

Lila winced as Susanna turned abruptly, and they trotted after her down the hallway. Susanna pointed to a large room on the right with French doors, extravagantly carved sideboards, custom skirted benches, and a long banquet table in alabaster wood. Floor-to-ceiling windows framed a patio and lush garden. "That's the Azalea Room, the main gathering space for residents."

Lila's shoes sank into the plush trellised runner extending down the middle of the long hallway. Gold sconces lined the wall, interspersed with landscape paintings.

Susanna gestured to a smaller room off the hallway wallpapered in a bright floral pattern of pinks, blues, and yellows. It was furnished with three round tables and bamboo chairs. Masses of sumptuous silk fabric hung from gold curtain rods. "This is the Hydrangea Room. You can reserve it for activities." She looked pointedly at Bea. "Neither of these rooms are suitable for children. The fabrics and rugs are quite expensive."

Bea peered into the room, making a show of looking up at the ceiling. "I'm surprised you don't have cameras in here. If someone spilled red Gatorade on that expensive rug, you'd never know who did it. I hope that doesn't happen," she said innocently.

Lila widened her eyes at Bea, mutely begging her for silence. Susanna managed to glare at Bea while leading them to the elevator with gold metal doors and filigreed decoration, framed in thick wood trim. There were small triangular beveled glass inserts at eye level, windows into the mechanics of the elevator beyond.

Reaching into her pocket, Susanna pulled out a key and key card and handed them to Lila. "The key is for the apartment. The key card opens the door to your floor from the stairwell. I checked on the unit earlier in the week to make sure all the systems were working properly." She hesitated. "I suppose you already know the state of the apartment."

"I never got the chance to meet or visit Gloria, but I know there's a fair amount to clean out," Lila said. "That's why I'm here."

For the first time, Susanna looked uncomfortable, and—was it possible?—even a little pitying. A shiver went down Lila's back; a feeling of foreboding. Mama had said the apartment was a little disorganized. Surely this wasn't one of her giant understatements, like when she'd said her second wedding would be a small, intimate affair and then invited four hundred people. She wouldn't do that to Lila, not after the last year.

"I'll let you get settled. Do not forget our discussion," Susanna said meaningfully.

"We won't," Lila said. "You won't even know we're here."

Susanna made a small noise of disbelief in the back of her throat and walked away.

"I don't think she likes us," Bea said.

Lila thought that was an understatement.

They took the elevator up to the second floor. The doors opened onto robin's egg blue carpet and cream wallpaper with a subdued vine pattern. There was an antique table with an ornate gold mirror above it. Lila caught a glimpse of her face; shadows beneath the eyes, lines etched around her mouth, hair straggling to her shoulders. People used to tell her she was pretty. Now she simply looked old and tired.

Lila and Bea walked down the hallway until they found a small gold sign that read *2B*. Lila unlocked the door and pushed it open. The air inside was musty and stale. It was strangely dark, as if it was midnight instead of mid-afternoon. After her eyes adjusted, Lila saw why—she was standing in a large living room and every square inch was covered in boxes, newspapers, furniture, and knickknacks piled all the way up to the tops of the windows, overflowing into the space as if the mess was its own organic organism that kept growing and growing. She could barely glimpse the dining room off to the left and the kitchen beyond. This was not a little disorganized like Mama had said. This apartment was a full-fledged disaster.

Flicking on the light, Lila leaned against the door, kneading her forehead. What had she done, moving here, leaving everything?

"Mama, we can't live here," Bea said, turning in a circle. It was a very small circle because there was almost nowhere to walk.

Bea's face worked—her lip pushing out, her forehead wrinkling, her eyes glossing with tears. She was frustrated and overwhelmed, close to buckling under the crush of her emotions. Lila's stomach clenched at the signs.

Lila tried to come up with the right reassuring words. "It's not so bad. I'll get this cleaned up in no time. I bet there are a lot of treasures in here too. Think of what we might find."

"It all looks like trash," Bea said.

Bea was right, it did.

"Why would you move us to this place?" Bea asked.

Because Lila didn't have a choice.

"Why couldn't we stay in our house?" Bea asked in a rising voice.

Because the government took it.

"This is part of the adventure," Lila said in an upbeat, slightly shrill voice. Her temple pulsed, signaling an incoming migraine.

Bea kicked at a nearby box. It toppled over into a couch, spilling out its contents of doll heads, which were not exactly the treasures Lila had promised.

"I'm not even excited about the murder now. I want to go home." Bea shouted the words.

"Stop yelling," Lila snapped, her words coming out louder than she intended. She exhaled, softening her voice. "We'll figure this out."

"This is your fault. Leave me alone." Bea flung herself around and stomped down the hallway.

Lila followed Bea to the edge of a bedroom and peered inside. The bed was buried beneath dozens of quilts in every imaginable color and an inexplicable pile of cowboy hats. Boxes lined the walls in teetering heaps. Layers of perfume bottles covered the entire surface of the dresser, and there was a bucket of lipsticks beside the door. Bea barged into the room and slammed the door behind her. Lila stared at the warped wood of the closed door. Her shoulders slumped. She had no idea what she could even say to Bea that would help. Trudging back down the hall, she brushed a stack of books off a blue mohair couch and sank onto the seat. The silence was frigid and absolute.

Chapter Three

Lila registered Bea at Liberty Falls Elementary the next day. They sat in the hard plastic chairs of the front office and waited for the principal to lead Bea to her classroom. The walls were a cheery yellow, and there was a large bulletin board decorated with construction paper flowers. The school secretary was occupied on the phone, and the office was quiet. Through the windows behind her desk, clusters of parents and kids milled around the front of the school, greeting one another from the concrete sidewalk. Except for a few polite smiles and nods, no one had given Lila a second glance when she walked into the school, which was a relief after the scathing looks she had regularly received at Meritt Academy.

Bea's posture was stiff and she clutched the straps of her backpack. She must have felt anxious about today, because she had barely spoken a word all morning. Lila had worried she'd only make the situation worse by saying anything, so she'd stayed quiet too. But this was her daughter's first day at a new school, and she had to give Bea some semblance of a pep talk.

Lila inclined her head. "It's okay to be nervous."

"I'm not nervous." Bea crossed her arms.

"Well, if you were," Lila said carefully, "I would tell you that you're going to do great. The principal said your teacher is really sweet, and I know you'll make new friends. You could try smiling a lot to show everyone you're friendly."

"That's so weird, Mama."

"Okay, how about starting up a conversation with someone at recess? Ask about their favorite movie."

"Also weird." Bea continued to stare straight ahead. "And most kids don't watch as many murder mysteries as I do."

That was probably true, possibly because their parents wouldn't let them.

"You could bring up your favorite books instead?" Lila suggested.

"More weird." Bea rolled her eyes.

Lila thought for a moment. "As a last resort, you could always mention how weird your mama is. I bet you'd have plenty to say about that."

Despite her rigid posture, a corner of Bea's mouth quirked up. "That would take a lot longer than recess."

Lila felt a little more cheerful after that. As far as pep talks went, hers wasn't amazing, but Bea *had* half-smiled. Lila was doing the best she could.

After Bea went off to her new classroom, Lila returned to the Primrose and parked in the side lot. Her beat-up Jeep Cherokee was out of place among the Lexuses and Audis. The government had confiscated her new Suburban a month ago. Ryan was the one who had insisted on the giant SUV in the first place. She'd teased him about how he'd only bought it after their neighbor across the street came home with the same car. Ryan had slung an arm around her shoulders and said, *Well, excuse me for thinking my pretty wife deserves a nice car.* That was him; always complimenting her up until the day he left. Maybe that's why she hadn't seen the end coming.

Their last conversation was carved into her memory. Ryan had called from the airport, explained that he was going away because of a misunderstanding with the business. When she'd tried to ask questions, he'd gotten quiet, and then said, *I'm sorry, Li, but we both know our marriage is over. I can't deal with you while I'm dealing with everything else.* She remembered her response: *What are you saying? Are you—are you leaving me?* Her voice had cracked, and it embarrassed her—that show of emotion when he sounded so matter-of-fact about the end of their marriage. Ryan let her question hang there in the air between them before continuing: *I guess that's what I'm saying. I want a divorce.*

Lila had not heard from Ryan since that call but maybe she shouldn't expect to. They weren't officially divorced yet, but he'd made it clear he was done with her. The divorce was only a matter of time. She had known things weren't great between them. He'd stopped texting when he went away on trips. She got bored when he talked about his opinions on politics. He'd watch her clean up the kitchen at night and never offer to help. They didn't talk about the little annoyances or frustrations; they were simply there, below the surface. They also hadn't had sex in . . . well, she wasn't exactly sure, but it had been a while.

Still, Lila had naively thought their problems were a phase. Ryan had still bought her extravagant gifts, and he had shown up at Bea's games and parent-teacher conferences. She'd figured if they ignored those small irritations, they'd eventually go away all on their own, especially when they had Bea to raise together. She hadn't seriously believed they would give up on their family. Ryan was supposed to be her future, but she'd failed to secure it.

Dejected, Lila trudged down the Primrose hallway toward the stairs. She noticed a hairline crack had spiderwebbed down the wall, faint and barely visible below the ornate sconce. It was the one imperfection she'd seen in the public spaces of the Primrose. Susanna would probably have it repaired by next week.

"Get off me." A feeble voice invaded the silent hallway.

"Mr. Kent, you must do what I say." Another firm and younger voice.

"You're assaulting me!" The feeble voice again.

Lila whipped her head around, searching for an authority figure to step in and stop whatever confrontation was taking place in the Azalea Room but no one was in sight. There was a scuffling sound, a bang, and more yelling. Her pulse accelerated. She had to do something. Shoving open the door, she spotted an elderly gray-haired man standing by the French doors and pulling away from a younger man in blue scrubs.

"Is everything okay in here?" Lila asked.

The younger man immediately dropped the arms of the elderly man, who stretched out his hand toward a nearby silver walker that was just out of reach. His body tilted, sagging toward the floor as he took a single, halting step. Lila jogged over and moved the walker directly in front of him. He leaned forward, his sun-spotted hands clutching the handles.

The younger man blocked her view of the walker. "Thanks for the help." He lowered his voice. "I'm trying to get him back to his room for his own safety."

Lila hesitated, matching his low voice. "Can I do anything?"

"No. I've got this under control." The younger man smiled down at Lila. "I haven't seen you before. I would have remembered. I'm Chris Angle. I work for Mr. Kent here."

Lila would have found Chris handsome once. She might have even blushed at the unmistakable interest in his smile, but now she barely registered the chiseled jaw. At this moment, she felt absolutely nothing except concern for the gray-haired man who was pushing his walker forward in a misguided but deliberate attempt to get away from them.

Chris turned, sensing the movement of the walker. His voice

hardened. "Mr. Kent, you can't be down here on your own. Why do I have to keep telling you this?"

Chris was obviously trying to do his job. Lila should leave him to it. She was backing away when Chris grabbed Mr. Kent's arm and yanked it from the walker. Mr. Kent made a small noise of distress. Lila halted. Well, that wasn't okay. She couldn't leave this poor man alone until Chris calmed down.

Lila stepped forward again, already suspecting this was a bad idea. "Mr. Kent, I thought I recognized you. It's me, Lila!"

Both men turned to stare at her.

"You two know each other?" Chris asked, releasing Mr. Kent's arm.

"We sure do. We go way back. I would love to catch up. You could take a break, and I can bring Mr. Kent upstairs to his apartment when we're done chatting," Lila said.

Mr. Kent was bent over his walker. Lila couldn't see his face and had no idea if he was even listening to her.

Chris tightened his mouth, the flirty smile gone at this point. "It's my job to stay with Mr. Kent. I can't leave him with someone he barely knows."

"We actually . . . we know each other well." Lila swallowed hard. Definitely a bad idea.

"How is that? You didn't seem to recognize him earlier," Chris said skeptically.

"It's been a few years since we've seen each other, but we had a—a special relationship," Lila said, unable to come up with a better lie off the top of her head.

Mr. Kent looked up and met her eyes from behind Chris's shoulder. His mouth twitched.

"I'll never forget our night in New York City," Mr. Kent said.

"Best night of my life." Lila bit back a smile.

"Are you saying you dated?" Chris looked from one to the other, his eyes comically wide. Lila didn't blame him. There was a fifty-year age difference between them.

"I don't like to label things, but I do prefer a more mature man," Lila said.

"And you always did say age is just a number," Mr. Kent said solemnly.

Chris scoffed. "If you two were so close, why are you still calling him Mr. Kent?"

That was a good question. Lila cleared her throat, buying time to think. "It's part of our role play—you know what, I can't go into the intimate details. It's private. You understand." Her face heated up until it felt as though it might catch on fire.

Chris frowned at both of them before throwing up his hands. "I don't know what's going on here, but I don't need this shit anymore. Tell Helene I quit." He stormed out of the Azalea Room, his footsteps echoing on the marble floor like rapid-fire bullets.

Lila flinched from the display of fury. A normal person would have calmly confronted Chris. A normal person did not make up a fake affair with an eighty-year-old man.

"Oh my God, I'm so sorry," Lila said, rubbing a hand across her face.

Mr. Kent's eyes crinkled at her. "I quite liked the role play bit."

Lila winced. "I panicked."

"To my benefit. I thank you for the assistance and the amusement." Mr. Kent turned and attempted to open the French door to the patio. The knob rattled, and he swayed.

Lila stepped around him and twisted the knob, pushing open the door and maneuvering around his figure. "Can I call someone for you?"

Mr. Kent waved her off and pushed his walker outside. "I prefer that you didn't, but you could join me if you like."

Lila hesitated at the door. She should have gone back upstairs to work but couldn't help worrying that Mr. Kent would end up sprawled out in the middle of the patio in a matter of seconds without some supervision.

"I've got a few minutes," Lila said and stepped onto the patio, hovering behind Mr. Kent in case he slipped.

He pushed his walker across the brick patio toward a black wooden bench and maneuvered around so he could sink onto the seat. The bench was set beneath a tall tree with wide-spread limbs and knobs of bark like cinnamon crumble. Cherry-red azalea bushes formed a flower wall on either side of the tree. The air was warm with a slight hint of a breeze. Lila took the seat beside him.

"Good girl." He patted her arm as if he was helping her and not the other way around. "You may call me Conrad, and you are Lila Shaw. I make it my business to know all the residents of the Primrose."

"It's good to meet you for real this time," Lila said, smiling at him.

Conrad listed to one side. He had rounded shoulders beneath a pale blue button-down and navy suit jacket with a pink pocket square. His face was a web of wrinkles, and he stared up at the trees, which cast shadows on the ground, painting an intricate pattern of leaves and sunlight on the brick. He folded his hands in his lap, and an expression of peace crossed his face.

"I like to get out here every day," Conrad said. "Gardens are good for the soul."

A comfortable silence swelled into the space between them. Lila gazed at the fervent green of the bushes encircling the brick patio and found herself breathing deeper.

"How far back do the woods go?" Lila asked.

"Oh, quite far. There are pathways that lead all the way down to the cliffs overlooking the river. I used to walk that way until they fenced off the area after a young girl fell and died."

Lila turned to look at the tree branches behind, feeling uneasy now. She would have to keep Bea away from the cliffs. Her stomach tightened at the thought of her daughter sitting alone at her new desk and pretending to fiddle with her pencil so she didn't have to look up into a classroom of unknown faces. Lila hoped Bea's teacher smiled at her and that she had someone to sit next to at lunch.

"I've lived here thirty-three years. Mostly good years, a few bad ones." Conrad cast his eyes down. "My granddaughter died here."

Lila straightened. Awareness quivered through her. She realized all at once that this was Conrad Kent, the grandfather of Sophia Kent, the unsolved murder victim associated with the Primrose. Sophia's death was famous nationwide back in 2002. Wealthy, pretty, beloved Sophia was only sixteen when burglars broke into her grandfather's penthouse. She was alone at the time. The killer was never caught.

"I'm sorry," Lila said.

Conrad didn't respond immediately. His eyes fixed on a point far away. "It never seemed fair that Sophia was the one to die instead of me. She was in my apartment when they found her. I thought about selling it." His voice wavered, his eyes watery. "But it's my home."

Lila looked away, not wanting to witness his resounding grief. She was familiar with that anguish; the way it seeped into your bones and marrow, inhabiting every inch of your body. Her first instinct was to flee but how could she ignore his obvious distress?

"You shouldn't blame yourself for Sophia's death or for wanting to stay in your home, although—" Lila hesitated before placing a hand on his arm, the tender skin depressing beneath her fingers. "I understand why you do. It's hard to not feel depressed when something terrible happens and you couldn't stop it."

"That's true. I know this all too well." Conrad nodded thoughtfully. "I suppose happiness takes its own courage, doesn't it?"

"I wouldn't know," Lila said, pulling back her hand and laughing to cover her discomfort. She was self-conscious of her own candor.

Conrad's face creased in a smile. "I don't believe that."

Lila stood, relieved to see Conrad's eyes were now dry. "I should probably get back upstairs. Can I help you to your room?"

"No, thank you. I'm going to sit here a spell. I'm often tired these days."

Lila stood and brushed off her pants. She didn't like leaving Conrad alone and vowed to tell Susanna where he was on her way back upstairs. "I'll look forward to seeing you again soon."

"As will I." Conrad looked straight at her then. His expression sharpened. "And do let me know if you find anything interesting in Gloria's apartment."

Lila tilted her head, sensing this wasn't an idle remark. "Is there something interesting to find?"

Conrad closed his eyes. When he spoke, his voice was soft. "Too soon to tell, but take care of that daughter of yours. The Primrose isn't as safe as it appears."

Lila stared at Conrad, a shiver running up her back at his strange words. His eyes remained closed. He breathed in deeply, his chest rising and falling, seeming to have gone to sleep. She backed away, the air suddenly cold.

Chapter Four

A few days later, someone slipped an envelope under the door of apartment 2B during the night. Lila found it because she had cleaned the apartment's small entryway over the past few days. She'd hauled out several loads of trash and lugged them into the dumpster at the side of the building. Now the entryway held only the envelope, a crystal chandelier, and a beautiful mahogany console that had been buried beneath two years of old tabloid magazines, most of which were about alien babies.

Lila scooped up the envelope as she shuffled Bea out the door. Lila's name was typed across the front. She stared at it for a moment and slipped it in her pocket. Whatever it was, it could wait a little longer. She needed all her energy to get Bea out of the apartment on time for school. After a week, Bea had not yet taken to Liberty Falls Elementary. She said the other students were mean, and the teacher refused to answer her question about whether anyone was murdered on school grounds. Before school, Bea put on her shoes as slowly as possible, dressed as slowly as possible, and walked as slowly as possible to the car, despite Lila begging her to move *just a little bit faster*. By the time they reached the Primrose parking lot, Lila would finally snap at Bea to *speed it up*, and Bea would snap back to *chill out*.

The regular morning battle meant Lila didn't even remember the envelope until she returned to the Primrose after dropping Bea at school. She sank into one of the kitchen chairs and slid her nail under the seal of the business envelope before unfolding the letter. She noted the letterhead—*Law Offices of Craigmont and Forrester*. Her heart started pounding. A letter from a law firm was never good.

Dear Mrs. Shaw,

I represent the interests of the Greyhaven Trust. I am writing to request a meeting with you this evening at 7 p.m. in the Azalea Room to discuss a legal matter of monetary significance. If you are unable to attend, please let me know at your earliest convenience.

Light refreshments will be served.

Sincerely,
James R. Forrester
Attorney-at-law

Lila stared at the paper for several seconds, frozen in place. *A legal matter of monetary significance?* Was this a civil suit against Ryan? If that was the case, she had nothing to say. After he was charged with health-care fraud and conspiracy, Lila had spent months convincing the FBI she wasn't involved with his crimes. She sat back, lightheaded, as she remembered all those meetings in stale government offices, the questions lobbed at her, none of which she could answer. Her ignorance didn't stop the government from seizing their bank accounts immediately and then, later, the cars, the furniture, the houses.

The truth was Lila hadn't known Ryan was scheming the government and his investors out of millions. She was busy meeting friends for lunch, volunteering at Bea's school, obsessing over the antique Oushak rug that her mother-in-law, Patricia, insisted she buy. *A goddamn lady of leisure,* the FBI agent had called her. The insult burned because this *goddamn lady of leisure* had not bothered to ask her husband the simplest questions about where all their money was coming from. Lila had never questioned how they suddenly had a bank account balance that allowed them to vacation in Harbour Island, redecorate their living room, and purchase a beach house on Figure Eight Island.

Lila should have suspected something wasn't right. Ryan was *her* husband; she was supposed to know him better than anyone. Was it stupidity, selfishness, or naivete on her part? She worried that she'd ruined Bea's life by not stopping Ryan. Lila's heart pounded almost painfully and she shrugged off her sweater, suddenly hot and clammy at the same time.

Gripping James Forrester's letter, Lila wanted to tear it into pieces. She stuffed it into her purse instead. This wasn't something to ignore.

At seven o'clock that evening, Lila told Bea she had to attend a quick meeting downstairs and instructed her to stay put in the apartment. After slipping on a sweater and jeans, Lila made her way down to the Azalea Room. She was afraid of what might come next; it was a familiar feeling these days.

When she stepped inside the Azalea Room, she was surprised to find it filled with at least forty other people. She scanned the room, trying to get a sense of what was going on. There was a long buffet table covered in platters and chafing dishes. The twin crystal chandeliers anchoring each side of the room were dimmed. Susanna fussed with a lectern in front of the French doors to the patio. Lila recognized most of the other people from the lobby or the parking lot. These were obviously residents of the Primrose. Lila exhaled, her breath loosening for the first time since she'd opened the letter. She remembered the light refreshments referred to in the letter. Perhaps this had something to do with the building's finances and was more of a social occasion than anything else. Whatever this was, it had nothing to do with Ryan.

"Wow! Hi. You're here. This is so exciting! You must be Lila. I'm Zoe Walters, the Primrose concierge." Zoe held out her hand. She was beautiful with glowing brown skin and straight white teeth. She was young and wore a stylish wrap dress of red and pink stripes. Lila immediately felt plain and underdressed.

Lila reached for Zoe's hand. "How do you know who I am?"

Zoe grinned. "You're under fifty and new, both of which are unusual here."

Lila couldn't help smiling back, charmed by Zoe's enthusiasm. She nodded to the room. "Do you know what this is all about?"

"I don't." Zoe lowered her voice. "But it could have something to do with Conrad Kent. His daughter-in-law, Helene, asked me to organize the refreshments."

Zoe gestured to a woman standing by the lectern. Her hair was an ash blond, swept back into a low bun. She could have been anywhere between forty and sixty-five, and was objectively beautiful with amber eyes, pale skin, and a high forehead, unmarred by wrinkles. Her immaculate Balmain cream tweed blazer only made her more intimidating.

Lila frowned down at her own shapeless blue sweater. Five months ago, she had boxed up most of her expensive, beautiful clothes and shipped them off to an upscale consignment website when she needed money for electric and gas bills. She had admonished herself (sternly!) that it was stupid to cry over dresses, but she'd still slumped over the steering wheel and swiped away tears on the day she'd taken those boxes to UPS. Her days of pretty were over.

"I met Conrad a few days ago. Is he here?" Lila asked.

Zoe's eyes swarmed with tears. "I'm sorry to say he's not."

Lila's stomach dropped. Something must have happened to

him. Before she could ask Zoe anything further, two women hobbled up. They wore matching sweater twinsets—one in purple, one in yellow—identical blond perms, and enormous diamond earrings. A gentleman in a black polo that strained over his stomach trailed behind them. His khaki pants were hiked up, and the few strands of hair he had left were plastered across his head.

"Zoe, I presume you're going to introduce us," the purple twinset said.

Zoe blinked back her tears, composing her face. She raised her eyebrows at Lila, a warning of some sort. "Lila Shaw, meet Iris and June Willoughby. They're sisters and live on the third floor. And this is Brock Anderson. He's on the fourth."

Brock stuck out his hand, glancing down at Lila's chest. "Brock Anderson at your service. President of River City Bank."

"Brock, you are president of nothing," June said. She was the one in yellow.

"I'm the retired president," Brock said, his florid face reddening further. "It's customary to still use the title."

"I don't think that's correct," Iris said.

"You wouldn't know," Brock snapped at her before turning back to Lila. "Now tell me, darlin', are you married? I don't see a ring."

Zoe stepped forward, attempting to maneuver Brock away. "Brock, did you try the rosé tonight? It's light and refreshing. Let me pour you another glass."

"I'd love to take you out for dinner as a neighborly gesture," Brock leaned around Zoe and smiled at Lila. His teeth were pale yellow and pointed like a dog's.

June studied Lila with a critical look on her face. "Everyone was right. You are very pretty, but I wish you'd wear something more flattering. In my day, if you wanted to catch a man, you needed to dress the part. I'd recommend a miniskirt."

"Or a low-cut blouse," Iris offered.

"Or that," June agreed. "It reminds me of the Oscar de la Renta cocktail dress I wore to a Christmas party in 1978. Now that had a low neckline. I couldn't wear a bra, and I can tell you plenty of men noticed."

"Do you like steak houses?" Brock asked hopefully.

"She might not want men to notice her, or she could be bisexual. Lots of young people are these days," Iris said.

"I kissed a girl or two in my youth," June said. "It's not a big deal, despite what Fox News says."

"I don't mind bisexual women," Brock said.

Lila swallowed. This conversation was completely out of control. Zoe stared at her, pressing her lips together and trying not to laugh. Lila found her own mouth curving upward for the first time all day.

"Excuse me." A loud voice filled the room, amplified by a microphone. All the heads in the room swiveled toward the lectern, and voices quieted down to a hushed silence. A man in a navy-blue pinstripe suit stood at the microphone. His dark hair was slicked to one side in a precise part. He pushed his glasses up his thin nose, looking nervous.

"Yes, thank you. Thank you very much for your attention." The man at the lectern nodded to the room. "My name is James Forrester."

"What are we doing here? Your note was unacceptably vague," one woman said, her voice carrying through the room.

"At my age, I like a little more notice before an engagement," another woman in a brightly colored caftan called out. "It takes some of us time to get out the door."

A man banged a cane against the wooden floor. "Seven o'clock is too late for a meeting. I like to drink my bourbon and get in bed by seven thirty."

A murmur went through the crowd, appearing to agree with the bourbon drinker.

James patted his hairline, flustered by the unruly audience. "The abbreviated notice period and in-person meeting were both conditions of the trust. I do apologize."

"I should hope so," Iris yelled louder than was strictly necessary.

James patted his forehead again. Lila could see the perspiration from where she stood.

"I'm here at the behest of Helene and Alice Kent." James looked to Helene, who stood to the left of the lectern.

Helene stood perfectly still and composed but her shoulders tilted toward the younger woman at her side who must have been Alice. Alice clasped and unclasped her hands, her face pinched. Based on the women's matching features and last names, Lila immediately guessed they were mother and daughter.

James continued. "There's no easy way to say this. Conrad Kent died two days ago."

A loud din rose from the crowd; sounds of disbelief, surprise, and shock were evident in their voices. Lila looked out onto the patio. A pang struck her chest. The light was fading outside but she could glimpse the bench where she'd sat with Conrad only a week ago. They'd shared a brief but real connection.

"If you'll quiet down for a moment," James said into the microphone. But it was to no avail. The residents of the Primrose were just getting warmed up.

A clamor of outrage broke out in the room, all voices talking at once. June loudly proclaimed that she was furious she hadn't heard the news as she and Conrad were *very* close owing to their brief fling in 1986. Brock stabbed at his cell phone and announced he was getting in touch with Conrad's business manager immediately about the failure to call him. Another woman was banging her walker on the floor and yelling about unacceptable surprises. In other words, it was complete bedlam, and no one seemed inclined to quiet down.

"Please," James implored into the microphone. "I only need a few minutes of your time. This has to do with Mr. Kent's trust."

That got their attention. The crowd went silent, mouths closed tight, eyes open wide, everyone looking straight at the lectern.

"Thank you." James dabbed at his temple. "As I was saying, Mr. Kent established the Greyhaven Trust a few weeks before his death. As trustee, I am charged with carrying out the terms."

"What does this have to do with us?" a man in a wheelchair yelled.

"You are all potential beneficiaries of the trust," James said.

There was a collective intake of breath in the room. Lila frowned, utterly confused. How could she be a beneficiary to a trust of someone she'd only spoken to for fifteen minutes?

"The trust money is a reward to any of you who can provide information that leads to the arrest of Sophia Kent's killer or the closure of her case."

Utter silence followed.

James waited several beats before continuing. "I realize this is a shock, but I can assure you it's all perfectly legal. Rewards are common in solving crimes these days, and Mr. Kent believed someone—" he swallowed, paused "—he believed someone in this building saw something the night of Sophia's murder. It was his dying wish to provide closure to her mother and sister."

James looked over at Helene and Alice again. Helene stiffened and stared straight ahead. Alice's face was still pinched and red as if she was trying not to cry.

For a long moment, no one spoke. Then someone called out, "How much is the reward?"

James hesitated and looked to Helene, who nodded back at him. "Two million dollars."

Well, that did it. The silence in the room cracked open all at once. Questions were now shouted at a furious rate—questions about suspects and motives and police. James tried to answer each one, though he barely got a word out before someone asked another question.

Two million dollars. Hope surged inside Lila at the very thought of that much money. Two million dollars would solve all her problems. She and Bea could find a place to live, they could move away from everything and finally escape their past. They would be safe.

But—

But that was ridiculous, wasn't it? Lila had no information about Sophia Kent's murder and no way of solving it herself. She hadn't lived there when Sophia died. Her inclusion in this potential reward was probably a mistake. More than that, she didn't have the expertise, resources, or anything else to actually figure out who killed Sophia. It was silly to even imagine. Lila shook her head, dislodging any misplaced optimism. Conrad Kent's trust changed nothing for her. Lila backed out of the room, slipped into the hallway, and climbed up the stairs to her daughter.

Chapter Five

Bea stood in the entryway of the apartment, bouncing on her toes. The light from the small crystal chandelier illuminated her hair, arcing around her head, almost like a halo. There was something different about her face. She was smiling.

"We have to do it," Bea said immediately, her voice vibrating with excitement.

Lila followed Bea into the living room, a smile growing on Lila's face as well. She could hardly believe how Bea was acting. This was the Bea she rarely saw anymore, the one who loved reading fantasy novels and started a neighborhood newspaper. This was the girl who didn't hate everything or wear a dirty Atlanta Braves T-shirt every day.

"What has gotten into you?" Lila asked.

Bea stood in front of her, hands clasped. "We have to solve Sophia Kent's murder and win the reward."

Lila stared for a moment, then groaned and collapsed onto the beige chenille couch, which she'd cleared off only that morning. It had been covered in old VHS tapes and fur coats.

"How do you know about the reward?" Lila asked.

Bea was practically jumping up and down. "Because I snuck downstairs. You did a decent job of hiding the letter from Mr. Forrester, but I found it and didn't want to miss the meeting in case it was important."

Lila had hidden the letter in a pocket of her purse. She wondered if Bea was in the habit of regularly searching through her things and suspected she wouldn't like the answer.

"I told you to stay put in the apartment," Lila said in a stern voice, though she wasn't surprised. Bea rarely did what Lila told her to do.

"We could win two million dollars," Bea said. "We would be rich again."

"We were never rich," Lila said automatically. She now knew how true this statement was. They were living off stolen money for the last two years.

"We could buy a car that doesn't make those weird gurgling noises and eat steak for dinner sometimes. We could find a school I actually like." Bea's eyes were shining in a way they had not in quite some time.

Lila's throat closed up. All her poor daughter wanted was a working car, a school she liked, and occasionally a steak. Lila couldn't even provide that much, and Bea would rather put all her faith in some insane idea of solving a murder than in Lila.

Pulling Bea toward her on the couch, Lila put an arm around her. "Things will get better. You'll finish out the school year here, I'm going to find a job, and we'll find the right place to live. I'll fix everything. I promise."

"But if we solve the murder, that will fix everything."

"We aren't equipped to solve a murder."

"I learned a lot about solving murders from Jessica Fletcher on *Murder, She Wrote*," Bea said hopefully. "We could at least make a murder board in the dining room. All I need is some string, a giant bulletin board, photos of possible suspects, and a copy of the police file."

Lila considered how best to dissuade Bea of this line of magical thinking. "What if we make some cookies instead of a murder board?"

"We can do both. Duh," Bea said.

Lila sighed. "I'm sorry but I wouldn't know where to start with an investigation. It's not something we can do. But I don't want you to worry about money. I've got it under control."

Lila's smile was tremulous, flicking down at the edges. Bea could probably see through her lie. Lila didn't have a single aspect of her life under control. Not one.

Bea got up from the couch. "You won't even give us a chance. Why don't you think we can do it?"

"Because we can't," Lila said automatically.

"Nothing is fun anymore since Dad left." Bea's face flushed.

Bea was right in a way. Ryan had been the fun parent; the one who told Bea silly jokes and tossed her into the water at the country club pool. Lila filled out the school forms, bought bananas and yogurt for snacks, and made the pediatrician appointments. She was maybe missing the maternal instinct for fun and now it would never kick in because there were too many things to worry about—things she couldn't tell her daughter. Bea didn't know about Lila's struggle to find a job and that the government had taken their house.

Lila wanted to protect Bea, but Bea was making everything more difficult by demanding they solve an impossible murder for fun. Lila couldn't imagine insisting her own mama do something so ridiculous. Lila had accepted Mama's decisions, not questioned them. Why couldn't Bea do the same and not always push for more?

"I'm not discussing this," Lila said.

Bea glared at her. "You're the worst."

"Bea, enough complaining. I'm only being realistic," Lila said, exasperation creeping into her voice.

"I hate realistic," Bea said, her face crumpling. "I hate everything." With that, she slid past the four easy chairs with protruding stuffing and picked her way down the hallway to her temporary bedroom where she slammed the door.

Lila massaged her temples. The springs of the couch bit insistently into her thighs. She agreed with Bea about one thing. She hated being realistic too, and everything that went along with it.

* * *

Lila lay awake in the darkness, her satin comforter pulled around her, thinking about Sophia Kent. Lila was used to the way the clock slowed down late at night. Sleep never came quickly these days.

After Bea went to bed, Lila had researched Sophia on the internet. She had been curious after the meeting that night. In the fall of 2002, there was a rash of robberies in the Primrose. At the time of the murder, all the residents were attending a building-wide cocktail party on the patio. The theory was the same burglar who'd robbed the other apartments had expected Conrad's penthouse to be empty at that time. Sophia surprised the burglar with her presence, and he panicked, grabbed a knife off the counter, and stabbed her. The burglar was never caught.

Sophia was sixteen at the time of her death. She was still in school, still living at home, still growing up; she was someone's daughter, just like Bea. Sophia's life was cut short with the flick of a knife. Girls were fragile and breakable. It was so much responsibility to keep Bea safe all on her own since Ryan had left.

Lila remembered their last anniversary dinner at La Seine. They'd barely seen each other in the weeks leading up to it; Ryan was traveling and busy with work dinners. But he was always good at celebrations. That night, he'd reserved the private room and had a small blue gift box waiting at her seat. *I've missed seeing you,* Lila had said, feeling her heart soften toward him for the first time in a while. Ryan had smiled and said, *I've missed you too. I'm going to try to be home more, I promise.* In that candlelit-soft-music moment, she could tell Ryan meant what he said. But he was back to traveling the following week for a work crisis and staying out late with his friends at a golf tournament the next weekend. Nothing changed and a month later, he was gone for good.

A sharp cry rose from Bea's bedroom. Lila threw off the covers and hurried down the hall, weaving around the stacked boxes in the dark. She was in Bea's room a second later, flicking on the light.

Bea was sitting up, her eyes wide with panic. She hugged her arms to her chest.

Lila crossed to the bed, sinking to sit on the edge. She put an arm around her daughter. "It's okay, honey. You're safe. I'm here."

Bea buried her head in Lila's chest. Lila patted her, making soothing sounds. Bea's fury from earlier was miles away, forgotten in this moment. Lila hated Bea's nightmares but loved the way she would lean into Lila when she awoke, the softness of Bea's hair against Lila's bare arm.

"Another nightmare?" Lila asked eventually.

Bea pulled away and slid back beneath the covers. Lila kept her hands still, though they longed to pull Bea close again. She didn't know what scenario ran through Bea's head when she woke up crying; Bea kept her dreams to herself. Lila worried about this in the middle of the night. She worried about so many things.

Lila leaned over and tucked the blanket around Bea, tight the way she preferred it. "I could stay for a while."

"No." Bea didn't have to think about it.

Lila tried not to mind the quick dismissal. She wanted to extend this moment a little longer. "Are you excited about kickball club tomorrow?" She had optimistically signed Bea up for the after-school activity, hoping it would help Bea adjust to Liberty Falls Elementary.

"Not really. It means I'll have to spend more time at school, and school is the worst."

"Come on. That's not true." Lila smoothed the hair back from Bea's face. "Mrs. Maisley is nice, and I know you've made at least one new friend."

Bea closed her eyes. "I haven't. No one likes me anymore."

Lila's heart contracted. She swallowed back the thickness in her throat, sticky like molasses. Bea's little face was turned away on the pillow. Lila could tell she was trying not to cry. She wished Ryan were here, if only so someone would reassure her she was doing the right thing. Instead, here she was on her own, making major life decisions on behalf of another human.

"People do like you, especially me," Lila said in a firm voice.

"I'm not talking about this," Bea said.

Lila wanted to say more, she wanted to say the right thing, but she didn't know what that was. She straightened, patting Bea's legs.

"Call if you need me." Lila crossed to the door and turned off the overhead light, coating the room in darkness once more. Bea had never needed a night-light, preferring darkness since she was a baby. How was it that Lila knew the way Bea liked to sleep but was clueless about what was going on inside her head these days?

"When is Daddy coming home?" Bea asked suddenly.

Lila closed her eyes against the question. The first month after Ryan left, Bea had asked this constantly, each time another lashing on Lila's heart. Lila had explained the situation as best she could—the FBI thought Ryan had stolen some money, and he'd left and couldn't contact them because he was trying to prove his innocence. She'd assured Bea that Ryan was coming back as soon as he had enough evidence to clear his name.

For a while, Lila had hoped that was true. But after her meetings with the FBI, she didn't believe Ryan was innocent. She'd assumed he would cut a deal and return to Virginia after a few months. That seemed less and less likely as time passed. She hadn't heard from him since the day he'd left and was beginning to fear they might never hear from him again. Lila couldn't lie to her daughter forever, but she couldn't tell her the truth either. It was too painful. Bea didn't even know her parents were getting a divorce. How could she handle that after Ryan's disappearance? Lila could barely handle it herself.

Lila forced a casual lilt into her voice. "Don't worry. Daddy will be home soon."

Her heart sank with the lie.

Chapter Six

Bea and Lila entered the lobby of the Primrose the following evening. Bea looked particularly dejected; her Braves T-shirt hung down to her knees and red dust smeared down one cheek. Apparently, kickball club hadn't gone well.

"Kickball is moronic," Bea announced loudly into the quiet lobby. "I hate it."

The Willoughby sisters and Brock Anderson were sitting on the couches across the room and turned to stare.

Lila bent down to Bea. "Not so loud."

Bea huffed at the admonishment.

Lila couldn't entirely blame her. She was frustrated with herself more than anything. There was a time when she had scheduled Bea's every free hour with soccer and softball and tumbling. Then Ryan left and their lives fell apart. Bea had spent the past seven months watching television after school while Lila answered angry phone calls during her customer service shifts or hid in her closet and quietly cried. Now her daughter didn't even want to play kickball. Lila had dampened Bea's natural love of sports with months of inactivity. Well, she was going to fix it.

"Kickball is fun and a good way to make some friends," Lila said firmly.

"But I didn't make friends. No one wanted me on their team, and Nora Raynor called me a dumbass when the coach wasn't listening." Bea loudly emphasized *dumbass*.

Zoe and Susanna stood beside the grand piano, their heads bent over a clipboard. They both looked up, startled at Bea's pronouncement. Zoe gave Lila a sympathetic look. Susanna glared at her.

Lila resisted the urge to tell Bea to not yell *dumbass* into the fancy Primrose lobby. Her daughter was upset, understandably so. Anger heated Lila inside as she imagined Nora yelling at Bea for no reason. She wanted to storm up to the school right now and tell Nora exactly what would happen if she didn't leave Bea alone. Lila would call Nora's parents and the principal; hell, she'd go to the school board if she had to. Bullying was no joke these days.

"Nora does not sound like a nice girl," Lila said as they turned onto the hallway. "I'll call the school to report this."

"Mama, no. That's embarrassing. I can handle Nora."

Lila paused, considering her daughter's track record. "I don't want you to get in trouble for taking matters into your own hands. Remember what happened at Meritt Academy."

Bea nodded as if she agreed. "Don't worry. I learned my lesson."

Lila relaxed. For once, they were on the same page.

"I won't let the teacher catch me this time," Bea said.

"Wait, no. Don't do anything to Nora. Tell *me* if she says something else."

"I'll think about it." Bea picked up her pace.

Lila sighed and hurried after her. Lila worried Bea had every intention of dealing with Nora herself, and Lila had no way to stop her.

"Let's hurry. I'm starving after all that stupid kicking," Bea said.

"I'll fix you a snack before you tackle math homework," Lila said.

"Actually"—Bea slowed, contorting her face into an exaggerated grimace—"I'm feeling really sad because of Nora. I should probably rest when we get upstairs. After my snack."

Lila wasn't buying it. "Does this sudden feeling of sadness have anything to do with not wanting to start your math homework?"

Bea exhaled. "I keep telling you math is pointless for my future as a detective."

"And I keep telling you to learn it anyway." Lila nudged Bea. "It's not that bad."

Except it was pretty bad. Lila was already anticipating the fight over the next hour. Bea would get upstairs to the apartment and need a snack. She would sit down at the table with the math worksheet and immediately take a break. Once Lila coaxed her back to her seat, she would request a different pencil, a fresh sheet of paper, and then another snack—anything to delay actually doing her homework. If things went as they usually did, Lila would finally lose her temper and yell that Bea couldn't get up from her chair for any reason whatsoever. Lila would then regret the yelling, especially when Bea said she needed to use the bathroom and was she still not allowed to get up from her chair for any reason whatsoever?

When Lila and Bea reached the elevator, two people were already waiting. A woman dressed in a fur coat, layers of gold necklaces, and Gucci high heels pushed a walker in front of her. She looked back at Bea and Lila, and wrinkled her nose as if she smelled something awful. A bald man carrying a cloth satchel stood a few steps behind her. He didn't turn around.

The older lady looked Lila up and down. "I suppose you're the single woman living in 2B." *Single woman* sounded like an insult.

"Yes, I'm Lila Shaw and this is my daughter Bea," Lila said, hoping her polite tone softened the woman's obvious disdain. She wasn't looking to make friends, but she also didn't want anyone to complain about her to Susanna.

The older woman frowned before responding in a grudging tone. "Evelyn Harrison." She gestured to the man who hadn't looked up from the floor. "This is Jasper Field. We both live on the second floor too."

Jasper nodded at Lila once before staring back down. The gold arrow on the elevator moved slowly from the fifth floor to the fourth and then the third. Silence stretched out among the three of them. It was awkward. Lila wished they'd taken the stairs.

Evelyn turned back. "You're lucky to live here. The Primrose is *the* premier building in Richmond. You might not know that since you're not from here." She made it sound as if Lila's non-Richmond origins were offensive to her.

"It's very beautiful," Lila said.

"Of course it is," Evelyn responded.

The elevator doors finally opened and all four of them got in. Evelyn huffed, conveying that she didn't appreciate having additional people in the elevator. Jasper backed into the corner, making himself as small as possible. No one spoke again as the elevator heaved itself upward with a clank of gears. It had only risen a few feet past the first floor when the elevator halted. The doors remained firmly closed, and the mechanics of the elevator went abruptly silent.

Lila stared at the display panel waiting for a light to come on, for the doors to slide open, for the bell to chime signaling a new floor. Nothing happened. Her heart sank. They were stuck.

"This is entirely unacceptable," Evelyn said, banging her walker against the elevator floor. "For goodness' sake, can one of you press the call button before we all suffocate in here?"

The air was close and heavy, and the honey wood paneling seemed to slowly encroach on the small bit of space they did have. Lila stepped forward and pressed the white call button.

A beep sounded. Susanna's staticky voice came out of the speaker. "Is there a problem?"

"Yes, there's a problem," Evelyn yelled. "Isn't it obvious? The elevator is stuck again. This is unacceptable, Susanna!"

"I'll call maintenance right away," Susanna said calmly.

"It's your job to see the elevator is serviced properly. I know everyone important in Richmond. Everyone! I will make sure that word of this incompetence spreads to all the right people," Evelyn said.

"We'll get right on it," Susanna said and clicked off.

"Florence would never stand for this," Evelyn huffed. "Not that I'd talk to her about it."

Evelyn continued to bang her walker on the floor of the elevator every few seconds, punctuating her unhappiness with the current situation. She kept saying *unacceptable* in a loud voice. Bea was staring at the floor, fighting back giggles.

At the same time, Jasper puffed out audible breaths. Lila glanced behind. His face was drawn and pale. He had braced both his hands on the side wall. Something was clearly wrong. Lila faced forward, her eyes trained on the elevator doors. She didn't want to get involved.

But Jasper's breathing grew more labored until it was impossible to ignore. Lila abruptly turned around to face him.

"Are you all right?" Lila asked.

Jasper shook his head frantically. His eyes bulged. "I can't breathe."

"Is he dying?" Bea asked in a loud whisper that everyone in the tiny elevator heard.

"No," Lila said, pressing Bea backward to give Jasper some more space.

"I might be," Jasper puffed out.

"Is it possible you were poisoned?" Bea asked, sounding hopeful.

"I doubt it, but I'm claustrophobic," Jasper said and dropped his head against the side of the elevator, wheezing out shallow breaths.

"No one is dying. I think you're having a panic attack." Lila knew about panic attacks. She'd had one or two of her own when the FBI raided her house.

Lila eyed Evelyn, who was still banging her walker around. "Any chance you can stop that for a minute?"

"Why would I do that?" Evelyn said.

"Because it's making us all feel worse," Lila said.

Evelyn narrowed her eyes, which were coated in thick mascara and purple eye shadow. "I am Evelyn Harrison and I will not have a rude young woman tell me what I can and can't do with my walker. It costs over two thousand dollars, I'll have you know."

Lila had no idea why the price of the walker was relevant to their current conversation. She turned back to Jasper, ignoring Evelyn for the moment.

"Why don't you sit down," Lila suggested.

"What on earth is the matter with him?" Evelyn said.

"He's dying," Bea said unhelpfully.

Jasper slid down the wall and put his head between his knees.

"I don't want to share an elevator with a corpse," Evelyn yelled. "You are not allowed to die in here. Unacceptable!"

The elevator seemed to be getting warmer. Lila wiped the beads of sweat from her upper lip.

"For the last time, no one is dying," Lila said. So much for not getting involved. She crouched down next to Jasper and patted his shoulder. "Take a deep breath in, let it out slowly."

"C-can't," Jasper said. His voice was barely discernible from between his legs.

"Try again," Lila encouraged.

Jasper merely squeezed his hands on his knees.

Lila tried to come up with something to help. Maybe she could take Jasper's mind off their current situation by distracting him. She looked around the elevator, searching for anything that might work. Jasper's cloth bag had dropped to the floor, the contents spilling out. Among the sacks of flour and sugar, she noticed a paperback with the title scrolled in cursive below a knife dripping vibrant red blood. It was a mass-market murder mystery; the kind Lila had loved to read before Ryan convinced her historical biographies were a better use of her time.

Lila grasped the book. "Is this one good?"

Jasper looked over and nodded. His face relaxed for a moment before tensing again.

"Do you like mysteries?" Lila asked, trying to engage him.

Jasper breathed out, shallow and wheezing. "I enjoy guessing the twist." He exhaled again. "I used to be a detective with the Richmond Police Department."

"You were a real detective?" Bea clambered down beside him, suddenly interested. "What kind of crimes did you solve?"

A corner of Jasper's mouth lifted. "Property mostly. Robberies, arson, that kind of thing."

"Cool," Bea said. "Have you ever seen *Murder, She Wrote*? It's my favorite show."

"That doesn't seem at all appropriate for a five-year-old," Evelyn said.

"I'm ten," Bea said, glaring up at her.

Evelyn shrugged. "You're quite small for ten."

"At least I'm not old," Bea shot back.

"Bea!" Lila admonished. "We don't talk about people's ages."

"I'm not old," Evelyn insisted, although all signs pointed to the contrary.

"Are too," Bea whispered under her breath.

Jasper cleared his throat. "I've watched every episode of *Murder, She Wrote*."

"Me too!" Bea said, genuinely excited. "Do you have a favorite season?"

"I like the second," Jasper said.

"My favorite is the fifth. It's the bloodiest," Bea said.

"I don't know why we're talking about an old television show," Evelyn said.

"Because it's awesome," Bea said. "The best episodes are when more than one person dies. More murders to solve."

"You mean you like the intricate plots," Lila corrected, thinking it sounded better.

Bea jutted out her chin. "No, I like the stabbings. It's too bad they didn't have an episode where a kid was the killer. No one would have guessed that twist. Not even you," Bea said to Jasper.

Jasper blinked. "You might be right about that."

Lila was unable to even look at Jasper or Evelyn for several seconds. What must they think of her parenting with Bea going on about kid killers and multiple murders? Ryan would have immediately cut this off, changing the subject to something like the latest Marvel movie. He was always good at distracting Bea. Lila frowned, considering this. Ryan was only good at distracting Bea when he was actually around, which he wasn't now. At least she was here.

"I'm certain I could sniff out any murderer on any television show, even if it was a child. No one likes to believe children are capable of evil. Obviously *I* know better. It's why I don't trust the young," Evelyn said, staring pointedly at Bea.

"I wouldn't say children are evil," Lila said.

Jasper cleared his throat. His breathing had noticeably evened out.

"But some are," Bea announced. She gave Evelyn what could only be described as a demented smile.

"My five-year-old niece destroyed all my peonies one spring, and I'd paid the landscapers a pretty penny to keep them properly pruned," Evelyn offered as proof.

"I probably kicked a peony bush once," Bea said.

"Exactly as I suspected," Evelyn said.

Lila looked sideways at Jasper, rolling her eyes upward to indicate her frustration with Bea and Evelyn. Jasper smiled then; a real smile that transformed his entire face. His eyes crinkled up, and his cheeks lifted.

The elevator clanked and whirred and began moving upward once again. Lila exhaled a sigh of relief. She straightened and offered a hand to Jasper, helping him to his feet. Bea gathered his spilled belongings and gave him the cloth bag.

"Are you going to be okay?" Lila asked. "Can I call someone for you?"

Jasper shifted his gaze to a point beyond her shoulder. "There's no one to call, and I'm—I'm fine. Thank you for your help."

"You're welcome," Lila said.

"A poisoning would have been exciting, but I'm glad you didn't die," Bea said.

Evelyn sputtered out something that sounded suspiciously like a laugh before she covered it up with a glare. "Children are disrespectful these days because they aren't raised properly."

The elevator doors opened onto the second floor. Evelyn pushed her way past Lila with her walker. Jasper slunk out next, hurrying to his own door. As Lila and Bea made their way down the hallway, Lila wondered if she would see neighbors again before she moved out of the Primrose. Though she still intended to keep to herself, she had to admit she was a little curious about Evelyn and Jasper.

Chapter Seven

It was only four o'clock on a Sunday afternoon, but the lobby was crammed full of Primrose residents, all clutching enormous glasses of wine when Bea and Lila wandered in from the library. There was a table draped in an ivory tablecloth off to the right with several bottles chilling in silver buckets. Lila stood and admired the scene, still in awe of the beautiful marble floors, crystal chandeliers, and gingerbread trim. The Primrose really was a stunning place to live, even if her actual apartment should be condemned.

Bea skipped ahead. A man wearing a tweed newsboy hat and two women materialized in front of Lila, cutting off her route to Bea. Lila recognized them as the trio in the lobby from her first day at the Primrose.

"Hello. I'm Florence Parker, and you're obviously our newest resident. Welcome to the Primrose. You've walked right into Sunday happy hour. This whole extravaganza was my idea. I've taken sommelier courses." Florence wore a pair of wide-legged camel trousers that Lila could have sworn were Stella McCartney. Everything about Florence—neat bob, straight shoulders, stylish pants—signaled she was the kind of person who was used to being in charge.

"We saw you move in last week and wanted to say hello, but we were avoiding Susanna that day because she hurt Edwin's feelings," the second woman said as she gestured to the man in the hat. "I'm Mary Dixon Carter. We all live on the fourth floor." Mary Dixon wore a sweater embroidered with a large and alarmingly lifelike cat face, along with feathered Balenciaga heels.

Zoe appeared at her side. "I see you've all met Lila."

Zoe handed Lila a glass of white, holding a bottle of wine in her other hand.

"Oh, I couldn't," Lila said, handing back the glass. "I'm on my way upstairs." She could see Bea stopped at the edge of the hallway, watching them suspiciously.

"Wine is good for your health. I learned that in my sommelier courses," Florence said.

"I'm really busy right now," Lila said.

Zoe pressed the glass into her hands again. "Have a few sips." She held up the bottle. "Anyone need a refill?"

"Oh me, please," Mary Dixon said. "I forgot to buy more wine at the grocery store."

Edwin's mouth turned down. "My ex-wife used to buy the groceries. I'm recently divorced."

"Edwin, you don't need to tell people that as soon as you meet them," Mary Dixon scolded him. "It makes you sound desperate."

"I am desperate," Edwin said sadly.

Not as desperate as I am, Lila thought. She took a big sip of wine, anxious to finish the glass and get out of there as soon as possible.

Zoe nodded to the wine. "What do y'all think?"

Edwin sighed. "I think divorce is hard especially when you're seventy-six and don't like Viagra, which limits my dating options."

"That might be why you got divorced in the first place," Mary Dixon said.

"It certainly didn't help," Florence agreed.

Lila looked from one person to the other, not sure what to even say to that. Without her noticing, Bea had crept up behind her. She pulled on Lila's hand. "Mama, what's Viagra?"

Zoe clapped her hands together. "Okay! Florence, Mary Dixon, Edwin, I noticed Brock hovering around the mixed nuts again. Will y'all make sure he doesn't eat them all like last week? But no pushing this time."

This sent Florence into action. She grabbed Mary Dixon's arm and pulled her off toward the back of the room, Edwin shuffling behind with his cane.

"Sorry about that. Wine night can get a little wild around here." Zoe lowered her voice to a conspiratorial tone. "They all insist on glasses poured to within a half inch of the top, which explains the frequent arguments."

Bea piped up. "I saw Mama drink a whole bottle of wine straight out of the bottle one time after the police raided our house."

A flush rose up Lila's chest. She honestly couldn't tell if Bea was trying to embarrass her or just make conversation. Either way, she wanted to sink into the floor.

Lila forced out a small laugh. "She's exaggerating."

"But I didn't even mention the second bottle," Bea protested.

"Bea, why don't you sit over there and start your new book while I finish up here." Lila gestured to a high-backed bench along the wall, needing to occupy her daughter before she shared any more humiliating stories.

"Fine." Bea looked up at Zoe. "I have a feeling Mama and I are going to have a talk later about wine bottles."

Zoe lifted her brows in amusement. "I have a feeling you're right."

Bea walked over to the bench, adjusted herself in the seat, pulled a library book out of her bag, and began to read.

"She's hilarious," Zoe said, grinning.

"She's certainly something," Lila said.

"How's it going upstairs?" Zoe asked.

"Making great progress," Lila said in a faint voice.

Yesterday, Lila had opened a cabinet and found a stack of at least thirty spiral notebooks, all of which were filled with handwritten, detailed notes about the comings and goings of the other Primrose residents. Lila was starting to think Gloria had suffered from agoraphobia in addition to the hoarding disorder. She seemed to have spent all her time spying on her neighbors and collecting detritus, saving everything from junk mail to bottle caps to dried-up pens.

"I heard the apartment was pretty messy. Are y'all okay in there? You can tell me," Zoe said, nodding encouragingly.

"Actually, the apartment is a wreck. I had no idea what I was getting into." Lila said it without thinking.

Zoe winced. "Do you have anyone helping you?"

"We don't know a soul here in Richmond," Lila said, then rushed ahead, regretting how pathetic she sounded. "But it's fine. We're making do."

Zoe clucked her tongue. "Yikes. Poor you."

Lila squirmed, embarrassed by her honesty and wanting to change the subject. She noticed Helene and Alice standing beside the piano, set off from the crowd. A long oatmeal-colored cardigan swallowed up Alice's small frame.

"How are they doing?" Lila asked, nodding to the pair.

"I'm not sure. Helene lives in the building and Alice is temporarily staying with her, but I rarely see either of them. They were both close with Conrad. Alice's dad died when she was a baby, and Conrad stepped in and acted like a father to her. But I don't think Helene is happy with his reward idea. I heard Brock ask her whether anyone had come forward about Sophia. She looked pissed and wouldn't discuss it. Brock had already consumed several glasses of wine and was slurring, so she may have just wanted to get away from him." Zoe grinned.

"I'm not sure I blame her," Lila said, remembering his long yellow teeth.

Zoe chuckled before turning serious and dropping her voice. "Everyone knows Helene despises publicity about Sophia and worries about the stress on Alice, who already has enough on her plate. She went through an ugly breakup with her fiancé recently. Helene had to get lawyers to file a restraining order against him."

Helene linked her arm with Alice's and led her toward the elevator. They were the same height, their heads turned toward each other, walking in perfect sync. Lila admired Helene's obvious devotion to her daughter. She looked to Bea and wished they would have that kind of relationship someday. At that moment, it seemed unlikely.

Zoe cocked her head to study Lila before seeming to come to some conclusion. "We should grab dinner. You must need a break."

Lila sipped her wine, buying time to think. She found herself flattered at the invitation and was surprised that she almost wanted to go. Maybe it was because she hadn't gone to dinner in so long, or maybe it was because Zoe seemed truly kind. She reached for her phone to text one of her regular babysitters and stopped, realizing she didn't have any babysitters in Richmond.

"I can't. I have Bea," Lila said.

"My sister is in college nearby. I'm sure she could take care of Bea." Zoe nodded as if the matter was settled. "I don't have my phone while I'm working, but I'll give you my number."

Lila hesitated still.

"Or I can DM you on Instagram," Zoe continued. "You've got an account, right?"

Lila did have an Instagram account, though she hadn't posted in months. But if Zoe looked up Lila's profile, she would still see an expertly curated grid of family vacations and sappy anniversary posts dedicated to Ryan. All happy, idyllic photos reflecting a perfect life that hadn't really existed. Sweat pooled beneath Lila's arms when she considered how miserable she'd been on some of those vacations, like the ski trip to Park City. Photos showed her laughing with Bea and Ryan, white-capped mountains in the background. The reality was Ryan had made nightly dinner plans with the new friends he met on the slopes, insisting Lila would love them. She hadn't wanted to eat with a group of strangers every night but she'd gone anyway, hiding her resentment beneath a new Moncler jacket as Ryan entertained the entire table with stories.

The woman on Lila's Instagram grid was a fraud. And as much as she wanted to befriend Zoe, what could the *real* Lila possibly talk to her about? Did Zoe want to hear about how Lila had cried every day for three months after Ryan left? Did she want to talk about the miserable customer service job Lila had gotten fired from? *No, definitely not.*

"I appreciate the offer but I'm busy with the apartment," Lila said without suggesting another time.

Zoe's smile dimmed. "No problem. I get it."

As Lila walked out of the lobby with Bea, she was discomfited at how she had brushed off Zoe's offer, but what else could Lila have done? It was too humiliating to show her actual life to a single soul outside of Bea.

As soon as they made it up the stairs and Lila unlocked their door, Bea raced inside. She was back in the entryway a moment later, holding a brown grocery bag and edging toward the door.

"What are you doing?" Lila asked. She stacked her library book on the coffee table, which she'd only recently unearthed from beneath a stack of boxes. It had pretty wood carvings down the legs, which now shone after Lila had wiped them down with wood polish.

"I have an errand," Bea said. "It's confidential."

Lila frowned. "But ten-year-olds don't get to have secrets from their parents."

"Why can't you let me have some privacy?" Bea's nose scrunched up in dismay.

"Again, it's the whole ten-year-old problem."

"This is like living on Alcatraz." Bea crossed her arms over her chest. "Fine, I'll tell you. I made something for Jasper and I want to give it to him."

Lila blinked, confused. "Do you mean Mr. Fielding, our neighbor?"

"He told me to call him Jasper." Bea's voice was defiant now.

"When was that?" Lila asked.

"You were busy in the bedroom yesterday, and I walked over to his apartment." Bea shrugged as Lila sucked in a breath. "You can't blame me. He was baking cookies, and I could smell them."

Lila had not seen Jasper since his panic attack in the elevator, but he had left a Tupperware container of the richest, chewiest brownies outside their door the following day. Based on the brownies, she would bet his cookies were equally delicious. But that didn't mean Bea was allowed to visit a stranger without permission.

Lila deflated. How had she not realized Bea had left the apartment yesterday? Shouldn't a sixth sense have kicked in? When she had discovered Bea had skipped school for two days after Ryan left, she had felt exactly the same—bewildered and dense, as if she was missing the natural good mother gene everyone else inherited.

"You can't leave the apartment without telling me," Lila said.

"I'm not a baby. I can walk six feet without getting kidnapped." Bea rolled her eyes.

"Maybe so but we have rules. You can't go see people I don't know."

"But you *do* know him. He's our neighbor, and he's a really good baker. He made chocolate chip cookies with peanut butter yesterday and gave me six to take with me."

"I didn't see any cookies."

Bea's gaze slid sideways. "I might have eaten them all. I'm not sure. But I'm telling you where I'm going now so I'm doing exactly as you wanted. You're the one who is always saying thank-you notes are important. I wrote Jasper a thank-you note for the cookies and brownies because I care about manners." She reached into her bag and held out a piece of red construction paper covered in multicolored writing in Magic Marker.

Lila didn't remember Bea ever caring about manners before. She suspected there was more to Bea's story, some angle she couldn't see yet. Perhaps it was as simple as Bea hoping for more cookies.

"Mama, come on," Bea said in a pleading tone.

Lila relented. "You can slide the note under his door. We don't want to bother him."

"Jasper said yesterday I wasn't a bother."

"I'm sure," Lila said doubtfully.

Bea huffed, sensing Lila didn't believe her. Bea disappeared into the hallway, letting the door slam behind her. Lila crossed the room and pressed her ear against the door. Nothing. She then heard footsteps in the apartment next door. There was a rumbly low voice and Bea's higher tone in response. Bea had not simply slid the note under the door as Lila had directed. Why was she surprised?

Chapter Eight

Lila opened the door to 2B. Bea glared back at her. The hallway lights blinked gold dots onto her Braves T-shirt. The glass door to the stairwell framed rising steps beyond Bea's shoulder.

Jasper stood in the hall beside his door, looking slightly dazed and holding the construction paper card. "I really don't think I could possibly do that," he said.

"Hi, Jasper. Nice to see you. We enjoyed the brownies. Bea, let's go," Lila said.

"I'm in the middle of something important here," Bea said.

Lila stepped outside the apartment, trying to figure out how to get Bea inside without causing a scene. "I think Jasper needs to get back to whatever he was doing."

"This is none of your business," Bea said in a loud voice.

Lila's face went hot. Bea shouldn't talk that way to her, especially not in front of someone she barely knew. Lila overcompensated with a sharp, raised voice. "Inside now."

Bea put her hands on her hips. "No!"

Jasper looked mortified. Sweat popped up along Lila's hairline. Bea was making Lila look like she couldn't control her child. While this was technically true, Bea didn't need to make it quite so obvious.

"This is the last time I'm going to ask you nicely," Lila said, all the while wondering what she would do if Bea continued not to obey—take away her Braves shirt? Sign her up for more kickball games?

"Leave me alone!" Bea snapped.

Across the hall, Evelyn's door swung open. She stepped into the hallway in a beaded dress and large emerald earrings, looking thoroughly annoyed. "What's going on out here? I can barely hear myself think with all the yelling."

"There wasn't much yelling," Jasper said.

"I'm sorry," Lila said quickly. "We'll be quiet." She would forcibly pull Bea inside if she had to. Evelyn was definitely liable to call Susanna, as was Jasper at this point.

Bea turned to Jasper, her face desperate now. "We can solve Sophia's murder. I know it."

Lila's heart sank as she realized why Bea wanted to see Jasper in the first place—this was about the reward. "Oh, Bea. We talked about this."

"Jasper was a detective. You said we didn't have enough experience to find Sophia's killer, but *he* does," Bea said.

Jasper looked stricken. "I retired two years ago."

"But you could solve it if you tried," Bea said hopefully. "You've got more experience than Jessica Fletcher and look how many cases she solved."

Lila rubbed her temple and gave Jasper an apologetic look. "I'm really sorry about this."

Bea kicked at the floor. There was a suspicious hitch to her shoulders, and Lila could tell she was trying not to cry. Lila's own eyes pricked.

"We're fine," Lila said to Jasper, or to herself. She wasn't sure which.

"It doesn't seem that way," Evelyn said.

"Excuse me?" Lila said, rearing back in surprise. Didn't Evelyn know the rules? Wealthy people always said everything was fine. She'd learned that from Patricia, who'd looked appalled whenever Lila mentioned catching a cold or Bea's struggles in math.

"You live in an apartment that doesn't belong to you. Your daughter is unruly. You're making a scene and disturbing your neighbors. I wouldn't say you're fine," Evelyn said.

Lila's throat worked to swallow. "We won't bother you again."

"I'm not holding my breath," Evelyn said.

"That's not nice," Jasper said softly.

"Jasper Fielding, I am known for many things—my impeccable style, my charitable contributions, my hostessing prowess. But I am not, nor have I ever been, known for being nice," Evelyn said in an exasperated voice.

Jasper shrank back against his door.

Evelyn lifted her chin toward Lila. "While I don't presume to give you advice, I do have some thoughts. Despite what Florence says, most people value my opinion. You should channel that young lady's energy into something useful. If she's so obsessed with Sophia Kent's death, why not engage in some clue searching in the apartment? There's obviously a reason we were all included as beneficiaries. Perhaps it's due to something hidden in this building."

Bea's face was blotchy with tears. She was quiet for once, her posture defeated. It was exactly the way she'd looked when Lila broke the news to her that Ryan had left. For a moment, she imagined how good it would feel if she could solve Sophia's murder for Bea. But that was unrealistic. How could she possibly find a clue to Sophia's death in all that mess? She wouldn't even know where to look unless . . .

"I—well—I actually did find these notebooks. I only glanced inside one or two, but it looks like Gloria kept diaries about her neighbors," Lila said before she could stop herself.

Evelyn took a step forward. "That's right. Gloria mentioned to me once that she made a habit of recording nuisance behavior. Perhaps she saw something the night of Sophia's death and wrote it down."

Bea's eyes lifted, blue and wide and hopeful.

"I suppose we could look through them. I doubt we'll find anything, though. This is just for fun," Lila said, trying not to think too hard about the fact that fun now included searching for clues in a murder investigation.

Evelyn crossed the hall and pushed past Lila with her walker, opening the door to Gloria's apartment. "Let's see what we're dealing with here."

Bea followed closely at the heels of Evelyn's black and tan CHANEL flats. Jasper gave Lila a disbelieving look, which she mirrored back to him.

"Will you come in too?" Lila asked, hoping Jasper would say yes so she didn't have to deal with Evelyn by herself.

Jasper took a deep breath and nodded, not looking happy but obviously taking pity on Lila and not wanting to leave her alone with a stubborn ten-year-old obsessed with murder and a bossy eighty-year-old obsessed with herself.

Evelyn stood in the room, looking around in disbelief. "This is a catastrophe."

Jasper's eyebrows shot to the top of his bald head.

"Do the police ever have to search houses as messy as this?" Bea asked.

"Never," Jasper said. "This is unusual."

"As I suspected. I hate unusual," Bea said.

Lila stepped across several boxes, four end tables, and a pile of folding chairs, reaching the giant hutch that dominated the far left side of the living room. She pulled out a stack of notebooks and carried them over to the middle of the room.

Evelyn plucked one from the top, opened it, and skimmed the contents. When she looked back up, her face was triumphant. "I was right about Gloria. My memory is like a steel trap. This will show my doctor that the ridiculous memory test he gave me a few months ago was pointless. I told him my family doesn't believe in cognitive decline." She lowered herself onto the mohair couch and looked expectantly at Lila. "You might as well bring them all over here so we can get started. I'd like a cup of mint tea as well."

Lila stared at Evelyn, wondering how she'd managed to barge in and take over. "I think I only have chamomile."

"It's not my favorite, but it will do," Evelyn said.

Evelyn reached onto the coffee table, picked up another notebook, and handed it to Bea. Soon they were both flipping through the pages. Bea hummed under her breath. Lila shrugged at Jasper, who shrugged back and sat down in one of the large club chairs, also picking up a notebook. He bent over the pages, instantly absorbed. The "clue searching" was happening whether Lila liked it or not.

After preparing the tea, Lila carried over the rest of the notebooks and took the seat across from Jasper. She opened one and began to read. Each page was neatly labeled by date, and the entries were daily and varied. *8:14 a.m. John Lee spotted outside, going for a jog (probably for the best as he has gained ten pounds). 10:48 a.m. Andrew and Wilma Winthrop return to apartment 2C, arguing about whether Wilma spent too much money at the antique store (most likely, she did). 2:32 p.m. Ava Currington leaves by the front door wearing sweatpants (inappropriate).*

After a while, Jasper held a green notebook aloft. "I think I found something. This one covers the time period around Sophia's murder."

"Don't dither around. What happened on the day of the murder?" Evelyn demanded.

Jasper flipped the pages. Lila's stomach was somersaulting inside. Bea was bouncing on the couch, her entire face alight. This was utterly crazy, but was there a chance Gloria had left a clue about Sophia's killer?

Jasper scanned the page, and his shoulders slumped. "There's nothing here."

"Can I see it?" Lila asked. She took the log and read the entry for the day of Sophia's death. Jasper was right. There was nothing of significance. It was all about people coming back to their apartments with coffee, and the noise of the cocktail party downstairs (which Gloria was furious about), and the police arriving at 8 p.m. Nothing to indicate who had killed Sophia.

"It was a good try," Jasper said gently to no one in particular.

Bea's movements stilled; her lip quivered. Lila reached out to touch Bea's arm. Bea shrugged her off. Lila's hands opened and closed, futile in their efforts to hold onto something. She picked up the log again for want of something to do. Scanning a page, she spotted the word *robbery*.

"Hey, this is interesting," Lila said, hoping to cheer Bea up with another crime, which was pathetic, but what else could she do? "Gloria mentions a robbery in here."

"Yes, there were several robberies in the building around that time. I almost moved after Sophia was killed, but I'd recently had the new drapes hung and they're silk," Evelyn said.

"What does it say?" Bea asked, looking mildly interested.

"Let me see." Lila read the page. "Okay, here we go. *November 14, 2002, 2:30 p.m. Suspicious person exits apartment 2D in ski mask, enters stairwell, and walks upstairs, as observed through glass door. Mia Clockworth arrives home at apartment 2D at*

4:10 p.m. and screams (noise violation). Building manager arrives at apartment 2D at 4:13 p.m. (could have been faster). Police arrive at 4:40 p.m. (tracked dirt onto carpet). Police knock on my door at 5:30 p.m. I did not answer (obviously)."

Lila reread the words, their significance sinking in. Despite the absurdity of this situation, something vibrated inside her. "Hold on. I want to understand this. In the stairwell, the doors to each floor are locked. Our key cards only unlock the door to the floor we live on. Was the same system in place in 2002?"

"The stairwell doors have always been locked since I lived here. Before the key cards, each resident had a regular key that only opened the door to their floor," Evelyn said.

Lila jabbed her finger at the page. "Do you know what this means?"

"Gloria saw the burglar and should have spoken to the police. She never answered her door, so I'm not surprised by her lack of cooperation," Evelyn said.

"It's more than that," Lila said. "If Gloria saw the burglar walk *upstairs*, they wouldn't have been able to enter any other floor unless—"

"The burglar lived on that floor," Evelyn finished in a loud voice. "That's exactly what I was about to point out to you."

Jasper's eyes were wide, his face intense. "If the burglar lived in the Primrose, that would explain why they never caught anyone on the security cameras entering the building."

"We found an actual clue," Bea said, bounding to her feet. "We're like a real-life police unit except two of us are super old."

Lila stared at Bea and her chest expanded, air rushing in to fill it. She couldn't even admonish Bea for calling Evelyn and Jasper old. Not when Bea looked so damn happy.

"We could solve the murder," Bea said excitedly.

"All we know is the burglar may have lived in the building, and the same burglar may have killed Sophia Kent," Jasper warned.

"But that's more than the police know. Now we can make a list of suspects. I'll get some paper." Bea looked at each of them, her face splitting into a grin. "I can't wait to get started. This is so fun." With that, she hurried from the room.

Lila eyed Evelyn and Jasper, both of whom were staring after Bea. A flush rose up Lila's neck. This was weird. She didn't want to rely on two people she barely knew for anything, much less investigating a twenty-one-year-old murder with her daughter.

Lila cleared her throat. "Thank you for coming to help today, but I'll talk her out of this."

Evelyn patted the double strand of pearls at her neck. "She is quite a determined young lady. That's not something you see much anymore. I'm awfully busy, of course, with all my social obligations, but I could help make a list of suspects. I do know everyone in the building, and I wouldn't be sorry if a few of them went to jail."

Jasper lowered his gaze to the floor and spoke in a soft, halting voice as if afraid someone was going to interrupt him. "I could pass along some investigation tips to Bea."

"But we can't actually investigate. That's ridiculous," Lila said.

Evelyn frowned. "What's so ridiculous? Jasper was a detective, and I'm excellent at uncovering secrets, in addition to having a genius-level IQ. Why couldn't we solve the murder?"

"Maybe because we don't know what we're doing," Lila said, a bit desperate now for someone else to come back to reality.

"Speak for yourself," Evelyn said. "Right, Jasper?"

Jasper was staring at his hands, hunching over in his chair. He risked a glance up at Evelyn and nodded quickly when she glared at him. Lila wasn't sure if he agreed with Evelyn or if he was simply afraid of her. Maybe both.

Bea raced back into the room, holding a sheaf of notebook paper. She skidded to a stop at Lila's side and wrapped her arms around Lila's shoulders in a hug. Lila froze, a lump instantly forming in her throat. How long had it been since her daughter spontaneously hugged her? Lila pulled Bea closer, looking up at her face. For once, Bea didn't pull away. Bea's eyes were shining; they literally caught the light and sparkled. How could Lila possibly not go through with this insane idea if it made her daughter look like this? Maybe it *was* ridiculous. Ryan would probably think so, but Ryan wasn't here. This was Lila's decision. She'd try to solve Sophia Kent's murder, she'd investigate, she'd play along. She'd do anything to reconnect with her daughter and bring back the cheerful girl who'd gone missing at the same time as her husband.

Chapter Nine

Bea begged to stay home to work on Sophia's murder investigation. She reasoned that the reward of two million dollars was worth more than finishing fourth grade. Lila sent her to school, promising Bea could work on the investigation when she got home.

Lila was sorting through a box of twelve-year-old power bills and expired cans of Campbell's chicken noodle soup. She had to carefully check every inch of the apartment because valuables were mixed in with all the trash. Only yesterday, she'd discovered a huge emerald ring inside of an aspirin bottle and a seventy-seven-piece sterling silver set hidden beneath molding linens, all of which she set aside for Gloria's son, Stanley.

There was plenty to do in the apartment, but she hated the silence and how lonely it made her feel. There was no reason for her to miss Ryan. He'd left her with a disaster. She wanted to hate him and a lot of the time she did. But despite her best intentions for hatred, she did miss some things: his big laugh, the way he teased Bea out of bad moods, how he could walk into a party not recognizing a soul and walk out with ten new best friends. Tears gathered behind her eyes in a painful burn. Ryan had known her better than anyone, and he hadn't wanted her in the end. Now whenever she tried to think about the future, her mind went blank. All those endless days and months of emptiness, by herself; no one to care for her, no one to love her, just... *no one.*

Picking up her phone, Lila scrolled through her contacts, wanting to fill the quiet with another voice. She stopped at Daphne Bryant, her fingers hovering over the name. Daphne was her closest friend in Norfolk, her oldest friend too. They'd bonded when they were in choir together at Meritt Academy, back when Daphne hadn't cared that Lila couldn't afford a Coach bag or the junior spring break trip to Mexico. They'd served as bridesmaids in each other's weddings and signed their children up for the same baby music classes. But their friendship was strained these days. It wasn't Daphne's fault they no longer had the same things in common like noncriminal husbands and stable lives. A flush rose up Lila's chest as she considered one of their last conversations where Daphne had offered her a loan. Lila had refused, but for one long moment . . . oh, how she'd wanted to take the money. How she'd considered swallowing her pride. Bea had needed new shoes, the mortgage had been due, she'd lost her job. The *yes* was right there on the tip of her tongue, and she was humiliated at her own desperation.

Lila scrolled past Daphne and called Mama again instead. She'd tried to reach her several times since moving into the Primrose and had been sent to voice mail every time. But Mama picked up this time.

"Honestly, Lila, what is going on? You keep calling me over and over," Mama said.

"Hi, Mama. It's good to talk to you too."

Mama's voice softened. "I'm sorry. I'm always happy to hear from you, but what is so important that you've left me four messages? You know I'm in the bridge championship at the club this week."

"I forgot about that. It's just . . . you never told me the apartment was this big of a mess," Lila said.

"Is that all? I'm sure I mentioned it needed some organizing."

Mama laughed, a high, delicate sound. Lila could see her sitting in the light-filled sunroom of Stanley's home, adjusting the sleeves of her prized Carolina Herrera tulip-print blouse.

"We can't even walk in here," Lila said. She still couldn't believe Stanley had let Gloria live like this. Had he ever visited his mama? And if he did, why hadn't he tried harder to improve her living situation?

"My goodness, Lila, Stanley gave you a place to live, didn't he? All he asks in return is a little cleaning." Mama's voice took on an edge.

"It's a lot more than a little cleaning."

Mama was silent for several long beats. Lila's stomach twisted at the silent rebuke.

"This arrangement took some convincing on my end. I can't control the state of the apartment too," Mama said.

Mama was reminding Lila of certain truths. Mama lived with Stanley, but she had no claim to his fortune. Though Stanley and Mama had dated for eight years, they weren't married. There were unspoken rules by which she had to abide to keep her position, and those rules did not allow her to push too hard when it came to supporting her daughter mired in scandal.

"I know," Lila said quietly.

Mama sighed. "I wish I could help more. I know this is an awful time for you. Ryan left you with nothing. I only wish you'd finished college."

Lila didn't remember Mama wishing that in the past. When she'd broken the news that Ryan had asked her to marry him, Mama was overjoyed. *Meritt Academy finally paid off*, she'd said as if the entire point of private school was to marry into the wealthy Shaw family.

Ryan had proposed at his college graduation party. They'd discussed dating long distance; she would finish her final year at Clemson and join him in Norfolk afterward. But that night, he'd pulled her outside on the patio of the Kappa Alpha house. The moon shone onto the brick pavers, the party a distant roar. He'd knelt beneath that pool of light and held out his grandma's two-carat diamond ring. *I don't want to wait. I already know I'll love you forever.* The combination of moonlight and diamonds and the security of forever was irresistible. She'd said yes without even thinking. He'd announced their engagement afterward to the entire party. One of Ryan's fraternity brothers made a joke about getting tied down. Ryan had shrugged, unembarrassed, his face flushed and handsome. *Dude, I don't care. I love her.* The guys had groaned good-naturedly, and the girls had looked at Lila with new respect, trying to calculate how she'd done it. There was no more discussion of finishing her final year of Clemson.

"I'll do my best on the apartment," Lila finally said.

"That's my girl. You need a positive attitude to get anything done. How is the job hunt going?" Mama asked.

Lila's gut squirmed. She'd applied for a few online positions—personal assistant, online sales, claims adjuster. So far, she hadn't gotten a single call back. She wasn't surprised since she'd spent the past ten years raising Bea. "I've applied for a few things. I'm hoping for something that lets me be around in the afternoons when Bea gets home from school."

Mama clucked. "Honey, you may not find a job that operates on your schedule. You might have to lower your standards."

"Trust me. They're not that high," Lila mumbled.

Mama exhaled as if her words pained her. "Stanley has kindly given you a roof over your heads, but he was very clear that the arrangement with Gloria's apartment is temporary."

"I know, and I am grateful," Lila said stiffly.

"I know you are. We owe Stanley a lot."

Mama always said that—*we owe him a lot.* Lila's father died in a car accident when she was only six. They were left with no savings, a rental apartment with mold that spread across the ceiling like black splotchy clouds, and a VW Bug with a dead battery. Mama had gotten herself a secretary job at a law firm. They got by. Barely. Lila remembered the time their electricity got cut off for five days and walking home from the grocery store, plastic bags cutting into her arms, because there was no money for gas.

After a few years, Mama had married Doug. He was a lawyer, she signed a prenup. They moved into his house. Lila tried not to mind that Doug never looked her in the eye or asked about her day. She tried not to cry when she thought about her own daddy running alongside her bike when he took off the training wheels. Mama said that kind of crying about another man would only make Doug upset, and Lila needed to stay quiet because they owed him a lot. When the marriage ended in divorce after three years, and Mama started dating David, then Pat, then William, Lila didn't cry. She didn't raise a fuss when Mama went on vacations without her or failed to show up at a chorus recital because a boyfriend needed her for a work dinner. The boyfriends never lasted too long, maybe because Mama chose them for the lifestyle they could give her more than anything else. But she was taking care of Lila as best she could, and they owed the men a lot.

Mama continued. "I know you'll get through this terrible situation. And I bet you can find someone new in Richmond. You're still so pretty. You should put yourself out there."

Lila bit her lip. She would never put herself out there again.

"I'm not ready for that," Lila said.

"He isn't coming back to you."

"I am well aware we're getting a divorce," Lila snapped.

Mama went silent again, making her opinion known—Lila was making a mistake, wasting her looks and not finding a new man—before changing the subject.

"Make sure to send a condolence note to the Kents. We heard about Conrad. They're a prominent family. Don't forget, you're a representative of Stanley's while you're living at the Primrose," Mama said.

"I met Conrad before he died. He was nice."

"Of course he was nice. He was one of the wealthiest men in Virginia. I understand he was friendly with Gloria too," Mama said.

"Really?" Lila straightened. "Did Gloria ever talk about him . . . or his granddaughter Sophia?"

"Is there a reason she would?"

"Sophia was murdered in the Primrose over twenty years ago. Don't you remember? It was a big story at the time. I thought Gloria might have mentioned it to you."

It was silly to ask but maybe Mama knew something about Sophia's murder that she could tell Bea about later.

"Why are you asking me about some girl's death? I don't like discussing such gruesome subjects," Mama said, an audible shudder coming across the phone line.

"Conrad left a reward for anyone in the building who provides information that leads to solving her murder."

"My goodness, that's certainly something, isn't it? I can't recall Gloria ever mentioning a murder."

"Maybe you should ask Stanley about it," Lila said.

Twenty-one years had passed since Sophia's death. Years when the police, amateur detectives on the internet, and investigative reporters didn't produce a killer. Lila still couldn't understand Conrad's reasoning for the reward. Surely if someone at the Primrose knew who had killed Sophia, they would have come forward by now . . . although, perhaps not. Perhaps the residents of the Primrose had reasons to keep their secrets.

"I hope you're not thinking *you're* going to solve a murder."

Mama sounded alarmed. "You need to keep your head down. We don't need any more publicity involving you."

Lila's cheeks burned. "I'm not solving anything. I was only curious."

Mama's delicate laugh tinkled once more. "Oh good. The whole notion sounds ridiculous anyway. As if you could solve a murder. Look at what was happening right under your nose with Ryan's crimes. Not that I blame you for not understanding numbers and business. It's all Greek to me too."

"I had nothing to do with his business," Lila said stiffly.

"Exactly," Mama said soothingly. "Now, honey, I really do have to go. I'm due at the club in a half hour. Let's talk in a few days."

"Yeah, okay." Lila slumped back. Her entire body felt heavy as if buried beneath layers of sand. She wasn't sure what she'd expected from the phone call but whatever it was, that wasn't it.

Chapter Ten

Lila stood, pushing the box of expired soup cans out of her way. She bounced her foot on the floor and tapped her fingers on the counter. Mama's words looped through her head—*we owe him a lot, put yourself out there, as if you could solve a murder.* All at once, Lila strode out of the kitchen. Time for a change of scenery.

The Primrose was situated at the end of Grove Avenue, the main thoroughfare that ran right through the middle of Richmond's Near West End. The area was dotted with established neighborhoods and stately homes, stunning stone churches, red-brick private schools, and a stretch of three blocks with upscale shops, restaurants, and specialty stores.

Rise Up Cafe was tucked away off a quiet corner down a small side street. There was a patio out front with black metal chairs and tables, and it always had a crowd of young mothers in designer workout clothes and expensive strollers. Lila recognized the type; she used to be one of them.

The cafe was busy midmorning with the regular mama and stroller crowd, a few retired men in golf shirts, and college students in sweatpants. The rich scent of coffee permeated the air. The bakery case contained an array of scones and muffins. The walls were a pale yellow, bathed in sunlight from the large bay window in front.

Lila ordered a regular coffee, the cheapest thing on the menu. She was told it would take a few minutes since they were brewing a fresh pot, and she grabbed the only empty table. Pulling the laptop out of her old Louis Vuitton tote, she stared at the familiar brown and beige pattern and the cracked leather of the handles. It was the first designer handbag she had ever bought, after they'd celebrated their first year of business. It had made her feel like she belonged, like she wasn't the girl at Meritt Academy whose mama couldn't afford the True Religion low rise jeans everyone else wore on the weekends. It was the one bag she hadn't sold yet. Lila shoved the bag away, under the table, and opened her laptop, navigating to the job-posting websites she frequented.

Scrolling through the websites unearthed nothing new. She heard the barista call her name and looked up. There were several people standing near the counter and by the front window of the cafe, obviously hoping a table would open up. Lila needed to save her seat but didn't want to leave her laptop or bag unattended. Reaching into her bag for something to serve as a table holder, she found only lip glosses, some stray Kleenex, and one of Gloria's old novels.

Yesterday, Lila had unearthed a large collection of space erotica from a cardboard box with titles like *Revenge of the Sexbots* and *Space Cavities*. This particular book was called *Thrust* and had an illustration of a man with a very prominent bulge in the front of his spacesuit beside a rocket ship out of which a mostly naked woman was descending. Bea had charged into the living room while Lila was holding the book. Panicked, she'd stuffed it into her handbag. She pulled it out now. It was the best thing available. She made sure to turn it over so only the back was visible and placed it on the table.

After grabbing her coffee from the counter, Lila returned to find someone had hijacked her table. The man was somewhere in his thirties with brown hair curling in five different directions and a pissed-off expression.

Lila cleared her throat, waiting for him to look up. He didn't. She cleared her throat again. He still ignored her. Finally, she said, "I'm sorry, but I think you made a mistake. I was already sitting here." She let out a nervous half-laugh. "I guess you didn't see my book?"

The man continued to look down at his phone. "I saw it."

Lila exhaled and stared at him, hoping he would get up or move. This was *her* seat and every other table was filled.

The man looked at her. "Do you mind not hovering? I have to take a call."

"Are you asking me to leave?" Lila asked in astonishment.

The man smiled then. "Thanks for offering." He held out her book. "You forgot this. Interesting choice, by the way. Do you think *Thrust* is referring to the rocket ship or . . ." He raised his eyebrows and let his voice trail off.

Lila blushed and snatched the book out of his hand. "This isn't mine."

"Great. Then we're in agreement on me keeping the table."

"I didn't mean it that way," The skin on Lila's chest prickled. "What I meant was the book belongs to someone else, but I did use it as a placeholder."

The man made a big show of looking around. "It belongs to someone else, huh? Is that someone imaginary?"

Lila narrowed her eyes. "Books are a universal sign for seat saving. Everyone knows that."

This guy knew it too, but he wasn't moving. He was betting on the fact that she was a demure, little woman who was too afraid to argue back with him. It wasn't a terrible bet when it came to her. She had never fought with Ryan. Life was easier and more pleasant without arguing. Mama had taught her that too. But right now, she had no interest in being pleasant to this guy or anyone else who pissed her off. Lila sat down in her original seat across the table. For good measure, she banged her coffee cup in front of her, claiming the spot.

"You do realize you're acting childish." The man glared at her.

"You're the one acting childish," Lila said, unable to believe she was even talking to a stranger like this, but not caring for once.

"I need privacy for my call."

"Then maybe you shouldn't have it in a coffee shop," Lila answered. She opened her laptop, making it clear she wasn't going anywhere.

His phone began to ring. "That's my call."

Lila looked down at her laptop screen, pretending she hadn't heard him.

He picked up his phone and answered the call, twisting away from her. "Hi, John. Thanks for calling."

Lila pretended to be reading something on her laptop. She sipped her coffee and eavesdropped. The guy deserved it. He was in a public place, sitting at her table.

He continued. "Yes, I understand. Sure I can have a proposal drawn up by tomorrow. Someone at the department has agreed to talk." Another pause. "I've requested a copy of the Kent trust, and I have a few interviews already lined up at the Primrose."

At this, Lila looked up. He was talking about the Primrose and Conrad Kent's trust. Who was this guy? He met her gaze and frowned, signaling that he didn't appreciate her listening in on his phone call. Did he live in the building? No, he couldn't. He wasn't old enough, and she'd never seen him before—she would have noticed those absurdly wide shoulders.

"Look, can I call you back in ten minutes? I'm having a problem with our connection. Okay, I'll call you. Bye." He hung up the phone and looked straight at her. "Do you enjoy listening to other people's calls?"

Lila snapped her laptop shut. "Why are you talking about Conrad Kent's trust?"

The man leaned forward, his eyes gleaming. Something about having all that attention and those green eyes directed right at her made her blush. She shrank back in her seat.

"What do you know about the trust?" he asked.

"I live in the Primrose," Lila said.

His eyes squinted at her. "You're not over fifty-five, are you?"

"No," Lila said, offended that he even asked. "I'm living in the building temporarily."

His face softened into an appealing but obviously fake smile. "I think we got off on the wrong foot. Can I ask you a few questions?"

"Who *are* you?" Lila asked.

"Nate Donnelly. I'm a reporter for the *Richmond Journal*."

A reporter. Shit. Lila hated reporters.

"Why do you care about the trust?" Lila asked.

"I'm writing an article about Sophia Kent's death. It's a retrospective look at the crime and failed investigation. There's renewed interest with Conrad Kent's death and the two-million-dollar reward. I'm interviewing the police, the family, and several of the Primrose residents. How long have you lived at the Primrose? How do you feel about the trust?"

This wouldn't work on Lila. She didn't trust him one bit. Draining the rest of her coffee, she got up from the table.

"I'm not interested in an interview," Lila said.

"You're busy. I get it. If you give me your name and number, I'll call you. We can set up a better time to talk." Nate put out a hand to stop her, rising to a half-crouch. "I promise I'm a nice guy when I'm not waiting on a call from my editor. He makes me nervous."

Nate's hair was an absolute wreck, as if he'd spent the entire morning pulling at the strands. For one brief, insane moment, Lila imagined smoothing it down herself.

"I can't help you. I don't talk to reporters," Lila said in a stern, definitive voice.

She thought of the articles written about Ryan's crimes and how he'd left his wife and daughter. A red-hot fire licked at her neck. It was mortifying even all these months later to imagine total strangers reading about the worst thing that had ever happened to her and judging her as they did so.

"I find that most of the time, people don't talk to reporters because they're hiding something," Nate said in a light tone.

Nate had no idea how close he was to the truth. The last thing Lila wanted was any more press, which was sure to mention her connection to Ryan and the scandal from last year. Richmond and the Primrose were a fresh, if temporary, start for her and Bea. She didn't want Bea's new classmates to know about Ryan's crimes.

"I'm not hiding anything." Lila's voice raised at the end, drawing the attention of the four women sitting at the table to their right, all of whom wore some version of lululemon leggings and matching crop tops, their hair slicked back into sleek ponytails. They glanced over at Lila and Nate. Their eyes flicked off her immediately and landed on Nate for several beats before lashes dipped and lips tipped up in unmistakable expressions of interest. The looks made Lila frown. He wasn't that attractive.

Nate held up his hands as if in surrender. "No need to get all worked up."

"I'm perfectly calm." But that was a lie. Lila was definitely worked up. "I'm just not interested in talking to you."

"Ouch." Nate glanced at her bare left ring finger. "Most people don't shoot me down after less than five minutes."

"Maybe those people haven't heard you talk yet." Lila clutched the bag to her side as if it was a shield. "I'm leaving."

"It would have been nice if you'd done that five minutes ago when I was on the phone."

Lila spun around, pushing past the tables and banging her shin into a table leg. The lululemon mamas watched her with interest, whispering among themselves.

"Enjoy your space porn," Nate called after her.

"Enjoy being a jerk," Lila yelled back.

Lila stalked out of Rise Up Cafe. Her heart was beating fast, but a small smile hovered around her lips because right then, she wasn't sad and she wasn't lonely and she definitely wasn't afraid.

Chapter Eleven

Lila walked back to the Primrose feeling strangely cheerful. Maybe she needed to get mad at people more often. She admired the large planters of geraniums outside many of the shops and stopped to pet a yellow Lab who sniffed at her legs. A plan was forming in her head of what she could accomplish that day. She'd get the kitchen pantry cleared out and apply for at least two more jobs. Something was bound to come out of all these applications.

Walking down the hallway to the elevator, Lila spotted Iris and June Willoughby in the Hydrangea Room at one of the round tables and waved. In front of them were two decks of cards and monogrammed Tervis tumblers. The tumblers were filled to the brim with brown liquid and a collection of ice cubes. The bamboo-backed chairs in the room were white with splashy turquoise-and-green-patterned fabric on the seats that matched the hues in the floral wallpaper.

"Lila," Iris called out. "There you are! Come visit with us."

Lila stepped inside.

"Can we interest you in a Manhattan?" June asked, holding up her drink. "We've mixed up a big batch." She nodded to a bag slung over her nearby walker; a glass thermos peeked out of the top.

"It's a little early for me," Lila said, glancing at the clock above the door that showed it was only ten o'clock in the morning.

"Suit yourself," June said.

Large windows filled the back wall. It was cloudy outside, and the light inside the room was sparse, barely grazing the upturned faces of June and Iris and softening their features. There was something cozy about the patterned floral wallpaper, the way it encircled the room and enveloped Lila beneath petals and leaves.

"Do you know how to play canasta?" Iris asked. Her rings—blue sapphire and pear-shaped diamond—glinted as she deftly shuffled the deck of cards. "We're waiting on Florence and Mary Dixon, but we could kick one of them out."

"Mary Dixon," June said, nodding. "She's awful."

"The worst," Iris agreed. "She never opens and pulls on her pearls every time she has a good hand. No one should have that obvious of a tell."

"Do you have a tell?" June asked.

"Me? Ah . . . I don't know," Lila said.

"It would take us a while to learn yours anyway. So you would still be better than Mary Dixon," Iris said.

"You should play with us," June said.

Lila stepped back, putting distance between herself and this entire idea. She had work to do and wasn't here to socialize. She also suspected Iris and June would ask her a slew of personal questions, which she had zero interest in answering.

"That sounds fun, but I don't know how to play canasta. I hope y'all win, though," Lila said.

"We probably will," Iris said contentedly. "At least, we'll have plenty to discuss with Conrad's last bombshell."

"It's just like that old rascal to come up with a final surprise after his death. He was always so inventive." June shook her head, a bemused expression on her face.

"She means in bed," Iris explained.

"Oh, right." Lila shifted uncomfortably.

"But the reward won't do any good," June said.

"Why do you say that?" Lila asked.

"No one can solve Sophia's murder. The police spent years looking into it," June said.

"Four burglaries, a murder, and not one suspect." Iris tutted under her breath. "I consider us lucky we never got robbed. Can you imagine if we lost Mama's rubies? She would turn over in her grave, God rest her soul."

June nodded. "It was bad enough the burglar stole Catherine Lee's collection of Herend figurines. The octopus alone was worth thousands even if it did have a chip in the front leg. There are only a few left in the world. Catherine cried for days."

"At least she wasn't home at the time like poor, dear Sophia," Iris said.

Voices rose from outside the room. An older woman with a permed helmet of red hair and a Day-Glo orange caftan was walking with another woman who sported stiff brown curls and a dour expression. Susanna strode behind in a sharp black pantsuit. Her brows drew together as the threesome halted.

"June and Iris, did y'all reserve the room for today? I don't recall seeing your name on the electronic sign-up." The woman in Day-Glo orange had a syrupy-sweet tone, her syllables stretching in a pronounced Southern drawl.

June's face darkened. "We play canasta every week at this same time. The entire building knows that."

"Do they? I wasn't aware. Best to use the sign-up from now on. It is required. Rule forty-five of the building handbook." The woman nodded to Lila. "I'm guessing you're Lila Shaw. Welcome! I'm Ruth Bailor, president of the Primrose Board, and this is Emily Canterbury, vice president. It's a pleasure to finally meet you."

"Nice to meet you both," Lila said with a small smile.

"There's nothing nice about them," Iris muttered.

Ruth made no move to come closer, probably because Iris and June were glaring at her. Susanna was scrolling through her phone, tapping her foot on the marble, ready to get on with her day. Emily studied Lila, sweeping her gaze from head to toe. Lila kept the pleasant expression on her face even though the scrutiny made her want to squirm.

"I see you're already imbibing," Emily said, pointedly looking at her watch.

"Who cares if we are?" Iris said in a mulish voice.

"Ladies, I envy your schedules. It must be nice to not have anything to do. I wish I wasn't so busy all the time." Ruth wagged a finger at them. "Do be sure to use the coasters in the console drawer. Rule 407 in the building handbook!"

"I thought that young woman was here to clean out Gloria's apartment, not get drunk every morning," Emily said.

Lila's face went hot at the judgment in Emily's voice even though she wasn't drinking. "I only stopped to say hello. I'm heading back upstairs."

"Lila was asking us all about Sophia Kent and what went on with the robberies. I was about to tell her the building handbook doesn't address how to deal with an ineffective board during a crime infestation," June said sweetly. "Weren't you president back then, Ruth?"

Ruth's cheeks reddened, clashing with her orange hair. "That's hardly an appropriate topic of conversation."

"I didn't ask about the handbook," Lila said hastily.

Ruth's eyes narrowed to slits, aimed at Lila. What could Lila say to make this better? She didn't want to end up on the bad side of the board president but from the way Ruth was glaring at her, it was already too late.

"You'll have to excuse us. Some of us have important obligations and can't spend our day gossiping." Ruth shot Lila a final, hard look before setting off back down the hallway with Susanna and Emily.

Lila exhaled as they disappeared around the corner. "I think Ruth hates me already."

"She hates everyone, and that superior act isn't fooling us. We all know Ruth drinks at least three glasses of wine with lunch," Iris said.

"Ruth and Emily like to think they run this place," June sniffed.

"It's never a good sign when they're meeting with Susanna," Iris said. "It usually means they've come up with some new rule. Like when they tried to ban alcohol in the common rooms after Mary Dixon spilled that bottle of red wine in the lobby while walking in her Jimmy Choos."

June gulped her drink, downing half of it. "It's unfair. Mary Dixon can't help that she's clumsy and bad at canasta. Susanna thinks she can push through those stupid rules because the Kent family likes her. But Conrad only got her the job because he felt sorry for her after Sophia, and he's gone now."

June and Iris knew a lot about the residents of the Primrose and probably about Sophia herself. It wouldn't hurt to ask them a few more questions. Lila could already envision telling Bea how she'd interviewed witnesses.

"What do you mean about Conrad getting Susanna the job after Sophia?" Lila asked, sitting down beside Iris.

Iris and June looked at each other, raising thin penciled-in eyebrows before nodding in some unspoken agreement.

Iris motioned for Lila to lean closer and lowered her voice. "Susanna was Sophia Kent's best friend in high school. She was devastated after Sophia's murder."

That explained why Susanna had gotten so upset when Bea asked about the murder.

"She had to take a semester off from school, and I heard her parents checked her into a mental institution," June said.

"That's awful," Lila said, regretting that she'd asked. Susanna was entitled to her privacy, not a bunch of people talking behind her back.

Lila wondered what Iris and June would say about her when she left. They'd most likely speculate on whether she'd known about Ryan's illegal activities, which they were surely aware of by now. She should be used to people gossiping about her. Lila didn't want to care but she did.

June continued, oblivious to Lila's uneasiness. "Our theory is Susanna blamed herself for not getting Sophia help before she died. They were always together. She must have known Sophia had gotten herself into a terrible predicament."

"What kind of predicament?" Lila asked.

June sighed. "You didn't hear any of this from us."

"We don't like to gossip," Iris said.

"Of course not," Lila murmured.

"On the afternoon of Sophia's death, we were in the Hydrangea Room, setting up for a bridge game," Iris explained.

"We were avid bridge players back then," June said.

"Until we switched to canasta. It's more fun and goes better with cocktails," Iris said.

"That's true," June agreed.

Lila nodded, wishing they would get on with it.

"In any event, we were setting up for bridge when we heard Sophia outside on the patio. Helene had gotten her a cell phone, and she was yelling into it. You couldn't help but overhear," June said.

"We barely even cracked the door," Iris added.

"Sophia was crying and carrying on. It was really quite a scene. She said, *This is blackmail*," June said. "She used those very words. I'll never forget them."

Iris widened her eyes. "Then she said, *We have to meet tonight before it all comes out.*"

Lila sat back, shocked by what they'd told her. "Did you tell the police?"

"Well, no. We didn't want to tarnish Sophia's name by implying she was involved in anything unseemly," June said.

"Police investigations are inherently messy, dear. We really couldn't get involved. It wasn't appropriate," Iris added.

Lila couldn't believe this. Somehow, she may have discovered another clue. Everyone assumed Sophia was killed in a botched burglary, but the police hadn't investigated this blackmail angle because they hadn't known about it. And while blackmail seemed extreme for a sixteen-year-old, it wasn't impossible to imagine. What if Sophia had let someone take naked photos of her, or what if someone knew she'd cheated on a test? What if someone was threatening to tell Sophia's parents about something illegal she'd done and demanding money to stay quiet? But if Sophia *had* gotten herself into that kind of trouble, could she not have asked Helene for help? Lila hoped that Bea would come to her if she was facing a serious problem, but she might not. Bea wouldn't even share her nightmares.

"How is your project coming along? I heard Gloria's apartment is a wreck," June said.

"One time Gloria invited us over and I thought I was going to catch crabs again just by sitting down." Iris reached for the glass thermos and topped off her drink.

"Crabs are pubic lice," June explained. "They cause intense itching. Iris had a very hard time with them in 1975."

Lila swallowed, not wanting to discuss pubic lice with a pair of octogenarians. "I haven't noticed any bugs, luckily. Just a lot of papers." *And a million other weird things,* Lila thought. But for some reason, she didn't want to tell June and Iris this.

"I bet she kept copies of all her complaints. Gloria was constantly calling the building manager about noise violations and loitering." June finished her cocktail in one large gulp.

"She was always alone inside that apartment, staring out her window and spying on everyone," Iris said.

Lila's face went tight the way it did before she was about to cry. She was overwhelmed with sadness for Gloria and for herself. After surrounding herself with the intimacies of Gloria's life, Lila felt as though she knew her now, understood her even. Like Gloria, Lila'd spent the past year staring out her window, alone in her home. She'd refused to go to dinner with Daphne, unable to muster the energy. She'd skipped Meritt Academy's lower school holiday concert and all-school basketball game, pleading headaches to Bea. Instead of leaving her house, she would check Instagram on the weekends, scrolling through the images of women she'd once texted on a weekly basis and missing the sympathetic complaints about their kids' school projects (*I fucking hate poster board!*) and the follow-ups after a party (*your dress was gorg!*). Now she was too afraid to even like their posts. Her life was a shadow of what it was before Ryan left. Suddenly Lila couldn't breathe. It was as if someone had kicked her in the chest.

"I have to go now," Lila said.

"Good luck with the cleaning. And if you find a complaint by Gloria from April 13, 1992, please throw it away. It was not Iris's fault that she wasn't wearing underwear," June said.

"My dress was see-through." Iris lifted one shoulder.

"Accidentally though." June poured herself another drink.

Chapter Twelve

Later that day, Lila was looking over Bea's homework, which required her to complete a math worksheet and read for fifteen minutes. Lila took a deep breath, preparing for the required cajoling and persuading.

"I was thinking about Sophia in school and realized we need to concentrate on motive. On *Murder, She Wrote*, the motive for killing the victim always leads to the killer," Bea said as she paced around the dining room table.

"At school, you need to concentrate on school," Lila said.

Bea stopped pacing. "For your information, Mrs. Maisley chose me to read out loud to the class today and said I did a great job. I didn't mispronounce a single word. I don't think."

"Really?" Lila smiled, unaccustomed to Bea having anything positive to say about school. "Honey, that's amazing."

Bea shrugged. "Can we talk about Sophia now?"

Lila patted the seat next to her, and Bea sat down. "I'll make you a deal. You get your homework done. After that, I'll tell you about my conversation with the Willoughby sisters. They overheard Sophia talking to someone on the phone the day of her murder. It sounded like she was being blackmailed."

Bea's eyes lit up. "Blackmail? That's motive!"

"I know," Lila said, pleased at Bea's reaction.

"Mama, you questioned witnesses," Bea said, sounding impressed. "That's cool."

"It wasn't a big deal." But Lila was also slightly impressed with herself for taking the initiative to learn something new about Sophia's murder.

Lila had cleaned up around the dining room table earlier that day, clearing all the boxes out of the room. The dining chairs were old-fashioned and high-backed with comfortable blue-and-white-striped seats. There was an antique Persian rug beneath the table in shades of blue and pink, the colors vibrant. Light spilled out of the window and through the crystal and gold chandelier. Lila slid the homework papers over the table to Bea.

Bea picked up the pencil, getting right to work. Lila couldn't believe it. It was a small thing, but she was proud of her daughter for the way she went about methodically working through the questions. Her tongue protruded the slightest bit from between her small white teeth, the way it did when she was concentrating.

Bea turned over the worksheet to the second side. Her pencil scratched on the paper. She spoke without looking up at Lila. "Do you miss our old house?"

Lila bit her lip, considering how best to respond. Did she miss their beautiful clean home with a freestanding bathtub and custom closet? Yes, one hundred times yes. But she needed to stay positive for Bea. "Not that much."

"I miss it. I also miss when Daddy came to my softball games and called me his number one Bea."

Heat ballooned across Lila's chest. Ryan should be here. Bea shouldn't have to miss him.

"I'm sure Daddy wishes he could see you too," Lila said.

"Then why doesn't he call me?" Bea said under her breath.

"I've told you he can't contact us or the FBI could figure out where he's calling from and bring him into custody. He can't let that happen until he proves his innocence."

Sweat beaded on Lila's forehead. How long could she keep telling Bea this story? When should she admit that Ryan couldn't prove his innocence and maybe wasn't coming back ever? She wished he would at least send a postcard or an email, anything to let Bea know he still thought about her.

Bea stayed quiet for several seconds, still staring at her paper. When she glanced up at Lila, the look on her face morphed into annoyance. "You don't have to sit here watching me. I can do it on my own."

Lila put her hands up and backed away from the table. She pretended to unpack a box of cat toys in the living room, sneaking glances at Bea. What other thoughts were going through her daughter's head about Ryan? Did she suspect his absence might be permanent?

Ryan had been a great father until he left; showing up at all Bea's activities, making her giggle over the dinner table. He could calm Bea down when she was mad, better than Lila ever could. Lila missed having him to talk to about Bea; to discuss everyday things like how fast she read books and the funny way she mispronounced *awry*. It was one of the reasons Lila had wanted to make their marriage work. Bea deserved two parents, living together and supporting her, even if they didn't always get along. Lila should have tried harder. She closed her eyes against the sharp sting of tears. Ryan's abandonment had hurt Bea, but divorce would hurt her too. The only person Lila was more angry at than Ryan was herself.

When they first married, things were easier between them. Lila and Ryan had started the business together. His family had a medical manufacturing plant, and she and Ryan opened their own storefront selling wheelchairs, crutches, and walkers. They discussed which products to carry while sitting on their front stoop at night. He would leave a latte on her desk as a mid-morning treat and kiss the back of her neck by the office copier when no one was around. They were a team. Ryan was the face of the company—the charismatic president who interacted with the shareholders, most of whom he'd known since childhood—and she was behind the scenes, helping things run smoothly. It was after Bea that everything changed.

They had been in the hospital, coming home later that day. Lila remembered staring at her newborn daughter, marveling at the way Bea's eyelashes rested like black silk fringe against the petal pink of her cheeks. This tiny person was now hers to care for, to keep *alive*. It was astonishing. One second, she'd only had herself to worry about. Now she had a child. Her head dropped back on the pillow, suddenly heavy. She'd looked up into Ryan's gaze, surprised by the tears in his eyes. He never cried.

I think you should stay home with her, Ryan had said. *You mean not go back to work?* Lila had asked. There was a fluttering in her belly of unease or relief. No, it was relief. Surely it was relief. *I can take care of you both. My mama stayed home with me and I loved it. But it's your decision,* Ryan had said. Bea's weight had rested on her chest, featherlight but insistent. She'd wondered—what would she do with a baby all day?

Lila hadn't gone back to the office. She and Ryan hadn't discussed the possibility again. He'd assumed she would stay home after he offered, and she never corrected him. Was it the right choice or had she even made a choice? Now she wasn't sure. She'd gotten privately furious when Ryan had said, *I wish I could stay home and play with Bea,* as if her contribution to their household was less than his. Sometimes she'd wanted to snap at him for leaving his socks on the family room floor or his dirty coffee cups on the counter, but he'd worked all day, and her complaints seemed petty, so she'd wordlessly cleaned up instead. Maybe she shouldn't have stayed quiet. Maybe she should have told him how she felt.

A knock sounded on the apartment door. Lila blinked, back in the present. She hurried to the foyer and pulled the door open, welcoming the distraction. Evelyn stood in front of her, leaning on her walker and frowning as usual.

"One thing you should know about me, I don't like to be kept waiting. Please consider that for future appointments. Heavens, are you wearing that to our meeting?" Evelyn said and eyed Lila up and down, wrinkling her nose at the yoga pants and oversize T-shirt.

"What meeting are you talking about?" Lila asked.

Bea rushed down the hall. "Where are we going?"

"I arranged for us to drop off dinner for Helene and Alice Kent, to show our sympathy for Conrad's passing. It's also a perfect opportunity to question them about Sophia. I told you earlier today," Evelyn said, sounding annoyed. She was wearing a long pink dress and a diamond necklace, all of which looked better suited to a cocktail party than a midafternoon visit.

"Should I bring a notepad?" Bea asked eagerly.

"Probably not. I doubt your handwriting is acceptable since you're only seven," Evelyn said.

"I'm ten, and it's probably better than yours," Bea said. "I noticed your hands are shaky."

"Bea," Lila hissed in admonishment.

"My hands are perfectly steady. I could perform surgery with these hands, they are that steady. And my penmanship is excellent," Evelyn said.

Lila cleared her throat. "I'm sorry but I didn't know about any visit."

"I'm sure I told you earlier," Evelyn said.

"I don't think you did," Lila said.

"I suppose you forgot." Evelyn eyed Bea thoughtfully. "You can come too, but only if you don't say anything. They may be more inclined to talk to us if you're able to act rather sad and shy, and they feel sorry for you. You should change your shirt too. Perhaps something pink?"

Bea was wearing her usual Atlanta Braves shirt. It had a large ketchup stain from lunch.

"The shirt stays," Bea said firmly.

Evelyn tilted her head and studied Bea before nodding once. "Fine."

"I could tuck it in," Bea offered.

"That will have to do. But do act as if you're about to burst into tears. No need to give a reason. They'll assume it's because you don't have a father," Evelyn said matter-of-factly.

Lila breathed in sharply, unable to believe Evelyn had mentioned Ryan. "Bea does have a father who cares about her."

"But he's not here now," Bea said, unfazed by Evelyn's comment. "This sounds like a good plan. I might limp a little too."

"Excellent idea," Evelyn said.

"No one is limping," Lila said and went to track down one of the button-ups from her past life. As she walked away, she was almost certain that she saw Bea wink at Evelyn, and Evelyn wink back.

"Put on a little lipstick. It would brighten up your face, which resembles a corpse, I'm sorry to say. Please hurry," Evelyn called. "Jasper is meeting us at the Kents' in five minutes."

"Jasper knows about this?" Lila asked.

"Of course. I told you both." Evelyn turned and walked back into the hallway, Bea following closely behind.

Chapter Thirteen

Lila, Bea, Evelyn, and Jasper were standing in front of a door on the fifth floor a few minutes later. Jasper had already been waiting when the women arrived. He held two large bags of food, which Evelyn had ordered from a local caterer. Bea quickly filled Jasper and Evelyn in on what Lila had learned from the Willoughby sisters earlier that day. Jasper barely spoke, choosing to stare down at his feet. Lila wondered if he regretted his decision to help with the investigation. At the moment, she certainly did.

Helene Kent opened the door immediately upon their knock and invited them inside. The foyer of her apartment was spectacular with a round gilt-edged table upon which sat a huge fresh floral arrangement of roses and lilies, chinoiserie wallpaper in stunning aquas, and a patterned gold and blue rug, which probably cost as much as a small car.

Lila caught a glimpse of herself in the foyer mirror and was startled by her own face. She'd applied makeup for the first time in ages at Evelyn's not-so-subtle prodding. Lila was used to her pale, sunken cheeks. It was nice to see herself with color on her face. It had been a long time since she'd made an effort.

"Good afternoon. It's lovely to see you all, and so thoughtful of you to bring us supper," Helene said, holding out her elegant hand decorated with several large gemstones. She was swathed in a soft gray cashmere sweater. Alice stood beside her, brown hair pulled into a low ponytail.

Helene asked politely how Lila was finding the Primrose, and Lila lied and said the apartment was wonderful. Helene mentioned how delightful she'd found Stanley and Mama when she'd spoken to them at the premier of *Madame Butterfly*. Lila smiled in response, agreeing that, *Yes, Stanley is such a character,* and *Mama never misses the opera*. She hoped her adherence to these little niceties would smooth over whatever Evelyn had in store for this visit. Bea only smiled demurely and followed behind Helene when she ushered them into the living room. She was limping.

"Are you in pain, dear?" Helene asked Bea.

"I try not to let my injuries get me down," Bea said in a pious voice, dragging her foot behind her in an exaggerated way that looked completely fake.

"She's just fine," Lila said.

"I stopped crying myself to sleep last week," Bea said, settling into a plush armchair clad in an apple green stripe.

Evelyn nodded approvingly, and Jasper pressed his lips together as if holding in laughter.

"We were sorry to hear about Conrad's passing," Evelyn said.

"Thank you. He was ill for quite some time, and we're grateful he passed away peacefully in his sleep." Helene clasped her hands together. She'd perched on a tall-backed chair upholstered in a busy green and white floral pattern. The room itself was a pale celery color, and a large window overlooked the courtyard below.

"Helene, I must say we were all surprised by the announcement of Conrad's trust. Rather a crazy idea to pursue Sophia's murderer after all these years," Evelyn said. "Do you think his mind was all there in the end?"

Lila goggled at Evelyn's blunt remark. Alice dropped her chin and looked down, but not before Lila caught a flash of hurt across her face.

Helene stiffened. "Of course it was. Sophia was Conrad's granddaughter, and he never fully recovered from her passing. He wanted justice for her."

"It was a long time ago, though," Evelyn continued, oblivious to the effect her words were having on Helene and Alice. "I'm surprised he didn't offer a reward like this before if he never got over her death."

The tension in the room was thick as smoke and equally as choking. Helene's face turned to stone. Alice twisted her hands together. Jasper's eyes hadn't left the floor. Only Bea was looking from one face to the other with undisguised interest.

"I'm sure he had his reasons," Lila said quickly.

"Actually," Alice began in a halting voice, "Grandpa formed the trust because of me."

"Is that so?" Evelyn said.

Alice nodded. "I was only eleven when Sophia died, and I adored her. I had severe asthma and missed a lot of school back then. I didn't have many friends, but Sophia always had time for me and made me laugh. I wanted to be exactly like her. I even convinced Mama to buy me the kid version of Dr. Marten boots to match the ones Sophia always wore. Grandpa knew I would do anything to solve her murder. The trust was his last gift to me; one final attempt to find out what happened."

"How did you feel about the trust, Helene?" Jasper asked.

Lila looked up, startled to hear Jasper's voice. She'd almost forgotten he was there.

"I don't know what you mean," Helene said in answer.

"You must have an opinion on Mr. Kent establishing a reward to assist with apprehending Sophia's murderer," Jasper said.

Jasper's bashful nature had disappeared. He wasn't mean or forceful, but there was a direct look on his face as he studied Helene, waiting for a response. For the first time, Lila understood what Jasper must have been like as a detective—no-nonsense, practical, confident.

Helene finally lifted a shoulder. "My opinion is Conrad could spend his money as he wished. I'm sure he thought he was doing the right thing."

"But you preferred for him to drop the issue?" Jasper asked, picking up on the tension behind her words.

"I preferred for all of us to focus on the present. As you probably know, we established a charity in Sophia's name dedicated to helping victims of violent crimes. We've raised millions of dollars over the years." Helene glanced at Alice. "We can't bring Sophia back. We can only move forward."

"But I want to know what happened to my sister the night of her death. I want to see her murderer in jail." Alice's voice quivered slightly.

Lila sensed this wasn't the first time she'd voiced this belief.

Helene reached across the arm of her chair and took Alice's hand. "There's nothing wrong with how you feel, but I won't let Sophia's death define your life. You are more than her tragedy."

Alice glanced at her mother's hand. A tremulous look passed between them. Lila dropped her eyes, feeling like an intruder on a private moment.

"We both miss her," Alice said quietly to the room.

Helene's face spasmed—lines deepening, eyes squinting, forehead cracking. For the briefest of moments, every muscle in her face contracted into a look of utter and complete despair before smoothing back out to a neutral mask.

Lila shuddered at the split-second truth on Helene's face. She couldn't imagine what it was like for Helene to live through the death of her daughter, to lose the most precious thing in existence. Lila was no stranger to grief, having lost her father and now

Ryan. Yet she was certain that losing a child was exponentially worse than anything else in the entire world. She glanced over at Bea, tracing the spray of freckles across her nose. She couldn't fathom Bea's death, the hole her absence would create. Lila would probably fall right into it and never emerge again. But Helene had somehow managed to endure, bolstering up her other child while moving through her own life with purpose.

Lila shifted in her seat. "I'm sorry for everything you've gone through."

"As am I," Evelyn said. "But since Sophia's death obviously continues to pain poor Alice, I do wonder if you've ever considered whether someone in this building was responsible for the robberies and even Sophia's death?"

Lila winced. It was not a particularly smooth segue.

Helene seemed unruffled. "I can't imagine. I've known most of the residents for years. I'm sure the police fully investigated every possibility."

"Of course," Lila said, half rising to her feet. "That makes sense. Thanks for seeing us. Again, we're so sorry about Conrad and—"

Jasper nudged Lila and gave her a small shake of his head. She swallowed down the rest of her words and sank back down.

"Helene, do you really think the police investigated every possibility? For example, did they know someone was blackmailing Sophia before her death?" Jasper asked.

Alice gasped. "She would never have gone so far as to blackmail Sophia—"

"Alice, please." Helene turned to Jasper with a frown. "I have no idea where you got your information, but it's wrong."

"We heard it from a very reliable source," Evelyn insisted.

"And it was under oath," Bea said ominously.

Lila widened her eyes at this blatant lie.

Helene stood then, signaling their meeting was over. Her movements were jerky with anger. "I'm afraid Alice and I have a prior engagement. Thank you for the food."

Lila knew they were well past any socially acceptable visit. Helene wasn't going to air all her darkest thoughts and suspicions with four people she barely knew. Lila imagined what Patricia would say about the entire interview—it was undignified and tasteless to press someone for their deepest emotions. But Lila found she couldn't regret her part in this meeting. Alice knew something and had tried to tell them before Helene cut her off.

Evelyn remained in her seat. Her eyes squinted. "Is it hot in here? My heavens, all of a sudden, I am feeling faint."

"You do look pale," Bea said.

"Dear me. I see black spots. Is the room getting smaller? My vision is narrowing as I speak." Evelyn's voice grew fainter.

Bea rushed from the chair to Evelyn's side, remembering only after she'd taken a few steps that she was supposed to have a limp. To compensate, she dragged her leg the last few feet, more pronounced than before. She flung herself on the couch with Evelyn.

"Perhaps some water and a few saltines?" Evelyn said.

Bea looked imploringly up at Helene. "It could save her life."

Helene appeared alarmed and annoyed in equal parts, but her good manners won out in the end. "Of course. I'll be right back."

As soon as Helene disappeared around the corner, Jasper turned to Alice. "You knew about the blackmail."

Alice hunched up her shoulders, obviously uncomfortable. "No, I didn't. Why are you asking all these questions? Is this about the reward?"

Several seconds passed. Lila couldn't think of a way to answer Alice's question that didn't sound offensive or crazy.

Bea piped up, her small voice low but intense. "I want to know the truth. I don't like unsolved mysteries. I don't know where my daddy is right now, and I hate that."

Lila took two deep breaths, holding her face still with some effort. It was clear that for Bea, this investigation was about more than Sophia. It was a way to take control, to *do something* when her life was messy and out of hand.

Alice's eyes softened as she stared at Bea. She glanced in the direction where Helene had disappeared. "All I know is Sophia got into an argument with someone right before she died. I can't imagine this person would have blackmailed her, though."

At this point, Evelyn had abandoned all pretense of fainting and was leaning forward, hanging on Alice's every word. Bea's "hurt" foot was tucked under her as she too appeared mesmerized by Alice's remarks.

"Who was Sophia arguing with?" Jasper asked.

Alice vacillated before answering. "Susanna Moore. I heard them outside my room. Susanna sounded furious and said something like, *You promised you'd stay away from Jeremy. I'll make you pay for what you did.*" She looked at her entwined hands. "Susanna was in love with Jeremy Buckingham since kindergarten, but they were just good friends. He was close with Sophia too. Sometimes he would come over here to hang out, and I always suspected he might like Sophia in a romantic way. When I heard Susanna yelling at her, I thought maybe Sophia had started liking him back. I never told anyone though. I didn't want people to think of Sophia as someone who betrayed her best friend. When I was a kid, that seemed like the worst thing ever."

But it wasn't the worst thing ever. Not even close.

Chapter Fourteen

Lila pulled up to the small art gallery off a side street in downtown Norfolk. That morning, she'd received a text from Patricia informing Lila that she was back in Virginia for a few days and demanding that Lila meet her for lunch at Tidwell Gallery to discuss an important matter. The fact that it would require Lila to drive two hours with no notice didn't seem to even occur to her mother-in-law. Lila had thought about refusing but knew she couldn't. The *important matter* could pertain to Bea or her impending divorce or even Ryan's case. Lila mostly hoped Patricia hadn't called her all the way to Norfolk to lecture her about Bea's expulsion.

The brick building was narrow and several stories tall, located in a small, historic neighborhood with cobblestone streets and upscale restaurants near downtown. Lila used to come here all the time with friends. The first floor was a bright gallery space filled with large colorful, modern pieces. The second floor opened up into a bustling restaurant with a bar along the back, pale rose walls, and charming wood plank floors.

Straightening her long maxi skirt, Lila glanced down and sighed. She hoped Patricia didn't spot the unraveling hem on the right side, although she probably would. She would also probably scrutinize Lila's scuffed boots and ragged cuticles. Patricia noticed everything.

Lila walked inside and straight to the stairwell in the middle of the gallery. She climbed the stairs to the second floor and spoke to the hostess, who pointed her toward the back corner where Patricia was already waiting. Round tables were scattered around the room, and the windows were open, letting a spring breeze swish through the air. Every seat was filled, and a soft clamor filled the room.

In the left corner was a table of six women, all wearing KHAITE flats and carrying Bottega Veneta handbags. Lila had chaired committees with these women and organized playdates with their children. They were no doubt planning gluten-free snacks for the Meritt Academy Art Fair or custom-built sets for the lower school play. Charlotte Waverly spotted Lila, did a double take, and whipped her head back toward their table, whispering. The other five glanced over at her immediately afterward. No one waved or smiled.

It felt as though everyone was staring at Lila, judging her, and finding her lacking. She wondered what they were saying about her, although she could guess it was nothing good—*she looks terrible, her house is in foreclosure, how can she show her face, never really liked her.* She let her hair fall over one side of her face, blocking it from their view. Her fingers opened and closed, tugging on her skirt as she walked.

Patricia was seated under the window. Gold highlights glimmered in her light brown hair. She wore a cream silk blouse and remained seated as Lila approached.

"It's good to see you," Lila said.

"I ordered spinach salads for both of us. I thought you'd prefer a healthy option," Patricia said, eyeing Lila's hips as she sat down.

"Oh okay," Lila said. There was no point in mentioning that she didn't care for spinach salads. If she dared to do so, Patricia would only look at her blankly before saying something like, *Don't be ridiculous, Lila. Everyone likes spinach salads.*

"How is Florida?" Lila asked.

Patricia's lips turned up in a stiff smile. "Palm Beach is wonderful. I hated to leave, but I needed to check on the house here. The yard maintenance is abysmal. My roses are an absolute wreck." She sipped her ice tea. "And how is your new living situation?"

Lila cleared her throat. "It's a little challenging, but we're getting settled. New environments are always stressful."

Patricia nodded. "So true, and stress can take such a toll on your body. I'm sure you're busy, but you should still make time to take care of yourself."

Patricia took a sip of her tea. Lila wondered if she was going to offer to pay for a babysitter or a therapist.

"You can't afford to fall behind on Botox at your age, and you'll feel much better once you get back to your routine of working out regularly," Patricia said, looking pointedly at Lila's midsection.

Lila sucked in her stomach. She was now painfully aware of every line on her forehead. She'd known she wasn't at her best, but Patricia really didn't need to point it out.

"I presume Beatrice is enrolled in a new school?" Patricia asked.

"Yes. She's doing really well," Lila said, trying to muster some enthusiasm.

Really well was an exaggeration. More like, Bea still complained most days about her class, but Lila wasn't getting called by the principal. She counted that as a win after the last year. The teacher seemed more understanding too. Bea had objected to playing tag and argued that chasing other kids was the kind of thing a future serial killer did during recess. Mrs. Maisley had asked the playground monitor to encourage games of Simon Says instead.

A waiter in a white apron placed a water and salad in front of Lila, and another salad in front of Patricia.

"Can I get you anything further?" the waiter asked.

"No, we're fine," Patricia answered for both of them.

Lila looked down in dismay at the limp spinach leaves and sparse offering of goat cheese and pecans. It appeared Patricia had requested the salad without dressing.

"I must admit we are still disappointed about Beatrice leaving Meritt Academy. Three generations of Shaws have attended there. It's unthinkable Ryan's daughter won't graduate from his alma mater," Patricia said reproachfully. "I don't know how you could have let this happen."

Lila cleared her throat. "It was an unfortunate misunderstanding. Another boy was mean to Bea, and she reacted badly. We've talked about it. She understands she was wrong, and I don't think it will ever happen again."

Patricia continued to stare at her without expression. Lila resisted the urge to squirm in her seat. All of her rehearsed explanations hadn't seemed to sink in.

"She's had a hard few months," Lila offered as a final excuse.

Patricia put down her fork. "Well, Lila, we've all had a hard few months. Think of poor Ryan, who had to put his entire life on hold because of a business mistake."

"Ryan did more than put his life on hold. He abandoned us. We haven't heard from him in months," Lila said, stabbing at her plate.

"My goodness, there's no need for dramatics," Patricia chided. "We all know Ryan will return as soon as this legal issue is resolved."

Lila pressed her lips together. She wasn't at all convinced Ryan was coming back, but there was no use arguing with Patricia. She'd never listen to anything negative about her son.

Patricia abruptly smiled, the expression stretching unnaturally across her face. "I'm sure you know that I've always liked you. You're a breath of fresh air compared to some of the other girls Ryan dated. You're simple, sweet, understanding..."

God, she was making Lila sound like an imbecile.

"But I do worry about the stress you're under," Patricia continued. "I'm not *entirely* blaming you for what happened at Meritt Academy but I think we're both aware things would have been different if Ryan was around."

Lila stiffened. "I'm doing my best."

"Bless your heart, of course you are," Patricia said, her voice turning friendly. "But we know you've had trouble making ends meet and handling Beatrice on your own. Robert and I want to help you both."

"Really?" Lila asked, trying not to sound skeptical.

Patricia did not help her. Ever. She had never offered to watch Bea or keep her overnight. The only occasion during which she spent time with Bea was when she took her to an annual holiday performance of *The Nutcracker*. She insisted Bea wear an uncomfortable plaid taffeta dress and patent leather shoes, both of which Bea hated.

"There is a lovely all-girls private school down the street from our house in Palm Beach. It's one of the most highly regarded institutions in the entire country. The facilities are top-notch—stables, a swimming pool, a Michelin chef on staff. They have every possible amenity. Their graduates go on to attend Ivies. Best of all, I've already spoken to them. They are willing to take Beatrice immediately," Patricia said.

"But we live in Richmond now," Lila said.

"Yes, Lila," Patricia said slowly. "Obviously this would require Beatrice to move to Florida. Robert and I are willing to find a nanny and fund her education. Think of it. We could impose some stability and discipline. This doesn't have to be permanent, but it would give you a chance to get back on your feet while Beatrice is exposed to an exceptional education opportunity. This is best for everyone."

Patricia was proposing to take Bea away from Lila to live in an entirely different state. She didn't think Lila could raise her own daughter? That Bea needed discipline and stability? Maybe she was right. Lila wasn't doing a great job by any estimation. Bea had gotten expelled and taken up investigating a murder as a hobby. They fought . . . a lot. Bea didn't even seem to like her most of the time, and Lila sometimes felt the same way about Bea. She might be better off with Patricia and Robert at a fancy private school down in Florida. Was it selfish to keep Bea in Richmond, living in a disaster of an apartment?

Patricia looked at her expectantly. "I can make the arrangements today."

"No." The word erupted from Lila's mouth.

"No?" Patricia's face soured, her lips puckering as if they were glued to a lemon.

Lila sat back, having surprised herself with the vehement response. Her heart thumped in rhythm with her answer—*no, no, no*. She meant it. Bea couldn't go live with Patricia. Bea could barely stand to be around Patricia, who always lectured her and complained about her behavior. More than that, Lila wanted Bea with her, even if things got bad. She glanced back at the six women behind her, huddled over their table, probably still gossiping about her. Fine, things *were* bad. She didn't have a good reputation or any money or a job or a house. But she could still raise her daughter somehow. At least, she could still try. Lila would figure out how to make their relationship work without private schools or babysitters or Ryan.

"Bea is going to stay with me," Lila said firmly, brushing her hair back behind her ear.

Patricia picked up her fork again, looking disgusted. "Well, Lila. I hope you know what you're doing."

Lila nodded. "I do."

She didn't. She most definitely didn't.

Chapter Fifteen

Jasper and Bea were making cookies in Gloria's hideously outdated kitchen with avocado green appliances and stained linoleum floors. Lila and Bea had run into Jasper in the elevator, and Bea had offered to show him her snickerdoodle recipe. Jasper had initially refused but there was a moment of hesitation; three long seconds before he declined. Lila had wondered if that hesitation meant something. Before she could talk herself out of it, she'd leaned around Bea in the elevator: *We really would love for you to come over if you have time.* Jasper had blushed and stared straight ahead while answering, *Okay.*

Lila was perched on a stool at the kitchen island, watching them measure out the sugar but not really hearing anything they said. Patricia's offer from lunch still stung hours later; her assumption that Bea was better off with her grandparents. Lila hoped she'd done the right thing by turning them down.

There was a knock on the door and Zoe was on the other side.

"I came to drop off some mail." Zoe held out an envelope addressed to Lila in Mama's handwriting. It must have been the check she was waiting on.

Lila took it and dropped it on the foyer table. "Thanks for bringing it up."

Zoe stared into the apartment, her mouth widening in a comical circle. "Shit, this place really is a wreck."

"Yep, and this is after me working on it for weeks. It's actually a lot better," Lila said.

And it *was* better if still a disaster. Lila had managed to stack the boxes in one half of the family room. The remainder of the room now had several couches and chairs, none of which matched, all huddled together as if sheltering from the storm of the mess. Lila had called Goodwill and arranged for a donation pickup. She hoped that by removing at least three-quarters of the furniture, they could finally walk around without tripping over a chair leg.

Jasper leaned his head around the kitchen wall and raised a hand in greeting. Bea was right beside him.

"Could you come grab a drink? I'm sure you deserve it, and I need one after the terrible day I've had." Zoe's smile was rueful. She wore a black jumpsuit and caramel-colored heels. Her dark hair was pulled back. Her lipstick was cherry red.

"Your lips are very bright," Bea said to Zoe. "They remind me of blood."

Lila coughed. "She means that as a compliment."

"I do," Bea said, nodding her head. "Blood is cool."

Zoe raised her eyebrows. "Then thanks?"

"Did you know there are people called forensic scientists, and their job is to use bloodstains to re-create crime scenes? Sometimes the blood spatter is all over the floor and walls and the ceiling and the furniture, and they can still figure out what happened. Isn't that awesome? I learned all about it in school," Bea said, her face animated.

"You learned about bloodstains in school?" Lila asked.

"I researched blood spatter on the computer during my break," Bea said.

Lila hoped the school didn't monitor computer search histories.

"Mama, you should go out with Zoe," Bea said. "You'll like that, and Jasper can stay here with me."

"We can't ask Jasper to do that. I'm sure he has his own plans," Lila said.

"I doubt it," Bea said. "He's always in his apartment alone."

"Bea, enough," Lila snapped and immediately regretted her sharp tone, wishing she could calmly pull Bea aside and explain why it wasn't polite to remark on Jasper's lifestyle choices.

"I don't mind sticking around. We've got at least another hour on these cookies," Jasper said quickly.

"We'll go to this place across the street. You can be back when the cookies are done," Zoe said.

Lila massaged her forehead, mortified at how Bea had suckered Jasper into babysitting her. Lila hated the idea of Jasper helping her. She didn't want to start relying on anyone at the Primrose when she was only there temporarily. Yet drinking a glass of wine in an actual restaurant suddenly sounded great, especially with Bea scowling at her, making the prospect of hanging around the apartment distinctly unappealing.

"Okay. Give me a minute to change," Lila said. "I'm a mess."

Zoe tilted her head and examined Lila. "Fine but you already look good."

Lila's cheeks warmed at the compliment, and she went back to her room and pulled out a silk shirt she hadn't worn in a year. They left the Primrose and crossed Grove Avenue, heading toward a spot down one of the side streets. The restaurant had a deep covered patio in front with a fireplace around which several people were clustered. Inside, the lighting was dim; candles adorned each table. A long, polished wood bar dominated the right side of the restaurant and was half filled with patrons. Zoe knew the hostess, and they were seated at a corner table. After ordering glasses of sauvignon blanc, they talked about the other residents of the

Primrose, Bea's new school, and Zoe's family. Then, Zoe rested her chin in her hand and looked at Lila.

"I know about the legal stuff with Bea's dad. I wanted to put it out there so you weren't wondering. I swear I wasn't cyberstalking you but—"

"But everyone knows," Lila said flatly.

Zoe shrugged, confirming.

"I'm sorry you're going through that." Zoe looked at Lila in that way—the one in which you expect the other person to share more about the dilemma, the one in which you look sympathetic and open to hearing the full story.

Yet Lila's throat closed up; not a word could escape. The pre-scandal Lila had shared all kinds of embarrassing, private things about herself with Daphne and her friends. She'd talk about the cellulite patches on her thighs and how much her mother-in-law disliked her. But also important things, like how Mama had left her alone almost every weekend the spring she turned fifteen to travel with a new boyfriend. Now she knew not to confide so easily. Zoe seemed kind and understanding, but how could Lila trust anyone with her real feelings when they could use them against her? People disappointed you more times than not.

Lila smiled. "Thanks. I'm doing okay. Tell me about your terrible day."

"All right, yeah. It was the worst. I've got this stupid side hustle that is killing me."

"What is it?" Lila asked.

"My brother, Alex, and I inherited this building from our great-uncle. It's about fifteen minutes from here. It was vacant for years, but we got the permit to turn it into a club. It seemed perfect because a couple of breweries opened two blocks away, and we thought we could capitalize on the vibe of the area. We've basically gotten everyone we know to invest, and we've finally finished construction. But our opening is in less than a month, we've hired this expensive band, and we've sold almost no tickets." Zoe gulped her wine. "I'm really worried we're going to lose everyone's money."

Lila frowned, thinking of what Ryan had done to his investors. "That's a terrible feeling."

Zoe nodded miserably. "I don't even know what else to do to bring in customers."

"Who's the band?" Lila asked.

"It's this cool West Coast group that Alex found. They just got a recording contract, and I know they're going to be huge in a few years, but they're not well known yet. I thought people would want to check out the space." Zoe hung her head. "I assumed I could pull this together because I plan a few events for the Primrose but it's totally different."

Lila reached out a hand and patted Zoe's arm. "Hey, it's a good idea. You're going to make it work."

"I don't know."

"No, really. You can do this. You can convince the college kids to come by advertising drink specials on your socials. Tag local student groups on your posts. Then you need some kind of draw to get other people in the door who will actually spend money—the young professional types who are going out. Maybe you could hire a local band as an opening act? One that people know and will show up to see?" Lila stopped as she realized she was firing out suggestions without even taking a breath. "I'm sure you know this already. I didn't mean to overstep."

"Are you kidding?" Zoe had gotten out her phone and was typing on the screen. "I'm taking notes. Were you an event planner or something?"

Lila laughed. "Not unless you count serving on a lot of committees that organized overly elaborate charity functions. My biggest contribution was chairing the Meritt Academy Auction. None of these things were a big deal, though; it was just a little hobby."

The words—*little hobby*—stuck inside her head, a faint echo of a memory from last year. She had been excited when Ryan got home, wanting to tell him about her progress on the auction; she'd managed to secure a large donation and negotiated a better price with the caterer. Ryan had nodded along as she talked, but the Clemson game was on in the background and he kept glancing at the TV over her shoulder. When she'd finished telling him everything, he'd smiled, his eyes on the screen behind her. *That's great, Li. I'm glad you're having fun with your little hobby.* Anger replaced her prior disappointment. Ryan shouldn't have belittled what was important to her.

"But you were in charge of the auction thing?" Zoe asked, her question bringing Lila back to the present.

"Yes, but I had a whole committee behind me, and they did a lot of the work."

Zoe stared at her. "You should help me with this. I can't pay you much, but I could come up with something. What do you think?"

Lila sat back, shaking her head. "You can do this yourself or hire a real event planner."

"I can't afford a real anything. You would be doing me a huge favor," Zoe said.

Before Lila could decline again, a tall man stopped at their table. His blond hair flopped over his forehead into dark eyes. He wore an untucked button-down and threadbare khakis. He was lanky and handsome, holding a short glass filled with clear liquor and four limes floating in it like tiny sunken boats.

"Zoe, hey girl. What's going on?" The man grinned at them.

Zoe rose to her feet, and he pulled her into a one-armed hug. The man was older than Lila had first realized, maybe in his late thirties, with faint lines around his eyes and skin starting to weather from too much sun. "Teddy, what are you doing here?"

"This is my usual haunt these days," Teddy said. He looked at Lila, waiting to be introduced.

"This is Lila Shaw. She's our newest resident at the Primrose and lives on your mama's floor," Zoe said and then turned to Lila. "This is Teddy Harrison, Evelyn's son."

"I didn't know Evelyn had a son," Lila said.

Teddy beamed down at her, looking exactly like the aging former frat boy he probably was. "I didn't know Mother had a gorgeous new neighbor."

Lila shifted in her seat as Teddy's eyes skimmed over her. To cover her discomfort, she sipped her wine. "I've enjoyed getting to know Evelyn."

Teddy made a mock shocked face. "I think you're talking about someone else. No one enjoys getting to know Mother."

"Teddy, that's not true," Zoe protested.

"Oh, that's entirely true. She's an absolute demon. I love her, but she's mean as a snake." Teddy grinned, covering his callous words in a charming smile.

"Actually, Evelyn has been lovely to me," Lila said, exaggerating Evelyn's temperament but not wanting to agree with Teddy. "She's especially sweet to my daughter."

"Now I know you've got the wrong lady. Mother hates children. She basically stayed away from me until I was old enough to mix her cocktails. But if your daughter looks anything like you, I can understand why Mother is enchanted," Teddy said.

Lila nearly rolled her eyes but finished her wine instead, not responding to his cloying compliment. Zoe sat down, effectively ending their conversation. Luckily, Teddy got the hint.

"I better get back to my friends." Teddy gestured to the bar. "I'll look forward to seeing you both around the Primrose."

As soon as Teddy was out of earshot, Zoe leaned in close. "He's an asshole in case you didn't notice."

Lila burst into laughter. "Oh, I did."

"He rarely visits Evelyn and, as far as I can tell, he's never had a real job in his life. He invests in different restaurants around town and spends his family money. He's also in a band. Lead singer, of course."

"Of course."

Zoe shook her head. "I know Evelyn is tough sometimes, but I've always felt bad about her only son barely showing up for her. I think she's lonely."

"Really? She's always telling me how busy she is," Lila said.

"She says that, but do you ever see her going anywhere?" Zoe raised her perfectly shaped eyebrows. "Evelyn used to spend all her time with Florence Parker. They were best friends but there was a big falling-out a year ago and now they don't speak."

"What happened?" Lila asked.

"No idea." Zoe glanced at her phone. "It's gotten late. I should get you back, but thanks for listening to me complain. Promise we'll do it again sometime?"

Zoe seemed genuine in her request, and Lila was pleased. She had forgotten how good it felt to talk with another woman, to brainstorm solutions to problems, to listen. It was also good to remember that she wasn't the only one with challenges. She'd somehow forgotten that over the last few months. Everyone had problems, even perfect-looking people like Zoe.

"I'd like that," Lila said.

"And I don't want to push about helping with the club, but I really would love it if you wanted to get involved." Zoe held up her hands. "No pressure, though. Seriously."

Once again, Lila heard the ring of sincerity behind Zoe's words.

Lila had loved planning the school auction and the diabetes society gala. There was something about digging into all the details, finding ways to make each party special, that excited Lila.

"Okay maybe," Lila said before she could overthink it.

Zoe squealed and squeezed Lila's hands.

From behind Zoe, Lila spotted Teddy once again. He was surrounded by a small crowd of people, leaning back against the bar, sipping his drink, looking as if he owned the place. He was holding court, and the three women in the group were laughing hysterically at whatever story he was telling. Lila recognized an Ulla Johnson top, a Veronica Beard blazer, the honey blond hair that required highlights every six weeks. They were all close to forty, probably married with children. The guys standing next to them were the same age, slight beer guts hinting at the years to come and baseball hats that hid their thinning hair. They were drinking expensive cocktails, wearing expensive clothes. They'd probably all gone to the same private school where Teddy was known as the guy who always had the liquor and hooked up with the prettiest girls.

"You said Teddy is in a band," Lila said, an idea forming in her head.

"That's right."

"You could use his band for your opening act. Teddy and his friends can convince everyone they know to come to the opening, and I'm sure they know everyone who lives in the Near West End." She shot another glance at Teddy. He was still talking and probably on his fifth tequila soda.

Zoe thought about Lila's suggestion for a long second. Lila immediately wished she could take back her words. Who was she to tell Zoe anything about her business? Lila didn't even know whether Teddy's band was any good.

"That's genius!" Zoe exclaimed.

Lila exhaled, not having realized how much she wanted to be useful. "You know what? I would love to help you."

Zoe tipped her glass to Lila. "This is the best news I've had all day."

Lila smiled and hoped she could help Zoe pull off the opening.

Chapter Sixteen

During the past week, Lila and her misfit investigators had managed to meet with several of the building's residents to question them about the night Sophia Kent died. No one was particularly helpful. Edwin gave Lila all the details on his divorce and taught Bea how to play a new video game. Follow-up questions for the Willoughby sisters only resulted in June going into further details about her past relationship with Conrad, none of which were in the least bit appropriate for Bea to hear. Meanwhile Florence complained about Evelyn the entire time before loaning Lila a romance novel that she insisted would change her life. It was about a woman who fell in love with a living gargoyle and featured some very explicit sex scenes involving a tail. Lila wasn't sure where Gloria and now Florence had gotten their book recommendations, but it definitely wasn't *The New Yorker*.

Despite the lack of progress, Lila found herself getting caught up in the investigation. She told herself she wouldn't get attached to her neighbors, but she couldn't ignore that the Primrose residents were having a positive effect on her daughter. Bea was in a perpetual good mood, even willingly doing her homework. She smiled every time Jasper and Evelyn came over, peppering them with her theories. *What if Sophia was a spy for the government and killed in an operation gone wrong? Could Sophia have a secret boyfriend who murdered her out of jealousy? Had the blackmailer finally gotten tired of Sophia not paying him?* Bea had an unlimited supply of motives, mostly pulled from old *Murder, She Wrote* episodes. Evelyn told her the ideas were *preposterous*, though Jasper listened carefully to each one before poking gentle holes in it. They gathered most evenings to discuss their latest interviews and Bea's newest ideas with some of Jasper's baked goods even though they had no chance of solving Sophia's murder, and Lila was sure they all knew it, except maybe Bea... and Evelyn.

In some ways it was easier to debate Bea's outlandish theories rather than face the reality of Sophia's death. Yet Lila could never completely forget that Sophia was a sixteen-year-old girl who had tragically died, leaving behind a family. Her stomach turned every time she thought back to Helene's grief-stricken face, the one Lila had witnessed in her apartment. Helene was a mother like Lila, and Sophia's murder wasn't a theory to her. She was living with the reality of her daughter's death every day while Lila's daughter played down the hall.

That afternoon, Jasper had convinced Emily Canterbury to meet with him and Lila while Bea was at school. Evelyn kept insisting an interview with Emily was a waste of time because she hadn't lived at the Primrose during the murder. They decided to meet with Emily anyway. Emily's apartment was next to Conrad Kent's on the fifth floor. Her mother had owned the apartment at the time of Sophia's death and made the initial 9-1-1 call.

Emily sighed when she opened the door to let them in. Her hair was arranged in stiff brown curls around her gaunt face. She was frail looking; her lips pursed in a scowl.

Lila held out her hand, smiling. "I'm Lila Shaw. We met briefly the other week."

Emily stared at the outstretched hand, looking disgusted. "I don't touch other people's hands. No offense."

Lila glanced at Jasper, who was staring pointedly at the floor. "None taken. Lots of people are afraid of germs after COVID."

"It's not because of germs," Emily said before turning. "Come in. The reporter is already here. Let's get this over with."

Lila and Jasper exchanged glances as they followed Emily inside, both thinking the same thing. *What reporter?*

Emily's living room was in the back of the apartment. Windows overlooked Grove Avenue, and taffeta puffed along the top in rose-colored clouds. Her furniture was pink chintz and it all matched: Two sofas, two chairs, and an ottoman were clad in the same floral fabric with cabbage roses, green vines, and small sprays of yellow lilies. A glass coffee table was poised in the middle of it all with a potted orchid and stacks of books. Across from the coffee table was Nate Donnelly.

Lila froze.

Nate stood and gave her a big grin. "Lila Shaw, I hoped we'd see each other again."

Lila moved stiffly to one of the sofas. "That makes one of us." He'd found out her name. That meant he'd researched her. It wasn't a good sign.

Looking down at her same boring maxi skirt with the unraveling hem, Lila wished she could have worn the little red Dolce&Gabbana sundress she'd once owned. It had been the most expensive dress in her closet. The length was too short but at least it showed off her legs. Unfortunately, she couldn't say the same for the maxi skirt. Right then, she looked exactly like what she was—a tired, worn-out mama who'd spent the morning cleaning out a drawer full of clown makeup. Photos indicated Gloria and Stanley had gone through a mother-son clowning phase, which more than explained Stanley's lack of a high school girlfriend.

"You know each other. Good," Emily said in a no-nonsense tone.

"I didn't want to conduct two of these interviews, so I figured I'd combine them into one." She sat down in one of the chairs.

"Well, we aren't exactly here about the same thing," Lila said, frowning at Nate.

"That's true. We aren't here for the same reason," Nate said, tapping his pen against a notepad in his lap. He looked handsome and confident, the picture of a gentleman. "I'm here to write an article for a well-known newspaper. Why exactly are you here again, Lila?"

Lila glared at him. She'd googled Nate after their coffee shop run-in, so she knew he was an investigative journalist who wrote interesting stories about government corruption and crime, ran 5Ks for charity, and posted photos of his baby niece on Instagram. But none of that excused the fact that Nate was obviously determined to act like an absolute jerk at all times. Not even his cheekbones could convince her that he was a decent person.

Emily sat up straight, picking up on Nate's not-so-subtle implication that Lila and Jasper were there for a sinister reason. "I thought you were helping Alice Kent. My understanding is she's actively looking for her sister's killer and supports this whole reward scheme. I assumed you were operating as a private investigator in your retirement on her behalf?" She looked to Jasper.

Beads of sweat popped up on Jasper's upper lip showing his nerves.

"We are helping Alice." Lila cut in swiftly. Her answer was entirely true even if they weren't exactly working for her.

Nate opened his mouth to say something else—most likely something terrible and cutting—but Emily spoke first. "Let's get on with this. I have a hair appointment booked in an hour, and I need to call down to have my BMW pulled around."

"You bet. Let's jump right in. I was hoping to get your perspective on what happened to Sophia. I understand your mother made the nine-one-one call but you were also here in the apartment at the time of the murder," Nate said.

Lila's eyes widened at this piece of new information, which made Emily a much more interesting witness.

"I see you've done your research. You're correct. I was here at the time of Sophia's murder. The police saw no need to disclose my name to the press, and I'd like to keep it that way," Emily said, her eyes narrowing. "I'm a private person."

"I understand. I have no intention of releasing your name. I only want to understand what happened that night," Nate said in a confidential, chatty voice, which Lila instantly hated.

Emily nodded briskly. "I appreciate that. At the time of the murder, my mother owned this apartment and was ill. I was her primary caregiver. I left my teaching position and moved in here on a temporary basis only two days before Sophia died."

"That's incredibly generous of you," Nate said.

"Yes, it was a hardship, but I was happy to do it. Mother needed me," Emily said.

"I bet your husband missed having you home," Nate said.

Lila refrained from rolling her eyes. He was laying it on pretty thick. Surely Emily Canterbury wasn't going to fall for that.

Emily Canterbury did indeed fall for that. She fluttered her hands. "Sadly, my ex-husband didn't see things the way you do. He wasn't supportive of me helping Mother but sometimes you need to make the hard decisions to do what's right."

"Brave," Nate murmured.

Lila scoffed out loud, drawing the attention of Emily, who frowned at her. Lila pretended to cough, covering up her disdain. Nate was grinning at her as if he knew exactly what she was really thinking and enjoyed her discomfort.

"Emily, can you tell us about the night of Sophia's death?" Jasper asked, putting the conversation back on track.

"There was a cocktail party on the patio downstairs for all the building's residents. Mother was too ill to attend, and I didn't like to leave her alone, so I stayed behind too. I was heating up some soup in the kitchen when we both heard the scream from next door." Emily shook her head. "It was horribly loud and went on and on. It woke Mother up, and she immediately called the police."

"Did you look to see if anyone was in the hallway?" Jasper asked.

Emily shook her head. "I was too scared. I wish I had."

Something didn't add up. Emily didn't seem like the type who was easily frightened. She wasn't afraid to tell a guest that she wouldn't shake her hand simply because she didn't feel like it. Lila couldn't believe Emily hadn't run to the door to peer outside upon hearing the scream.

"The police arrived shortly thereafter. The commotion broke up the cocktail party. I'll never forget watching Conrad hurry down the hall to his apartment. There was a terrible look on his face as if he expected the worst, which is exactly what he got." Emily pressed her lips together, her countenance pale.

"I understand you worked at Stratford Academy as a teacher," Nate said. "Can you tell me about what Sophia—"

"Excuse me, but we have more questions about the night of Sophia's death," Lila interrupted, not willing to let Nate take back over the interview. She looked to Jasper for help, but he was staring around the apartment, his eyes flitting from object to object.

"Please go ahead, Lila." Nate sat back, crossing one leg over the other, looking amused. The sunlight gilded his hair and highlighted the golden skin on his face.

Lila's brain worked to come up with another question, something a detective would ask. "Did you notice anything, um, suspicious right before Sophia's death?"

Emily wrinkled her nose. "Suspicious like what?"

"Like . . . well, did you see any strangers hanging around the building, possibly in the stairwell?" Lila asked, avoiding looking anywhere in Nate's direction.

"No. I obviously would have reported that to the police when they questioned me," Emily said, frowning.

"What insightful questions," Nate said, grinning at Lila.

Lila glared at him, unable to hide her dismay.

"As I was saying," Nate said smoothly, drawing Emily's attention. "I understand you were a teacher at Stratford Academy. Was Sophia Kent a student of yours?"

At this question, Emily stiffened; her shoulders noticeably raised closer to her ears. For the first time, Lila spotted the large diamonds in each earlobe. When Emily clasped her hands in her lap, enormous gemstones—rubies, emeralds, diamonds—gleamed on both her right and left fingers. Lila studied Emily's entire outfit, noticing her Gucci loafers and the Hermès scarf knotted at her neck. For a former teacher, Emily was outfitted in lavish attire.

"I did know Sophia. I was her English teacher during her junior year before she died. She was smart and a pretty girl too," Emily said flatly.

Lila leaned forward. It wasn't Emily's words. The words were perfectly acceptable. But there was something in Emily's voice that said there was more to the story. Lila recognized that particular cadence in Southern women's voices—the compliment swathed in a monotone, the lack of emphasis or enthusiasm, the failure to gush in any way. That was not the way that ladies talked about a young girl unless they truly disliked her.

Nate and Jasper were both looking at their pads, scratching down notes, and absolutely unaware of Emily's unspoken opinion of Sophia.

"I suppose Sophia had a lot of friends?" Lila said.

"It did appear that way," Emily said and looked away.

"I read she was involved in several community service organizations," Lila said.

"That's what I was told," Emily said.

"The faculty must have thought highly of her," Lila said.

"We loved all our girls," Emily said.

Oh, she was making it perfectly obvious she had despised Sophia.

"So why didn't you like her?" Lila asked.

Nate and Jasper gaped at her, gasping a little. Emily dipped her chin, acknowledging that Lila had read her perfectly. Lila stifled a gasp of her own. She couldn't believe she'd come out and said what she suspected, and that she was right.

Emily refolded her hands in her lap, composing herself. "Most of the girls at Stratford Academy were privileged but not like Sophia. She was given everything she wanted—a Mercedes on her sixteenth birthday, a new wardrobe each season, elaborate parties for every possible occasion. It made her selfish and entitled." She held up her hands in defense. "I know that's an awful thing to say about a sixteen-year-old girl who died tragically, but it's true."

Once Emily started speaking, it was as if a dam erupted from inside her mouth. The words were tumbling over each other, spilling out at a rapid pace. Emily wanted to tell this story. She wanted to say these things about Sophia, and there was no way she was going to miss an opportunity to bash this girl.

"Was she well liked by her classmates?" Lila asked.

"I really don't know," Emily said. "She had a clique of girls who seemed to love her, though I wouldn't say she seemed particularly nice to anyone outside of her little group. Everyone forgot about that after Sophia's death. Most of this town would tell you Sophia was perfect, but it's not true. All those community service hours she supposedly did tutoring underprivileged kids? Lies. She skipped almost every session. And her stellar academic record? Also lies. Her grades should have been C's and D's, but her mother managed to fix all her problems by convincing teachers to re-grade her papers and insisting the school overlook her propensity for skipping class."

"Wealth has a way of controlling the narrative," Jasper said.

Jasper's words echoed inside Lila, a ring of honesty. She hadn't grown up with custom-made couches and six-hundred-dollar shoes. She'd gone to Meritt Academy on a scholarship and worked over the summer to buy schoolbooks and a pair of Gap jeans from the sale rack. It was only after she started dating Ryan in high school and spent time in his waterfront home with the original artwork and his mama's sneering disbelief at her old Dodge (*Bless your heart, is that safe to drive?*) that she really understood how her classmates lived. There were the country club memberships, the housekeepers, the constant house upgrades, the elaborate vacations to Europe and the Caribbean. For some reason, she'd started to believe that money made them smarter and more credible than everyone else. She'd taken Ryan's wealth for granted, assuming he knew how to maintain it and hold onto it. He'd tell her to *buy something pretty* and insisted *let's enjoy what we have.* His parents were always extolling him as a successful entrepreneur while they ate overcooked steak in the club dining room every Sunday night, further cocooning her in the myth of Ryan Shaw. She'd fallen for the lie—hook, line, and fucking sinker.

Nate stared at Lila as if he sensed the tumult of her thoughts before turning to Emily. "Interesting. I'm scheduled to talk to several of her former classmates later this week. I wonder what they'll say about her."

"They will all remember the story they were spoon-fed by the Kent family after her death; how Sophia was brilliant and generous and spent her time helping others. It's all ridiculous, but the

Kent family is powerful and they turned Sophia into a saint." Emily injected venom into the words. Her face was red, scrunched up, and angry looking. It was clear she had harbored these resentments for a long time, and Lila couldn't help but wonder if there was a more personal reason for Emily's dislike.

"I heard Sophia had a drug problem. Is that something the Kents may have covered up?" Nate asked.

Lila's mouth fell open. A drug problem? That was another surprise.

"Certainly," Emily said. "I have no doubt they would have kept any drug use private."

"There was cocaine in her system when she died," Nate said.

"How can you know that?" Lila asked. Had Sophia's family known she was using cocaine? Helene and Alice hadn't given any indication during their chat.

Nate smirked at her. "Private source. Real professionals have these sorts of contacts. I understand the police were looking for Sophia's drug dealer after her death. You don't know who that was, do you?"

Emily shrugged. "I'm afraid I can't help you. To be honest, I never fully believed the robbery theory of her murder. I'm sure Sophia had enemies, some of whom may even have appeared to care about her." Her eyes shuttered as she rose to her feet. "I must get going now."

Lila walked to the foyer with Nate and Jasper, her feet light on the floral-patterned rug. She was exhilarated by what they'd learned about Sophia, each interview getting them closer to the truth. No matter how ridiculous it sometimes felt to get so wrapped up in the investigation, Sophia Kent's murder was a lot more interesting than cleaning out Gloria's apartment. She couldn't wait to tell Bea about the interview.

Emily opened the door to shuffle them out into the hallway.

Lila noticed a silver frame on the claw-footed table against the foyer wall with a photograph of a younger Emily and an older woman in front of a roaring ocean. Lila peered closer and picked up the frame. She never could resist looking at other people's photos. The photo surprised her. Emily had been beautiful when she was young.

"Don't touch that," Emily snapped.

Lila stepped backward, taken by surprise at the hostility in Emily's voice. She bumped into Nate's warm chest, tipping slightly to one side as her right ankle wobbled. Nate's hands closed around her arms to steady her. Heat radiated from her skin. Her heart stuttered, her fingers slackened, and the frame crashed to the hardwood floor.

"Look what you've done," Emily screeched.

Lila shook off Nate's hands, stepping forward again. The glass on the frame had shattered into small pieces, scattered around the floor. Her face flushed.

"I'm so sorry! I'll clean this up," Lila said hastily.

"Get out," Emily said, pointing to the hallway.

Lila winced. "Are you sure I can't—"

"Just leave," Emily said.

"We're going." Jasper took Lila's elbow and helped her over the shards of glass, leading her into the hallway.

Nate trailed behind, quiet for once, although the suspicious sound of stifled laughter emanated from his direction. Emily slammed the door as soon as they cleared the threshold.

"I hope you didn't have any follow-up questions, because I don't think she's interested in talking to you again," Nate said, sounding amused.

"Oh, shut up. This is your fault," Lila said.

Nate held up his hands. "I didn't drop the frame."

"You startled me," Lila said accusingly.

"I can't help if I make you nervous," Nate said.

"You don't make me—I don't care if you—" Lila stopped stuttering and drew a breath. Nate wasn't worth arguing with. "Jasper, come on. Let's get out of here."

Jasper nodded, and the two of them walked away from Nate. Lila refused to turn around, but she felt his eyes on her until they turned the corner.

Chapter Seventeen

Bea and Lila spotted Mary Dixon waiting for the elevator later that day. Her face brightened as they walked up. Today she wore a pink denim jumpsuit and her platform Alexander McQueen tennis shoes. Her cane was hot pink.

"Oh girls, I'm glad I ran into you. After we talked, I remembered something else about Sophia that you might find interesting," Mary Dixon said.

They had interviewed Mary Dixon earlier that week, and she'd had nothing significant to share about the robberies or the murder. She had spent most of the time talking about her cats and showing Lila pictures of her grandchildren.

Bea twisted her mouth into a serious expression that made Lila want to pull her into a hug. She looked so cute and solemn. "Tell us everything. No detail is too small."

"Well," Mary Dixon said, lowering her voice. "I hate to speak ill of the dead, but I do recall seeing Sophia on the Primrose patio right in the middle of the school day on more than one occasion." She raised her eyebrows meaningfully. "Do you understand what I'm saying?"

"She had a date with a secret boyfriend?" Bea asked.

The gold arrow at the top of the elevator ticked down from the fifth floor to the fourth. It was moving as slow as ever. But Lila was used to it now and didn't mind waiting.

Mary Dixon clasped her chest. "My goodness, I have no idea about a secret boyfriend. All I know is she was skipping school."

"Oh." Bea slumped, obviously hoping for a more exciting piece of evidence.

"Bea did bring up a good point, though," Lila said.

"I did?" Bea asked.

"Sure, you did. You wanted to check if Mary Dixon saw Sophia meeting with anyone while she was skipping school," Lila said.

Bea puffed up her chest. "That's true. That's what I wanted to ask. And also why was she hanging around here instead of at her own house?"

Bea looked up at Lila for approval. Lila smiled at her. Bea had asked an excellent follow-up question.

"I never saw Sophia meet anyone and I'm not sure why she was at the Primrose." Mary Dixon looked away as if uncomfortable at this line of questioning. "I did mention the situation to Helene though. I worried about Sophia jeopardizing her education by cutting class."

"How did Helene react?" Lila asked.

"Did she lose her temper and start throwing things?" Bea asked eagerly.

"Not at all. She thanked me and said she would handle it. I hated to get Sophia into trouble but skipping school is very risky behavior."

"Skipping school is much worse than throwing a book at someone," Bea said in a solemn voice. "I wish more people would remember that."

"Why would anyone throw a book at someone?" Mary Dixon looked alarmed.

"Self-defense," Bea said. "Or because they deserved it."

"Do you know, sometimes I watch these girls complain on Tik-

Tok, and I think they'd be better off throwing something and getting out their anger," Mary Dixon said.

"I totally agree," Bea said.

The elevator arrived—*thank God*—before Bea had a chance to further explain or justify her own book-throwing tendencies to Mary Dixon. In the elevator, Mary Dixon asked if Bea would like to meet the kitten she was fostering that week. Bea wanted to go immediately, and Lila agreed to the visit. She got off on the second floor alone as Bea and Mary Dixon continued to the fourth. When she turned the corner past the elevator, Teddy was standing outside Evelyn's apartment, holding something wrapped in a plastic bag.

"What brings you over here?" Lila asked, slowing in the hallway. She did not feel particularly happy to see him but couldn't ignore him either.

Teddy leaned close to her and touched his lips to her cheek. They left a wet spot on her face, and she stopped herself from reaching up to swipe it away. His cologne had an overly spicy scent that clogged her nose. She quickly stepped back.

"Came to return a dish to Mother, but she's not here. She's awfully particular about getting her Tupperware back," Teddy said.

"She's not here because she gets her hair set every Wednesday afternoon," Lila said.

"Is that so? I guess I'd forgotten. What a shame I missed her." Teddy winked and smiled.

Lila was entirely sure that he'd returned the Tupperware precisely when he knew Evelyn wasn't home. Her neck stretched taut with irritation. Evelyn deserved more than that. She had used this container to bring Teddy something to eat, still trying to take care of him even though he was a fully grown adult and didn't seem grateful. Though perhaps it wasn't fair to expect gratitude for a mother's innate safeguarding of her child. She considered what she'd learned from Emily—about how Helene had polished over Sophia's mistakes. Lila understood Helene's need to make things easier for her daughter.

"I can give Evelyn the dish if you'd like," Lila said briskly.

"Thanks." Teddy stepped closer, holding out the Tupperware.

Lila reached for the plastic dish, tugging it toward her. Through the bag, it was evident the dish had bits of food still clinging to the inside. He hadn't even bothered to wash it. What an ass. Lila continued down the hall, but Teddy followed behind.

"Maybe I could wait for Mother at your place?" Teddy asked, stopping outside her door.

Lila did not take out her key. She barely knew Teddy and wasn't interested in entertaining him in her apartment. He didn't seem to notice her discomfort. Teddy Harrison was used to getting his way. Lila recognized this particular brand of Southern male—despite the wrinkles, receding hairline, and slackening muscles, he still envisioned himself as captain of the lacrosse team who deserved whatever he wanted.

"The apartment isn't ready for visitors yet," Lila said.

Teddy's smile flickered before returning full wattage. "How about I buy you dinner instead? You can consider it a thank-you for my band's gig at Zoe's new space. She said it was your suggestion."

Lila wasn't interested in going anywhere with Teddy. He was looking at her with uncomfortable intensity, glancing down at her chest, and crowding her by standing a hair too close.

"I wish I could, but my daughter is due home soon. Sorry," Lila apologized, not sure why she was apologizing for declining a dinner she didn't want to attend.

"How about tomorrow? We could go to Olivia's. Best Greek food in the city. I swear," Teddy tried again. "I'm a part-owner. Andrew

Bouras is the head chef. He's a phenomenal cook but his restaurant didn't make a dime until I stepped in to help. I turned the whole place around."

Lila internally groaned, listening to Teddy take all the credit for a restaurant he wasn't even running.

"I can't. I'm busy with the apartment," Lila said firmly.

Teddy held up his palms. "I tried. Now I'll have to sneak down the elevator and hope I don't run into Susanna again."

"You don't like Susanna?" Lila asked.

Teddy laughed, but it wasn't a nice sound. There was a malicious note behind it. Lila could tell he wasn't kidding about his dislike.

"I've known Susanna since we were kids. We grew up around the corner from each other. She's not what you'd call friendly."

Lila nodded. "She does seem a little prickly."

"Understatement of the decade. She's a bitch. Last year, I came over here to sign some legal paperwork for Mother. I snuck up the elevator without checking in. I mean, come on, it's not a big deal. Mother has lived here forever. Susanna found out what I'd done and called the police. She said I was an intruder."

"Wow," Lila breathed, imagining the scene between Evelyn and Susanna and the police. "I bet that didn't go over well with Evelyn."

"She wanted Susanna fired but, as usual, Conrad stepped in and defended her. He always had a soft spot for her because of Sophia."

Sophia again. It was interesting how many of Lila's conversations came back to Sophia Kent. It was as if the girl was mixed into the mortar of the building itself.

"Did you know Sophia?" Lila asked.

Teddy waved a hand. "A little. I was two years ahead of her at Stratford. I used to see her out at parties, but we weren't close. We would have these huge parties down at the cliffs behind the Primrose, and everyone would come. Sophia too. That was all before Melanie Livingston fell off the cliffs and died."

That must be the accident Conrad had mentioned on their first meeting.

"What happened there?" Lila asked.

Teddy's face fell. "It was terrible. It was the summer after our senior year. Melanie was drinking at one of the cliff parties and tried to walk home alone. I guess she got turned around and fell. Her body wasn't found until the next morning. They closed the cliffs down after that."

"That's awful," Lila said.

"Yeah. Sometimes awful things happen," Teddy said, looking morose. "Look at Sophia. People don't recover from that shit. I swear Susanna was never the same after Sophia died. She got bitter, you know?"

"I heard they were best friends," Lila said.

"They were." Teddy's teeth gleamed. "Well, they supposedly were, but sometimes it seemed like they hated each other. One time, Susanna got mad at Sophia for something—I have no idea what—and she punched Sophia in the face."

Lila was shocked at this news. "Really? Did Susanna get in trouble?"

"No idea. I only knew about it because I was at the party where it happened. They got into a screaming match outside, and when Sophia went to walk away, Susanna grabbed her arm and threw the punch." Teddy shook his head. "Half the party was standing outside watching. Susanna fully went after Sophia, jumped on her, intending to kick her ass. It was fucking crazy. Sophia was crying and trying to get away from her, but Susanna was furious. It was like she snapped or something."

"When was this?" Lila asked.

Teddy shrugged. "Not long before Sophia died. I saw Susanna crying at the funeral and couldn't help but think it was ironic to see her so upset after that argument. But hey, what do I know about how girls fight?" He smirked as if to say girls were such silly, ridiculous creatures, and who could possibly understand them?

"Most girls don't fight like that," Lila said quietly. "Do you think Susanna was capable of—I don't know—really hurting Sophia?"

"You mean did Susanna kill her?" Teddy reared back, seeming shocked by the question. "No way." He pressed his lips together, thinking. "I guess it's possible. Anything is possible, right?"

Lila managed to escape Teddy's company and lock herself back inside the apartment. She leaned against the door, her pulse racing. Had the police even looked into the fight between Susanna and Sophia? If Susanna had snapped once, was it possible she had snapped again and killed Sophia?

There was a ping inside Lila like a guitar string plucked against her chest. It was an uncomfortable feeling, a warning of sorts. After all their interviews and meetings and discussions, she never actually thought they would find the killer of Sophia Kent. This "investigation" was supposed to be fun, a distraction for Bea, a way to connect with her daughter. It wasn't supposed to be *real*, but it was starting to feel that way.

Chapter Eighteen

Zoe's club was located on a side street in an industrial area. The gray door was unassuming, the white brick exterior equally so. Upon entry, a warren of several smaller rooms was newly painted in moody dark grays and had seating areas with low modern couches and matching club chairs. The rooms opened up into a cavernous space with fifteen-foot ceilings and two-story columns. The stage was set several steps above the wood floor, and there was a long bar along the opposite wall.

"This place is amazing," Lila said admiringly.

Bea had disappeared as soon as they arrived and was off exploring somewhere, hopefully not making any trouble.

"Do you really like it?" Zoe asked, watching Lila closely.

Lila could tell her reply was important to Zoe. "I love it. I think it's going to be a huge success. It reminds me of an old speakeasy with those small rooms opening up to this. In fact . . ." She ran her hands along the cinderblock walls, tapping them thoughtfully. "You could make the opening party a speakeasy." She began to talk faster, considering the possibilities. "You could curtain off the first room or—or turn it into a little merchandise shop so it appears that there's nowhere else to go, and then everyone has to have a password to get in. You wouldn't need much in the way of decor; some candles and maybe a few flowers. I could see waitresses and bartenders dressed in 1920s attire, and you could serve sidecars and French 75's as the house drinks . . ." Her voice trailed off. "I love a theme party. I get carried away sometimes."

Zoe's face split into a huge smile. "Keep getting carried away. I have to call Alex about some logistics on the ABC license. I want to tell him about your ideas. Do you mind?"

"Sure. Go ahead. I'm going to take some photos of the space to put on Instagram. I noticed you didn't have many posts. I thought I could tag some of the local reporters and influencers."

"Yes, absolutely. Do that please." Zoe was already hurrying away, pulling out her cell phone. "And hey, Lila?"

"Yes?"

"You really are good at this. Thank you," Zoe said.

Lila turned away before Zoe could see how flattered she was by the offhand compliment. It wasn't as if she had done much. Yet Lila had to admit it felt good to hear that someone liked her suggestions. She remembered how much she had enjoyed working on her and Ryan's business before Bea was born—interacting with customers and employees and coordinating the store openings. She liked to plan things and maybe she *was* good at it.

There was a crash behind the stage. Lila hurried to the back of the room, noticing a small door in the wall. She pushed it open and found Bea in a storage room, standing beside an overturned stack of twelve metal cafe chairs that were strewn in all directions across the concrete floor.

"Bea, what are you doing back here?" Lila whispered. She looked over her shoulder, hoping Zoe wasn't on her way into the room to check on the crash.

"Just looking around," Bea said innocently.

"If you're just looking around, why are all these chairs on the floor?" Lila asked.

"Before you get mad, I want you to know that I was conducting a science experiment, and you're the one who is always saying that science is important."

"I'm talking about science in school. Not whatever this was," Lila said, pushing the words out from behind her clenched teeth. "What happened?"

Bea bit her lip, looking guilty. "The chairs were stacked up, and I wanted to see if I could climb to the top."

Lila blew out a breath. "You shouldn't have done that. You could have gotten hurt."

"But I didn't," Bea countered and nudged a chair with her toe.

"You also could have damaged the chairs."

"They look fine," Bea said, rolling her eyes. "It's not a big deal."

Lila found herself getting more and more annoyed at Bea's nonchalant attitude. "It's rude to make a mess like this and risk ruining Zoe's stuff. Do you understand *that*?"

"It was an accident."

"It wasn't an accident. You climbed those chairs on purpose!" Lila said, her voice rising.

"You're mad about nothing," Bea said, louder now.

"I'm mad because you won't admit you did something wrong," Lila yelled.

Bea glared at her. "Daddy never yells at me like you do."

Hot air rushed inside Lila, filling her up with fury. How dare Bea compare her absent father to Lila who was here with her every single day! "That's because he's not around."

"He's coming home soon, though," Bea shot back and stared hard at Lila.

Lila knew what Bea was waiting for—she was waiting for Lila to agree with her, to tell her Ryan was coming home any day now. But Lila was too angry in that moment to perpetuate the fantasy she had told Bea over and over. She pressed her lips together and began restocking the chairs in a pointed silence.

Bea's face crumpled. She whipped around and stomped out of the storage room.

Lila stopped stacking chairs. She leaned against the wall, the fight draining out of her. What was wrong with her? She should have agreed with Bea, reassured her that her father still loved her and wanted to see her. She should have remained calm and absorbed Bea's outburst without losing her temper. Gentle parenting was clearly not her strong suit. Why had she let her own anger get the best of her? Because she had no self-control. That was the cold, diamond-hard truth.

"Lila!"

Lila heard her name called from outside. She finished straightening the chairs and exited the storage room. Evelyn was hobbling into the room with her walker, accompanied by Jasper, who was looking around with interest. Bea was nowhere in sight.

"This place was impossible to find, and Jasper is the slowest driver in Richmond," Evelyn said.

"I'm cautious," Jasper said. "And you could have driven yourself."

"I'm not allowed to drive after my last speeding ticket. The judge was quite melodramatic about it and called me *a danger to myself and others*. I informed him that it's not dangerous to drive fast when you have my excellent hand-eye coordination, but he kept saying I was in contempt of court," Evelyn said, looking irritated. "Why did you text us to meet here?"

Lila frowned and picked up her cell phone. Sure enough, there was a text sent an hour ago to Evelyn and Jasper, telling them to come to the club.

"I'm sorry. Bea was the one who texted you, not me. I don't even know where she is right now." Lila ran a hand through her hair.

"I saw her hiding behind the curtain near the entrance," Jasper said.

Lila's shoulders tensed at this news. She'd yelled at her daughter, and now Bea was hiding from her. She shouldn't have lost her temper.

Zoe hurried back into the main room. "Alex loved the speakeasy idea. We're making lists right now of what we need." She stopped, catching sight of Evelyn and Jasper. "Oh hey, you two. I didn't know you were going to be here."

"Neither did I," Lila said quickly. Was there anything less professional than inviting your retired neighbors to a job site?

"I understand this is your place, Zoe," Evelyn said. "It reminds me of an old tool factory my daddy owned. Of course, his factory was more upscale, but this is still relatively nice. You may give me a tour now."

"I think Zoe is busy with some other things," Lila said.

Zoe flashed Lila a quick smile. "I don't mind giving Evelyn a tour. I'm sure you heard Teddy's band is going to play for the opening."

A quick pained expression passed over Evelyn's face. Lila bet Teddy hadn't told Evelyn about his gig. He probably didn't tell her much of anything.

Evelyn drew herself up. "If Teddy's band is playing, I should definitely walk around to make sure it's good enough for one of his shows."

"I'd love to show you the kitchen," Zoe said, leading her down the right side of the room.

Lila crossed the room to Jasper. "I'm sorry Bea texted without checking with me. She does that kind of thing sometimes."

Jasper smiled. "I don't mind. It's nice to be asked for my opinion."

"She hates me right now," Lila blurted out.

"I'm sure that's not true."

"No, it is. I yelled at her, and she said some things and I didn't . . ."

Lila waved a hand, embarrassed at the hot rush of tears behind her eyes. Why was she even telling him this? "It's not something you want to hear about."

"We all say things we don't mean when we get upset."

"Yes, but I should stay calm. I'm the adult."

Jasper shrugged. "You're also human, and Bea is a strong-willed girl."

Bea *was* strong-willed. Lila had always known this, but she'd gotten more stubborn and argumentative since Ryan left. Yelling at her never seemed to work. Lila wished she could find a way to connect with Bea better; maybe then she wouldn't resist everything Lila asked her to do.

Jasper stared off at a point in the distance. "Bea reminds me of my partner, George." He stopped, shook his head a little. "My ex-partner. We separated two years ago. He was emotional and determined like Bea, and he threw himself into his interests like her. I always admire that in people."

Lila had wondered about Jasper, whether he'd ever married or had children or had any family in Richmond. Now she knew that he'd had a serious relationship with someone.

"I'm sorry about your breakup," Lila said.

Jasper waved a hand. "It's okay. I've mostly recovered."

Lila wondered if she would ever *mostly* recover. She thought of Ryan's last words to her, the way her heart had stopped at *divorce*. She thought about how she woke up every morning, stretched, saw the flickers of sunlight on the bed, and then her stomach dropped when she remembered all over again. Ryan had left her. She no longer had someone to share stories about Bea with, to debrief after parties with, to make hard decisions with. It wasn't so much losing Ryan that still hurt. It was losing her family and the future she'd planned for them.

"We were together for thirty years before he left. I was shocked when he wanted to end our relationship, but George wasn't happy. I guess I'm dense sometimes." Jasper chuckled at himself but there was no mirth in the sound. It was clear that he was still smarting from the split. "I was sixty-two and on my own for the first time in decades. I stopped caring about work and retired from the police force. I wasn't contributing much anyway."

"I can't believe that's true," Lila said. "You're really good at questioning witnesses."

Jasper's cheeks reddened. "I don't know about that. It's a little embarrassing how I acted after George left. I spent a lot of time in my house, not going anywhere."

"I did the same thing after my husband left me," Lila said with a rush of sympathy for Jasper. There were days when she had barely gotten off her couch, much less out of the house.

Jasper's toe scuffed the floor. "It all worked out in the end. I'm happier alone. I only make poor decisions when I become too attached to something."

"I know all about making bad decisions too. I'd say moving us to the disaster of Gloria's apartment and letting Bea spend her time chasing down a murderer is proof of my incompetence as a mother." Lila tried to make it sound like a joke but it came out weightier than she'd planned, probably because it was all true.

Jasper frowned. "That's not true. After everything you've been through—" He stopped and looked straight into Lila's eyes then, not shying away. "I know about your husband's fraud. I think you're doing a great job. I can't imagine it's been easy."

"No, it definitely hasn't." Lila's body lightened with something—was it relief? How long had it been since someone said she was doing a good job as a mother and didn't blame her for their problems? She couldn't remember.

"Bea has had a lot of adversity with her father leaving and changing schools, and she still manages to stay positive most of the time. I would say some of that is due to the way she's being raised by you."

Lila's throat closed up, tears gathering behind her eyes again. She blinked them back, not wanting to embarrass Jasper with her sentimentality. She hadn't realized how much she needed to hear that she was doing okay. Jasper's words were a balm to that thing inside her that was raw and wounded.

"Thank you," Lila finally said when she could speak without risk of breaking into tears. "That means a lot to me. Sometimes I feel like I have no idea what I'm doing."

"I guess we all feel like that sometimes," Jasper said quietly. "And I don't think there is anything wrong with that."

Chapter Nineteen

Lila tracked Bea down after talking to Jasper. She gave Bea a short hug, apologized for raising her voice, and tried not to mind when Bea did not apologize back. While Zoe and Lila talked through some decor ideas for the opening party, Bea had a whispered discussion about the investigation with Jasper and Evelyn in the corner. Bea filled Lila in when they got in the car to go home.

"Susanna is my number one suspect," Bea announced. "Evelyn agrees with me."

"What about the blackmailer or the robber? There are other suspects too," Lila said. She didn't want Bea to focus on Susanna. After what she'd learned from Teddy—how Susanna had attacked Sophia right before her murder—Lila was beginning to think Susanna really could have hurt Sophia. She didn't want Bea anywhere near a real murderer. Susanna could also kick them out of the Primrose. They couldn't afford to offend her and accusing her of murder was definitely offensive.

"Yeah, but we don't know their names. Susanna is our best lead," Bea said. "She was mad at Sophia for stealing that Jeremy guy like Alice said."

"We don't know that for sure," Lila said.

"But we do know that Susanna was mad at Sophia. We need to talk to her. On *Murder, She Wrote*, Jessica always learns a lot from how a suspect reacts when they are questioned."

"I can guarantee Susanna's reaction is going to be angry," Lila said, turning on her left blinker and pulling into the Primrose parking lot.

"That's what Jasper said too. But Evelyn said she can tell when someone is lying because she's basically a human lie detector. She's going to accuse Susanna of murder and see what happens. I'm going with her in case Susanna tries to run."

"And what will you do if Susanna tries to run?"

"I'll run after her and stop her from escaping." Bea straightened in her seat. "I did ten push-ups in PE last week."

"Which is impressive," Lila said slowly. "But you're not allowed to chase people or accuse them of murder. It's—it's not polite."

"Mama, detectives are not polite."

"You're a fourth grader, not a detective."

Bea's chin jutted out. "I can be both."

Lila drew a breath. *Stay calm, don't argue,* she reminded herself. "You know what? You're right. You can be both. But I'm worried about what might happen if Evelyn accuses Susanna of murder. Evelyn is a little blunt sometimes. Susanna will probably get upset, and we don't want to upset her. Remember that she can ask us to leave the Primrose."

"I forgot about that," Bea conceded with a frown.

"I could try to convince Susanna to talk about Sophia. We might learn something just by doing that," Lila said. "What do you think?"

Bea considered this idea. "I guess we could try that first before the accusation."

"Good plan," Lila said quickly, relieved Bea had agreed.

Lila parked the car, and they walked through the parking lot toward the front doors. She had stopped Bea from approaching Susanna for now, but Lila had to come up with a plan for talking to Susanna soon. Otherwise, Evelyn and Bea might do it without her, which risked angering Susanna and jeopardizing their safety.

She couldn't lose sight of the fact that someone had murdered a girl and that someone was still out there.

They pushed open the front door and halted immediately at the scene in front of them. Evelyn was standing in the lobby, screaming at Florence. Florence screamed back. Several other residents were watching the scene with interest. The Willoughby sisters and Brock had made themselves comfortable on the taupe velvet couches with glasses of wine. Edwin was hiding behind a column off to the right. Emily was shaking her head and looking disgusted.

"You're the one who cheated," Evelyn yelled. She was holding out a finger, wagging it in Florence's face.

Florence stepped closer and frowned at Evelyn. Her normally neat gray bob was mussed in the back. "You're the one who threw a gin and tonic at the waitress and got us permanently banned from the card room at the club."

"That was an accident, and you know it," Evelyn shouted.

"It didn't look like an accident," Florence said. "It also wasn't an accident when you told Mary Dixon that my dress to the Bal du Bois was too tight."

"That was stating facts. You should be happy I refrained from mentioning that you shouldn't wear a strapless dress over sixty. You were seventy-four at the time."

"I was seventy-three," Florence snapped.

Bea was staring back and forth at the argument like it was a Ping-Pong match. Jasper was wringing his hands, slowly backing away.

"We should go. This is private," Lila said, attempting to shuffle Bea to the outer wall and around the two angry figures.

Bea stayed put, digging in her heels. "It's not private if they're yelling in front of everyone. What if Evelyn needs backup?"

Lila didn't even want to think about what kind of *backup* Bea planned to provide.

Susanna stepped into the middle of the argument. "Ladies, let's take this into my office, shall we? We don't want to cause a scene."

"Evelyn loves causing a scene even if it is unsavory," Florence said. "It's because she's from Maryland."

Evelyn's mouth gaped. "I moved to Richmond when I was two years old."

"Exactly. A native Richmonder would never act this way," Florence said smugly.

"She's right about that," Iris piped up from the couch, which seemed to make things worse.

Evelyn slammed her walker onto the marble floor close to Florence's prim, bow-toed Ferragamo flats. They were the same shoes Patricia always wore. Lila winced, imagining how it would feel if Evelyn slammed her walker directly onto Florence's toes. Susanna must have envisioned the same problem because she moved in front of Evelyn, subtly putting space between her and Florence's feet.

"Susanna, this is none of your concern." Evelyn huffed out her breath.

"Let them fight it out," Brock said loudly before finishing off his wine.

"I have some tea in my office," Susanna tried again.

"Florence only drinks her morning tea with bourbon," Evelyn said.

"There's nothing wrong with a morning bourbon," June insisted. Iris nodded in agreement.

Edwin leaned around the column. "My granddaughter's therapist said you shouldn't use alcohol as a coping mechanism."

"You know I would never take a sip of alcohol before noon," Florence screeched.

"I've seen you," Evelyn said, looking around to make sure everyone was paying attention. "You shouldn't lie."

Florence shoved her hands onto her hips. "I'm filing a complaint with the board. This is harassment."

"Come now, we don't need to file a complaint," Susanna cajoled. "Let's sit down and talk about this calmly."

Susanna's face had grown increasingly red and splotchy as Evelyn and Florence proceeded to snap at each other. She obviously had no idea how to make this stop. The two women needed a mutual distraction. Lila suddenly had an idea.

"Evelyn," Lila said, walking forward into the fray. "I'm sorry to interrupt."

"You should be," Evelyn snapped.

"But the thing is I found a vintage Pucci caftan upstairs among Gloria's things. Can you believe it?" Lila asked.

Evelyn and Florence both turned to stare at her. The room was silent as if the crowd was collectively holding their breath in the marble-floored lobby.

"I was thinking about selling it on one of those resale sites but I have no idea how much to list it for. Do you think one hundred dollars is a good price?" Lila asked.

"One hundred dollars? That's ridiculous," Evelyn said in outrage.

"She's right. Vintage Pucci is a treasure," Florence agreed. "You could easily fetch over one thousand dollars depending on the condition."

"And the colors," Evelyn said.

"That goes without saying. If it has the turquoise and pinks, I'd imagine it would go for higher," Florence said.

"She's right," Evelyn said.

Lila put her hands to her cheeks. "Oh gosh. I'm glad I ran into you two. Evelyn, do you think I could bring the dress over for you to look at?"

Evelyn dipped her chin. "That would be fine." She eyed Florence. "I have to go back to my apartment anyway. I'm expecting a call from my decorator."

Florence smoothed her gray bob. "And I'm late for my water aerobics class."

Without saying goodbye, Evelyn headed toward the elevator, and Florence turned and walked out the front door. The rest of the crowd dispersed. Lila sent Bea to accompany Evelyn upstairs. She could hear Bea asking if Evelyn knew how to throw a punch. Evelyn responded loudly that *of course she did.*

Susanna stepped up to Lila. "I thought those two were about to have a physical altercation. Thank you for your help."

"It was nothing," Lila said.

Susanna made a move back toward her office. The lobby was empty. This was the opportunity Lila had counted on when she broke up the fight. She could talk to Susanna now before Evelyn and Bea had the chance to do so.

"Wait, Susanna, do you have a minute?" Lila asked.

Susanna hesitated, clearly wanting to be by herself but also knowing she owed Lila for stopping the fight. "Sure, come with me."

Lila took a deep breath and followed behind.

Chapter Twenty

Susanna led Lila into her office. The room was small with windows looking out onto Grove Avenue. There was a dark wood desk and an upholstered armchair behind it. Two cream damask club chairs were positioned in front of the desk. The desk itself was spotless with only a small Tiffany lamp and a laptop.

Susanna gestured to one of the chairs. "Please sit."

Lila sank into one of the seats. It was hard as a rock and the back was too low, digging into her spine. She wondered if Susanna had bought uncomfortable chairs on purpose.

"What can I help you with?" Susanna asked in a brisk no-nonsense tone, opening her laptop.

Lila had to be careful here. She needed Susanna to deny any involvement in Sophia's murder so she could honestly tell Bea and Evelyn that Susanna wasn't a good suspect, all while not completely offending her.

"I wondered . . ." Lila began, swallowing, trying to come up with the right approach.

"Yes," Susanna said impatiently.

"Well, the thing is, I had a question," Lila said. *If only she could think of it.*

Susanna raised her brows. "I really am in the middle of something."

Susanna stared down at her laptop, typing something into it. Lila's shoulders tensed, rising an imperceptible half inch.

"There are some rumors going around the building after the announcement of Mr. Kent's trust," Lila finally said.

"Rumors are fairly common here. I don't pay them much attention," Susanna said, continuing to stare at her laptop, making it clear Lila wasn't worth her time.

Suddenly Lila was back in her old house on the phone with her manager, Troy. She'd called to let him know Bea was sick again—a cough this time—and she had to pick her up from school, which meant leaving her shift early. It had happened the week before too when Bea was running a fever, and two weeks before that when Bea had the stomach bug. Troy had been distracted on the phone, calling out directions to coworkers while she was talking. She'd finally managed to explain the predicament: *I'm sorry, I have to log off early, Bea is sick, it won't happen again, I swear.* Her stomach had tied itself up into tighter, more intricate knots with every syllable. Troy had gone silent. *This isn't going to work out,* he'd finally said. *I have to let you go.* He'd hung up as she was giving him more excuses and begging for her job. It was humiliating—the way he'd fired her so easily. He didn't care that she needed to pay her bills and make a living and care for her sick child all at the same time. He'd dismissed her as if she didn't matter in the least. And here was Susanna, doing the same thing.

Annoyance spread like a rash on Lila's body. Susanna could at least look at Lila while she was talking and pretend to listen. She was entitled to some basic respect.

Lila drew herself up, her words clipped. "Maybe you *should* pay attention this time because the rumors are about you."

Susanna looked up then, a crease between her brows. "What rumors?"

"People are talking because of the reward, and they're saying that you and Sophia fought before she died. There are questions as to whether you were . . . violent toward her in the days leading up to her death."

"Are you joking?" Susanna asked. She leaned forward, her posture menacing.

Lila gripped the arms of her chair tightly, forcing herself to remain still. She was not going to back down now.

"No, I'm not joking. People are wondering if, perhaps—" Lila stopped. There was no easy way to accuse someone of murder. Best to just come out with it. As Bea had said, *detectives are not polite*. "If perhaps you had something to do with Sophia's death."

"Excuse me?" Susanna said in an astonished voice. Her face drained of color.

"The rumor is you were mad about Sophia's relationship with Jeremy," Lila said. "I know you got into a physical fight with her before she died."

Susanna smoothed the wrinkle in between her eyebrows with her index finger. She closed her eyes for a long moment. When she opened them again, there were tears. "You have no idea what you're talking about. I would never have hurt Sophia. She was my best friend."

"But you were fighting with her before she died," Lila said.

"Not that it's any of your business but yes, we did argue. I was upset with her at the time, but we would have made up eventually. Instead, that fight was the last conversation we had. If you must know, it absolutely screwed me up for years. Maybe you can share that with the rumor mill," Susanna said bitterly. "We had tickets to a concert on the night she died, and I refused to go. If we hadn't fought, I might have been with her during the break-in."

Susanna looked utterly haunted by this. She was blinking rapidly as if trying not to cry. Lila was having a hard time believing Susanna had done anything to hurt Sophia. She had obviously loved her.

"I'm sorry," Lila said softly.

Susanna cleared her throat, regaining her composure. "Why are you even coming to me with these rumors? We're not friends, and I haven't been that nice to you."

"No, you haven't." Lila hesitated. She could come up with any number of reasonable explanations for approaching Susanna, but considering her pained reaction to Lila's accusation, Lila wondered if honesty wasn't the best answer. Maybe Susanna would be willing to talk to her if she knew Lila was only trying to help. "I'm researching Sophia's death with Jasper and Evelyn. Bea is obsessed with the crime, and I've gotten caught up in it too. I know it sounds crazy, but it's not fair what happened to your friend, and it doesn't sit right with me that her murder was never solved."

As soon as she said it, Lila realized how truthful her statement was. She kept telling herself the investigation was all for Bea and it *was* one of the only things making Bea happy, but it was more than that. Someone should pay for taking the life of a young girl. Every new clue or revelation she uncovered about Sophia made her feel as though she was accomplishing something worthwhile even when the rest of her life was a disaster.

Susanna tilted her head, studying Lila. "I don't think you have any chance of solving Sophia's murder."

"I don't disagree with you."

"But I suppose there is a chance Conrad's reward could lead to some new clues. No one else is looking into them, and Jasper was a detective."

"Are you saying you'll talk to me about Sophia?" Lila asked, holding her breath.

"I didn't kill her," Susanna said.

"Then tell me what you were arguing about before she died."

Susanna knocked her fist on the desk, remaining silent. Finally, she sighed. "This was such a long time ago. I doubt it will help. But back in high school, Sophia and I were close friends with Jeremy Buckingham. He's a year older, but we hung out all the time. He grew up across the street from me and lives in Boulder now. Right before Sophia's death, she found out a big secret involving him. She promised not to tell anyone and then she broke her promise. It changed his whole life. I was really angry with her back then."

"So it wasn't a love triangle," Lila said.

"The only love was on my end. I had a crush on Jeremy back in high school. It didn't help that my parents were dying for us to get together. Unfortunately, he had no interest in me like that. I was fairly awkward. My parents actually offered me a nose job at one point because 'it might help with boys.'" Susanna's lip curled in obvious disgust.

Lila immediately understood. She remembered overhearing Mama on the phone to a friend once, saying, *Well, it's sad. She's not that attractive, so I don't think she'll ever have that many options.* The following year, Lila had grown breasts and shed the last of her baby fat. Ryan had started hanging around. Mama had gotten a whole lot nicer to Lila, hugging her in the kitchen for no reason, asking her questions about her day, and buying her new clothes they could barely afford so Lila could eat with Ryan's parents at the club. Lila had basked in Mama's attention, but she could see now that it was terrible for Mama's approval to hinge on Lila's ability to land a boyfriend.

"It sounds like Sophia wasn't the best friend to you or Jeremy," Lila said, hoping to encourage Susanna to share more details about the fight or the secret.

"That's not true. She was a great friend. She always included me in plans even though I was not the most popular in high school. I didn't have a lot of friends. My sophomore year, these senior girls started a rumor that I was giving blow jobs to guys in the locker room, which was a complete lie. I hadn't even kissed anyone yet. It was embarrassing, as you can imagine." She shrugged at Lila's pained expression. "Yeah, teenagers are mean. When it first happened, Sophia was furious. She yelled at everyone who brought it up. She used to say, 'Don't worry, I'll handle it.' The rumors eventually died down, mostly because Sophia made them. People listened to her."

Lila leaned forward, thinking of Emily's unflattering portrait of Sophia. "Did Sophia have any enemies?"

Susanna considered this. "I can't think of any, but I'm sure there were people who didn't like her. Sophia was hilarious and fun, but she was also stubborn and only wanted to do things her way. It drove her parents crazy. Helene insisted Sophia sign up for AP Spanish during her junior year. Her college counselor had said she needed an AP language for college applications, but Sophia dropped the class without telling her parents and took intro theater instead. She hid the class change from her parents for two whole weeks, but Helene eventually found out and made her switch back into the Spanish class. Sophia was so mad."

Lila couldn't help thinking about Bea, who was already headstrong at ten, going places without telling Lila and harboring her own secrets. What would she be like at sixteen? Would she try to ignore Lila's good advice, same as Sophia had done to Helene? Probably, yes. Lila couldn't let Bea make a mistake that might affect her future, but she also couldn't control everything her daughter did. It was a nearly impossible line to walk.

Lila returned her focus to Susanna. "I've heard a few disturbing things about Sophia's behavior before her death."

"Like?" Susanna sounded wary.

"Like she was using cocaine and being blackmailed."

Susanna rubbed her eyes, slumping down. "I didn't know about any of that. Sophia *was* wasted at every party that fall. I just assumed she was drinking too much. I was naive at the time, and she was secretive those last few months."

"Secretive how?"

"She would disappear for entire days, and then she started skipping field hockey practice and tutoring. When I asked where she'd gone, she wouldn't tell me. There were also these phone calls on her new cell phone. She'd answer with 'I can't talk,' and then refuse to say who had called her. I was frustrated and felt left out. I'm sure that's part of why I got so mad when she told Jeremy's parents."

Lila couldn't help her curiosity. "Can you tell me what the big secret was about Jeremy?"

Susanna winced. "It happened a long time ago but it's still a sensitive issue."

"What if it connects to Sophia's murder?" Lila wheedled. "You never know."

Susanna exhaled, looking upward. "Here's all I can tell you. Jeremy was involved with an older woman. Sophia caught them together and was worried. He swore he'd break it off and begged her not to tell anyone, but she told his parents anyway. They actually pulled him out of Stratford Academy only two days before Sophia died and sent him to boarding school to finish out his senior year. I was heartbroken when he left, which was why I blew up at Sophia. But she made the right decision."

"Was he underage?" Lila asked.

"He was eighteen, but the relationship was not appropriate *at all*," Susanna emphasized.

There was something familiar about the story, but Lila couldn't pinpoint what. Why would Jeremy's parents have pulled him out of Stratford, and why was Susanna so adamant about the inappropriate nature of the relationship? Was it possible the woman was the mother of one of their friends or a coach or a teacher? Something clicked inside her brain—*only two days before Sophia died.* Jeremy left Stratford at the exact same time Emily Canterbury left her job... at Stratford.

"Was Jeremy having an affair with Emily Canterbury?" Lila blurted out.

Susanna gasped. "How could you possibly know that?"

Lila's heart raced as the puzzle pieces of the story snapped together. "I talked with Emily the other day. She did not like Sophia and mentioned leaving her position at Stratford Academy only two days before Sophia's death, which is when you said Jeremy left too."

"It's true, and it was horrible. Jeremy's parents were furious with everyone. They told Emily's husband and Headmistress Quillan what was going on. Jeremy was devastated because he thought he was in love with Emily even though she was a married woman in her forties and one of his teachers. His parents agreed not to sue the school or make the affair public as long as Emily left Stratford and agreed to never teach again."

Lila's mind circled through this information. She'd suspected Emily hated Sophia for personal reasons. Now she knew why, and the timing was troubling to say the least.

"Sophia exposed the relationship, which got Emily fired, permanently banned from teaching, and ended her marriage. This was days before Sophia died, and then Emily just so happens to be right next door during her murder," Lila said. "You didn't think that was a weird coincidence?"

"What do you mean? Emily wasn't living here at the time."

"She was. She had moved in with her mother."

"I had no idea," Susanna said slowly. "I wasn't around for most of the investigation. My parents checked me into a treatment center for some health issues. I never said anything to the police about Emily and, as far as I know, no one else knew about the relationship except for the school and her husband, and they certainly didn't want anyone to hear about it."

Silence sank between the two women, drawing them into a contemplative pit. Lila was thinking hard, trying to make sense of it all. A new possibility and a new suspect emerged from Susanna's confession. Had Emily Canterbury killed Sophia in revenge for ruining her life?

Chapter Twenty-One

Jasper suggested telling Conrad's lawyer what they'd learned about Emily. Evelyn offered to confront Emily directly on her own, insisting she could coerce her into a confession if they were alone. Bea wanted to break into Emily's apartment to search for clues. Finally, they decided Lila would deliver a batch of blueberry muffins as an apology for breaking her frame, along with a note asking her to *discuss an urgent personal matter of the utmost importance.* They reasoned the muffins would soften her up and the note would pique her curiosity, ensuring she called. Lila would then arrange to meet Emily, bringing Jasper and Evelyn along to question her.

Lila dropped off the muffins and note outside Emily's door the following morning and spent the next few hours cleaning out Gloria's kitchen cabinets, which included a drawer stuffed with sock puppets and a valuable first-edition Sherlock Holmes book. She finally got a text from Emily insisting she had a busy afternoon and could only meet in the next fifteen minutes. Lila knew Jasper wouldn't like her seeing Emily alone, but Emily was tiny and over sixty, and it was broad daylight. There wasn't much she could do to hurt Lila.

But when Lila arrived upstairs at Emily's apartment, her knocks went unanswered. She texted Emily again—*I'm at your door.* Emily didn't text back. Maybe she had changed her mind about the meeting. Lila decided she would come up to the apartment later with Jasper and Evelyn to catch her by surprise.

Lila stopped at the grocery store and dropped off some items at Goodwill before picking up Bea from kickball practice. As they turned into the parking lot of the Primrose, it was immediately obvious something was wrong. Five police cars crowded the circular driveway, and an ambulance with blinking red and blue lights stalled beside them.

"Mama, what's happening?" Bea asked.

"I don't know yet," Lila said, but a sense of foreboding gathered inside her.

A police officer guarded the front doors. He wore aviator sunglasses and held a clipboard in front of him. He eyed Lila suspiciously. Her own worried face reflected from the mirrored surface of his glasses.

Lila gave him a tentative smile. "Can you tell me what's going on here?"

The police officer shook his head. "Afraid not. No one is allowed inside at this time."

Bea reached for Lila's hand, squeezing it tight. Her hand was clammy. Lila gave her a reassuring nod, and her voice was nononsense when she spoke again. "We live here."

The officer lifted the clipboard. "Apartment number and name."

"Apartment 2B, Lila and Bea Shaw," Lila said.

The officer scanned the clipboard and stepped aside. "You can wait in the lobby."

The scene inside was jarring and chaotic. It appeared that all the Primrose residents were crowded into the lobby and spilling over into the Azalea Room. There were police officers blocking the hallways and entry points, refusing to let anyone pass.

Evelyn waved at Lila from the center of a small crowd and pushed her walker forward. "I don't know why the police are holding us hostage in our own building, but they can't keep me from my apartment. Do they know who I am?"

Lila eyed Evelyn, knowing her rising temper tantrum wasn't going to get her far in this mess. She gestured to a bench along the wall of the Azalea Room where Jasper was already seated. "Why don't you sit over there? I'll talk to Zoe and see if she knows anything."

"I can talk to Zoe too. I'm not an invalid," Evelyn snapped.

"I know that. But it's crowded in here, and the bench is a good place to wait this out." Lila lowered her voice. "Besides I see Florence making her way over there. If you get there first, she won't have a place to sit."

Of course, that did it. Evelyn took off toward the bench at a fast clip, shoving her walker ahead of her and narrowly beating Florence to the seat. Lila looked around and spotted Iris and June at the concierge desk with Zoe.

Lila walked up to them, keeping her voice low and Bea's hand still firmly in hers. "Do y'all know what's going on?"

Zoe shook her head. "No idea. The police showed up about thirty minutes ago."

"What about Susanna?" Lila asked. "Isn't she in charge?"

Zoe nodded. "She's involved. As soon as the first officers arrived, she led them upstairs." Her voice halted, cracking on the last syllable. "She looked upset."

"Do you think someone is hurt, or..." Lila's voice trailed off. She couldn't say what she really wanted in front of Bea. She wanted to ask if someone was dead.

Zoe's brown eyes were watery. "Whatever it is, it's not good. They don't send this many police officers for nothing."

"I think we better get out the extra wine from last week," June said. "It's the only way to calm people down."

"People seem fairly calm," Zoe said.

"Yes, but internally, we're all panicking," June said. "You may not know this, Zoe, as you're a tiny bit younger than us, but internal panic for older individuals can cause serious injury. You don't want another serious injury here, do you?"

Zoe considered this faulty logic and shrugged. "I could actually use some wine too. I'll go get it from the storage closet."

"Do bring white and red," Iris urged. "The people really need both."

"To help with the panicking," June added.

Bea had disengaged her hand and moved a little apart from the group. She was hugging her arms to her chest and staring around, a blankness in her eyes. There was something about her forlorn expression, about the Braves shirt dangling around her knees, about the knot in the back of her hair; it all made her look small and vulnerable.

Lila crouched down next to her. "Are you all right? There's nothing to be afraid of."

Bea shivered. "The police officers remind me of when they came into our house after Daddy left. They went through all our stuff, even my room, and they made a huge mess. I hated that. You were crying."

Lila closed her eyes for a moment, thinking back to that day. She was not prepared for the police to knock on the door with a warrant. She hadn't expected that strangers would rifle through her underwear where she kept her old vibrator or toss aside Bea's artwork as they searched her desk. Lila had felt like a criminal, and Bea was right. She *had* cried and later felt guilty that her tears made the situation worse for Bea. But she saw her behavior in another light now. Her crying was normal. It was okay for Bea to see normal emotion, and Lila could be afraid and still comfort her daughter at the same time.

Lila searched her daughter's eyes. "Whatever is going on here has nothing to do with us. You don't need to worry."

"I know, Mama. But it makes me feel . . ." Bea shook out her hands and wiggled her legs, expressing what her words couldn't. She was nervous and scared.

"It makes me feel that way too," Lila said honestly.

Bea's shoulders relaxed, and her body stilled. Lila sat back on her heels, feeling proud of herself. For once, she'd said the right thing—the *make it all a little bit better* thing—to Bea. Was there anything more important than comforting your own child?

Gazing around the Azalea Room, Lila noticed Jasper had pulled out a Tupperware container. "I see Jasper has brownies." She pointed toward a skirted table along the wall near the bench, draped in blue dotted fabric. "And if things get dangerous, you can always hide under that table. No one would find you there. It's safe."

"What about you?" Bea asked.

"I'll obviously come join you," Lila said.

"I don't know if underneath is big enough for both of us," Bea said, eyeing Lila's body.

"Maybe no one will notice if my butt is sticking out," Lila said.

Bea started giggling exactly as Lila had hoped and she scampered off to Jasper and Evelyn.

"What's the deal with all the cops?"

The voice came from behind Lila. She whipped around to find Nate Donnelly standing there. His button-down was untucked, giving him a cute, disheveled look. Not that she noticed that he was cute, more that he was chaotic and messy. His hair needed a cut and his tennis shoes were filthy. She tried to catalog more flaws before giving up.

"You're a reporter. Aren't you supposed to know that?" Lila asked.

Nate raised his brows. "I'm not here because of the police. I had an interview on the third floor before they arrived."

"I should go," Lila said.

"There's a chance I was an asshole when we first met," Nate said, surprising her.

"Chance?" Lila asked, an uplift to her voice.

"Fine. I was definitely an asshole. I'm sorry. It's not an excuse but I had gotten into it with my editor right before I saw you. He pushed back on the Sophia Kent story, doesn't think there's anything new to write about. He finally agreed to give me a few weeks to dig around and develop a new angle. If I can't come up with something good, he won't be happy, but that's my problem. It wasn't a reason to steal your table and act like a jerk."

"No, it wasn't," Lila said. She wanted to still hate him, but he sounded sincere. Her hard feelings softened a little.

"Speaking of Sophia, how *is* your investigation going?" Nate asked.

Lila kept her face impassive. "We're making progress."

Nate grinned. "Amateur sleuths always say that."

"Oh really. What about you then? Have you figured out who killed her?"

"I'm not trying to solve her murder. I just want to write an interesting article. I'll tell you one thing, though. I don't think it was a burglary gone wrong," Nate said.

"I don't either," Lila couldn't resist saying.

"Okay, Nancy Drew." Nate studied her. "We finally agree on something. Makes we wonder what else we could agree on."

"I doubt it's much," Lila said, wanting to turn away but also finding herself rooted to the floor.

"I know our tastes in books are different."

"I don't like space porn," Lila hissed, hoping no one heard her.

Nate continued as if she hadn't spoken. "I noticed your order at Rise Up—basic coffee with cream, same as me. I also know you like eavesdropping on conversations." Lila made a noise of protest, but Nate kept going. "Also same as me. And I know you're smart and intuitive. I'd say same as me, but I don't want to brag. Hell, who am I kidding? We both know I think that applies to me too." He smiled then to let her know he was poking fun at himself.

Lila couldn't help herself. She grinned back before reminding her face that she hated this guy. She worked her mouth into a frown. "You have no idea if I'm smart or intuitive."

"Not true. I watched you interview Emily Canterbury. Piece of work, by the way. You picked up on Emily disliking Sophia and got her to open up about it. I was impressed. I'm guessing you do that all the time."

"Do what?"

"Surprise people." He nodded to her, seeming embarrassed for the first time since she'd met him. "They probably underestimate you based on—you know—how you look, and then they find out there's a lot more to you."

"I can't tell if that's a compliment or not," Lila said.

"I meant it as a compliment," Nate said.

Nate simply looked at her then, his eyes catching her own. Heat built below her neck. For one insane second, she imagined what it would feel like to grab his face and pull him toward her into a kiss. Her lips parted and her throat worked before Lila remembered she was in the middle of the Primrose lobby and didn't even like Nate. She took a step back.

"I need to check on my daughter." Lila spun around and took off without waiting for Nate to say anything further. That was the weirdest interaction she'd had with him so far. It was still hostile but also . . . kind of . . . flirty?

Lila weaved through two clusters of Primrose residents, all of whom now held wineglasses, and back over to where Evelyn and Jasper were seated with Bea. The area around the bench was empty except for one man leaning against a nearby wall. Lila recognized him instantly. It was James Forrester, Conrad's lawyer. He wiped his brow and bowed his head, mumbling to himself, obviously upset about something.

"Mr. Forrester, are you all right?" Lila asked.

James looked up, a confused expression on his face. "Do we know each other?"

"I'm Lila Shaw, one of the residents here. I was at the meeting about Mr. Kent's trust."

"Oh, oh yes. I do remember seeing your name on the invitation list."

Evelyn looked over then. "Are you having a heart attack? You look ghastly."

"You look pale," Lila corrected. "Do you need to sit down?"

"Me? No, no, of course not. I'm just—well, I suppose I'm—to be honest, I'm—I'm in *shock*!" James almost shouted the last word.

Lila's heart pounded. He must have known something about what was going on at the Primrose. "Would it help to tell me what's wrong?"

"I don't know if it's professional but, at this point, I don't know if I care. It's not attorney-client privileged. I should have said no when Conrad asked me to do this, but he was a long-time client of the firm, and I felt like I didn't have a choice." He began pacing back and forth, mopping at his face.

James abruptly stopped, breathed, and seemed to come to a decision. "Emily Canterbury called and left a message today. She said she knew who killed Sophia Kent."

Lila froze. There was a sharp intake of air from Evelyn and Bea in unison. Lila put out a hand to stop them from saying anything further, afraid it would quiet James for good.

"Who was it?" Lila asked softly.

James shook his head. "I don't know. I tried to call Emily back multiple times, and she didn't answer. Finally, I couldn't wait any longer, so I drove over here. I knocked at Emily's apartment. No one answered, but the door was cracked, which I thought was strange. I stuck my head in the apartment, intending to call her name, thinking maybe she hadn't heard me. That's when I saw her."

"Saw who?" Bea asked. "We need as many details as possible."

"I saw Emily on the ground. She was lying there, and her eyes were open and staring, and her chest was covered in blood." James opened his eyes wider than ever as if he was seeing Emily all over again. "She was dead. I called nine-one-one and then I called downstairs. Susanna ran up there, and the police came after. I heard them say she'd been shot." He wiped his mouth, looking as if he might vomit.

There was only one explanation for Emily's death. Someone had shot her to keep her from telling the truth about Sophia's death. That meant Sophia's murderer had killed again. There was a whooshing in Lila's ears, and the edges of her vision darkened. Lila had knocked on Emily's door only hours before. What if the killer was inside the apartment while she waited, inches away? Suddenly, she wondered just what in the hell she had gotten herself and her daughter into.

Chapter Twenty-Two

Susanna strode into the hallway between the foyer and the Azalea Room, looking harried. Her face had splotchy red marbling to it and her dark bob was ruffled around the edges. The crowd of residents rushed toward her. A clamor of voices rose, shouting out questions about when they could return to their apartments and what happened and shouldn't Zoe open more wine?

Holding out her hands to silence them, Susanna spoke. "The police have opened up the building. You can all return to your apartments now. I'm sorry for the delay."

"But is it safe?" June asked. "Why are the police here?"

Brock pushed his way to the front of the crowd. "We have a right to know what's going on in our own home."

"The police will make an announcement soon," Susanna said.

"We deserve to know now." Florence stepped forward then.

Evelyn still sat on the bench with Bea, looking very smug. She leaned over to Lila. "Poor Florence is the last to know everything."

Susanna looked helplessly at the officers behind her in the hallway. One of them nodded and strode off. The residents of the Primrose continued to grumble, getting louder by the second.

"Please be patient," Susanna said.

"I will not be patient if my life is in danger," Mary Dixon said, waving her cane in the air. "I can't defend myself in these shoes. I knew I should have worn my platform sneakers today."

"Do you think those young, handsome officers would like a glass of wine?" June asked. "I'm sure they're thirsty after all their hard work."

A man with pockmarked skin and thinning gray hair approached Susanna. His mouth was a narrow line bisecting his face. "Folks, settle down please. I'm Detective Roberts. There is no need for any alarm at this point. We have searched the building and there is no present danger. You can feel safe returning to your apartments."

If Detective Roberts thought that would satisfy this group, he was sorely mistaken. The clamoring only grew louder, and the crowd drew closer.

Florence yelled, "I'm calling the mayor!"

Brock yelled, "I'm calling the governor!"

Detective Roberts finally flung up his hands. "All I can tell you is that someone died in the building, but we believe it's an isolated incident."

"Has rigor mortis set in?" Bea called out.

"That's not important now," Lila whispered. The last thing she needed was Bea lobbing questions at a cop and drawing his attention to them.

"It is so important," Bea insisted. "They estimate time of death based on how stiff the body is."

"My knees are already stiff. Would that affect my rigor mortis?" Edwin asked Bea.

"No, because when you die, your entire body gets stiff, even your eyelids," Bea said.

"My knees are excellent," Evelyn announced to no one in particular.

"We're in the process of notifying family members about the death." Detective Roberts looked darkly at the crowd, frowning especially hard at Bea. "This is an active investigation."

Now all went quiet, absorbing the announcement. The confirmation of an investigation and a death had dampened their frustration. They slowly dispersed, talking amongst themselves, trying to determine who had died. Lila reached out a hand and gripped Bea's shoulder, wanting to get her back upstairs to the safety of Gloria's apartment. But before she could usher her daughter away, one of the police officers approached her.

"Lila Shaw?"

"Yes," Lila said.

"Detective Roberts would like to speak with you immediately," the officer said.

Lila stiffened. "Am I in trouble?"

"Not for me to say," the officer said, his face impassive and unfriendly.

Evelyn rose unsteadily to her feet. "What's this all about? She doesn't have to go anywhere with you and—"

"We'll take Bea upstairs," Jasper said, cutting off Evelyn's tirade. He leaned into Lila and whispered, "Don't say *anything*," before ushering Evelyn and Bea down the hallway.

Lila followed the officer toward Susanna's office. A fog of apprehension seeped into her vision, blurring the familiar walls of the Primrose. Her mind flashed back to all those months ago when the FBI had called her into Ryan's home office. Agent Pike had sat behind the heavy wood desk, flipping through a stack of papers. He had gestured for her to sit as if this was his house and not hers, and the rapid-fire questions began—*Where was Ryan? Who had access to their accounts? Where was the money? Where were the payments?* Over and over, one after another, until she was hoarse from answering, *I don't know, I swear I don't know.* Lila's gaze sharpened, back in the present. No, *no*. She would not allow herself to panic this time. She had done nothing wrong.

Detective Roberts was waiting in Susanna's office behind her desk. He looked too big for the room with his massive shoulders. He didn't bother to stand when Lila approached, only nodded to the officer who closed the door.

"What's going on here?" Lila asked instantly.

Detective Roberts gestured to one of the club chairs. "I have a few questions for you."

"About what?" Lila asked, grateful for the chair as her legs had gone quivery with the serious expression on the detective's face. She was maybe starting to panic.

"Were you inside Emily Canterbury's apartment today?"

Lila's pulse quickened. "No. I left a note and some muffins outside her door earlier this morning, and I stopped by again this afternoon, but she didn't answer the door."

"What time was this?" Detective Roberts asked.

"Around one o'clock."

Detective Roberts sealed his meaty hands flat to the desk. His wedding finger was bare but there was a faint white line where a ring had once rested. Lila wondered if he was recently separated or divorced. She'd sold her wedding and engagement rings to pay off credit card bills.

"It's funny you aren't asking about Ms. Canterbury's well-being," Detective Roberts said.

"That's because I spoke with James Forrester a few minutes ago and heard what happened." Lila swallowed.

"Then you know Ms. Canterbury was shot and murdered."

"I didn't know for sure. That's terrible." Hearing the word—*murdered*—sent a fresh shock through Lila's body.

"Your note was found in Ms. Canterbury's pocket; the note in which *you* requested an urgent meeting. We also have Ms.

Canterbury's cell phone, which shows she asked you to come to her apartment, and you texted back that you were outside her door."

"I already told you she never answered the door."

"So you say." Detective Roberts crossed his arms.

The walls closed in on Lila. Her chest tightened. "Are you . . . are you implying I had something to do with her death?" Her voice came out high and shaky.

Detective Roberts raised his eyebrows as if asking her to answer her own question.

Lila shook her head. "I didn't shoot anyone. I would never hurt Emily. I haven't seen her in days."

"I understand you two had some problems. She wanted you removed from the building. You and your daughter. She called Susanna to complain yesterday."

"I had no idea about that." Lila privately fumed that Emily had tried to get her kicked out of the building when she'd done nothing wrong except break a picture frame. She swallowed hard as the realization hit her that she was only hearing about this after Emily had died. It was all so horrible.

"Are you saying you didn't know Ms. Canterbury had asked Susanna to revoke your residence status because you had never gone through the formal approval process?"

"Yes, that's exactly what I'm saying," Lila said.

"What about the note you left for Ms. Canterbury? Why would you write that you needed to meet to discuss an 'urgent personal matter of the utmost importance'? I assume this was about your living situation here at the Primrose and Ms. Canterbury's intention to have you removed?"

"I didn't know she wanted me removed. I planned to talk to Emily about Sophia Kent. It had nothing to do with me." Lila's voice shook. Did she sound like she was lying?

"Strange that your note refers to a 'personal matter' but now you're claiming you wanted to talk to Ms. Canterbury about a girl who died over twenty years ago? I'm confused as to how a decades-old murder was an urgent, personal matter for you." Detective Roberts looked skeptical.

"It was personal to her," Lila said. Her breathing quickened and a weight settled onto her chest. She couldn't draw a deep enough breath. Was she going to suffocate right here in this room before Detective Roberts?

"What did you say to Ms. Canterbury when you met with her this afternoon?"

"I didn't meet with her. I swear." The words were strangled.

Detective Roberts slammed a fist on the desk, startling her. "Enough! It's time to start telling me the truth."

The door behind her opened suddenly. Jasper appeared at her side. He crouched down beside her. "Lila."

Lila gripped his forearm, staring into his kind face. Blood rushed back through her veins, the weight on her chest lifted. She breathed.

Jasper nodded at Detective Roberts. "Craig."

"Jasper," Detective Roberts sneered. "Why are you interrupting my interview?"

"Lila's daughter needs her." Jasper helped Lila to her feet.

"The daughter is going to have to wait," Detective Roberts said, rising also and leaning forward until he hovered menacingly over the desk.

"Are you charging her?" Jasper asked.

Detective Roberts stared at him for a long moment before responding. "Not at this time."

"Then we're leaving." Jasper gripped Lila's hand in a tight embrace and maneuvered her toward the door.

"Ms. Shaw?" Detective Roberts called after her.

Lila turned back.

"Don't leave Richmond. We're going to speak again soon," Detective Roberts said.

Jasper hurried Lila out into the hall, past the two police officers stationed near the Azalea Room, and around Mary Dixon and Florence, who were pretending to rest on a bench but mostly waiting to see what happened next.

"Is Bea all right?" Lila asked as they rushed down the hall toward the elevator.

"She's fine. I needed an excuse to get you out of that room."

Lila stopped, her body still trembling with adrenaline. "Jasper, am I in trouble?"

Jasper's face was grave. "You're currently a suspect in Emily Canterbury's murder."

Chapter Twenty-Three

Evelyn and Bea were waiting in Evelyn's apartment. Evelyn led them into a living room with a gilt and glass coffee table, extravagant silk window treatments, and floral-patterned couches. The rug underneath was a sumptuous Turkish design in salmon pinks and sky blues.

Bea rushed to Lila, stopping short at her feet. "Do they think you murdered that lady?"

"Of course not." Lila said this with a mostly straight face. She could feel a muscle twitching by her eye.

"Why did the police stop you then?" Bea's eyes narrowed.

Lila would bet the *TODAY* parenting guides didn't provide tips for talking to your child about your false murder accusations. Her instinct was to keep lying, to avoid panicking her daughter, but Bea knew something was wrong and deserved some explanation. "The police think I met with Ms. Canterbury before she died, and they asked me some questions. I didn't meet with her, though, and I told them that."

"They might not believe you if someone framed you for murdering her. It happens all the time in *Murder, She Wrote*."

"No one is framing me. That's only on TV shows. I didn't do anything wrong, and the police will come to that conclusion soon if they haven't already," Lila said, hoping this was true.

Bea examined Lila before nodding to herself, seemingly

reassured. "Good because next week is my first kickball game, and I know you wouldn't want to miss that."

Lila didn't know whether to laugh or cry that Bea was thinking about her kickball game when someone had just been murdered in their building.

Lila stooped down to Bea's level, needing her to take these next words seriously. "But, honey, we're done with the investigation into Sophia Kent. It's not appropriate with everything going on in the building right now."

A small line formed between Bea's eyebrows. "But we know more than anyone about Sophia."

"Maybe so, but no more investigating," Lila said firmly.

Bea wanted to keep arguing. Lila could tell by the way she opened and closed her mouth, but she merely kicked at the floor and stayed quiet, which was astonishing in and of itself. Lila turned on an episode of *Murder, She Wrote* and sat Bea in front of Evelyn's television.

Jasper, Evelyn, and Lila reconvened on Evelyn's small patio overlooking the front of the Primrose. The ambulance was still idling outside, and a stretcher now appeared with a black bag on top of it. Emily's body.

"I can't believe this is happening. It's so exciting," Evelyn said. She stopped when she saw Lila's face. "Well, not for you obviously. But they can't really think you would kill Emily. She probably had lots of enemies. I never liked her."

Jasper paced the small balcony. "I spoke with one of my friends at the department. Emily was shot twice in the chest. She never stood a chance of surviving."

"Why didn't anyone hear the shots?" Lila asked.

"The killer must have used a silencer," Jasper said.

Lila sank into one of the patio chairs, worried she might get sick. Knowing the method of murder somehow made the entire thing more real. "Do they really believe I shot someone? I don't have a gun. This is a nightmare. What am I going to do?"

Jasper stopped pacing. "Their motive is weak. Despite Emily's complaints about you, Susanna already told the police there were no plans to remove you from the building, which means there was no reason for you to harm Emily. They also don't have any physical evidence tying you to the crime scene. If they did, they would have arrested you. That's the good news."

Lila closed her eyes. "What's the bad news?"

Jasper hesitated. Beats of silence passed.

"Oh, Jasper, just come out with it," Evelyn snapped.

"All right, all right. The bad news is Craig Roberts, the lead detective. He's lazy, and he tends to home in on a suspect without considering other options," Jasper said.

"And he's homed in on me?" Lila asked.

"Based on Emily's movements and when James found the body, they believe she was killed between twelve thirty and two o'clock today. That text you sent Emily puts you at the scene at the time of the murder," Jasper said.

"I don't have an alibi," Lila said faintly.

Jasper was quiet, not denying the obvious problem.

"What about the fact that Emily was murdered right before she revealed Sophia Kent's killer? She intended to tell James Forrester *today*. The two cases are clearly connected. Sophia's murderer killed Emily to keep her from talking," Evelyn said.

"I agree it's a good theory, but that doesn't mean Craig Roberts will look into it. It was embarrassing enough when the department couldn't solve Sophia Kent's murder the first time. I doubt they will take the chance of reopening the case a second time and failing again. They're going to avoid linking the two cases if they can," Jasper said.

"We have to find the murderer ourselves then," Evelyn said matter-of-factly, as if that impossible task would fix everything.

Lila was already shaking her head. "No way. I don't want anything more to do with this. I can't have Bea anywhere near this kind of danger."

"I'm sorry, dear, but you don't have the luxury of ignoring this. You're the primary suspect. We need to clear your name." Evelyn sighed. "I swear sometimes it's hard for me to always be the brave one."

"We are not detectives," Lila reminded her. She glanced at Jasper. "Okay, I know you were a detective, but that doesn't mean any of us have the resources to solve a murder. We should let the police do their job, right?" She looked at Jasper, hoping he would back her up. After all, he was the experienced one here.

Jasper avoided Lila's eyes. "We keep Bea out of it, but otherwise I agree with Evelyn. If we can find enough evidence to point to a legitimate suspect in Sophia's murder who could have also killed Emily, the police would have to take the connection between the two cases seriously. I've already asked Susanna to dig up the old building records to see if anyone was delinquent on their accounts at the time of the burglaries and needed the money. It could provide a lead."

Lila sank down in her seat, wishing she could sink straight into the core of the earth and burn into nothing. How had she managed to get herself into even more trouble? If she thought a fraud accusation was bad, a murder accusation was a whole lot worse, especially when she was expected to solve the crime herself with the help of two geriatric investigators.

"Someone killed Emily *today*. This isn't a cold case anymore. The investigation could get dangerous," Lila said.

"I'm a bit of a daredevil," Evelyn said, nudging her walker out of the way. "Besides, I can't leave you to your own devices. Without me, you're bound to get yourself arrested. I'm not particularly fond of you, but I do believe in charity work. If you get thrown in lockup, Bea won't have anyone to look after her. She'll essentially be an orphan since her father is a deadbeat. I've always prided myself on helping orphans."

Jasper lowered himself into a seat. "I'm, uh, enjoying the investigation. I forgot how much I like this sort of work." He glanced away, his cheeks reddening. "And I like you and Bea."

Lila looked from Jasper, still staring at the other side of the balcony, to Evelyn, who was craning her head to get a better look at the stretcher below. It had been one thing for them to band together and investigate Sophia's death when the possibility of actually solving anything and thereby attracting a murderer's attention was nonexistent. Now the stakes couldn't be higher. Lila might end up in jail; she could lose her daughter, the one person she cared about more than any other. Her heart stuttered in her chest. The possibility of losing Bea was terrifying enough, but then there was the risk in investigating a killer who was still at large. She was potentially putting her life in the hands of two people she barely knew. Though the last person she'd trusted with her life—the one she had devoted nineteen years to—she also apparently hadn't known at all. A hard ball formed in her stomach. People were out for themselves. She knew this and yet, did she really have a choice? She needed help, at least until the police eliminated her as a suspect.

Lila exhaled and nodded once. "What do we do first?"

"You'll be pleased to hear I've already gotten started," Evelyn said. "I told everyone in the building that we believe Sophia's death is connected to Emily's murder, and we are investigating the murders and burglaries too. I asked anyone with information to contact us."

"But what if the murderer is someone *in* the building?" Lila asked.

"Then they're probably scared since they know we're coming after them," Evelyn said in satisfaction. "There's nothing like an element of danger to make one feel alive."

*　*　*

ZOE KNOCKED ON Lila's door later that evening.

Lila had dreaded answering, afraid it was the police showing up to arrest her. She'd spent the evening sitting in the living room, watching the local news for any coverage of Emily's murder. Every noise made her startle, and she was almost unbearably cold. All she could think of was Detective Roberts's grim face snarling in her direction, telling her *they would speak again soon*.

Zoe held up a bottle of wine. "I came to check on you. Today was rough. I thought you might need a drink . . . or three."

Lila stared at her, taking in Zoe's casually ripped jeans and gray sweatshirt that slid off one shoulder. She'd gone home after work and changed before coming back to the Primrose. "Are you picking up your paycheck?"

Zoe pulled her brows together, confused by the question. "No."

"You forgot something at the concierge desk?"

"No."

Did that mean Zoe had come back to the Primrose . . . just to check on Lila? She must not know about what had happened earlier. Lila felt obliged to tell her. It wasn't fair for Zoe to unknowingly associate with a potential criminal.

"I was questioned by the police today about Emily's death. I'm a suspect," Lila said. The words sounded hollow as they escaped her lips. She still couldn't believe she was saying them out loud, that they were real.

"I heard. Why do you think I'm here? I know you didn't kill Emily. The whole idea is ridiculous."

"But you barely know me," Lila said.

Zoe laughed. "Lila, please. No one actually thinks you murdered someone except for that police officer. What an asshole, right? I saw him push past Mary Dixon, and I thought she was going to clobber him with her cane. He better watch his back is all I can say. I once saw her trip June when she took the last glass of wine."

"I know you're here because you feel sorry for me, but I'll be fine," Lila said, trying to give Zoe an out.

"I do feel sorry for you since you're accused of something you didn't do. But I'm here because you're my friend, so I showed up to try to take your mind off this bullshit for a while."

Lila stared at Zoe, not speaking and trying to process everything. She knew how this was supposed to work after last year. Even friends distanced themselves from you in a scandal.

Zoe put her hands on her hips. "What's going on? You're acting weird. Can I come in or are you going to keep me out here in the hall forever?"

Lila stepped aside, and Zoe walked into the foyer and immediately pulled Lila into a hug. Her arms were tight and warm. A lump lodged itself in Lila's throat, and she leaned into Zoe. It had been some time since she'd let anyone comfort her. It felt strange and wrong and nice.

"I'm really sorry about today. That must have freaked you out," Zoe said, stepping back.

Lila nodded, not trusting herself to speak without crying. There was something about Zoe's calming presence and the lack of judgment that made her feel a little warmer.

"It's not going to amount to anything. Don't worry," Zoe said.

Lila looked over at Bea, who was lying on the floor in the next room, drawing in her notebook. Her hair hung in her eyes, tangled at the back of her head in its usual knot. Lila resisted the urge to go straight to her, to smooth the knot and pull her into Lila's lap as she did when Bea was young. Lila would do anything to keep her daughter from getting hurt.

Zoe followed her gaze. "Susanna has hired some security guards to patrol the building, and there is twenty-four-hour monitoring of the security cameras in the lobby and front halls. Don't worry. Now can we please open this wine?" Without waiting for a response, Zoe made her way into the kitchen. "You've done so much work. It looks a lot better in here." She reached for the wine opener on the counter, uncorked the bottle, and plucked two glasses out of the newly organized cabinet, pouring a large amount of wine into each one.

"Do you want to talk about the murder or something else?" Zoe asked.

"Something else, please," Lila said.

They moved into the dining room and sat at the table. The windows were uncovered and displayed the now familiar landscape of Grove Avenue with its rows of lit-up restaurants, each storefront unique from its neighbor and equally as charming with shutters and window displays.

"I had a call from the editor of the style section at the *Richmond Journal* today. They interviewed me about the club opening." Zoe clapped her hands together, unable to hide her glee.

"Really? That's amazing. I didn't expect an interview. I emailed the editor yesterday and asked her to include the club opening in their weekend calendar. That feels like a lifetime ago," Lila said.

"They're going to run the story this week in advance of the opening. And our ticket sales are way up after you got some of those local Instagram influencers to start promoting the opening and tagging our account. We've got a ton of new followers."

Lila couldn't help smiling. Here was an area of her life where she was managing to do something positive for someone who deserved it. Things did work out for the best sometimes.

"Oh, and before I forget, Susanna asked me to give these to you or Jasper." Zoe pulled out a sheaf of papers from her handbag. They were spreadsheets covered in numbers.

"What are these?" Lila asked.

"Accounting records for the Primrose."

Lila grabbed the stack of papers, flipping through the pages, which were organized by month, year, and tenant name. They were the records Jasper had requested. "I can't believe Susanna gave these to you. I didn't think she would want anything to do with me at this point."

"Why? Susanna likes you, and she *doesn't* like everyone," Zoe said. "She thought it was ridiculous that detective was harassing you." She lowered her voice and nodded to the pages. "Take a look at how far behind Brock Anderson got on his homeowners association fees."

Zoe reached across the table to pour herself more wine. She appeared to be settling in for a while, and Lila was glad. Turning her attention to the papers, Lila studied the records and noted Brock Anderson's name listed every month in 2002 as not paying his homeowners association fees. He was thousands of dollars in debt, more every month. There was a notation at the bottom of the account in September about foreclosure proceedings. However, in November, his account showed as fully paid. That was right after the robberies concluded and Sophia was killed, which raised the question, where had Brock gotten the money to pay off his debt?

Chapter Twenty-Four

Lila was up all night tossing, turning, and wrapping the covers around herself. It was impossible to sleep when her brain was spinning through one dark question after another. If the police charged her with a crime, would social services take Bea away? How could she afford a lawyer when she didn't have a job? Would a judge grant bail for a pending murder charge and, if so, could Mama pay it? Finally, Lila went deep down an internet rabbit hole researching *a typical day in the life of a prisoner*. The results weren't comforting. Somehow she still managed to get up when the alarm went off and went through the motions of toasting a bagel for Bea. She dropped Bea at school and trudged back into the Primrose lobby, her head fuzzy and pounding like she was hungover.

Ruth was waiting inside. Lila hadn't spoken to her since that day in the Hydrangea Room, but she could tell from the way Ruth looked at her with a slight sneer that Ruth wasn't a fan of Lila.

"Oh, Lila, my goodness. I'm surprised you've left your apartment," Ruth said, pursing her lips to indicate she did not approve of Lila's decision. She was standing next to the grand piano and brushed an invisible speck of dust from the lid, a covetous expression on her face.

"I come home from taking Bea to school at this time every day," Lila said.

"Still, with everything going on . . ." Ruth smoothed down her caftan. The hot pink flowers clashed hideously with her orange hair. "In any event, it's lucky I ran into you because we do have a problem, and I'm simply not comfortable meeting in private."

Lila's arms were suddenly heavy as if waterlogged while she waited for Ruth to come out with whatever imagined problem she had created.

"I'm afraid our bylaws specify that residents who commit violent criminal acts are not eligible to remain in their apartments," Ruth said primly. "Rule 202."

"I didn't commit a violent criminal act," Lila said.

"The police think you did," Ruth said and clucked her tongue in a way that made Lila's skin crawl. "Poor Emily, so helpless. I must confess I'm nervous just standing in front of you." She made a point of looking at the security guard who was stationed in the corner of the lobby.

Lila couldn't believe the nerve of Ruth Bailor, accusing her of murder right to her face. She would have laughed at the utter ridiculousness of Ruth waiting for her and then pretending to be afraid of her if it also didn't mean her place at the Primrose was in jeopardy. She and Bea still had nowhere else to go and now they couldn't leave the city.

"You're going to have to vacate Gloria's apartment immediately," Ruth continued.

Lila lifted her chin and smoothed her wrinkled T-shirt, aware of the dark circles under her eyes but not caring. "I wasn't charged with a crime." She seized on what Jasper had said to Detective Roberts. "There's no proof I did anything wrong. You can't kick me out."

Ruth's face darkened. "I don't know who you think you are, but the bylaws—"

"I'd like to see them," Lila interrupted. "Read them for myself. I'm guessing you can't evict someone because of a rumor."

Ruth blinked, not used to anyone telling her off. "I'll have to check them again."

"You do that. But don't threaten me unless you have your facts straight," Lila said firmly.

"Or maybe don't threaten her at all." The voice behind Lila was sardonic.

Lila whirled around. Nate had managed to sneak up behind her again while she was talking to Ruth. He wore a pale green polo shirt that matched his eyes.

"I told you not to return here." Ruth looked more annoyed than ever.

"That's true," Nate said, smiling. "But then June and Iris invited me for tea, so I'm back."

"They're not allowed to invite you back. You are banned from this building," Ruth said.

"I recall you saying that when I tried to interview you last week. So I checked the bylaws myself because I expected you might bring them up again. It turns out the bylaws don't allow you to ban guests without a full board vote and evidence of violence, disruption, or lewd behavior. I know I wasn't violent, and I didn't make any kind of scene when I was here. I'm almost certain I kept my clothes on when we talked last so I'm assuming I wasn't lewd, but correct me if I'm wrong."

Lila instantly pictured Nate without his shirt on. He was slender with a tennis player's build; she'd bet his arms were muscled and he probably had a six-pack. A flush crept up her cheeks at the image.

"You were disruptive," Ruth said furiously. "This whole article is disruptive."

"Was there a board vote?" Nate asked.

Ruth stomped her foot. "Not yet but there will be."

"Good luck at the next board meeting then. I've gotten close with Mary Dixon and Florence. They're both on the board, aren't they? Mary Dixon said I remind her of her son. What a compliment," Nate said.

Ruth's wrinkled lips pressed closed, the lipstick tacky and sticking at the sides. She pointed a bony finger at Nate and then Lila, looking absolutely livid. "I'll be in touch soon. About both of you. I wouldn't get too comfortable here." She stalked off down the hallway.

Lila watched her go, her lips turning up.

"Horrible woman," Nate said.

"I can't believe you read the bylaws," Lila said.

Nate laughed. "I thought they might come in handy with her."

Lila patted her hair, hoping she'd remembered to brush it on her race out the door.

"I understand you're a dangerous woman to be around," Nate said, raising his eyebrows.

Lila stiffened at the implication. "I didn't kill anyone."

"I'm only kidding," Nate said hastily. "I don't think you're stupid enough to leave Emily a note asking for a meeting and then shoot her on the same day. You'd have a little more subtlety than that, right?"

"That's right," Lila said in surprise. Nate made a good point. She should have thought of that herself. She'd make sure to tell Detective Roberts next time she saw him. She shivered, wishing she'd never have to see Detective Roberts again.

"Now that we've established you're not a murderer, we should go to dinner," Nate said.

"I'm still not interested in an interview," Lila said.

"I wasn't asking for an interview."

Lila stared as the implication of what he was asking dawned on her. "Wait. Are you—you're not . . . Are you asking me out on a date?"

"Yes. but I'm obviously doing a bad job of it if you sound that confused." Nate grinned.

Lila was speechless. No one had asked her out in nineteen years, not since she started dating Ryan in high school. She didn't know how to date—what to wear, what to talk about, how to *kiss*. It was ridiculous to even consider. She would make an absolute fool of herself, not to mention that she was technically still married.

"I can't," Lila finally said.

Nate ran a hand through his already disheveled hair. "Right. Implying you might have murdered someone wasn't the best first line. Let me start over. Do you like sushi?"

Lila shook her head.

Nate bit his lip. "I really thought you would say yes to that. Damn."

Lila couldn't help feeling flattered at his obvious disappointment and a little sorry that she had turned him down. "Look, I can't go but it's not because of you."

Nate's eyes lit up, sensing an opening. He stepped closer. Lila inhaled his scent, some subtle woodsy cologne. Her stomach dipped. Fine. Maybe she was a little bit attracted to him but that didn't mean she was ready to date anyone.

"Forget sushi. What if I told you I know the best Italian place in town? How about Thursday night?" Nate asked.

"No, really it won't work."

"It's because I hate space porn."

"I'm not in a place where I can get involved with anyone," Lila said.

If she dated Nate, she would only mess it up like she had messed up her relationship with Ryan. She also had Bea to worry about. Bea didn't know her parents were getting divorced yet.

"Oh." Nate ducked his head. "I thought you were single. I heard you were living here on your own when I asked around."

"You asked around about me?"

"Well, yeah." Nate looked distinctly embarrassed, which made him even cuter. "I also googled you."

Nate didn't say anything about what else he must have learned over Google—Ryan's fraud and current status as a wanted fugitive. No wonder he'd thought she was single. He knew Ryan had left her. That fact was all over the news.

"I'm getting divorced," Lila said, pushing out the words reluctantly. There it was—her admission that she'd failed at her marriage. Would there ever come a time when she could say the word *divorce* without feeling ashamed?

Nate grimaced. "I'm sorry, and I get it. Ending a relationship is hard enough without all the shit you went through. I barely got through my divorce two years ago."

"Now *I'm* sorry," Lila said.

"It's okay. I've gone to therapy, worked on myself. Gotten in touch with my feelings." Nate chuckled as if he was joking, but Lila sensed he was serious. "I know why my relationship ended."

"What happened?" Lila couldn't help asking.

"We ended things amicably. That's not to say it was easy. I slept on my couch for two weeks with a bottle of vodka after I signed the divorce papers. It was brutal. But we got married really young and grew apart. Jennie is a jewelry designer and she was spending all her time growing her business, and I was spending all my time researching stories for the paper, and neither of us was spending time on our marriage. We stopped talking to each other and eventually realized we didn't have much in common. Jennie is engaged now to a great guy. We're still friends." Nate pulled at the collar of his shirt, looking distinctly uncomfortable. "I bet you're wishing you had ended this conversation five minutes ago."

But it was the opposite. Lila appreciated his vulnerability. It made her feel less self-conscious of her own marital failures.

"We could go to dinner as friends," Lila said, wanting to offer something to make up for her rejection.

"Friends?" Nate questioned before breaking into another smile. He smiled easily. "Okay, yeah. That sounds good. Let's do it."

They exchanged cell phone numbers and made a plan to meet up soon.

"I'll send you the address of the Italian place," Nate promised. "And hey, if you want to take advantage of my body *as a friend*, I can live with that."

"You wish," Lila said, rolling her eyes. She started on her way down the hall but turned at the last second to watch Nate leave.

Nate reached the double doors, pumped his fist in the air, and gave a little hop. It was an obvious celebration that Lila had agreed to go out with him, even as friends.

Lila turned back around, a smile spreading over her face. It had been some time since Ryan had shown that much enthusiasm about her. In college, he used to call her three times a day and stop by her apartment every night even though his friends were always dragging him out to another beer pong tournament or a football game. When had it all changed? Had it been the expansion of the business, or the reality of parenthood and adult life? Ryan had spent more and more time at work or golfing or playing pickleball, and even when he had been home, they watched TV in separate rooms. Their house was quiet. Distance had expanded between them and she'd willfully ignored it.

Lila remembered straightening up Ryan's home office a few months before he left. He had been supposedly working late. There was a phone on his desk, buried beneath papers. It wasn't Ryan's latest-model iPhone; it was a simple flip phone she'd never seen before. A text message had come through from an unfamiliar number: *at Ramada, where are you.* She had frozen, her veins icing solid. Ryan was texting with someone on a second phone and meeting that person at the Ramada, a rundown hotel in a seedy neighborhood. An affair, she'd thought. She'd stared at the dark screen for over an hour, not knowing what to do next. In the end, she'd left the phone and walked away. She had told herself Ryan must have arranged to meet an investor at the Ramada restaurant, and she was overreacting. Now she could see the truth—she hadn't wanted to know that he was cheating on her because that would mean she'd have to do something about it.

Lila expelled a harsh exhalation. Where was Ryan now? Would she or Bea ever see him again? There were no answers, but she did know one thing for certain. If she could go back, she would have talked to him about the phone . . . about the distance . . . about all of it. Maybe she couldn't have fixed what was wrong, but she could have faced the reality of her life. She'd rather have known the truth, even if it broke her heart.

Chapter Twenty-Five

started a club," Bea announced when she got into Lila's car that afternoon.

Lila stared at her, unable to keep the surprise from her face. The clouds had turned the sky a morose gray, but a small ray of sunlight poked through the mist, illuminating the blacktop of the carpool line in front of them. She started forward in her old Jeep.

"You started a club with other kids?" Lila asked.

"Duh, Mama," Bea said. She had knotted her Atlanta Braves T-shirt on the side instead of letting it hang down around her jean skirt.

A club was a good sign by any measure. It meant Bea was making friends at her new school, which meant this move to Richmond wasn't a complete disaster, if you didn't count the possible murder charge.

Jasper had called earlier and said the lab was processing the evidence from Emily's apartment. His friends at the police department had promised to share the results. Would they find something to tie Lila to Emily's death? But how could they when Lila hadn't done anything wrong? Lila kept reminding herself of that fact as she cleaned out an entire bedroom closet to keep busy and quiet her mind.

Lila turned to Bea, determined to show her how excited she was about the club. "Tell me more."

"It all started when we were talking about Ms. Canterbury's murder at recess."

Lila hit the brakes, causing the car to come to an abrupt stop. The car behind her honked. She raised a wave in apology and made herself breathe.

"Why were you talking about Ms. Canterbury's death at school? Remember we discussed how crime and school don't go together."

Bea sighed. "I know you say that, but the other kids were interested when I told them how an old lady was shot and killed in my building. Mama, that doesn't happen every day."

"I'm aware of that," Lila said between gritted teeth. "What does Ms. Canterbury's murder have to do with a club." She was afraid of what Bea might say next.

"I was trying to tell you that before you interrupted me." Bea looked annoyed. "As I was saying, me, Nora, Evie, Layton, and a few other kids were all talking about Ms. Canterbury getting killed and how the police came and our building is now a crime scene. Everyone wanted to hear about when they took her away on a stretcher in a real-life body bag."

"You saw that," Lila said weakly.

"I was staring out the window because I didn't want to miss it," Bea said patiently. "I thought maybe I would see the actual dead body but no luck. After I told them all about the body bag, I said we should start a club where we talk about different murders. We would take turns picking a new one every week."

Lila gripped the steering wheel. Oh, she was definitely going to hear about this from Bea's teacher. No one wanted a ten-year-old to start a murder club.

"Does your teacher know about the club?" Lila asked.

"Duh, Mama," Bea said again. "We have to tell her to start an official school club."

Lila turned onto Grove Avenue, her patience wearing thin at Bea's remarks. "You're telling me that your teacher let you start a club about murders? I find that hard to believe."

"We had to change it to a detective club where we learn about famous crimes and find out how they were solved. Mrs. Maisley said the crimes can't be murder or anything violent. She suggested a famous art heist from Paris. It's not as good as murder but still cool. She even said her uncle is a detective and might come talk to our club." Bea paused here. "Don't worry, Mama. He isn't the detective on Ms. Canterbury's case. I would not invite him to my club."

"That's good to know," Lila said faintly. She wondered if Bea was making this entire thing up.

"And I'm not lying about this, in case you were wondering," Bea said.

"I wasn't," Lila said guiltily, staring straight ahead at the road.

"Nora Raynor said it was the best club she'd ever heard of, and she never joins clubs. Everyone is afraid of her, but I like her now. Her favorite show is *Law & Order* but when she described it to me, I said it didn't sound like something you would let me watch yet."

"You're right," Lila said.

"Well, Nora has three older brothers," Bea said as if that explained everything. "I told her about *Murder, She Wrote*, and she's going to check it out tonight."

Bea smiled in her seat, looking out the window, humming to herself. Lila's mood lifted. Sure, Bea had started a club about criminals, which wasn't the most conventional way of making new friends. Still, it seemed to work for her. And if it worked for Bea, it worked for Lila.

Lila pulled into a parking space at the Primrose and put her car into park. When she looked back up through the windshield,

Mama was standing on the sidewalk waving. Her blue floral dress was unwrinkled despite the drive from Norfolk. Saint Laurent sunglasses pushed the blond hair off her forehead. There was a smile fixed on her face but Lila could tell, even from behind the glass, that it was strained. Her stomach sank.

"Mimi is here," Bea said enthusiastically, unbuckling her seat belt and opening the car door.

Lila leaned into the headrest for a moment before slowly climbing out of the car.

Mama hugged Bea to her side. "I missed you."

"Missed you too," Bea said.

Mama's gaze flicked to Lila, her lips briefly tightening. "We have a few things to talk about, don't we?"

Lila flinched. This definitely wasn't a pleasure visit.

Mama pulled back from Bea, examining her. "I see you're still wearing that old T-shirt." She looked over at Lila. "Doesn't this sweet child have anything else to wear?"

"I like this shirt," Bea said in a stubborn voice.

"That doesn't mean it's appropriate for school," Mama said, still smiling.

Lila took a deep breath. "It's Bea's favorite shirt, and she can wear it to school if she likes. I personally think it's unique."

Mama cleared her throat and changed the subject. "How are you liking Richmond?"

Bea shrugged. "The apartment was a hellhole."

Mama's eyes widened.

"I'm learning about blood in school," Bea continued.

"That's not entirely accurate," Lila said as Mama's eyes bugged out further.

Bea nodded. "You're right. I'm learning about bloodstain patterns, and I've made a lot of new friends. Some of them are super old. I've also been busy with a murder—"

"Hey, Bea?" Lila interrupted, making her voice breezy. "I see that Edwin pulled up and could use some help with his groceries. Would you give him a hand getting them out of the trunk?"

"Sure. Edwin is one of my new, really old friends. He's looking for his next wife," Bea said.

Mama looked slightly dazed as Bea ran off to the other side of the parking lot. "What is going on around here?"

"Nothing is going on. I'm cleaning out the apartment. We're making the best of the situation. The residents here are great, and they love Bea—"

"I don't care about the other residents," Mama said in a low, hissing voice that Lila remembered from every time she'd gotten in trouble in her childhood. "I heard you were arrested in Stanley's apartment."

"That's not true," Lila said, swallowing hard.

Mama let silence linger and curl around them, somehow still expressing her disapproval even when she wasn't saying anything. Finally, she said, "Let me ask this another way. Are you under suspicion for murdering a woman who lived at the Primrose?"

Lila dragged her toe along the sidewalk, not meeting Mama's gaze. "It's complicated."

Mama sputtered. "It—it always is with you. Why can't you keep things simple—go to the apartment, clean it out, find a job. Why do you need to involve yourself in another disaster?"

"There's no disaster. She is working really hard on the apartment," Bea said, appearing from behind a parked car beside them. "You should come up and see it."

Mama rounded on her. "Bea, this conversation doesn't involve you. Eavesdropping is rude."

"But it's not eavesdropping because you're outside and everyone can hear you," Bea said in an earnest voice.

"Don't be disrespectful," Mama said, her words clipped.

For a second, Bea's face fell at the rebuke before readjusting into a deep, familiar glower. But Lila had seen the minuscule shift; Mama's comment had cut into Bea, and Bea's defense was always her anger.

Lila lifted her chin. "Actually, Bea is only stating a fact. That's not disrespectful."

"She shouldn't state anything when adults are talking. That's the time for children to stay quiet," Mama said.

That's what Mama had always told her—stay quiet when she was upset, when adults were around, when things went wrong. Lila had done it. In fact, she'd stayed quiet her entire life, but Bea wasn't like her. Bea was opinionated. She said what she was thinking and sometimes Lila didn't like it, but she didn't want to change her either. She liked that Bea could be loud.

"I don't want Bea to stay quiet," Lila said in her own loud voice.

Bea lifted her head. She looked at Lila from across the sidewalk, and then she smiled wide and big. It creased up her eyes and brightened her entire face. It was the best smile Lila had seen in a long time.

"I'm going to help bring Edwin's groceries upstairs," Bea said after a moment. "I wanted to tell you where I was going."

"Thanks," Lila said.

Mama exhaled when Bea was out of earshot. "I'm sorry for snapping at Bea. I'm upset. Stanley is horrified with everything going on and blames me for letting you move into the Primrose. He heard from the president of the board. She is livid. This puts Stanley in a terrible position."

Lila tipped her head down, closing her eyes. Of course, she should have suspected Ruth would have called Stanley to complain when she couldn't get Lila kicked out on her own. Ruth wanted to make Lila's life difficult, and it was working. But maybe Mama was exaggerating Stanley's reaction because *she* was upset at having to listen to him gripe about her daughter again.

"I didn't do anything," Lila said. "This is a big misunderstanding. You have to believe me."

Mama sighed, her frustration seeming to ebb. "Sweetheart, I do believe you, but Stanley wants you to vacate Gloria's apartment."

Lila choked on her own breath. "We have nowhere else to go."

"I know. I told him that, and I had to work very hard to convince him to let you stay. He's agreed for now. But, Lila, if there are any more problems or complaints, he's going to insist on you leaving."

Lila knew Mama was telling the truth. She was Stanley's girlfriend and only had so much control over him. He was paying her bills, letting her live in his waterfront mini-mansion, and buying her expensive clothes and dinners; bankrolling her entire lifestyle. Mama couldn't afford to lose him. She didn't have a backup plan and she wasn't getting younger. Lila glanced at her reflection in the car window, zeroing in on the lines scrawled across her forehead and the droop to her cheeks. That's the problem with being pretty when you're young—no one tells you that *pretty* is not a marketable skill in middle age. Mama knew that well enough too. Stanley was a final option for her, which meant they were yet again at the mercy of a man who could decide to end things whenever he wanted.

"I'm sorry I made things harder for you with Stanley," Lila said, and felt a pang in her chest. Mama was doing her best, even if that wasn't enough.

"I'm worried about you and Bea," Mama said softly. "How much trouble are you in?"

Lila slumped down. "A lot. I could go to jail."

"What are you going to do?" Mama asked.

"I'm going to handle it," Lila said in a weary voice.

Mama's eyes filled with tears. "I wish Ryan was here to help you."

But Lila didn't. She was done waiting around for Ryan to save the day. He had made her feel safe once, but she'd become complacent and lethargic about her own life. That kind of inertia wasn't a choice when you were a murder suspect and facing jail time.

A crushing weight pressed on Lila's chest. If she went to jail, she would lose Bea. Patricia would move her to Florida and put her in the fancy school and make her wear fancy dresses that she would hate, or Mama would take her back to Norfolk and spend all her time shushing Bea so she didn't disturb Stanley. She couldn't let that happen. No one else knew Bea the way she did. Bea was challenging and difficult at times, but she was also funny, creative, empathetic, and amazing. Lila was finally starting to understand her, to figure out how to talk to her, to really connect with her. Bea needed her, and Lila needed Bea too. It was time for Lila to protect them both. She was the only one around who could solve their problems, even if that meant solving a murder at the same time.

Chapter Twenty-Six

Lila was feeling more clearheaded after her talk with Mama. Up in the apartment, she riffled through the paperwork Zoe had dropped off last night and decided a visit with Brock Anderson was in order. She wanted to know how he had managed to pay off his debts in 2002. While she considered the best way to go about meeting with him, she noticed Bea was sitting at her laptop and reading something on the screen. She'd deliberately moved the computer so it was facing away from Lila and kept glancing over at her.

After a few minutes, Bea got up. Lila waited until she'd left the living room before opening the laptop and checking the search history. Sure enough, Bea was reading everything she could find on Emily Canterbury. There wasn't much about the murder yet. The police had only released her name that morning. The second search term in the history was Sophia Kent. Bea had been looking up the old *Dateline* segment again.

Closing the computer, Lila exhaled a heavy, low sound that resonated through the empty living room. She'd told Bea no more investigation, but it shouldn't surprise her that Bea was unwilling to let go of Sophia Kent's murder and the new connection to Emily Canterbury. Bea wasn't one to give up lightly on anything she cared about. It was one of her best and most challenging qualities. Lila knew yelling at Bea wouldn't accomplish anything. Bea would lash out and continue to do as she wished. She'd have to find a way to reason with her daughter, though she wasn't sure how to do that yet.

Crossing the room, Lila knocked on Bea's bedroom door and cracked it open. "How about a hot chocolate at Rise Up for an afternoon snack?"

"You never let me get hot chocolate anymore," Bea said suspiciously.

"I think we both deserve a treat. Yesterday was a long day," Lila said.

Bea studied Lila. "Can we talk about Sophia on the way there?"

"You already know the answer to that question, which is no," Lila said. "In fact, we aren't going to talk about Sophia anytime soon, but we still have plenty of other fun things to do like getting hot chocolate."

Bea scowled, and Lila was certain she would refuse to go. Instead, she began pulling on her tennis shoes. "I want whipped cream."

"Obviously."

"Actually, I need double whipped cream because I live in a building where someone got killed. Stress can make people hungry, Mama."

At Rise Up Cafe, Lila ordered a hot chocolate and a coffee, which she desperately needed after staying up all night. She collected them from the counter while Bea went to use the restroom. The cafe tables were empty during this midafternoon lull, save for one.

From across the room, Lila noticed Helene and Alice seated at a table in the corner. Lila approached to say hello but as she drew nearer, she realized they were in the middle of a heated disagreement. Lila froze, not wanting to interrupt.

"I'm worried he's only after your money," Helene said.

"That's not true. Why can't you believe he cares about me?" Alice said.

Lila took a step back to avoid drawing attention to herself. It would be awkward if they saw her at this point and knew she'd overheard them.

"I'm sure he does care for you, but why would you give him another chance? He cheated on you. Everyone knows about it. He embarrassed you," Helene said angrily.

"I don't care about that or what everyone thinks they know. He didn't cheat on me. He has always denied it, and I believe him."

"You can't see him clearly the way I do." Helene reached out her hand, placing it on Alice's arm. "I don't want you to get hurt again."

Lila turned soundlessly, slinking backward further.

"It's my decision," Alice said in a soft voice.

"Oh, Alice, this is a mistake." Helene sounded sad. She stood, tucked her Hermès Birkin handbag under her arm, and swept out of the restaurant.

Alice turned to watch her mother go and spotted Lila, only two tables away. Alice's brow lifted. The veins in her eye were a delicate, pink spiderweb. She looked as if she had been crying.

"I guess you heard all that?" Alice asked.

Lila winced. "Some of it. I'm sorry. It wasn't intentional."

Bea appeared at Lila's side, and Lila handed her the hot chocolate. Bea cupped it in her hands, her face lighting up as she inhaled.

"Hot chocolate with double whipped cream, as promised," Lila said.

"What a nice mama to get that for you," Alice said. Her smile was forced.

"It's a bribe," Bea explained.

"It's a treat," Lila corrected.

"A bribe-treat," Bea amended and looked at Alice. "She's trying to distract me from thinking about the murder yesterday, but I don't think hot chocolate can make up for a violent death, do you?"

Alice looked taken aback. "No, not really."

"It's good that she tried," Bea said. "I'll wait outside, Mama."

Lila stifled a laugh as she watched her daughter leave. Bea wasn't one to sugarcoat anything.

"You have your hands full," Alice said.

"You have no idea," Lila replied. She took the seat across from Alice. "Is everything all right? I'm not trying to pry. I just want to make sure you're okay."

Alice shrugged. "Mama means well, but she's overprotective. I guess that's what happens when you lose one of your children. She worries about me all the time."

Lila sipped her coffee, thinking of Sophia's young and innocent face. "That's understandable."

"The problem is that sometimes she's irrational. I wish she would trust me," Alice said, sounding deeply frustrated.

"I get that too," Lila said.

"I was engaged last year. His name is Wyatt. We were really happy until someone saw him leaving a bar with another woman. Mama was the one who told me. Wyatt said it was nothing, a misunderstanding, but there were all these rumors flying around town and Mama got in my head, saying she'd never trusted him. I broke it off." Alice's face was drawn. "We started talking again a few weeks ago after Grandpa died. He explained nothing happened that night at the bar. I believe him and I still love him. I told Mama we're getting back together, and—" She blew out a mirthless half-laugh. "You heard her response. She thinks he's after my trust fund."

"I'm sure she only wants to help," Lila said.

"I guess, but she's always like this with anyone who gets close to me. She's suspicious, unfriendly. Grandpa used to help run interference, but I don't think she has liked a single one of my boyfriends." Alice made a face. "Granted, I do have questionable taste. I dated one guy who owned eight snakes, and he kept them all in his bedroom."

"Well, I married a criminal, so your taste isn't any worse than mine," Lila said, trying to lighten the mood.

Alice smiled a little at that. "Maybe not. But Wyatt is different. I wish I could make her see that, but I'm worried she'll never give us her blessing."

Lila wasn't sure what to say. Alice was a grown woman; she seemed smart and sensitive, the kind of person who was a decent judge of character. She could understand Helene wanting her to remain cautious, but she should also let her daughter make her own decisions about her love life. Helene sounded overprotective and even a little controlling. Although Lila could understand why. She'd already lost Sophia.

"I'm sure you can talk it through," Lila said reassuringly. "Give Helene a chance to get used to the idea of Wyatt again."

"Maybe you're right. Thanks for listening." Alice hesitated. "And I'm sorry about this mess with Emily. I heard the police questioned you yesterday, which is ridiculous."

"Thanks for saying that. I hope they find out what happened," Lila said and glanced out the large picture window to the small patio where she glimpsed Bea bent over her drink. "I don't like to think about a murderer at the Primrose."

"It's terrifying," Alice agreed. She leaned toward Lila, lowering her voice. "The timing is suspicious too. Emily called James Forrester yesterday and left a message saying she knew who killed Sophia."

"I heard. I ran into James in the lobby."

"It doesn't make any sense. If Emily knew who killed Sophia, she would have told the police years ago. It makes me wonder if she was suffering from dementia before she died."

"She seemed fine earlier this week," Lila said.

"That's true. I guess she was after the reward." Alice frowned. "Emily never liked my sister. I went to a fundraiser dinner for our charity last year. Mama gave a speech, and on the stage was a portrait of Sophia. Emily was at my table. She'd had too much to drink and leaned over to me, pointed to the stage, and said, 'She's not who you thought she was.'"

Lila sucked in a breath. "That's really tactless."

"I got up and left. I hadn't spoken to her since, and now I can't. I guess we'll never know who she intended to accuse of Sophia's murder, and it's all I can think about right now. You—well, you actually inspired me the other day," Alice said shyly.

"Me?" Lila was surprised.

"I figured if you could investigate Sophia's murder, then I could too. We've still got a box of Sophia's stuff from her old room. I guess Mama didn't have the heart to throw it away. I knew it was wishful thinking, but I went back through everything, hoping there was some clue I'd missed."

"Did you find anything interesting?" Lila expected the police had pored over Sophia's room after she was murdered.

"Not really. It was a lot of what you'd expect—photos of Sophia and her friends, yearbooks, a few old stuffed animals, and school papers." Alice took a sip of coffee. "There was this one weird thing."

Lila looked at her expectantly.

"There's an English teacher at Stratford Academy—Mrs. Pritchard—she's been there forever. She makes all her students spend ten minutes journaling at the beginning of every Friday class. I found Sophia's journal from the class. It was mostly blank, but the last entry reminded me of you asking about blackmail. It was dated the month before she died."

"What did it say?"

"It's probably nothing, but it creeped me out. Sophia wrote two lines—*I can never pay back what I've taken. He's coming for me.*"

"Who's *he*?" Lila asked, shivering at Sophia's words, which had creeped her out too.

Alice looked disconcerted. "I have no idea. But I'm beginning to think there was a lot I didn't know about my sister."

Chapter Twenty-Seven

Lila didn't know what to make of Sophia's journal entry. It might be nothing more than typical teenage angst, or it could mean exactly what it said—Sophia had stolen something, and someone was coming after her for it. But what could she have taken? Lila hadn't heard of any theft connected with Sophia except for the Primrose burglaries. Was there a chance she was involved in those? Lila was more determined than ever to get as much information out of Brock as she could and arranged to meet him for dinner that night.

Turning out of the Primrose parking lot, Lila glanced reassuringly at the Proenza Schouler jersey dress she'd managed to hold onto from her earlier life. It was black and simple with long sleeves and a mid-length skirt. She'd kept it because it was impeccably cut, she looked amazing in it, and her heart had literally *hurt* when she'd thought about giving it up.

The Old Dominion Country Club was over a century old and the most exclusive club in the state, according to Brock, who was a member. Brick columns bordered the entrance to the long drive that wound around to a striking redbrick clubhouse. A discreet gold plaque affixed to one of the columns announced, *Private Club. Members Only.* It was there to keep the wrong people out and the right people in. Lila had no idea which one she was anymore. She used to belong to a club exactly like this with Ryan until she couldn't pay the dues anymore.

The golf course stretched out alongside the road and, beyond that, the tree line cradled the vibrant greens. The parking lot was packed with gleaming SUVs adorned with Stratford Academy stickers and University of Virginia logos. Lila pulled into the circular drive in front of the clubhouse. A valet dressed in a spotless tuxedo shirt and black trousers rushed to the driver's side and opened Lila's door. Inside, a hushed silence extended to the top of the high ceilings and thick triple crown molding. Heavy gold-framed paintings hung on the walls, and Lila caught a glimpse of her pale face reflected in one of the mirrors above the delicate wooden tables flanking the entrance to the formal dining room.

Brock's face lit up when he saw Lila, and he walked toward her, his arms outstretched. He kissed her cheek, smelling strongly of cologne, and not the subtle, expensive kind.

"I'm glad we're doing this," Brock said. "When you called, I knew it was fate. It's steak night."

Lila forced a smile. "Can't wait."

Brock winked at Lila. "I don't even mind that you may have killed Emily. I never liked her much anyway."

"I didn't kill anyone," Lila managed to spit out.

"I'm only joking with you. I know a pretty thing like you would never hurt a fly," Brock said, leering down at her figure.

Lila set her jaw. She reminded herself that she was the one who had initiated this dinner. While she knew Brock wouldn't outright confess to committing the robberies at the Primrose, he might say something to give himself away or at least provide another clue to follow up on. Brock didn't strike her as the most savvy or discreet individual. She would learn more about him from his reaction. Unfortunately, that meant sitting through an entire meal with him.

"I've already got us the best table in the room, and I ordered their most expensive bottle of red," Brock said.

"Sounds perfect," Lila said, trying to sound enthusiastic.

The dining room was filled with round, white-skirted tables and tapestry upholstered chairs. Heavy brocade curtains framed the tall windows and glass patio doors. Two brass chandeliers hung from the two-story ceiling, looming over the cavernous room like gold-toned spiders.

It was the sort of reassuring country club decor Lila had grown accustomed to after she'd married Ryan. There was nothing too flashy or ostentatious about any of it; this was Virginia after all. Old money was threadbare antique carpets that cost thousands of dollars, lump crab cakes served on RITZ crackers, and private school charity auctions where someone bought a yellow Labrador retriever with a hunting pedigree for the price of a new car. Lila had learned the unspoken rules of this life, one of which was that the money didn't run out. People didn't drop out of the club because they lost a job or had a bad month in the stock market. The money was bigger than that. Ryan had invited Lila into his world and lulled her into believing she was part of the never-ending club too. But she should have remembered the rules of her own childhood—for someone like her, there was no safety net.

At the table, Brock started off talking about his condo in Park City and his other condo in Boca Raton, then his stock portfolio, and his yearly trip to Las Vegas. Lila needn't have worried about making conversation. He talked enough for both of them.

The waitress came to take their order. Lila simpered and asked Brock to choose her meal. Sipping occasionally on her wine, Lila made sure Brock's glass was continuously full and nodded enthusiastically when he suggested ordering another bottle. She needed him loose-lipped and relaxed when she finally got to the point of this dinner.

After the waitresses brought out their steaks and refilled

Brock's wineglass for the fourth time, Lila saw her chance. "Have you lived at the Primrose for a long time?"

"Twenty-three years. I moved in after my last divorce. My second wife got the house on Oak Lane, and I didn't want another big house to take care of, so I bought a place at the Primrose. Been there ever since. Not much of a singles scene unfortunately." Brock smiled with all his yellow teeth. "That is, until recently."

Gross. Lila swallowed down bile.

"The homeowners association fees are a little steep, aren't they?" Lila asked.

Brock cut his steak and took a bite. When he spoke, Lila could see chewed-up red meat in between his incisors. "I never noticed."

Lila wrinkled her forehead. "Brock, I feel I should tell you something as your friend. There's been talk."

Brock grinned. "About you and me? That's not surprising. People are always trying to set me up with girls." He slugged his wine, and a few red drops splashed onto his chest from the corners of his mouth. "I don't like to brag but I'm known as quite a catch around here."

"Oh, I can see why, although the talk I'm referring to isn't so much romance as it is about your finances."

"My finances?" Brock frowned.

"Some people have said you don't pay your homeowners association fees on time."

Brock sputtered. "It's not true."

"I'm sure you wouldn't lie to me but there's proof. Gosh, I'm uncomfortable even telling you this." Lila twisted her hands together, trying to convey her distress.

Brock reddened. "Proof?"

"Yes, well, I hate to bring this up. I suppose someone discovered we were getting to know each other." Lila nearly choked on this statement. "And they sent me an anonymous copy of the Primrose accounting ledger."

It felt risky and her reasoning was flimsy, but Lila had no other way to ensure Brock understood she already knew about his debts. Otherwise, he would continue to deny it. He was the kind of man who wouldn't admit to a failure unless someone was waving it in his face like a red flag in front of a bull.

Brock put down his fork, his brows drawn together in fury. "Those records are private. I'll have to speak to the board about this."

Lila made a sympathetic noise, encouraging him to go on.

"There may have been a time when I was a little behind on my fees but that's only because I had some more pressing debts at the time. My finances are all cleared up, I can assure you," Brock said.

"How did they get cleared up?" Lila asked sweetly.

"Sugar, we need to get to know each other better before we talk about money." Brock's smile was tight.

Lila knew it was now or never. She reached out a hand and placed it on Brock's arm. "You must think me silly to worry about these things, but financial security is important to me. I could never get serious with anyone who I didn't trust."

Brock cleared his throat, his gaze glued to Lila's hand on his arm. "A girl has to look out for herself. I suppose it wouldn't hurt to tell you I called in a favor. No financial issues since then. I was president of River City Bank, you know."

"You mentioned that," Lila said. "What type of favor, I wonder?" She sighed and squeezed his arm lightly. "I'm sorry to ask but I do have to be careful. There are so many con men out there."

Did that even make sense? Lila wasn't sure.

But Brock was nodding as if he agreed with her. "That's true. It's good to stay cautious but there's nothing to worry about here.

I had an understanding with Conrad Kent. It was all aboveboard, I can tell you that."

Lila leaned forward. Finally, they were getting somewhere.

"You must have done something important for Conrad Kent to owe you a favor. He was one of the most powerful men in Richmond," Lila said, sounding impressed.

"That's true, and I was a close confidant of his."

"I'm sure," Lila murmured, pouring him more wine.

Brock took a sip, his eyes red-rimmed now. "This is a secret, you understand?"

"Yes, of course," Lila said, staring as if he was the most fascinating person she'd ever met.

"Conrad's granddaughter got herself into some trouble at the bank. Sophia stole her mama's checkbook and wrote some checks to herself after forging Helene's signature. Sophia tried to cash them at my bank. The total amount was suspicious. The bank teller came to me directly. Everyone was aware I knew the Kent family personally. I called Sophia into my office. Poor girl admitted everything; she was embarrassed and remorseful. I felt sorry for her. I helped make the whole thing go away after I called Conrad. As the head of the family, I thought he'd want to know. Conrad was grateful for my discretion and cleared my debt with the Primrose. He saw fit to reward my compassion in helping a young girl through a difficult situation."

Despite Brock's assurances that he was only acting altruistically, it sounded a lot like Conrad had paid Brock not to prosecute Sophia for check fraud.

"You're such a kind gentleman," Lila said admiringly.

Brock waved his hand as if to dismiss her praise, nearly knocking over his glass of wine while doing so.

"I'm curious, though. Did Sophia tell you why she needed the money?" Lila asked.

"She was real dramatic. A troublemaker, if you know what I mean. She cried in my office, begged me not to call her granddaddy, though I did anyway. She said she owed someone money, claimed he was going to hurt her if she didn't pay him. Said she was desperate. I think it was drug-related, if you can believe it."

"Oh my goodness! Was she buying or selling?" Lila asked, her heart suddenly racing. This tracked with Nate's revelation that Sophia had drugs in her system when she died.

"She didn't come right out and say, and I didn't ask," Brock said, slurring his words. "Too bad. Such a pretty girl."

Lila's increasingly pointed questions should have put Brock on notice that this was no longer a conversation about his financial potential, but Brock had drunk way too much wine to make that connection.

"Did you tell the police about this incident after Sophia died?" Lila asked.

Brock was in the process of taking a sip of wine. He paused, the glass halfway to his lips. "Now, sugar, I promised Conrad discretion. I couldn't go back on my word. Conrad was sponsoring me for a club membership at that time. Besides, I didn't want to embarrass that poor family with what Sophia had done."

"You're saying you never told the police," Lila said slowly.

Brock sipped, another drop of wine dribbled down his weak chin and onto his white shirt like blood spatter. "It was a family matter. You understand."

Oh yes, Lila understood. Brock had gotten paid off and he didn't want to jeopardize that payoff or his club membership even if it would have helped solve Sophia's murder. But if the police had known that Sophia was in debt to a drug dealer who had threatened to hurt her, they might have solved the crime twenty-one years ago.

Chapter Twenty-Eight

After dinner and two bottles of wine, there was no way Brock could drive himself home. Lila poured him into her car and managed to get him inside and into the elevator at the Primrose. Luckily, he was too drunk and busy talking about himself to attempt a goodnight kiss.

Lila collected Bea from Evelyn's apartment. After settling Bea into bed, Lila texted Jasper and Evelyn with a summary of Brock's drunken confession. Jasper indicated he would call his police contact the following day and try to convince them to follow up on this new lead. It might be impossible to find a drug dealer from back in 2002 but at least it was something.

An hour after Lila had tucked Bea in, she was reading in her own bed. It turned out Gloria had the complete collection of Agatha Christie novels, and Lila was enjoying reading her way through the mysteries.

There was a pitter-patter of feet. Lila set down her book. She looked up to catch sight of Bea hovering around the bedroom door.

"What are you still doing awake?" Lila asked.

Bea stepped into the room, her eyes bleary in the sudden light. "I couldn't fall asleep."

"Do you want some water or a snack? You could read for a while. That usually makes me sleepy," Lila said.

"Maybe," Bea said but made no move to leave the room. Instead, she crept closer, standing at the foot of the bed, picking up the edge of the covers and twisting them.

"Is there something you want to tell me?" Lila asked.

Bea shrugged. This was her usual response when it came to her feelings.

Sophia was heavy on Lila's mind these days. It seemed as if the poor girl had kept so much of her life hidden from everyone, including her own mother, and it had only led to sorrow. Lila wanted something different for Bea. Everyone had little secrets, but she wanted Bea to tell her the big things. That would never happen if they couldn't talk to each other.

"I can't ever sleep when I have something bothering me," Lila continued matter-of-factly. She sensed Bea had something to say, but Lila knew she would only scare her away if she pushed too hard. Picking up her book, Lila pretended to read while watching her daughter from beneath her lashes and giving her the space to speak.

Bea continued to twist the covers in her hand. Finally, she said, "I'm mad because you made us stop the investigation."

Bea's voice was quiet, dipping down at the end of her sentence. Her eyes filled with tears. Bea had said *us*, not *me*. Lila realized all at once that Bea wasn't angry, she was hurt.

"I can tell you're disappointed," Lila said.

Bea nodded, her chin jerking up.

"I understand. I wish we didn't have to stop too."

"Then why do we?" Bea asked, sinking down onto the bed.

Lila put down her book and scooted to the edge of the comforter until she was beside Bea. "Ms. Canterbury was killed, and the police don't know what happened yet. But there's a chance it has something to do with Sophia Kent. It's my job to protect you.

I can't have you involved in something where you might get hurt. Do you understand?"

"I guess," Bea mumbled.

"I did have fun working together on the investigation, though."

Bea didn't say anything, but her body went still. Her head inclined the slightest bit toward Lila. She was listening.

"I know I didn't go out much this past year. It was . . . a hard time for me," Lila said haltingly. "I was sad a lot, but that didn't have anything to do with you. I'm better now. At least, I'm not as sad."

Lila wanted to reassure Bea with her words, but she also realized they were true. Her face no longer ached with the effort to keep it from collapsing into tears. Her chest was not completely hollow, and she could go minutes, hours even, without thinking of her lost life with Ryan. She was still sad, but not *as sad*. Maybe that was something Bea should hear now especially because things could change in an instant. Lila's thoughts suddenly flashed to Detective Roberts snapping handcuffs on her, roughly dragging her out of the apartment while Bea screamed at him to stop with tears streaming down her face. Lila blinked, pushing the image from her mind. She needed to focus on Bea right now.

Lila continued. "I was thinking maybe we could start a new hobby together like a cooking class or an art class or a book club."

"A mystery book club?" Bea asked.

"Definitely a mystery book club."

"We could ask Jasper and Evelyn to join too," Bea said.

"I'm sure they would like that." Lila's chest expanded at Bea's hopeful expression.

"Okay, Mama," Bea said and remained seated on the edge of the bed.

"Okay, Bea," Lila said and stayed beside her.

* * *

THE THUD STARTLED Lila awake. She'd drifted off to sleep. Bea had fallen asleep beside Lila, Bea's chest rising and falling with even breaths. Yet something had woken Lila. She sat up, listening. There it was again. A thud out in the hallway.

Lila froze, breathed, listened. She glanced at the bedside clock. It was 2 a.m. Someone had broken into her apartment.

Lila ran through her options. She didn't want to alert the intruder that she was awake. Maybe if he thought she was still asleep, he would avoid coming in here altogether. The last thing she wanted was a confrontation. The intruder could have a gun, a knife, anything. They could harm Bea! A cold sweat broke out over her entire body as panic enveloped her. Her body tensed, prepared to leap out of bed and run. But to where? There was nowhere to go.

Exhaling, Lila relaxed her hands. She needed to be smart about this. First, lock the door. Next, call 9-1-1. *Do not wake Bea,* she told herself.

Pulling back the sheet, careful not to disturb her daughter, Lila swung her legs over the edge of the bed, landing softly on the floor. She eased herself off the mattress. There was shuffling from out in the living room, a rifling through boxes and papers. Her chest constricted. Blood pumped rapidly through her veins. She picked her way across the room, avoiding the clothes on the floor.

She didn't breathe as she reached the door and turned the small gold lock into place. The click of the mechanism was impossibly loud in the room. All of Lila's limbs locked into position as if trapped in amber. The shuffling in the living room stopped. Had the intruder heard her? Lila held her breath, afraid the smallest exhale would give away the fact that she was awake.

The noises started in the living room again. Good. Now Lila

needed to get to her cell phone without making a sound. The flimsy lock wouldn't keep someone out of the room for long, but it would at least slow them down.

Lila stepped across the floor, her toes touching down softly. Another step. Almost there. Her cell phone was plugged in, resting on top of the dresser. Another step. Without warning, her shin scraped against a pile of shoeboxes she'd intended to move all week. The boxes toppled over, crashing to the floor.

Shit.

Bea stirred in bed. Footsteps started up the hallway, moving closer. Lila stopped worrying about being quiet. She sprinted the last two steps. Her entire body was tight with adrenaline.

Lila grabbed her cell phone.

"Mama?" Bea sat up, her shape indistinct in the darkness.

"It's okay," Lila whispered.

The footsteps in the hall stopped right outside the door. Lila could hardly breathe now. Her heart was in her throat, almost as if the organ was thudding against her neck.

Hands shaking nearly uncontrollably, Lila punched in 9-1-1 on her cell phone. It rang once. The operator picked up.

"Nine-one-one, what's your emergency?"

The lock jiggled on the door. Lila clenched the phone to her ear, pressing the plastic into her cartilage until it was painful.

"Someone has broken into my apartment. I'm at the Primrose on Grove Avenue, apartment 2B. Please send someone immediately. Hurry." Lila's voice broke on the last syllable.

The lock jiggled again.

Bea's voice was frightened now. "Mama, what's going on?"

"It's okay, it's okay," Lila said to Bea.

"Ma'am, are you in a safe location?" the operator asked.

"No," Lila said. "I locked the bedroom door but they're trying to break in."

"Can you get to a safe location?" the operator asked.

"There is nowhere else to go. We need help now," Lila said.

Bea was up, crossing the room quickly to stand by Lila. Lila put an arm around her, squeezing her tight, hoping that Bea didn't feel how much her body was shaking.

The operator was talking, saying she had dispatched the police. Lila focused on Bea staring up at her. Even in the darkness of the room, Lila could see her big blue eyes filled with tears.

"I'm scared," Bea whispered.

"I know," Lila whispered back. "Me too. But the police are on their way."

Lila bent down to Bea's level. "Go hide under the bed. If someone breaks in, you run if you get the chance."

"What about you?"

Lila didn't answer, she gently pushed her daughter back toward the bed. Bea crept down and disappeared underneath. Lila exhaled. Okay. If the intruder broke into the bedroom, at least Bea was hidden and maybe the police would arrive before he found her or she would have a chance to escape if Lila distracted him long enough.

Lila raised her voice then, not knowing what else to do. She shouted at the door. "The police are on their way. You better get out of here."

The jiggling stopped.

The operator was asking if she was all right. Lila didn't answer. She closed her eyes, thinking of the contents of the room. She needed a weapon. There were a million coat hangers in a pile on the floor, the costume jewelry from the dresser, the odd turban collection in the closet. Then she remembered the stilettos. She'd found them that afternoon. They were gold Manolo Blahniks, never worn. The heels were like daggers, and Lila had put them aside on top of the dresser, thinking they'd fetch a good price for

Stanley on a resale site. She reached for one of the shoes now. If worse came to worst, they could do some damage.

Shuffling forward to the door, Lila held up the sharp heel of the shoe. There was breathing outside the door, soft and steady. The intruder was so close, only separated from Lila and Bea by inches.

Seconds later, the footsteps receded down the hallway. There was only silence in the room and outside the door. Lila stayed at the door, the stiletto raised and ready until the voice of a police officer filled the apartment, announcing his arrival.

Chapter Twenty-Nine

The police stayed for an hour, inspecting the apartment. The only thing obviously missing was the Primrose accounting records, which Lila had left on the dining room table. The police said there was nothing to indicate the lock was tampered with, meaning someone may have used a key to get in. Evelyn and Jasper were inevitably woken up by the commotion and came next door. Evelyn insisted Bea and Lila spend the rest of the night in her sumptuous guest room under a spotless white coverlet with down pillows so soft, Lila fell asleep immediately.

The following morning, Lila offered to let Bea stay home from school. Lila was worried that Bea was traumatized by the events of the last night, but she seemed fine. She told Evelyn it was exciting hiding under the bed, as if she had been in an actual episode of *Murder, She Wrote*. Apparently, the characters hid under the bed with some regularity. Bea said she would prefer to go to school so she could tell the Detective Club about how she was part of an actual investigation. Lila thought the normalcy of a school day would be good for her.

Lila had no idea how someone had gotten a key to her apartment—Susanna said that there were no missing keys at the front—but Lila wasn't taking any chances and called a locksmith to come later that day. While there was no proof the break-in had anything to do with the murders, Lila was certain it did. The only thing missing was the Primrose accounting information and it seemed like too much of a coincidence that an intruder would have broken into their apartment right after Emily's murder.

After dropping Bea at school, Lila returned home and stopped in the small alcove with the Primrose mailboxes. Detective Roberts clomped into the space behind her and stood still, waiting for her to turn around. Lila didn't react immediately. She took a moment to unlock and pull the mail from her mailbox, buying time to compose herself.

Detective Roberts breathed behind her in clamorous exhales that sent a new quiver of dread through her with every breath.

"Ms. Shaw," Detective Roberts finally said, his voice booming in the small space.

Lila clicked the mailbox shut. "Yes, Detective." She faced him then, backing up to put space between them.

"I heard there was some trouble in your apartment last night," Detective Roberts said.

"There was a break-in," Lila said.

"That's mighty suspicious, isn't it? You have a break-in right as we're investigating you for murder. What do you make of that?"

"I don't know what to make of it except to tell you it was scary."

Detective Roberts snickered, a sound that was less joyous and more menacing. "According to the officers, nothing was missing."

"That's not true. Some papers were missing."

"So you claim." Detective Roberts leaned against the wall. He was wearing a sports coat with threads hanging from the buttonholes. "I looked into you, Ms. Shaw. Found out about your legal troubles back in Norfolk."

Lila swallowed. "Then you know those were my husband's legal troubles, not mine. I was cleared of any wrongdoing."

"The way I understand it is they didn't have the evidence to prove you were involved, but that didn't mean they believed you. Frankly, the FBI thought it was ludicrous you didn't know what was going on under your nose. Your husband stole a lot of money. Were you oblivious or stupid or complicit in the scheme? No one could ever decide. But unlike the feds, I'm not so easy to fool," Detective Roberts said.

"I never thought you were," Lila said.

"You staged that break-in to make yourself look like a victim. I don't buy it. The cute, helpless, innocent act doesn't work with me. You've got a new grift here at the Primrose—living for free in your mom's boyfriend's apartment—and you didn't want to lose your access to all these wealthy elderly folks who you plan to take advantage of."

"That is not true," Lila said.

"Emily Canterbury was the one thing standing between you and your next con. When she threatened to remove you from the building, you had to stop her. You killed her when your daughter was at school. That's despicable."

Lila drew herself up. "It's also false. I would never hurt anyone. Have you looked into the connection between Emily and Sophia Kent? I know Emily contacted the Kent lawyer before she died and said she knew who killed Sophia."

Detective Roberts scoffed. "Oh, come on now. Emily didn't know who killed Sophia. If she did, she would have told someone a long time ago."

"Then how do you explain her calling the lawyer on the day she died?" Lila said.

"Stop stalling, Ms. Shaw."

Detective Roberts took two steps closer until he was only inches from Lila. Lila's back hit the gold turnkeys of the mailboxes. She was trapped in this alcove. If Detective Roberts arrested her, who would break the news to Bea? Lila understood Bea needed time to process her feelings and her defiant exterior often hid a hurt interior. No one else could get through to her like Lila.

"Are you arresting me?" Lila asked. Shallow breaths tugged at her rib cage.

Detective Roberts stared down at her. His brown eyes were flat, a muddy puddle of disdain. Lila willed herself not to look away.

"Not yet," Detective Roberts finally said.

Lila slipped off to the side. "Then we're done talking."

Detective Roberts sneered at her. "We're done talking for now. Next time it will be down at the station in handcuffs. I know you killed Emily Canterbury, and I'm going to prove it. You're better off telling me the truth. It's only going to get worse for you."

A red haze filled Lila's vision. The thought that she could get arrested had seemed more like a bad dream than anything else until this second. This was real, and Detective Roberts would do everything possible to convict her and take away her life with Bea.

"Leave me alone," Lila said and whirled around, heading toward the stairs.

"You're making a mistake," Detective Roberts called after her.

And maybe she was, but she'd rather make a mistake than dissolve into a quivering, crying mess in front of this asshole. It wasn't until she reached the stairwell and let the door swing closed behind her that Lila realized how badly her legs were shaking. She collapsed on the stairs and her entire body shook with great, wrenching sobs.

* * *

LILA DRIED HER tears before returning to her apartment, though she was sure her red face gave her away. Evelyn had insisted on sitting with Lila all day, supervising the steady stream of visitors since the morning. After her run-in with Detective Roberts, Lila was grateful for the company. She didn't want to be alone with spiraling thoughts, all of which eventually came back to her ending up in jail, unable to care for Bea.

Apparently, word had gotten out in the Primrose about the break-in, and Lila was on the "condolence circuit," according to Evelyn. By the time Bea got home from school, Zoe had stopped by with coffee. Brock had brought by a fifth of whiskey and offered to comfort Lila in person, but Evelyn said Lila was too overcome to receive any visitors (she did keep the whiskey, though). The Willoughby sisters had baked her a dessert that they referred to as a better-than-sex cake, and both insisted it wasn't true but they liked the name. Ruth Bailor had written a sympathy note, which suggested Lila might want to vacate the apartment for her own safety, and Alice Kent had dropped off a gift certificate for a pedicure. Bea was reading on the floor of the living room and Evelyn was on the phone, lobbying Susanna to hire personal bodyguards for Lila and herself. There was another knock on the door, and Lila opened it to find Florence and Mary Dixon. They both held out casserole dishes.

"We thought you might be hungry after your ordeal," Mary Dixon said.

"Thanks." Lila was touched. "That's really kind of you."

"I made turkey tetrazzini. It's my mama's famous recipe," Florence said.

Bea appeared at Lila's elbow.

"I made macaroni and cheese. I thought you would like that," Mary Dixon said to Bea.

"Macaroni and cheese is my favorite as long as Mama didn't make it," Bea enthused.

Lila nudged Bea. "Come on, you love my cooking."

"I do love when you burn stuff, and we have to order pizza for dinner," Bea said. "It happens a lot."

Florence and Mary Dixon exchanged glances. Lila swallowed

down a sigh. Someday Bea would stop embarrassing her, but that day wasn't today.

Lila took the casseroles and placed them on the foyer table. "I appreciate this."

Mary Dixon lowered her voice. "We just feel awful for you. I heard there were four intruders ransacking the whole apartment."

"That's true," Bea said without any evidence to support her statement. "But we had a plan where Mama called nine-one-one, and I was going to distract them if they broke down the bedroom door by getting them to chase me into the hallway."

Lila cleared her throat. "That wasn't exactly the plan, and I don't think there were four intruders."

"You're right. There were probably five," Bea said, nodding seriously.

"My heavens," Florence said, her eyes enormous.

"It must have been terrifying," Mary Dixon said, clasping her hands together.

"It was a little," Bea admitted. "But Mama stayed calm the whole time and that kept me calm. We're good under pressure. Right, Mama?"

"That's right," Lila said. Her eyes pricked with tears. Despite all her bluster, Bea was still just a kid who'd been scared last night.

Bea skipped off back toward her room.

"What a brave girl. You let us know if you need anything else. I'm sorry you're dealing with this in our building," Mary Dixon said. "It's normally very safe. I accidentally fell asleep on the lobby couch one night last year."

"More like passed out after too many glasses of wine," Evelyn whispered. She had crept up behind the door, not showing her face to Florence or Mary Dixon.

"And no one took advantage of me despite my vulnerable state. I thought we were all safe here. It's terrible to think we must remain on high alert in our own homes," Mary Dixon continued, oblivious to Evelyn's remark.

"Crime is becoming all too common these days. I hope you're especially careful with a young daughter," Florence said.

"I've already changed the locks," Lila said.

"Quite right. Best to be proactive, dear. In that regard, please do tell Bea that I checked and my Taser does have an age restriction of eighteen and up," Florence said.

"You were talking to Bea about Tasers?" Lila asked.

"Yes, in the lobby when the police were here because of Emily. We were all discussing our various protective methods," Florence said. "Bea was quite interested in hearing more about my Taser."

"I only have a key chain knife," Mary Dixon said, looking upset.

"Sadly, none of our weapons could have saved Emily. I still can't believe she's gone. It makes you realize you can lose people in an instant," Florence said quietly.

Florence's voice was normally so loud and authoritative. It was odd to see her subdued. Lila could have sworn there were tears shining in Florence's eyes.

"I'm sorry. I didn't realize you were close with her," Lila said, reaching out to briefly squeeze Florence's hand.

Florence shook her head. "Thank you, but we weren't close."

"Emily was awful," Mary Dixon said before making the sign of the cross. "May God still rest her soul, of course."

"Of course," Lila said.

Florence glanced down the hall as if searching for something. Lila realized Florence was staring directly at Evelyn's door. Florence's head drooped, her back bowed, and even her Saint Laurent handbag hung limply off her shoulder.

"I wouldn't mind making amends with certain people, especially old friends. As I get older, I can't recall what I was ever mad about in the first place. I don't want to die with any regrets," Florence said. Her eyes were suspiciously bright again.

Lila resisted the urge to turn and look at Evelyn.

Mary Dixon patted Florence's arm. "We're late for canasta."

Florence nodded and looked at Evelyn's door once again before they were off.

Lila closed the door and stared pointedly at Evelyn, who was pretending to study the casserole dishes.

"Florence used the cheap tinfoil. Such a pity. It rips easily and you can't reuse it. Mary Dixon used too much cream in this macaroni and cheese. Bea won't like it," Evelyn said.

"Stop that. Are you going to pretend like you don't know who Florence was talking about just then?" Lila asked.

"I can't imagine what you mean," Evelyn said, avoiding her gaze.

"Florence misses you. I think you should ask her to lunch," Lila said.

Evelyn looked up. Her wrinkles deepened and her lips sagged downward. She looked small and vulnerable. Lila's heart contracted. Evelyn acted as if she was tough and nothing bothered her, but that was far from the truth.

"She hates me," Evelyn said softly.

"I can tell that isn't true. If anything, it seems like she wants to reconcile."

Evelyn tapped her red nails against the silver handle of her walker. "We had an awful fight a year ago. She said some things about my Teddy, and I said some things about her Catherine. Unkind things, you understand. I'm usually a model of diplomacy, but I can be quite cutting in my remarks at times."

"I've noticed that," Lila said neutrally.

Evelyn's throat worked to swallow. "There's a chance Florence only said those things to protect me. She did it in an unacceptable way, highly inappropriate in her language. She's not known for her tact like I am."

"But maybe that's not a reason to hate her forever."

"I suppose there's an argument for your point of view. I find that occasionally, only occasionally, mind you, I miss Florence's company. We did grow up on the same street, and she was my maid of honor. Did you know that?"

Lila rubbed Evelyn's shoulder. Evelyn didn't pull away.

"Sounds like you have an important history with Florence," Lila said.

Evelyn nodded. She bent over to examine the casseroles once more before looking up at Lila. "Florence's casserole is quite terrible, though. Her mama used to make this whenever someone died and it was terrible then too. Well, poor Florence can't help her genes, can she? I should give her one of my recipes for future condolence food."

"You do that." Lila smothered a smile.

She promised herself that she would find a way to arrange a surprise meeting between Florence and Evelyn if they didn't do it themselves in the next week. Those two needed to work out their differences. They couldn't throw away seventy-five years of friendship. And despite Evelyn's protestations, Lila knew she was lonely. No one stopped by to visit her, and she didn't seem to go anywhere. She'd eaten supper by herself every night until she began inviting herself over to Lila's apartment. Evelyn needed to let the past go because Florence was right about one thing—no one wanted to die with regrets.

Chapter Thirty

Lila spotted Helene on the patio through the glass French doors in the Azalea Room when Lila ventured downstairs to get some fresh air later that evening. The sunlight was waning. Shadows gathered in the corners of the garden, tinting the bushes a dark charcoal. Helene's head was tipped up, exposing her long neck. She was sitting on the bench. It reminded Lila of her meeting with Conrad only weeks before, though it seemed as though years had passed since then.

Helene's version of Sophia—the one she'd described the other week in her apartment—was not complete. After all Lila had learned, she had more questions for Helene. Maybe Helene had hidden facts about Sophia to protect her reputation, which Lila understood, but she had to get as much information as possible; her own life depended on it now.

Helene's gaze shifted to Lila when she pushed open the glass door and stepped onto the patio. Helene's face tightened for a brief moment before settling into a gentle, concerned expression with wide eyes and downturned lips.

"How are you? I heard about the break-in," Helene said.

Lila took a seat on the bench beside Helene. "Thanks for your concern. We're okay. It was scary, but luckily no one was hurt."

"And Bea? She's handling the aftermath all right?" Helene asked.

Lila shrugged. "I think she liked the excitement."

Helene nodded. "Children are resilient."

"Sometimes they are," Lila agreed.

"Well then, I'm glad you weren't harmed."

Helene's words sounded final. She was dismissing Lila from the patio. Lila fought her natural instinct to comply. Mama would have told her to smile and make a graceful exit. Ryan would have made a charming joke and ushered Lila back inside. It was awkward to sit out here with someone who wanted her to leave, but she knew Jasper and Evelyn wouldn't budge if they were in the same situation. Evelyn would ask some slightly rude questions, and Jasper would get that determined look on his face and speak in his quiet voice that carried more authority than he seemed to realize.

"Did you know I met Conrad before he died?" Lila asked.

Helene smiled faintly. "Yes, he told me. His health-care aide also mentioned your name when he gave his notice."

Lila swallowed, sensing the unspoken reprimand. "He was a little rough with Conrad, and I tried to help. I didn't mean for him to quit."

"Hmmm" was all Helene said.

The light faded a bit more, the shadows deepening on the patio. The stone pavers bisected with white mortar looked like puzzle pieces. Helene's hands were folded in her lap. She wore a soft black cardigan with pearl buttons, and pearl and diamond earrings.

"I'm sorry again about Conrad's passing. I enjoyed my one conversation with him. It seemed as if y'all were close?" Lila asked, turning it into a question to force Helene into a response.

"We were. My husband died when the girls were young. After that, it was just the three of us and Conrad. He helped raise them. Now that he's gone . . ." Helene trailed off, not finishing the sentiment. "It's been difficult losing him."

"I understand." Lila considered her next words. She had to get

Helene to open up about Sophia. "I get the sense you aren't crazy about the trust Conrad set up."

"No, not particularly. It's stirring up quite a bit of trouble."

"I guess you already know Emily called James Forrester before she died and planned to tell him who killed Sophia."

"James informed me." Helene's face gave nothing away.

"I think Emily's and Sophia's deaths are connected."

"I'm sure you do." Helene turned to face Lila directly. "That would take the police attention off you, wouldn't it?"

Lila met her level gaze. "I didn't kill Emily."

"So you say." Helene's shoulders shifted toward the door again, away from Lila.

It was time for Lila to stop talking around her questions and simply get to the point. "I've learned some things about Sophia these past few weeks. She was having problems right before her death—skipping school and activities, not getting along with her friends. There are allegations of drug use and blackmail too."

"I knew Sophia skipped a class or two and experimented with drugs a few times. She may have gotten into a couple disagreements with friends, but none of that was out of the ordinary for girls her age. Certainly no one was blackmailing Sophia. If she thought that was true, it was only because she was overly dramatic on occasion," Helene said dismissively.

"It sounds like it was more than that. Susanna said that Sophia was secretive and drinking too much those last few months before she died," Lila said. "Did Sophia talk to you or ask for help?"

"Susanna told you about the psychiatrist, didn't she?" Helene's mouth tightened. "It's true I didn't think Sophia needed to see a professional, and I told her so when she asked. She was having a few difficulties. Nothing we couldn't handle."

The hair on the back of Lila's neck rose at Helene's unwitting revelation. Lila had not known Sophia wanted to see a psychiatrist and she didn't think Susanna knew either. That fact suggested Sophia was struggling with something before she died. She thought of the journal entry, the forged checks, the secretive phone calls. Was it all about her drug use or something else?

"What kind of difficulties was Sophia having?" Lila asked.

"They weren't significant, I can assure you." Helene waved a hand at her words as if to wave away the mere suggestion that there was a problem with Sophia. "Sophia overreacted to things like most teenage girls. She was quite headstrong at times, but I had it under control. She would have been fine."

But Sophia wasn't fine. She was dead. Helene had tried to fix Sophia's mistakes and hide her problems, and it hadn't worked. In the end, her control hadn't mattered.

Lila could see it now. Control was a slippery slope when it came to daughters. She wanted Bea safe and sometimes needed her to listen. But she also wanted a girl who was confident and independent. Neither of those qualities were controlled. They were sometimes unmanageable and wild, just like Bea. Mama had made sure Lila was under control when she was growing up, and Lila had carried that same restraint into her own unhappy marriage to Ryan. She wasn't exactly sure how to balance it all, but control over her daughter wasn't what she wanted. She didn't want to be her mama or Helene.

Lila chose her next words carefully. "Do you think there's a chance that if Sophia wanted to see a psychiatrist, she thought the problems were more significant than you did? Significant enough to lead to her death?"

Helene eyed Lila, her lip curling at the edges. "I've seen the articles about your husband in the newspaper. That's quite a public scandal. Please understand me when I say this. We aren't like you. Our family handles problems privately when they arise. We don't collapse and make a fuss, and we don't announce our issues to the world." She stood, her face icy and distant. "If you'll excuse me."

Lila stood halfway. "Wait, Helene. Don't you want to know what happened to your daughter?"

Helene stilled. "I know what happened to my daughter. She died. You can't understand what it means to lose a child until it happens to you. I hope it doesn't. I wouldn't wish that fate on anyone. I live with her death constantly."

Despite Helene's insults, Lila was truly sorry for her. No one told you in advance that motherhood came with a prescription for a daily dose of fear. It only got worse when your child stepped out into the world without you.

"I know it's hard to talk about her but—"

"No, you don't." Helene's face hardened. "And I won't see Sophia's reputation destroyed, and Alice dragged down with some unsavory allegations about her sister. I suggest you drop this line of inquiry immediately. It's upsetting to me, and if it continues, I will make sure to call Stanley Ranger and the Primrose Board and everyone else I can think of to have you removed from this building."

Helene turned and strode off the patio, her heels clicking on the stone.

Lila sank down onto the bench. Helene wasn't president of the board like Ruth but she had even more power and sway over this community. Mama had made it clear if Stanley got any more complaints, Lila would have to vacate the Primrose. A complaint from the connected, intimidating Helene Kent would certainly be the last straw for Lila. The problem was if Lila stopped digging into Sophia's murder, she might end up in jail herself.

Despite Helene's threat, Lila called Susanna immediately to ask if she was aware Sophia had wanted to see a psychiatrist before her death. Susanna professed ignorance and the lack of knowledge seemed to sadden her.

"I'm starting to feel like I didn't know her at all," Susanna said.

Lila tried to reassure her. "Mental health is so personal; Sophia didn't know how to tell you." Lila didn't have the heart to tell Susanna she might be right; no one knew the real Sophia.

* * *

BEA WAS ALREADY in bed, and Lila was straightening up the family room when her cell phone rang later that night. It was an unfamiliar number with a Norfolk area code. Lila's entire body tensed. What if it was Stanley on the other end of the line, calling to tell her to get out of the apartment because Helene had already made good on her threat?

"Hello?" Lila answered tentatively, her hand rigid against the phone.

"Ms. Shaw, this is Gerald Partridge, your husband's lawyer. I'm sorry to call you so late in the evening, but I have some news."

Lila wasn't sure if this was better or worse than Stanley. The last time Gerald had news, she'd lost her house. "What is it?"

"Ryan was apprehended in Honduras earlier today by the FBI. He's on his way back to the United States."

Lila's legs wobbled. She sank down to the couch, her back pressing into the cushions. There was a noise in her ear like rushing water, and Gerald's voice sounded as if he was speaking to her from the bottom of a river. All the vowels were jumbled, the consonants slurred.

"I—I'm sorry," Lila interrupted. "Are you saying Ryan was arrested?"

"Yes, I'm saying exactly that," Gerald said. "I spoke to him briefly, and he wanted me to call and let you know so you could tell Bea."

Tell Bea? How did Lila explain any of this to her daughter? She didn't want to tell Bea her father was going to jail, and her parents were getting divorced.

"Okay," Lila said faintly, still trying to process this information. "What happens next?"

"As you know, Ryan was charged with conspiracy and fraud last fall. There's a trial coming up in Norfolk. He will plead not guilty," Gerald said.

"But he—he fled the country."

"Yes, and that doesn't help his case. There will certainly be additional charges related to that behavior, but it doesn't change the fact that there is little evidence against him. We're going to fight this thing."

Ryan was accused of working with a fraudulent telemedicine company to submit thousands of false claims to Medicare for reimbursement, paying illegal kickbacks and bribes for patients, and stealing from his own company. He had fraudulently billed the government for twenty-two million dollars.

"I don't understand. It was his company," Lila said.

"True, but Ryan relied on his CFO to manage the finances and oversee the medical reimbursements, and he himself was unaware of any fraudulent behavior."

But that didn't make sense. Ryan had always been involved in every aspect of the business. That's the way he liked to run his company.

Gerald continued. "Of course the CFO has a different story, but there's no evidence of any communications between your husband and the telemedicine company involved in the fraud. Aside from all that, there's no money trail between Ryan and the fraudulently obtained funds. Someone moved that money into an untraceable offshore account before the FBI raid. All I care about is there's nothing to prove it was your husband."

Lila was lightheaded, unable to respond. Gerald talked some more about the court procedure and promised to keep Lila updated on the next steps for Ryan's case before getting off the phone.

Afterward, Lila sat motionless in the darkened room. Her brain considered this latest development, swirling it around like froth on a wave. Ryan was pleading not guilty. Was it possible he was innocent? She didn't believe it.

Ryan's face was suddenly there behind her eyelids—the firm jawline, the blue eyes, the little half-smile at her over the kitchen table when Bea said something funny. They used to walk around their first neighborhood every weekend talking about plans for the future. He'd paced the hallway with Bea when she had those terrible high fevers, insisting Lila sleep. Ryan would scoop Bea up and turn her upside down to make her laugh when she was on the verge of a tantrum. It wasn't all bad.

And yet, it wasn't good.

Lila hadn't spoken up when Ryan skipped meals for last-minute pickleball games or work dinners. Instead, she'd seethed inside, ignoring him when he got home. She'd stopped asking about the business because she felt she wasn't a part of it anymore. When Ryan had turned over in bed to look at her expectantly, she'd pretended to sleep because she hadn't wanted him. Sex had felt like too much work for years. Yes, he'd left her and fled the country and destroyed their life with fraud—she'd probably never forgive him for that—but it wasn't the sole reason their marriage was over.

The marriage was over because they no longer loved each other, and that had happened well before Ryan left town. They had nothing in common any longer except Bea, no reason to stay together except their daughter. Lila had told herself that was enough and things might get better someday, but she didn't really believe it.

Two miserable parents didn't make a happy family or a happy life. Yet telling that to Bea was not something she wanted to do. Lila wanted her daughter to remain innocent, still hoping her father would resume his life with them. She wanted her daughter to have both parents at home in the way Lila hadn't.

Pain pulsed behind her eyes, and her throat tightened almost painfully. How would Lila tell Bea that Ryan was back . . . but he wasn't coming home to them?

Chapter Thirty-One

Lila had intended to cancel her dinner with Nate, not wanting to leave Bea alone after the break-in and the news about Ryan's arrest, which she was still keeping to herself. But Bea came home from school in a great mood, relaying a story about how she had described the entire break-in to her class during their sharing circle that morning. Zoe then stopped by the apartment to get Lila's opinion on the signature cocktail for the club's opening party. When she heard Lila planned to stay in, Zoe insisted on watching Bea herself. She offered to paint Bea's nails, and Bea clapped her hands and rushed off to finish her homework before the manicure. There was nothing else for Lila to do but go to dinner.

Lila arranged to meet Nate at the restaurant. She applied makeup and put on her Proenza Schouler dress. She only regretted her efforts when Bea caught sight of her and frowned. "You can't outrun a murderer in a dress that tight," Bea said. Lila mumbled something about *having a business meeting and not a murderer meeting* and fled from the apartment while pretending not to see Zoe winking at her. There was nothing to wink about. This wasn't a date, she kept reminding herself.

The restaurant was close by, nestled between a high-end gift shop and a specialty grocer. She walked in to a gleaming wood bar with sparkling bottles on glass shelves behind it. The decor was dim lighting and white tablecloths. A fire crackled from the fireplace in the corner. Voices murmured below soft, old-fashioned jazz.

Lila spotted Nate in the back at a small table set slightly apart from the others. He stood when she approached, a wide smile on his face. He appeared to have combed his hair for once.

"You look great," Nate said, leaning over to kiss her on the cheek.

Her cheek throbbed where his lips had landed. Lila was momentarily flustered, almost tripping over one of the heels she'd borrowed from Gloria's closet. She backed up into her seat.

Lila noted that he had a glass in front of him filled with ice cubes, a lime, and the remnants of a drink. "Am I late? I thought we said seven."

Nate laughed ruefully. "You are right on time. I got here a half hour early. I wanted to get this table in the back. And I guess I was excited."

Lila's cheeks warmed. Now she was especially glad she hadn't canceled, although this was only a quick dinner. Between friends.

"I could use a glass of wine," Lila said. "It's been a long week."

Nate motioned to the waitress and asked for her wine suggestions, listening carefully to her descriptions. Ryan had always looked around as their waiter talked about the specials, eager to return to the conversation at the table and whatever funny story he had been telling.

"The pinot please," Lila said when the waitress finished speaking.

The waitress nodded and left the table.

"Tell me about this long week," Nate said.

Lila raised her eyebrows. "Do you want the good news or the bad news?"

Nate sat back, looking amused. "I'll take both."

"The good news is I'm not under arrest yet. The bad news is

someone broke into my apartment." She said it lightly as if it was a joke, though of course it was deadly serious.

Nate's eyes darkened. "Holy shit, Lila. Were you home during the break-in?"

Lila inclined her head. "Yep."

"That must have been horrifying. What time was this? Was anyone hurt?"

"No one was hurt. The police got there before anything happened. It's not that big of a deal."

"It's a huge deal. Are you kidding?"

"We're both fine," Lila assured him.

Nate's fists clenched on the table as if he was going to somehow defend her, which was ridiculous because he barely knew her and he wasn't there during the break-in. Still, Lila found herself utterly transfixed by his reaction. She shifted in her seat, imagining what it would have been like if Nate had been there, how he might have defended her. But if he had been there, he probably would have been in her bed *with her*.

"Was anything stolen? Do the police have a suspect? Where are you staying?" Nate fired off questions one after another, quickly, like bullets exploding from his mouth.

Lila held up a hand to calm him. Maybe this was what it was like to date a reporter. Not that they were dating. They were *friends*.

"As far as I can tell, the only thing missing was some paperwork. The police don't have a suspect, and we've been sleeping in our apartment because I already changed the locks."

"Are you scared?" Nate asked.

Lila considered his question that went right to the heart of the entire issue. Her first instinct was to make a joke but what came out of her mouth was the truth. "A little, but I don't have anywhere else to go and I'm not going to let someone scare me away."

Nate studied Lila. "I respect that. If this helps, it's a safe building in general. I researched the Primrose history as part of my article, and I've found no criminal activity since Sophia Kent and those robberies in 2002." He drummed his fingers on the table. "I'm sure you already considered this, but the break-in has to be connected to Emily Canterbury, right?"

"I thought that too. The entire building knows I'm a suspect in Emily's murder. The intruder might think I have evidence proving I was involved in her death."

Nate nodded thoughtfully. "That, or they could think you had evidence pointing to someone else. Evelyn did announce you were investigating Sophia's murder."

"You heard that," Lila said.

"It was hard to miss. She made sure to tell everyone." Nate grinned.

"Nate? Hi!"

A woman stopped at their table, a big smile on her face. She wore a bohemian red and blue dress and a wrist full of gold bangles. Her dark hair was twisted into a casual knot at the back of her head. Nate stood up and kissed her on the cheek.

"Lila Shaw, this is Jennie Blair," Nate said, gesturing to the woman who was now directing that smile down at Lila. "My ex-wife."

Lila had googled Jennie after he'd mentioned her name the other day. Her gold bracelets with their intricate filigree designs were featured in *Harper's BAZAAR* last year, and Lila could see why. She was talented, beautiful, and a little intimidating.

Lila started to stand, and Jennie waved her back down. "Please don't get up. I'm interrupting, I know. But I couldn't resist coming over. Now I see why Nate wouldn't stop talking about you."

Nate shook his head and sank back into his seat. "Really, Jennie?"

Jennie laughed. "What? You haven't mentioned anyone in such a long time. I can't help being curious after you kept talking about Lila, the gorgeous woman who stole your table."

He'd discussed her with his ex-wife and called her gorgeous? Jennie looked genuinely delighted to meet Lila, and Nate didn't seem anxious or uncomfortable around his ex-wife. He rolled his eyes but in a way that showed he found her funny rather than irritating.

"Actually he stole *my* table," Lila said, raising her eyebrows at Nate.

Nate leaned toward Lila, a little smile on his lips, seeming to forget about Jennie entirely for the moment.

"I guess you two have worked out your furniture differences," Jennie said.

"I think your friends are calling you over," Nate said, still gazing at Lila.

Jennie held up her hands as if surrendering. "I'll go. I can see how meeting the ex-wife isn't the best way to start a first date. Really nice to see you, Lila."

"You too," Lila said.

Jennie waved and sashayed away toward the front of the restaurant.

Nate groaned. "I swear I didn't tell her this was a date. She sometimes jumps to conclusions."

"She seems great, and it's fine," Lila said.

Nate wasn't kidding when he said he had a good relationship with Jennie. There was unmistakable warmth between them. Would she and Ryan ever have that? Right now, she couldn't imagine it.

Lila's wine appeared. They ordered salads and pasta. She took a sip of her drink. The liquid traveled down her throat and into her stomach, warming its way through her body.

"How did you become an amateur detective anyway?" Nate asked.

"I would not call myself any kind of detective. The investigation started out as a way to entertain my daughter."

"Your daughter likes murder investigations?"

"Loves them." Lila laughed. "Bea's favorite hobby is murder."

Lila thought about Bea's wild theories and her way of convincing anyone, even grown-ups, to participate in her schemes. It was impressive. No one could call her ordinary.

"You said it 'started out' as a way to entertain Bea. But what about now?" Nate asked.

Lila shrugged. "Now I'm investigating because I don't have a choice. We—meaning Jasper, Evelyn, and I—think Sophia's death is connected to Emily's." She explained how Emily had called James Forrester on the day she died.

Nate sat back. "That's quite a motive."

"The problem is the lead detective seems to have settled on me as his prime suspect and isn't interested in any other motives except mine," Lila said, grimacing. "Jasper thinks if we can find enough new information about Sophia's murder, the police will look into the connection between her death and Emily's."

"It's not a bad idea," Nate mused. "I can include the connection between the two deaths in my article too. It could at least help with public opinion."

"That would be great. And you've already helped some. You told us Sophia had drugs in her system when she died."

Nate nodded, looking pleased. "I found a retired cop who had worked on the case. He's the one who told me about the drugs. Apparently, the family was able to keep it out of the press. They're a powerful bunch—the Kents. They held a lot of sway over what did and didn't make it into the news."

"It was a good tip because since then, I talked to a witness who says Sophia owed money to a drug dealer."

"You're good at getting people to open up." Nate's gaze was fixed on Lila. His green eyes glowed in the candlelight.

Lila flushed. "It was nothing."

"It wasn't nothing. Do you know how hard it is to convince someone to trust you with their secrets?"

Lila sipped her wine, taking a moment to compose herself. She didn't want Nate to see how flattered she was by his assessment. She was used to people underestimating her. Half of Norfolk thought she was a clueless idiot after Ryan left her. But with Nate it was the opposite. If anything, he gave her too much credit.

"How is your article coming?" Lila asked.

"It's a different portrait of Sophia Kent. I'm not here to crucify a sixteen-year-old dead girl, but I hope a more honest account of who Sophia was might show people that we're all human. No one is a saint."

Lila waited for him to ask her the name of the witness who had told her about Sophia's connection to the drug dealer. He must have wanted that information for his article but Nate nodded to Lila's glass. "Do you want some more wine?"

Lila frowned, unable to stop herself from asking, "Don't you want the name of the witness I found?"

"Not if you don't want to tell me. And I wouldn't want to spook the witness and risk screwing up your investigation."

Lila could tell he meant it. He'd rather forgo a scoop for his article if it meant helping her. She had misjudged him entirely when he'd stolen her table at the coffee shop. He was a good guy, concerned about other people, and definitely not a jerk. She found herself liking him more the longer she talked to him, and she couldn't deny that he was good-looking. Really, really good-looking.

The realization of the extent of her attraction crashed into her all at once. Her stomach flipped. She *liked* him. He was the kind of person she could really care about if given the time and opportunity. But Lila had no interest in falling for anyone again; not after what had happened with Ryan. Her entire life was turned upside down; her expectations and plans for their future crushed. Lila had cried every day for months and she'd struggled to get out of bed for weeks. Her mind would snap back incessantly to their final conversation as if the memory was a magnet. Even though she knew she was better off without Ryan, his rejection of her and their life was a scar she would carry forever.

Lila couldn't put herself through that pain again. It was better for her to focus on Bea and not get distracted by another man who would only let her down, especially one like Nate. The truth was she'd rather be alone. It was better to struggle with occasional loneliness than risk another broken heart.

Lila suddenly pushed back her chair and stood up. "I have to go."

Nate rose, looking alarmed. "Is everything okay?"

"I forgot Bea has a big project due tomorrow. I need to help her with it," Lila lied.

"Could you wait for our meal to come out first?" Nate asked.

Lila shook her head. She didn't trust herself to spend more time in his company. "I can't. I'm sorry. You're a great guy."

Nate frowned, his eyes crinkled at the edges. He looked upset and hurt. "Did I say the wrong thing?"

"Just the opposite. Really. But I have to go." Lila spun around and walked out of the restaurant. She didn't turn to wave or smile one last time. She couldn't. She was afraid if she did, she would return to the table and find him even funnier and kinder and more handsome than she already did. Lila wouldn't risk another disappointment. She couldn't pin her future on anyone but her daughter and herself.

Chapter Thirty-Two

Lila lay awake for some time. Her mind ran on a loop, replaying her dinner with Nate, her abrupt departure, and that sad look on his face before she walked away. She was still thinking about it the following morning when she put on her tennis shoes.

"I'm ready," Bea called from the living room.

Lila pulled her hair back into a ponytail as she left the room. Should she call Nate? They weren't really friends. They weren't anything, and now they never would be. She hoped he wasn't too upset with her.

Bea was standing by the door, her backpack already slung over her shoulders. Lila still hadn't told her about Ryan's arrest and how their life would never go back to normal. Lila dreaded hurting her daughter. Her stomach cramped.

"Finish your breakfast before we leave," Lila said briskly to cover her unease.

"But I don't feel like eating eggs this morning," Bea said. "My friend Evie only eats what she wants. Her mama said it's important for parents to accept their kids' feelings about food and to not judge them."

Lila had never heard of Evie's mama until this very second, but Lila already didn't like her much.

"Evie's mama said we should listen to our bodies when it comes to food," Bea continued.

"Interesting. And what does Evie's body normally tell her to eat for breakfast?"

"Pop-Tarts," Bea said hopefully. "Those feel right to Evie and me too. We could pick some up on the way to school."

"Well unfortunately for you, Pop-Tarts don't feel right to me, so you can eat these eggs and get some protein, which will help you to focus better in school, or you can grab a piece of bread from the pantry."

Bea frowned. "Pop-Tarts have fruit in them. That's healthy."

Lila glanced at her phone, noting the time. She wasn't going to argue. "If we wait too much longer, you'll miss the sharing circle. Your call."

Bea stalked to the table and took two large bites of egg. "It was worth a try."

"You made a pretty good case," Lila agreed.

"I know." Bea ate another bite.

Lila was relieved and a little disbelieving that Bea had given in without much protest. She could handle this parenting thing—unless she went to jail. *Jail*. The very idea dissolved every other thought in her brain. Her balance teetered. She clutched at the couch to steady herself. Why was she worrying about Nate or Ryan or anything else when her life was on the verge of another total implosion?

After dropping Bea at school, Lila headed straight to Jasper's apartment. The space was sparse with dark leather couches and iron chairs, none of which looked like Jasper. The only thing that did look like it belonged to him was the kitchen. Bea's homemade thank-you card was taped to the refrigerator door, the well-used mixing stand perched on the counter, and large glass containers of flour and sugar stood nearby.

"This place could use some color," Evelyn sniffed and sat down on one of the chairs.

"George decorated it before he left," Jasper said.

"It's nice there's no clutter," Lila said diplomatically.

Lila secretly thought the apartment was depressing but didn't want to hurt Jasper's feelings. The place reminded her of what her own house had begun to look like after Ryan left. She had to sell off pieces of furniture and art, leaving pockets of empty space; a daily reminder of everything she'd lost.

"I was always reluctant to change anything. Everyone says George has great taste," Jasper said, looking around a little uncertainly.

"I disagree. After all, he let you go," Evelyn said.

Jasper cleared his throat and looked away, smiling a little. Lila could tell he was embarrassed and pleased. She wanted to hug Evelyn.

"I thought about buying some red pillows for the couch," Jasper said, taking the seat beside Lila.

"Red isn't my favorite color, but I suppose it's a start," Evelyn said. "Now, have the police said anything about the piles of evidence we've turned over? We're essentially doing their jobs for them."

Jasper shook his head. "Not much. My sources tell me Craig Roberts continues to insist Lila is responsible for Emily's death." He turned to Lila. "It might be time to engage a lawyer. If he tries to question you again, you need one with you."

A lawyer meant money she didn't have. Lila winced at the thought of her bank account. "Thanks for checking with the police."

"You know, I haven't minded," Jasper said, sounding surprised. "It was nice to talk to some of my old colleagues. Speaking of, I was able to get my hands on the abridged version of Sophia Kent's case file. I made a FOIA request weeks ago. We've got witness summaries, investigator notes, photos of the crime scene, and the medical examiner report. I reviewed most of it last night and came up with a new lead."

"Don't keep us in suspense," Evelyn demanded.

"The police talked to Lionel Garrett on several occasions. He's an antiques dealer. At the time, he was a known fence for stolen goods. The police could never pin anything on him but suspected his involvement in the 2002 robberies."

"I understand perfectly. You want us to interrogate this Lionel Garrett," Evelyn said. "Good idea. Sophia's drug dealer is a dead end after all these years."

"I don't know about that, but we should approach Lionel. Enough time has passed that we could catch him off guard. He might trip up and tell us something useful," Jasper said.

Lila took the file and flipped through the pages. She stopped at the photo of Sophia strewn across her grandfather's kitchen floor; her limbs askew, her short dress tangled around her body, her legs ending in a pair of CHANEL heels. There was a gaping red slash in her arm and a wide pool of blood around her torso. It was the first time Lila had seen a murder photo that wasn't on a true crime TV show.

Jasper nodded to the file. "The knife severed the brachial artery in her arm. Without treatment, she lost consciousness and bled out."

"It's horrible." Lila looked at the photo more closely.

There was something about the photo that bothered Lila; it was the first time she was facing real violence without the filter of a news broadcaster. She shut the file, wanting to clear the image of Sophia's lifeless body from her vision. Terrible things had happened in this very building. They could happen anywhere.

Evelyn stomped on the floor to draw their attention. "I suppose we'll have to go undercover to interrogate this Lionel fellow." She sighed as if this was a terrible thing for her to endure. Her gleaming eyes said otherwise.

Jasper shifted in his seat, looking uncomfortable. "I thought we could just visit his shop and ask him a few questions."

"That won't work. He will kick us right out of his shoddy little store. We have to lull him into trusting us. I understand how these antiques dealers work. I've got plenty of experience with haggling," Evelyn said.

Lila exchanged a look with Jasper. "I agree with Jasper. We should be honest and—"

"Honesty is overrated in a criminal investigation," Evelyn cut her off. "Lila, pull together a box of junk from Gloria's apartment—ceramics and assorted china should work—and let's meet downstairs in twenty minutes. I'll explain the plan on the way."

Evelyn's voice left no room for further argument, and Lila had to admit she would try anything to come up with a break in Sophia's case that could also eliminate herself as a suspect in Emily's murder. Within a half hour, they were driving through the West End in Jasper's Honda toward a neighborhood near the downtown area.

Lionel Garrett's antique store was tucked away on a side street between a butcher and a small cafe. The sign was blue with gilt lettering: *Garrett Antiques*. The front window held a display of an old typewriter, a dark wood desk with elaborately carved legs, and two chairs with needlepoint backs.

They pushed open the glass door to Lionel's shop. A bell jingled, announcing their arrival. From the back, a gentleman emerged in a navy sweater, dark charcoal slacks, and carefully combed white hair.

Lila lifted the box in greeting. "I heard you purchase on consignment."

"I'm the owner, Lionel Garrett. Nice to see you." Lionel came forward, extending his hand to Evelyn first, then Jasper. Lila's hands were full, but he nodded at her too.

The shop itself was dim, crowded with various items. There was plenty of furniture—old dining chairs, a beautiful burl wood table, Swedish grey end tables, several camelback sofas covered in faded upholstery. On the shelves surrounding each wall were rows of books, figurines, teacups, and plates with painted flowers. The walls had dark oil paintings of serious men with beards, sailboats, and country estates. The floors were covered in red and gold Persian rugs. Toward the back was a small counter with a register and the glimpse of an office beyond.

"I'll need a few minutes to look at your items. Feel free to browse in the meantime," Lionel said, taking the box from Lila.

Lila walked down the aisles taking in the various items. Patricia was an antiques aficionado. When she was still trying to mold Lila into a proper wife for Ryan, Patricia had taken her to some places like this in Palm Beach. Lila had bought whatever Patricia told her to, too afraid to express her own opinion at the time. She had learned a few things from her mother-in-law about antiques. To Lila's eyes, the store and everything in it looked legitimate. She feared this whole excursion was a bust.

Evelyn stopped at a particular chest, walking around it. "This is quite a good example of early eighteenth-century craftsman." Her voice was begrudging. "He does have some nice things."

Lionel appeared at the end of the aisle. "There are a few pieces I can take. You get fifty percent of the profit. How does that sound?"

"That sounds fine," Lila said.

Lila followed Lionel back to the counter. She eyed Jasper and Evelyn, who pretended to look at a shelf of rare books. According to Evelyn's plan, this was where things would get interesting.

"Some of these bird figurines are quite good sellers. Nothing too rare here, but you've got a few lovely specimens," Lionel said.

Lila stood by the register. Lionel handed her an information form and a pen. From her vantage point, she could see into Lionel's small office behind the register area. There was a heavy wooden desk, a high-backed chair with tapestry upholstery, and a cozy threadbare patterned rug. His desk contained a laptop, a stained glass lamp, and a small collection of ceramic animal figurines—a horse, a sheep, and an octopus.

"I must say I'm impressed with your inventory," Evelyn said.

"Thank you," Lionel demurred. "I noticed you admiring the armchair in the corner. It's Biedermeier nineteenth century. If you're interested, it's one of a matching pair."

"I already have two similar chairs in my living room. But I am always looking for new antiques. I understand you're the place to go for certain *specialty items*." Evelyn emphasized the words and widened her eyes as she said them.

"I go on several buying trips a year and have some wonderful pieces in my storage unit. If you tell me what you're looking for, I may be able to accommodate you," Lionel said.

"What about rarer pieces, the ones that don't normally come on the market. Can you help us with those too?" Jasper asked.

Lionel gave Jasper a tight smile. "Again, I simply need an idea of what you're looking for. I'll help if I can."

"What kind of help can you give? Is it the kind that's not available to the general public?" Evelyn asked.

Was it Lila's imagination or was Evelyn beginning to sound like a stereotypical mob boss; vaguely threatening and with a slight New Jersey accent?

Lionel shrugged. "I'm afraid I don't know what you're asking for."

"I think you do," Evelyn said.

Lila risked a glance at Lionel's expression. His lips were pursed in annoyance. This plan was going south fast.

Jasper leaned in over the counter. "We understand there are some things only certain customers are allowed to see. We'd like to see those items."

Evelyn opened her handbag and pulled out a large wad of cash. Lila's eyes went wide. She'd never seen that much money in one person's hand.

"We've brought untraceable funds," Evelyn said.

Lionel stepped back. His face was tense, set into tiny lines of displeasure. "I'm sorry. I don't think I can help you. This is an aboveboard establishment. I don't have certain items that I only show to special customers. All my antiques are of impeccable provenance, and they are available to everyone via credit card, debit card, or cash if you prefer."

"I get it. You're playing hardball. Two can play at that game. We have some questions for you," Evelyn said, shoving the cash back into her Gucci handbag.

Lionel crossed his arms over his chest. He looked furious.

The atmosphere was tense and stifling. Lila couldn't even look at Lionel. Her vision tunneled to the figurines on Lionel's desk. Lionel spoke, something about being outraged and offended. Evelyn raised her voice back and, yes, there was the slight New Jersey accent again. A voice whispered in the back of Lila's mind. What was it she needed to remember? Something about an octopus . . .

The answer snapped into her head. She stepped back suddenly, tripping over a stool, startling herself with the revelation. They all went silent, staring at her.

Catherine Lee had an octopus stolen, a rare Herend piece. Surely this wasn't it. It would be crazy for Lionel to display a stolen piece. Although . . . it was in his private office and it had been twenty-one years. After that long, someone might get sloppy, cocky even, thinking there was no way they would get caught.

Stepping around the counter, Lila strode into Lionel's office. She picked up the octopus.

"Excuse me?" Lionel said from behind her. "That room is off-limits to customers."

Lila turned over the octopus, noting the Herend seal on the bottom, the blue spots on the eight legs, the jeweled eyes, and the chip in the front leg. *The chip.* June had said the octopus had a chip in the leg. There was no doubt. This was Catherine Lee's stolen octopus.

"That is a delicate piece. Put that down immediately and leave the store before I call the police." Lionel's voice wobbled over the words.

"Where did you get this?" Lila asked, clutching it in her hands.

"I don't know. I've had it for some time," Lionel said.

"Have you had it for twenty-one years? Because that's how long ago it was stolen from the Primrose," Lila said.

Jasper looked at Lila. "Are you certain?"

"June Willoughby described it perfectly. Catherine Lee had a rare Herend octopus with a chip in its leg exactly like this one," Lila said.

"I don't traffic in stolen goods. I'm sure this is a mistake or a duplicate," Lionel blustered, but his face was red with fear. "You can't be serious."

Jasper stepped up to him. Jasper's shoulders seemed to widen, his chin set firmly. He looked straight into Lionel's eyes. "You better tell us exactly how you came into possession of this figurine or I'm going straight to the police. I am a retired detective, and I guarantee they will take me seriously."

Lionel deflated and leaned heavily against the counter.

"We're waiting," Jasper said. "You tell us or you tell the cops."

Lionel sighed. "It's not what you think. I wasn't lying before. I don't take stolen goods, not knowingly. But back when I was getting started, I may have overlooked the provenance of some pieces. I'll admit I made some questionable decisions in those early days. Working with that woman was one of them."

"What woman?" Evelyn asked.

"I don't know who she was or even what she looked like. She convinced me to meet her in a parking garage at night. She was wearing a trench coat and a hat pulled over her face and a cheap black wig. She brought me a few boxes of valuable ceramics, jewelry, silver, and glassware," Lionel said.

"You must have known they were stolen. You don't meet someone in a parking garage at night in a disguise if you're not hiding something," Jasper said.

"I'm not admitting to anything except to say that there was a network back then, a pipeline for stolen goods. The people involved were pros. This woman was not part of that network," Lionel said.

"How did she find you?" Lila prompted.

"No idea. She called me out of the blue and wanted to meet. She's the one who brought me the octopus."

"How many times did you meet with her?" Jasper asked.

"A handful. All in the parking garage. I would assess the inventory, we would agree on a price, and then we met again and I brought her the money." Lionel hung his head.

"When was this?" Lila said.

"It was back in 2002, right before I opened this shop. The sale from those items gave me enough money to afford the down payment." Lionel looked miserable.

"You never told the police." Jasper said it as a statement.

Lionel was quiet but his silence was answer enough.

Evelyn sniffed. "Sir, you are no gentleman, and I am going to inform all of my friends they should not shop here."

Lila knew she needed to get him to tell her everything possible. He was scared, hoping they wouldn't turn him in. This was the opportunity to get information.

"There must have been something distinguishing about this woman. Hair color, eye color, anything?" Lila asked.

Lionel shook his head. "I can't remember. I never got a good look at her face but—" He stopped, thinking hard. "There was something. She pushed up the sleeve of her trench coat when she was handing me one of the boxes. There was a birthmark on her inner arm near her elbow. It looked like a four-leaf clover. I only remember because I thought she was going to need all the luck she could get."

"What about her car? You said you met her in a parking garage. Did you see what car she drove?" Jasper asked.

"It was something dark. I don't know. I remember there was a small pink sticker on the back windshield. That's it," Lionel said.

Evelyn, Lila, and Jasper all stared at each other. The pink sticker sounded like the Primrose parking emblem. They'd suspected the burglar was a resident of the Primrose, but now it was confirmed. More than that, they knew the burglar was a woman.

Lila stood up, still holding the octopus. "I'm taking this back to Catherine's family."

"Are you going to turn me in?" Lionel asked.

Jasper gave him a withering glance. "I'm a detective. Yes, I'm going to turn you in."

"I'll deny everything," Lionel said.

Jasper held open the door for Evelyn and Lila. "Good luck with that."

Chapter Thirty-Three

Jasper dropped Lila and Evelyn back at the Primrose, then went straight to the police station to explain what they had learned from Lionel. Lila walked through the wooden double doors into the now familiar marble lobby.

She gazed fondly around at the weekly flower arrangement, this one made of peonies and roses, at the taupe velvet sofas and the grand piano. She felt her shoulders relax. In a short time, Lila had grown to appreciate the calm of the hushed lobby. The shimmering gold finishes, soft upholstery, and welcoming faces promised graciousness and comfort. Even with the break-in, this place felt safe.

Evelyn continued up to her apartment, but Lila had arranged to meet Zoe for coffee in the Hydrangea Room and headed straight there. Florence and Mary Dixon sat at a table with a pile of knitting material. Lila stopped, assessing them with fresh eyes. They looked so innocent and harmless, and maybe they were, but one of the women in this building had robbed several apartments and possibly killed Sophia Kent and Emily Canterbury. All of them were potential suspects now, as much as she hated to think of it.

Zoe was waiting at another table with two cups of coffee. They'd agreed to have a quick meeting about the club opening. Lila had continued to post on social media—an artful photo of a flower from the proposed table arrangements, a photo of the headliner band, a picture of the signature cocktail, and a black-and-white shot of the unassuming entrance with the caption *Do you know the password?* Their Instagram following grew every day.

Lila settled into the chair across from Zoe. She wanted to get upstairs and make a list of burglary suspects but that would have to wait.

"Are you ready for this?" Zoe asked. "We sold out opening night!"

"You're joking," Lila exclaimed.

"I wouldn't joke about that," Zoe said.

"We bought tickets," Florence said, overhearing the conversation. "Most of the building is going."

"Edwin is hoping to meet his next wife," Mary Dixon said. "He said music makes women more open to commitment."

"I can confirm that." Teddy walked in then. His tight jeans belonged on someone twenty-five years younger.

"I saw you two and thought I'd make sure we are set on logistics for next weekend," Teddy said.

"I understand you've already spoken to Jim, our sound guy," Zoe said.

"Yep. Okay for us to come by Saturday afternoon for a quick rehearsal to get the feel of the space?" Teddy asked.

"Of course. I'll be there all day," Zoe said.

"Perfect," Teddy said. "The guys are pumped. We've put it on our socials and sent out emails to everyone we know."

"Thanks for spreading the word," Lila said. Maybe he wasn't as big of a jerk as she thought. He may have helped to make the party a success.

Teddy smirked at Lila. "I hope you'll be there. People say I'm a natural on the stage."

And he was back to being an asshole.

"Please don't get all modest on us," Lila said wryly.

Zoe shot Lila a delighted look, but Teddy didn't seem to hear, distracted by his cell phone. That was probably the way Teddy went through life—looking only at what interested him and ignoring everything that didn't.

"I've got to run," Teddy said.

"Are you going up to visit Evelyn?" Lila asked. "She just got home."

Teddy frowned. "Can't. I have somewhere to be. I only stopped by to pick up some mail from the front desk." He was already turning away, preoccupied with his phone again.

"You should make time to see her," Lila said louder.

Teddy turned back. "Excuse me?"

"I said you should make time to see her. She's your mother," Lila said.

"Is she paying you to like her or something?" Teddy's laugh was hollow, and he waited for her to join him, to let him off the hook with an accompanying laugh at Evelyn's expense.

But Lila wasn't interested in letting Teddy off the hook. She gave him a blank stare. Why should she pretend to find him funny? Evelyn wasn't perfect, but he took advantage of her. It wasn't fair for him to get away with it. No one called him out. Lila doubted he would care what she thought but she also refused to go along with him.

"I'd say it's more like she's paying to support you," Lila said.

"Funny, Lila," Teddy said, deadpan.

Zoe's eyes grew comically wide across the table, but she kept her mouth closed. When it was obvious no one planned to smooth over the awkward silence, Teddy shrugged and left the room, slithering out of their space like the reptile he was. When he was nearly at the door, he passed Florence and Mary Dixon and tripped over a long half-unrolled ball of yarn that had fallen off their table.

Teddy hit the floor, landing on his butt. Zoe looked at Lila, and the two of them burst into giggles. Teddy was less amused.

He scrambled to his feet, his face red. He pointed at Mary Dixon. "You could hurt someone!"

"Teddy, I'm sorry," Mary Dixon said, her lip quivering.

"Oh, calm down, Teddy. There's no need to yell. It was an accident," Florence snapped at him.

"She could have thrown my back out," Teddy yelled.

Florence clicked her knitting needles, looking unconcerned. "Don't be so dramatic."

Teddy got closer to their table and gestured to the pile of fabric in Mary Dixon's lap. "I better not have a bruise from that ugly piece of shit." He turned and strode out of the room.

The Hydrangea Room hushed. Lila could have heard a dust particle hit the floor. She looked over at Mary Dixon and was dismayed to see her bent over her knitting, her shoulders shaking with silent tears.

Lila hurried out of her seat, sinking down next to Mary Dixon. "Don't be upset. Teddy is a jerk. He shouldn't have yelled at you like that."

Zoe crouched down on Mary Dixon's other side, rubbing her shoulder.

"I am going to tell Evelyn all about this as soon as I get out of here," Florence announced. "That Teddy Harrison is bad news. I told Evelyn he was trouble."

"This isn't Evelyn's fault," Lila said evenly.

"I know that, Lila. Evelyn did her best with Teddy. She was a terrific mother. She's not responsible for her son turning into a douchebag," Florence said.

At her words, Zoe and Lila looked at each other over Mary Dixon's back. Mary Dixon looked up too, her face tearstained. "Did you just call Teddy a douchebag?"

"Yes," Florence said defiantly.

Mary Dixon raised her eyebrows; her tears turned into laughter.

Zoe and Lila joined in. There was something so ridiculous about proper Florence Parker calling someone a douchebag.

Mary Dixon shook her head. "I don't know why I got so upset. I suppose Teddy always reminded me of my son. I never thought Teddy would speak to me in that way."

"He's awful," Lila said.

"I suppose so," Mary Dixon said sadly. "I always gave him the benefit of the doubt because he was Evelyn's son. I never wanted him to get in trouble but perhaps I misjudged the situation. Conrad dying, and that meeting with the lawyer about the reward, and now Emily's murder—makes me think I should have told someone what I saw."

Lila sat back on her heels. The hair on the back of her neck stood up. "What are you talking about?"

Mary Dixon looked down, playing with the knitting in her lap. The green and yellow yarn crisscrossed together like the variation in a new leaf, falling down to her chunky Prada loafers. "I thought about it the other day when Bea asked about Sophia and a secret meeting. The night of her death, I did see something. I was setting up for the cocktail party. You remember I was on the committee?" She turned to Florence.

Florence nodded. "You were in charge of decor and did an excellent job."

Mary Dixon visibly exhaled, soothed by Florence's compliment. "I was the only one on the patio that night. Ruth hadn't shown up when she was supposed to, and I had to carry all the ice out there by myself. I was arranging the wine in the buckets when Sophia came tearing out of the woods. She was furious. I didn't want her to see me, because I was sure she'd end up embarrassed by the state she was in. I moved behind the magnolia tree on the edge of the patio, and that's when I saw Teddy."

"Teddy?" Lila asked, feeling confused. What was Teddy doing on the patio the night of Sophia's murder?

"He was following Sophia. She turned around and yelled at him to leave her alone. She ran inside, and he ran after her." Mary Dixon shook her head. "I never told anyone. I didn't want to get Teddy in trouble since he's from a good family."

How many transgressions were excused because of a good family? Lila was definitely not from a good family, at least not the kind Mary Dixon meant; she didn't have wealth or an impressive family name. Patricia had made that clear from the first time Ryan brought Lila home. But it turned out that a fancy name and money didn't equal a good life or make you a good person.

"But why would Teddy get in trouble?" Zoe asked Mary Dixon.

"Sophia was dead an hour later," Mary Dixon said. "And Teddy looked . . . he looked . . . I guess I would say he didn't look like himself. He was red and angry and kind of weaving around. It seemed as if he had too much to drink."

Or maybe he had taken drugs. Sophia had drugs in her system when she died—specifically, cocaine. Teddy was with her right before the murder. He'd chased after her; he'd looked angry. What if Teddy had given Sophia the drugs? What if there was a confrontation? What if Teddy had killed her?

Lila sat utterly still. The flowers on the wall blurred together into ambiguous shapes and colors. Her stomach was a cold pit, endless and deep. She knew what she had to do, but the task itself was impossible. How was Lila going to tell Evelyn the truth about her son?

Chapter Thirty-Four

Lila paced her apartment, trying to figure out how to talk to Evelyn about Teddy. She had procrastinated with other tasks all afternoon—picking up Bea, cleaning out the linen closet, vacuuming the old rugs—and she still didn't have the courage to approach her friend.

Lila's phone rang. It was the Richmond Police Department. She picked up immediately. "Hello?"

"It's Detective Roberts." The deep voice rumbled. "We're going to need you to come into the station tomorrow for some more questions."

Lila pressed the phone to her ear. This was what Jasper had warned her about. She took a deep breath. "What if I refuse?"

Detective Roberts chuckled. It was not a pleasant sound. "That's your prerogative. But your fingerprints are in the apartment, your note was in Ms. Canterbury's pocket, we can place you at the scene of the murder, and you have motive. If you choose not to show up, I'll work on an arrest warrant."

Lila's heart stopped. *An arrest warrant!* This was her worst nightmare coming true. What would happen to Bea with two parents in jail?

"I guess I don't have a choice. What time?" Lila asked in a shaky voice.

"Four o'clock. Ask for me as soon as you arrive," Detective Roberts said.

Lila gingerly pressed the button to end the call as if the phone screen might sting her hands. She'd thought things were bad when Ryan left, but this was so much worse. This might be the end of her entire life. Bea's tiny face popped into her head: blue eyes, tangled hair, freckles across her cheeks. Tears flooded Lila's eyes. She couldn't lose her daughter.

Lila's time to save herself was nearly up. She had to talk to Evelyn as soon as possible about Teddy. He was a jerk, and she wasn't sorry to see him in trouble for however he was involved in Sophia's last hours, but she hated to hurt Evelyn.

Evelyn and Jasper had already planned to come over after Bea got home from school so Jasper could fill them in on how things went with the police and Lionel Garrett. Lila had bribed Bea into doing her homework in her own room by agreeing to watch two *Murder, She Wrote* episodes with her that night. It wasn't a hardship. She wanted to spend as much time with her daughter as possible right now.

Jasper and Evelyn arrived and sat on the blue mohair couch. By now, Lila had managed to clean out most of the apartment. The living room rug in shades of blue and cream was in perfect shape under all the boxes and furniture, and the window provided a flood of light into the space now that it was cleared of debris. Goodwill had removed boxes and furnishings, and Lila had hired another company to sell the more upscale furniture online and would send all the proceeds to Stanley. All that remained was a single sofa and two floral-patterned chairs, a carved wooden coffee table and glass end tables, and the built-in bookshelves. After weeks of work, the apartment finally looked like actual humans lived there. Lila had stacked a group of boxes in the corner with papers, jewelry, other valuables, and family photos she thought Stanley might want, but the space was otherwise clear. She was proud of the progress she'd made.

"It's amazing what you've done here," Jasper said.

"It does look relatively normal," Evelyn said. "Aside from the need for new rugs and upholstery and window treatments."

Lila took a deep breath. This was hard. The waiting and the worry about getting arrested was bad enough, but now she had to tell Evelyn that her son might be a killer.

Jasper sighed. "I heard from my contacts this afternoon. Detective Roberts wants you for more questioning."

"He already called. I have to go tomorrow. I contacted the lawyer you suggested," Lila said. She didn't know how she was going to pay the woman but also knew she couldn't show up at the police station without help.

Jasper shook his head. "I was afraid of this."

"What about Lionel's confessions? Could that help?" Lila asked, sounding desperate.

"I met with two of my old colleagues today who are helping out with Emily's case. They said they would try and run down the lead but it's complicated. The Sophia Kent murder is technically an unassigned cold case, and Roberts is treating Emily's death as a separate event entirely. The fact that he's calling you into the station isn't a great sign. They may not have much to tie you to the murder, but this also probably means they don't have anyone else."

"I've always thought lawyers were a waste of time and space, but I suppose they're a necessity here," Evelyn said. "My daddy said talking about money is tacky and I agree of course, but there are exceptions. For example, I could loan you funds to cover a lawyer." She cleared her throat, staring at a point off Lila's shoulder. "Or we don't even have to call it a loan. I could give you the money."

Lila's eyes pricked with painful tears. Evelyn wanted to help her not knowing she was about to destroy Evelyn's world with the news about Teddy. Lila rubbed her eyes and mustered up her courage.

"Evelyn, I have something to tell you. There's another suspect in Sophia's death," Lila said.

"But that's good news," Evelyn said.

"It would be except—" Lila swallowed. "I don't know how to say this. It's about Teddy."

"Teddy?" Evelyn asked, frowning. "What does Teddy have to do with Sophia."

"Mary Dixon saw Teddy with Sophia less than an hour before her murder. He chased her from the woods into the building. Mary Dixon said he was furious with Sophia, that he was shouting at her and appeared drunk," Lila said.

Evelyn's face paled. Jasper flinched.

"You think my Teddy killed Sophia?" Evelyn asked softly.

"I don't know. But I do know this is something the police should hear about. Mary Dixon never told anyone about seeing Teddy that night. She didn't want to get him in trouble. I'm sorry, Evelyn. I hate for you to go through this, but it's time for the whole truth to come out," Lila said.

Evelyn's eyes were sad and downcast. "I promise you that Teddy did not kill Sophia."

"You can't know that," Lila said. "I'm not saying this to hurt you but it's the truth."

"Evelyn, she's right," Jasper said quietly.

"No, you don't understand. I know Teddy couldn't have killed Sophia. Not because I believe in him or I think he's incapable of it." Evelyn looked up, meeting their gazes at last.

"Then how can you be so sure?" Lila asked.

"Because Emily Canterbury confirmed his story," Evelyn whispered.

"What are you talking about?" Lila said.

Evelyn clasped her hands together. "Teddy was nineteen when Sophia died. He was supposed to be in college but had decided to take a year off. I should have known it was a bad idea but I had a hard time saying no to him. He was about to turn twenty, which was when he would come into the first portion of his trust fund. However, the trust had strict provisions in it. He would lose access to it if he violated any of them, one of which prevented him from using drugs. Not only was he using drugs back then, he sold them to pay for his habit." She closed her eyes. "Teddy was Sophia's drug dealer. On the night of her murder, she wanted cocaine for a concert she was going to. After he gave it to her, she admitted that she couldn't pay him. Apparently, she owed him quite a bit of money by that point. It was money he owed to his supplier, who was an unsavory character as you can imagine. When Teddy got upset with her, Sophia claimed she could pay him later that night and was meeting with someone who had access to all the money she needed. He didn't believe her so he followed her up to Conrad's apartment."

Lila held her breath, unable to believe what Evelyn was saying.

"What happened next?" Jasper asked.

"Teddy watched Sophia go inside the apartment and waited in the hallway. He passed out. He had taken a significant amount of drugs that night too. The next thing he knew, Emily Canterbury was shaking him awake. She told him he had to move because the police were on their way. He came straight to my apartment. I was already there, getting ready to leave for the cocktail party, and he told me everything," Evelyn said.

"How do you know he wasn't lying?" Lila asked.

"I didn't," Evelyn said. "He was high and not making much sense, and I was scared of what he might have done. I went to Emily myself the next day. She said Teddy was telling the truth. She heard Sophia scream that night and looked outside into the hallway. She saw someone running out of Conrad's apartment, and then noticed Teddy passed out in the hall."

"This means Emily saw Sophia's murderer," Lila said slowly.

"I believe she did," Evelyn said, nodding. "When I asked her if she told the police who or what she'd seen, she said no. She told me that she had her reasons for staying quiet and presumed I did as well."

"It's hard to imagine why Emily kept this to herself, but she must have decided to finally come forward after Conrad set up the reward," Jasper said.

Lila sat totally still, listening to this story. Heat rose up her arms and chest. How could Evelyn not have told them this before? Emily had seen Sophia's killer and planned to expose that person to James Forrester to collect the reward. This was another clear connection between Emily's death and Sophia's case, and yet Evelyn hadn't said a word even though Lila was on the verge of arrest.

Evelyn continued. "I've never told anyone. I was afraid if it came out that Teddy was dealing and using drugs, he would lose his trust. I sent Teddy to rehab and lied to the police about where I was during the murder. I've always felt guilty."

"Not guilty enough to come clean," Lila said. She could barely keep her voice modulated as her anger expanded, swelling to fill every inch of space inside her body.

"I know this sounds terrible," Evelyn said, her voice breaking.

Lila looked away, unable to bear the sight of Evelyn's remorse. This was an important piece of evidence that could keep Lila out of jail. Lila had thought they were friends. She trusted Evelyn. In the end, people only thought about themselves, even people who supposedly cared about you.

"Were you ever going to tell me?" Lila asked.

Evelyn looked distraught. "I never thought Emily's investigation would get this far. I was sure the police would drop you as a suspect."

"Nonetheless, we need to tell the police about what happened that night with Emily and Teddy," Jasper said. "We can go over together. I understand why you never said anything, but it's time to confess everything, even if it gets you and Teddy in trouble."

Lila's fists clenched. "You *understand*? Are you joking? You *understand* why Evelyn lied? Do you have a backbone, or do you go along with what anyone tells you?"

Lila was glad to see his face darken. She wanted someone to yell at her, and she wanted to yell back. Fight was broiling inside her.

"I understand Evelyn wanted to protect her son. I'm not saying that was right but, yes, I do understand," Jasper said.

Jasper's tone was neutral and calm in the face of Lila's anger. That only made her more furious.

"Well, I don't understand. I don't get why Evelyn would have lied to us for weeks. I thought we were all in this together. When I nearly got arrested, I thought you were both my friends and doing everything possible to help me, but you weren't. You were holding back crucial information because you didn't want your horrible son to get in trouble. This is the same son who spends no time with you and has zero respect for you." Lila breathed hard. Her voice was loud, nearly shouting.

"Lila, calm down." Jasper reached out an arm.

Lila twisted away from him, popping up to her feet, stepping backward.

Evelyn hauled herself up with difficulty. "I'm so sorry."

Lila crossed her arms. "I don't forgive you. I want you both to get out."

"I didn't do anything. I'm only trying to help," Jasper said.

"I should never have gotten involved in this investigation or with either one of you. I don't know what I was thinking. I'm about to get arrested and lose my daughter. Do you understand that? Do you even care?" Lila couldn't stop the words from spewing out of her mouth. It was as if the entire last year was all coming out at the same time—all the anger, all the pain, all the unfairness of Lila being accused of things she'd never done and being let down by people who were supposed to love her.

"Get out." Lila pointed to the door.

Evelyn looked unsteady and wobbled backward. Jasper took her arm and handed her the walker. The two of them made their way to the door. Bea burst out of her room.

"Where are you going?" Bea said, running up to Jasper and Evelyn.

"Bea, they need to go now," Lila said.

Bea rounded on her. Her face was red and blotchy like it got before she started to cry. "Why are you making them leave?"

"It's all right," Jasper said calmly. "We will see you soon."

"Mama, what's happening?" Bea asked. Tears slid down her face. "Why are you so mad?"

Evelyn and Jasper were at the door now, heading into the hall. Evelyn's face crinkled up and there were tears in her eyes.

"I'm not talking about this right now," Lila said.

The door shut firmly, leaving Lila and Bea alone in the apartment the way they had been for months. They should have stayed that way all along.

Bea's face grew dark as she contemplated the silence. "You make everyone hate us."

"Excuse me?" Lila asked, her anger rising higher to meet Bea's.

"Daddy hates us, everyone in Norfolk hates us, and we made friends here and now they hate us too. This is your fault!"

"I'm not going to listen to this. Go to your room."

"I won't." Bea stomped her foot like a toddler.

"You will." Lila crossed the room and pointed toward the hall. "I'm not arguing about this with you. I'm in charge and what I say goes."

"I hate you," Bea said. "I hate you so much."

"You know what? Sometimes I hate you too." Lila spat out the words before she could stop herself.

Lila's body prickled with heat, fury, and frustration. She didn't want to be anywhere near her daughter or anyone else. She strode down the hall to her own room and slammed the door, blocking out everything from her life.

Chapter Thirty-Five

Lila lay on her bed for a long time, her body radiating anger. The last time she was this upset was when Ryan left; she'd had the same unending pit in her stomach. How could she trust anyone? Why did Bea blame her for everything? This could be her last night of freedom, and Lila continued to make mistakes and put herself in situations where she was taken advantage of. She didn't want to live this way. It was too tiring—letting people get close until they inevitably disappointed her, leaving her with nothing in the end.

Thoughts continued to churn through Lila's brain. She pulled the coverlet up around her like armor against the outside world. The pillow muffled the sounds of the street, protecting her from the onslaught of voices and demands. It was quiet and warm, and her body went limp. Without warning, she fell asleep.

When she woke up, Lila could tell some time had passed by the dimming of the light and the shadows darkening the corners of the room. She checked her watch—two hours had gone by. Her head throbbed. The anger from before was still there, simmering below the surface, but it wasn't as intense. She shouldn't have lost her temper with Bea like that. Her body flooded with shame as she relived telling Bea that she hated her. That was unacceptable, no matter how angry she got. Bea was a child, *her* child, and no child should hear that. She would calmly talk to Bea, apologize, and work through this fight. Lila had to make it right with her before tomorrow.

Lila opened her bedroom door and went to Bea's room. It was empty. The living room was empty too, and the kitchen and the dining room. A sour taste formed in Lila's mouth, and her heart beat a little faster. Where was her daughter?

Lila rushed into the hall and knocked on Jasper's door first. No answer. Then she went to Evelyn's door. No answer there either. She texted them both, asking if they had seen Bea, but didn't get a response. She shouldn't be surprised. They probably didn't want to talk to her after what had happened earlier.

Lila called down to the lobby and got Susanna on the phone.

"Have you seen Bea?" Lila asked, getting straight to the point.

Susanna's voice was brisk, distracted. "She came through here over an hour ago."

"By herself?" Lila asked, unable to stop the quake in her voice.

"Yes, she was by herself. I didn't think anything of it." There was a soft intake of breath. "Lila, is something wrong?"

"I don't know where she went. We had a fight." Lila's voice broke on the last word. Before she could stop herself, she was crying softly into the phone.

Lila's chest was taut as if a rope was knotted around it and pulling tighter by the second. The streetlights winked on outside; it had grown fully dark in the small space of time since she had woken. Bea was missing. She was only ten and she was outside in the unruly dark alone. She could be hurt or worse. What if whoever had broken into their apartment and killed Emily had taken Bea too? This was Lila's fault. It was all her fault.

"I'm coming up. We'll find her. I'm sure she hasn't gone far." Susanna's voice was firm, and she hung up the phone before Lila could say anything else.

Lila sat with the phone in her lap, replaying her last conversation with Bea. There was an ache deep in her bones.

Susanna called all the neighbors in the Primrose from Lila's apartment. No one had seen Bea since she'd left. When Lila spoke with the police, they agreed to send someone over. She tracked down the number for Nora Raynor's mother, Elaine. Nora had not seen or heard from Bea, but Elaine insisted on calling the rest of the class parents in case anyone else had. The responses trickled in on her cell phone—no one knew where Bea was.

Lila texted Mama to let her know Bea was missing but ignored Mama's phone call in return. She couldn't bear to talk to anyone, knowing it would only make her break down.

The police finally arrived; a round-faced woman with red hair and kind eyes and a dark-eyed man with a rigid jaw and bushy eyebrows. They asked questions and requested a recent photo. They explained how they would canvass the neighborhood and call in other officers to help. Lila nodded, the words entering her brain and exiting just as quickly.

The minutes passed slowly as if they were mired in molasses, trickling past Lila second by second. It was eight o'clock and Bea was still missing. It was eight fifteen and Bea was still missing. It was eight twenty and Bea was still missing.

Lila couldn't sit still. She got into her car, tears leaking from her eyes. Driving around the West End, she peered into alleyways and circled parking lots. She drove down the side streets that she and Bea had walked together. She scoured the darkness for any sign of her daughter, but she was nowhere to be found.

The air in the car was thick, pressing on Lila's chest. This was it—the worst had finally happened. Bea was gone. Lila's life was over without her daughter. She could survive losing all her money and her husband and her house and her friends and anything else in this world. But this? This she could not survive. She could not lose Bea.

Breathing in and out, Lila deliberately tried to calm herself. Her face streaked with tears. She pulled into a parking space at the grocery store and rested her head on the steering wheel. *Think*. Should she call the police and see where they'd searched? Check the school again? It made sense. Bea felt comfortable in school. Where else did she feel comfortable? Perhaps the library or Rise Up or the ice cream shop.

Or . . . or . . . Lila turned the key in the ignition, yanked her car out of park, and pressed her foot on the gas, peeling out of the parking lot. Bea would have gone to a place that Lila told her was safe because despite their fight and their clashes, Bea trusted her. Lila wasn't certain of a lot of things, but she was certain of that.

Lila sped back to the Primrose, parked, and sprinted inside. She flew down the hallway and raced into the darkened Azalea Room and to the skirted table along the right wall, skidding to a stop.

Lila knelt beside the table and held her breath. *Please, please, please make her here.* She lifted the heavy blue dotted upholstery fabric.

Bea was curled underneath the table, her hair spilling onto the rug. Lila placed a hand on Bea's little red cheek. Bea woke with a start. When she saw Lila, she started to cry.

Chapter Thirty-Six

Lila pulled Bea into her arms. Relief surged through her, leaving her jittery and elated at the same time. Her daughter was safe for now. She tightened her hold.

Bea's hiccupped sobs eventually subsided. She pulled back and looked up at Lila with a tearstained face. "What are you doing here?"

"I came to get you," Lila said simply.

"How did you know where I was?"

"I was the one who told you this was a good spot to hide. It took me a little while to remember that," Lila said.

"Were you worried?" Bea asked anxiously.

"I'm always worried when you're not with me. That's part of being your mama."

"I heard people talking about me in the lobby. They said I was lost, but I was too embarrassed to come out. I didn't mean to be gone so long."

Lila shook her head. "I don't blame you for wanting some space after our fight. We both said a lot of awful things. I should never have said I hate you even if I was angry. I'm sorry about that, and I hope you know I don't feel that way."

"Even though I get mad sometimes and yell?" Bea sounded so young and uncertain.

"Yes, even then. I want you to tell me when you're mad, and you can even yell if you want. But next time you have to tell me where you're going, okay?"

"Okay." Bea nestled closer into her arms. "And promise you won't leave me like Daddy did? I'll be good from now on. I won't even read your text messages anymore or fake another fever to stay home from school."

Lila tipped up Bea's chin. "I'm not going anywhere, and Daddy didn't leave you either. We talked about this. He had to go away because of problems with his business."

"You keep saying that but . . ." Bea's voice faltered. Her hands balled into fists.

"Tell me what you're thinking," Lila said.

Bea screwed her eyes closed. Lila let the seconds pass, waiting for Bea to say something. She concentrated on the rise and fall of Bea's chest, the air blowing through the vents above, the patterned rug scraping at her feet. Lila realized for the first time that she'd kicked off her shoes in the lobby in her haste to reach Bea.

"I was getting demerits in school," Bea finally said, opening her eyes. "You didn't know about most of them. I told Daddy instead. He said to try harder to follow the rules, but I didn't. Maybe if I wasn't so much trouble, he could have taken us with him."

Lila stilled, absorbing Bea's confession. How often had her daughter agonized over this regret?

"The demerits didn't matter. I promise. Daddy was never going to take you with him," Lila said.

"Why not?" Bea asked, her fists still balled at her sides.

Lila took Bea's hands, unlocking her fingers. "Because you need to live somewhere safe where you can go to school and follow a routine and eat healthy food and sleep in a warm bed. Daddy didn't know where he was going or how long he would be there. He would never have put you in an unstable situation like that. He loves you too much."

Bea's eyes filled with tears. "If he loves me, when is he coming home?"

Lila's heart cracked at Bea's pain. She wanted to tell her that their family would go right back to normal, tomorrow or the next day or the day after that. But that wasn't fair to Bea. She deserved to know the truth even if it was hard to hear.

"I know Daddy wants to see you, but I'm not sure when that will happen." Lila swallowed hard, preparing herself for this next part. "I've tried to figure out a good way to tell you this but there isn't one. Daddy was arrested two days ago and moved into a jail. We don't know for how long yet."

"But he was trying to prove his innocence," Bea said uncertainly.

"And I don't know if he can do that. The courts have to decide. But sometimes people, even good people like Daddy, make mistakes. When they do, they have to face the consequences of their actions. None of this changes how he feels about you, though."

Bea sat back, taking this in. "You're getting a divorce, aren't you?"

Lila froze. "Why would you say that?"

"You don't like to talk about him since he left, and now he's going to jail." Bea hesitated. "I've wondered about it for a while."

Lila bowed her head. It made her sick to think Bea had worried about her family's future in silence. She'd thought she was protecting Bea by hiding the divorce, but she'd only delayed the inevitable. If Lila had only been honest with Bea months ago, she might have comforted her daughter sooner and helped her understand what was happening.

"You're a really smart girl." Lila took a deep breath. "And you're right. We are getting a divorce. Daddy and I realized that we can't get along anymore, even before he left. This isn't caused by anything you did. I promise you that. Even though things will be different, I will always be your mama and he will always be your daddy. That's not going to change."

"What if I'm sad about it?" Bea asked, a tear slipping from her eye.

Lila's chin trembled. "It's okay to feel sad, and it's okay to feel mad too. Sometimes I feel both those things when I think about the divorce. It's normal and understandable. You can feel any way you want, and I'm here to listen. I love you."

Bea stared at her hands. "I know that."

"Do you want to talk about this some more?"

"Not yet," Bea said, "but I will."

"That sounds like a plan."

Lila bent down and kissed the top of Bea's head. She was worried about how much bad news she'd piled on Bea, but she was also hopeful that she'd finally done the right thing, and that Bea would keep talking to her about what was important. Maybe that was the best she could hope for.

After several seconds of quiet, Bea spoke again. "Mama? I don't want you to stay mad at Jasper and Evelyn either. I know Evelyn is sorry for lying to you about her son."

"Did you overhear our conversation?"

"Duh, Mama. Jessica on *Murder, She Wrote* is always eavesdropping. That's when you learn the best stuff."

Lila bit back a smile, then sighed as she thought of Evelyn and Jasper. "The stuff with Evelyn is complicated."

"People make mistakes, and you should listen when they're sorry about it. It's like when Nora called me a dumbass, and I forgave her. Or when I secretly poured hot sauce in her water bottle, and she forgave me."

"Hold on. When did you pour hot sauce—"

"The point is forgiveness," Bea interrupted. "You and I made up even though we had a big fight and both said bad things. Don't you think that means you should make up with Evelyn and Jasper too?"

Lila hugged her tightly. "I'll think about it."

"All right," Bea said. "I'm too tired to come up with any more excellent arguments. Can we go home?"

"Yes, we can." Lila pulled Bea up and led her back upstairs to their apartment.

* * *

Lila and Bea's footsteps echoed in the hallway. Jasper flung open the door to his apartment and hurried outside. Evelyn hobbled out behind him. Jasper's shirt was untucked, and there were mascara rings beneath Evelyn's eyes. They both looked disheveled and pale.

Jasper rushed forward, leaning down to Bea. "Are you hurt?"

Bea shook her head.

Jasper wrapped Bea in a huge hug. He looked over at Lila, a smile breaking over his face. Lila smiled back.

"I'm okay," Bea said shyly.

"We heard you were missing," Evelyn said in an accusing tone. "Children going missing is unacceptable. You made things difficult for the rest of us."

"Some people like difficult," Bea said.

"Yes, well. I am one of those people," Evelyn said, not looking at Bea. Her voice was suspiciously shaky as she spoke.

Bea went to Evelyn, wrapping an arm around her waist. Evelyn took her hand off her walker and hugged Bea back. Her wrinkled face was taut with emotion.

Bea released Evelyn and peered into the open door of Jasper's apartment. "I hope you've got cookies in here because being a missing person really made me hungry." She disappeared inside, presumably to help herself to whatever baked treat Jasper had available.

Jasper, Evelyn, and Lila stood in silence. The lights shone on Jasper's bald head and Evelyn's thinning brown hair. They both looked small in the long hallway. For a moment, Lila wished she could hug them the same way that Bea had. All her anger from earlier had slid away. Bea was right. It was better to forgive people when they made a mistake.

"I'm sorry about the argument. I shouldn't have yelled at you," Lila said. "But you should have told me about Teddy's connection to Sophia earlier."

"You're right. I should have told the police twenty years ago and made Teddy face the consequences of his actions rather than cover up his mistakes. That was *my* mistake and I regret it. I especially regret that I made you think I didn't want to help you, because I do. I care about you and Bea." Evelyn gripped her walker tighter and stared straight ahead. "I can't tell you why. Bea is a terrible young girl, and you have no fashion sense and are obviously penniless."

"But you love me anyway?" Lila asked, coming forward then.

Evelyn nodded stiffly.

Lila hugged Evelyn before turning to Jasper. "I shouldn't have blamed you. You were only trying to help."

"That's right. You shouldn't have blamed me," Jasper said, drawing himself up.

Lila smiled. She was proud of Jasper for standing up for himself, even when it was to her.

"Accept my apology?" Lila asked.

Jasper nodded. Even though Lila knew it would embarrass him, she rose up on her tiptoes and kissed him on the cheek. When she pulled back, Jasper ducked his head and shuffled backward but he was smiling.

Jasper cleared his throat. "We still have the problem of you going to the police station tomorrow. Evelyn and I went to Detective Roberts directly this evening, and we told him about Teddy selling Sophia the drugs and what Emily saw that night."

"You did that?" Lila looked to Evelyn.

"I should have done it a long time ago," Evelyn said.

Tears gathered in Lila's eyes. Evelyn waved them away. "Enough of that. We aren't going to sit here crying like a bunch of idiots. We need to do something. Detective Roberts still thinks you're responsible."

"That means we have until tomorrow to solve Sophia and Emily's murders," Lila said. She was scared but she wasn't hopeless. They could find a solution somehow.

"Let's think about this. We know Sophia planned to meet someone the night of her death to get the money she owed Teddy. The Willoughby sisters overheard Sophia mention blackmail. We assumed she was the one being blackmailed, but what if—what if she was doing the blackmailing?" Lila said.

"You think Sophia discovered the identity of the Primrose burglar and tried to blackmail her for money." Jasper's eyes narrowed as he considered this possibility.

"It's possible," Lila said. "And what about that birthmark Lionel mentioned? If we can figure out who has that birthmark on their arm, we could uncover the identity of the burglar and give the police an actual suspect in Sophia's murder. When you combine that with the new information you provided about Emily seeing the murderer, they'll have to at least investigate the person. And I'm sure whoever murdered Sophia and Emily left some kind of trail behind for the police to look into."

Jasper cocked his head. "But how are we going to find the birthmark?"

"Ladies my age do not typically show their arms. It's one of the first places to really go downhill on a body," Evelyn said. "We could tell everyone there's a disease going around the building and they all need to get a shot in their arm. I'm certain the Willoughby sisters have spread some form of herpes around."

"I think we might have trouble convincing people, especially those not having sex with June or Iris," Lila said.

"Fair point," Evelyn acknowledged.

Lila was thinking. What would convince wealthy, elderly women to gather in one place and roll up their sleeves? Something that wasn't suspicious, something that was irresistible and fun, something that was . . . free.

"I think I might have an idea," Lila said. The plan was already forming in her head when her cell phone started to ring. She pulled it from her pocket and squinted at the screen—*Norfolk Correctional Center*. Her hand clenched around the phone. Ryan was back.

Chapter Thirty-Seven

Lila was having trouble taking a full breath. Her gasps were shallow, audible. The phone trilled again like an alarm in the hallway. Evelyn and Jasper eyed her with concern.

"Are you all right?" Jasper asked.

"Just give me a minute here," Lila said faintly. She pushed open her door, stepped into the apartment, and answered the call.

A robotic voice filled Lila's ear. "This is a call from an inmate at the Norfolk Correctional Center. You are receiving this call from Ryan Shaw. To accept, press one, to reject, press two or hang up."

Leaning against the wall, Lila stared down at her phone screen. Her eyes watered. Ryan waited at the other end of the line, after all those months of silence. She grimaced and pressed one.

"Li."

That one syllable cut Lila's heart. The voice was so familiar, she could have placed it in her dreams. It had whispered to her in classrooms and in bed and on the couch and in hospital rooms.

"Why are you calling me?" Lila whispered.

"Your mama called mine and said Bea was missing. Is she okay? What's going on? My parents are on standby. What can we do?" Ryan asked, talking low and fast.

"Nothing. Bea is fine. I found her, and she's home." Lila's voice sounded as if it was coming from far away. The walls wavered in her vision. None of this seemed real.

"Thank God. I was so worried," Ryan said fervently.

Lila blinked, the apartment coming into stark focus. Wait one second. Now he was suddenly worried about Bea? After eight months of no contact?

"Well, there's nothing to worry about. I can handle Bea without you," Lila said. It was true. She'd done everything herself since Ryan left. She hadn't done it perfectly, but she'd kept parenting Bea and pulled herself together after they lost their house.

Ryan was silent for several beats. "I was concerned. I only wanted to help."

"I guess that's a nice change from abandoning us," Lila snapped.

"That's not fair. I know I left you in a bad situation, but it was hard for me too. I wasn't sure what else to do." Ryan's voice broke on the last syllable.

Lila slid down the wall, pulling her legs up, making herself small. Ryan's voice flooded her with a litany of emotions, anger and sadness and regret. Maybe he hadn't known how bad it would get for them. Except . . . no. *Hell no!* Ryan should have faced up to what happened with his business right away, and he shouldn't have abandoned Bea. He'd owed Lila the courtesy of a real discussion about the breakdown of their marriage, not a phone call on his way out of the country.

"You shouldn't have run," Lila said, her voice tense. "We lost the house and all our friends. Bea was devastated when you left and never contacted her. I don't forgive you for any of that."

"Wow. Okay. You still have a lot of anger," Ryan said, sounding surprised.

"Of course I do!" Lila retorted.

"I'm sorry, but I didn't want to go to jail," Ryan said. As far as apologies went, it wasn't a good one. "Will you put Bea on the phone?"

Lila was already shaking her head. "Not tonight. I need to first have a discussion with her about whether she is ready to talk to you."

"I guess I have to accept that for now," Ryan said shortly. "Hopefully I can make this all up to her in person soon. I'm not sure how much you know about the case, but I didn't handle the medical reimbursements. The government has gone through all my text messages and emails. They've interviewed everyone who worked for me, and there's nothing to connect me to the fraudulent telemedicine company. I have nothing to hide."

"You have *nothing* to hide?" Lila's voice was soft, barely audible to her own ears.

"Exactly," Ryan said.

But it sure seemed like he had something to hide. Lila remembered Ryan's secret flip phone and the text about meeting at the Ramada. She had feared he was caught up in a shady affair, but what if it was a shady business deal all along?

Ryan was talking again, explaining more about his case and how he was going to get off, maybe serve a few months in a minimum-security prison for fleeing the country. Lila interrupted, unable to hold her accusation inside for one more second.

"I know about your second phone and your meetings at the Ramada."

"I—I don't know what you're talking about," Ryan said loudly.

Yet even from one hundred miles away, Lila could hear the fear lacing his voice. There was a slight shake to each syllable. Ryan was scared and he was lying.

"I found the phone, and I saw the texts. You know what I think? I think you were meeting with that telemedicine company in secret and using that second phone to communicate with them," Lila said.

"This is ridiculous," Ryan blustered.

"No, it's not. I bet the FBI can find someone who remembers you from the Ramada. I heard those bartenders have worked there for years."

"You can't talk to the FBI. You're my wife," Ryan said, sounding desperate.

"Except I won't be your wife for long since we're getting a divorce. A divorce you initiated. Besides, I *can* talk to whoever I want and testify against you if I choose. I looked up spousal privilege months ago. I can waive it."

Ryan's tone turned wheedling. "Come on, Lila. Why would you want me to go to jail? Is this revenge? Is it because I asked for a divorce? I'm sorry I hurt you, but we were married a long time and I'm still Bea's father."

"And Bea needs to see that when you do something wrong, you accept the consequences. You stole money. You can't just get away with that!"

Ryan was quiet, his breath the only sound in her ear. Lila dropped her chin onto her knees. Yelling wasn't going to fix this situation. She was angry and would stay angry for a long time, but this was about more than just her.

Lila exhaled. "Look, Ryan, you were right about the divorce. It's time. I don't want revenge, but I do want you to return the money you took. Patricia is paying Gerald Partridge a lot to defend you. I bet he can get you a great plea deal."

"You've changed," Ryan said softly.

"Maybe," Lila said.

Or maybe this was the person Lila had always been inside but had pushed down to accommodate Ryan. Lila wouldn't go back to staying silent or keeping the peace at the expense of her own opinions. In some ways, it wasn't all Ryan's fault that he'd missed so much of the real Lila. While he could have tried harder to see her, she could have tried harder to be seen.

* * *

Nate was standing on the porch of his small craftsman house when Lila pulled up in her Jeep with Evelyn. She could just make out his face, which was impassive beneath the light from the lanterns framing his front door.

"He doesn't look happy," Evelyn said.

"Give me a minute," Lila said.

Lila unfolded herself from the car and rubbed her hands on the legs of her jeans. The walkway to his porch seemed a mile long when she finally stopped at the base of the stairs.

"It's pretty late for an unannounced visit," Nate said.

Nate was right. It was after ten o'clock. It was rude to show up on his doorstep at night, especially when she'd walked out on their dinner. But she'd called first, and he'd ignored her. From the comfort of her living room, she had decided the obvious choice was to come over and talk to him in person. Her obvious choice seemed more like a bad idea at the moment.

"I'm sorry. I did call but you didn't answer," Lila said.

Nate looked at her with steady eyes. "That was on purpose."

"Oh right. Yes." Lila scuffed her foot against the step. She noticed weeds around his flower beds. Not terrible, but not perfect. For some reason, that gave her comfort. Ryan always liked everything so perfect and beautiful on the outside. She thought Nate might spend more of his time on things inside.

"He was zombie-ing you. Don't be offended. It happens to everyone these days," Evelyn called out from the car window.

Evelyn had insisted on coming with Lila in case she needed "backup." Lila now realized this was also a bad idea.

"You brought a chaperone," Nate said, sounding amused.

"I'm not a chaperone. If you wanted to kiss her, I would look away," Evelyn yelled in a voice that half of Nate's neighborhood could hear. "Although I don't condone necking outdoors in the open. It's tacky, especially when a man has zombied you."

"I think she means ghosted," Lila said quietly.

"Ah." There was laughter in Nate's voice, and Lila was encouraged.

"Look, I know I acted weird at dinner," Lila began.

"It's hard for her to trust people but she's working on it," Evelyn called out.

Lila gritted her teeth. "She's not completely wrong." She crossed her arms, then uncrossed them again. "I told you I'm getting divorced but what I didn't tell you is that I was blindsided when my husband left. I knew things weren't good but thought we could make it work."

"There are always signs, dear. I'm surprised you didn't see them, but you were probably more gullible back then," Evelyn yelled. "That's not a bad thing in a girlfriend, Nate."

Lila ignored Evelyn. "I had a terrible few months where I lost everything, and I ran out on our date because—"

"Because she likes you. I can tell," Evelyn said helpfully.

"Will you excuse me a minute?" Lila asked Nate.

Nate nodded, his mouth quirking up. Lila marched back to Evelyn and leaned in the car window. "You need to let me do this without commenting."

"I'm helping to move things along. We don't have all night," Evelyn said.

"I appreciate that, but I need to do this on my own. It's part of my—let's call it my personal growth."

Evelyn harrumphed. "I hadn't thought of it that way. All right. I'll stay quiet."

"Roll the window up," Lila said.

Evelyn sighed but rolled the window mostly up.

Lila walked back to Nate. "Sorry about that. She wants to help."

"What did she say about you liking me?" Nate asked.

Lila laughed a little. Her heart pounded, and she realized how nervous she was. Well, why shouldn't she be? She hadn't done this in nearly twenty years.

"She is right. I do like you," Lila said, pushing the words out of her mouth before she could take them back.

"What happened at dinner then?" Nate asked. He no longer looked angry with her, but he wasn't smiling either. He stepped down off the porch until he was level with Lila.

"I guess . . . I'm afraid of falling for someone and messing it up and getting hurt again." Lila closed her eyes, unable to look at Nate, but she made herself keep talking. "I avoided conflict with my husband, which led to a lot of resentment and disappointment. Eventually, I shut down and he shut down and our marriage couldn't recover. I don't want to do that again, and I'm scared that I will."

"I understand that."

It was the lack of judgment in his tone that made Lila open her eyes and look at him.

"I can't jump into a serious relationship. I have Bea to think about, and I don't know where I'm going to live, and I'm a murder suspect. But I do like you. I know that." Lila laughed, sounding slightly hysterical. "I can't believe I'm telling you all of this. I don't even know if you're still interested."

Nate stared intently at her. "I'm interested. My divorce was hard too, but I don't want to be alone for the rest of my life, so I keep trying even though I'm only attracted to smart, beautiful women who run out on my dates, investigate crimes in their spare time, and read space porn."

Lila couldn't stop the smile from spreading over her face. She could feel it stretch all the way up to her eyes.

"Now that you mention it, I did think you might want to read

Thrust since you're a writer. It's a work of creative genius—the space exploration is actually a metaphor for—" Lila stopped. "You know what? I don't want to ruin the plot."

"I'd brave it on your recommendation." Nate smiled.

"So." Lila smoothed her hair and stared up into his eyes. They looked dark underneath the moonlight, and she swore her knees liquified as she took in the sharp planes of his face. "Could we start slow, maybe go out again?"

The words were out before she could even think about them. She'd come over here to ask him for a favor. Her intention wasn't to ask him for another date. But here he was in front of her, making jokes, understanding why she was afraid, and looking incredibly good while doing so. Lila found she didn't want to resist Nate. Even if this never worked out or went anywhere, she was okay with that. Lila wanted to move forward, and Nate seemed like a decent start.

Nate put his hand on her waist. Her skin burned where he touched. He pulled her close. She was barely breathing. Her mouth was dry when he tipped up her chin. His lips hovered above Lila's for a moment before he brought them down to hers.

"I'm not looking." Evelyn's voice carried across the yard.

Lila pulled back, her lips on fire and her head spinning. Nate laughed.

Lila shook her head, wanting to hug and strangle Evelyn at the same time. "I should probably get back, but I actually came over here to ask for a favor."

"You didn't come over here to make out with me?" Nate asked.

"That was a bonus."

Nate held out his hands, his mouth lifted in a smile. "What do you need, Lila?"

"I need your help throwing a fake party tomorrow afternoon at the Primrose," Lila said.

"Not that I don't pride myself on my ability to hang streamers, but is there another reason you need me specifically?"

Lila hesitated. "I need a jewelry designer for the party."

Nate rolled his eyes and chuckled. "I can call Jennie tonight."

"But don't you want to know what the plan is first?"

Nate shook his head. "Nah. I trust you."

Evelyn leaned out of the car. "I always say that an accommodating man is the most useful kind of man. I like this gentleman, Lila."

Lila didn't reply. She wrapped her arms around Nate and kissed him again.

Chapter Thirty-Eight

The Azalea Room was full the following morning with every female resident of the Primrose and a few of the males who wanted to see what all the commotion was about. June and Iris secured a table near the back. Florence and Mary Dixon were in the front with Edwin. Ruth talked to Helene by the patio. Brock was stationed by the sandwiches. The sun shone through the window. Somehow Zoe had managed to pull together a lunch of sandwiches and soda. Susanna paced by the podium, having been talked into this plan after making it clear she didn't think it would work.

Jennie had set up a table of jewelry near the front in a display worthy of a high-end jewelry store. She'd acted thrilled at Nate's invitation to hold an impromptu jewelry show at the Primrose, even though her usual clientele was forty years younger.

Evelyn stood at the podium. "Ladies, and the gentlemen who weren't invited, I'm glad you could join us this morning. As I wrote over email, we've convinced Jennie Blair to come for a one-time exclusive event here at the Primrose. No other building in the country has this opportunity, and I was able to personally arrange this private luxury jewelry show. You are all welcome."

Florence smiled proudly. Evelyn had insisted on giving opening remarks even though Lila had said opening remarks weren't necessary for a jewelry show. But Evelyn wasn't going to miss a chance to take credit.

Evelyn continued. "Jennie's jewelry rivals some of my best pieces, many of which are Cartier and Van Cleef & Arpels. My late husband, Richard, had excellent taste and doted on me. Not only has Jennie provided us with an array of high-end pieces to try on and purchase, you are all entered into a raffle simply by attending this event. The winner will receive one of Jennie's bangles. Don't forget to get your wrist measured before you leave as each bangle is custom fit to its wearer."

A murmur went through the crowd at Evelyn's statement. This was, of course, the reason for the high turnout. Lila knew rich people liked free stuff as much as everyone else if not more. She had made sure to include the raffle on the invitation to entice them all to the event, if the complimentary lunch wasn't enough (which it was for most everyone).

Ruth raised her hand. "I don't recall seeing this meeting in our online reservation system. As the chairman of the board, it's my responsibility to check it every evening. If you didn't reserve the room, you'll need to vacate it immediately."

"Oh, I did reserve it," Lila said. "You can check. I did it at two a.m. this morning."

"That's not enough notice," Ruth said.

"Actually it is. Rule 72.3—common rooms may be reserved with no less than six hours' notice," Lila said.

Ruth lowered her hand, looking annoyed.

Jennie stepped forward then. "I'm so happy to be here with you. Thanks for coming on short notice. I know you're all busy. My work is influenced by Greek—"

"I canceled a podiatrist appointment for this," Iris said loudly.

"I was supposed to meet with my trainer but I rescheduled," Brock said. "He's the most exclusive in town, but I have him on speed dial and he always makes time for me."

"Men weren't even invited," June said.

"But I told Edwin to come. His feelings get hurt if he's not included in building events," Mary Dixon said.

"That's true." Edwin nodded. "And I might need some jewelry for my next wife."

"Let's get on with this. Jennie doesn't have all day, and I have a salsa lesson in a half hour," Florence said.

"Florence does know how to speed things along," Evelyn whispered to Lila.

"As I was saying," Jennie started again.

Lila silently wished her good luck, knowing this crowd.

Jennie managed to get through a small presentation, after which the residents of the Primrose filed up to the front of the room to examine her jewelry collection. Lila waited with a tape measure off to one side of the podium, ostensibly to measure for the custom bangle but really to check for the birthmark.

Florence came first. She pulled up the sleeve of her white silk blouse and held out her arm. Lila took the tape measure and wrapped it around the widest part of Florence's wrist as Jennie had shown her. Turning Florence's arm under the guise of proper measuring, Lila examined the skin on her inner arm. Bluish veins ran beneath the skin like the curved branches of an ironwood. There was nothing that resembled a four-leaf clover.

There was a chance no one had the clover on their arm. Perhaps the woman who had stolen from the Primrose all those years ago had died or moved away or the clover itself had faded into folds of skin, no longer visible as a beacon of guilt. What if Lionel had lied about the entire thing in an attempt to lay the blame of the robberies on someone else? This plan was a long shot but it was also their *last* shot before Lila was due at the police station to face a possible arrest for murder. Glancing down at her phone, she saw the minutes ticking past. Her heart rate increased. The bundle of nerves and frustration and fear tied up inside her grew heavier.

Looking up, Lila met Jasper's eyes. She read the question on his face and shook her head to let him know it wasn't Florence. Jasper tipped up the corners of his mouth in a small smile and crinkled his eyes. It was an encouraging look; a reminder that there was still time.

Mary Dixon stepped up next, holding out her arm. "I never win anything but I have a lucky feeling today."

Lila smiled and measured Mary Dixon's wrist, turning over her arm. Helene was next. Brock insisted on getting measured as well because he said it was prejudicial to men to not allow them to participate in the raffle. Lila didn't feel like arguing with him and she measured his pudgy arm. No one had a birthmark resembling a clover on their skin.

June and Iris Willoughby finished trying on every piece of Jennie's jewelry and made their way to Lila. Jennie had brought a small portable credit card reader and was doing a brisk business as various residents purchased bracelets, charm necklaces, and signet rings. The gold from the display glinted in the sun, drawing its own light. The chatter in the room was loud and cheerful, but Lila had almost lost all hope. The list of suspects was rapidly dwindling, and her chances of arrest rapidly increasing.

Ruth pushed her way in front of the Willoughby sisters, cutting them off before they could step up to Lila's measuring station. She wore one of her Day-Glo caftans. Today it was the kind of fuchsia that could burn retinas with its intensity.

"Ruth, you cut in front of us," June said, sounding outraged.

"Oh, were you getting in line? I didn't see you," Ruth said, smirking.

Lila looked from June to Ruth. June whispered to Iris, something like, *No, I won't push her this time.* June finally shrugged and stepped behind Ruth.

Lila held out her hand with the measuring tape. Ruth extended her arm. The sleeve of her caftan fell away when Lila turned the arm over. Lila's body froze. *There*, right in the middle of Ruth's pale arm, was a small mole in the unmistakable shape of a four-leaf clover.

Lila gasped and gripped Ruth's arm tighter.

"You're hurting me," Ruth complained, pulling back her arm.

Evelyn was handing Jennie her credit card. She looked over at Lila, her eyes widening. She shoved the card reader out of the way and hobbled toward them. Jasper advanced at the same time.

"Step back," Jasper directed Iris and June.

"What's going on?" Ruth said, adjusting the sleeve of her caftan over her arm.

"She has the birthmark," Lila said to Jasper and Evelyn. She dropped the measuring tape, staring at Ruth's small brown eyes, now narrowed in her direction. Lila's mind was wiped blank of every thought but the revelation that Ruth Bailor was the Primrose burglar.

Jasper leaned in close to Ruth. "We need to talk to you in private immediately."

It was obvious now that something was happening, which was bigger than Jennie's jewelry show. The atmosphere in the room shifted; the crowd quieted and no one even pretended to look at jewelry anymore. June and Iris joined Florence near the sandwich table. They whispered among themselves, shooting glances at Ruth.

"I'm not sure what is happening but I have a meeting. You'll have to wait," Ruth blustered.

Lila leaned toward Ruth and whispered, "We know you're the Primrose burglar."

Ruth's mouth opened and closed like a fish tossed out of water. "What? That's ridiculous. I would never. I'm president of the board. I—I—" She looked to Susanna, who stood off to the side, her face white with shock. "Susanna, tell them to stop this harassment immediately."

"I would advise you to hear what they have to say," Susanna said in her crisp voice.

A chorus of whispers erupted at Susanna's refusal to come to Ruth's aid.

"You either talk to us now, or we go straight to the police with everything we know," Jasper said.

"You can have five minutes of my time," Ruth said imperiously, but her fingers clutched at the sleeve of her caftan, opening and closing on the material. She blinked and followed them out of the Azalea Room. The other residents stared in disbelief, sensing a reckoning was upon them.

Chapter Thirty-Nine

Lila pushed the door to the Hydrangea Room closed behind her. Jasper stood by the exit with his arms crossed. His jaw was clenched as he stared down Ruth.

Evelyn sat at one of the small round tables, pushing her walker to one side. Ruth glared at her from the middle of the room, but Evelyn patted the seat beside hers. "You might as well sit down."

Ruth didn't move. "This is ridiculous. I don't have to listen to you accuse me of a crime. I only came because you were causing a scene."

Jasper raised one eyebrow. "You might want to listen. We met with Lionel Garrett yesterday."

"I don't know who that is," Ruth said coolly.

"He's an antiques dealer in Richmond and a well-known fence. Is that the right term, Jasper?" Lila asked.

"That's it, although I suspect Ruth already knows that. We found evidence that Lionel was involved in moving some of the stolen goods from the Primrose back in 2002. He's already talking to the police," Jasper said.

"I don't know what that has to do with me," Ruth said.

"Don't treat us like imbeciles, Ruth. I have a genius-level IQ. We know you're the one who sold him the stolen goods from the Primrose. He's already identified you," Evelyn said, lying through her teeth.

"I had nothing to do with any theft, and I'm guessing after

twenty years, any identification from Mr. Garrett would be difficult, assuming he even got a good look at the face of whoever sold him the goods." Ruth smirked, knowing she had a good point.

"He might not have gotten a good look at your face, but he did get a good look at your birthmark—the one on your forearm that resembles a four-leaf clover. He remembered that very clearly," Lila said.

Ruth scoffed. "Lots of people have birthmarks. If you actually think I would confess to a crime I didn't commit, you're out of your minds. Now my guess is you three still think you're going to solve Sophia Kent's murder and, by extension, Emily Canterbury's. I know you're worried about Lila here getting arrested for Emily's murder, but we have to let the police do their job. I called Detective Roberts the other day to check on the investigation. He's such a nice man, so diligent about catching criminals. It's certainly not my problem he believes Lila is guilty, other than we shouldn't have a murderer living in our building. Once Lila is arrested, I will make sure the board votes her out. Even the members who you've somehow managed to charm won't have a choice when you're in jail."

Lila wasn't sure what else to say. Her shoulders drooped, her body cold. Ruth was right. They had no real evidence of anything. The only suspect in Emily's murder was Lila. She had hoped Ruth might confess when they presented her with proof of her theft, but Lila shouldn't have expected so much. Ruth wasn't the type to cave. She was the type to dig in until the end.

Evelyn toyed with the diamond bracelet on her wrist before looking up at Ruth with a small smile. "You may be right about the police. Perhaps they won't thoroughly look into Lionel's story and his claims about your birthmark. However, I can promise you one thing. I will tell everyone in Richmond about what you did, and I will make them believe it."

"No one will listen to you," Ruth said, her voice jittery. She moved closer to Evelyn.

"Oh no? I chaired the Children's Hospital Ball for five years in a row, I was on the board of the Richmond Symphony and the Virginia Opera *at the same time*. That's unheard of, Ruth. I was Chairman of the Stratford Board of Trustees, I founded the Society of Highway Beautification and I was president of the West End Garden Club for ten years. Do you really think I don't have any clout in this town? Women may not like me. Let's call a spade a spade—most women despise me, but they *will* believe me." Evelyn looked up at Ruth, but it had never appeared more as though she was looking down on someone. "In any event, rumors tend to take on a life of their own in this town. I'll make sure this one ruins you and I highly doubt you'll still be president of the Primrose Board after the dust settles on this."

Ruth finally sank into one of the chairs. Her hands gripped the edge of the table, her knuckles whitening with the effort. It was obvious Evelyn's arrow had hit its target. Threatening to call the police was one thing; Ruth could survive that. But threatening ostracism by the entire society of the Near West End of Richmond was entirely different and much worse to someone like Ruth.

Ruth's voice was faint. "Let's say hypothetically I was the burglar. What if I could convince you I had nothing to do with Sophia's death? Would that result in a different outcome?"

Jasper shook his head, but Evelyn gave him a steely-eyed gaze that made him stop.

"If you were hypothetically to tell us everything you knew about the burglaries and Sophia's death, and *if* we believed you, I think I could see my way into keeping this between us. I can't speak for Jasper of course," Evelyn said.

"The police are already talking to Lionel. If they find out about you, I'm not going to cover for you," Jasper said.

"You don't have much evidence," Ruth said. "I'm sure of that. Some old accounting records don't implicate me."

Lila stared at her, realizing Ruth or someone she'd hired had stolen the accounting records from her apartment on the night of the break-in. "Were you the one who broke into my apartment?"

Ruth smiled. "How would a retired housewife like myself go about breaking and entering? I suppose I could have made a copy of the spare key Gloria gave to me right before she died, knowing it might come in handy someday. I might have been curious about what kind of evidence you collected after Evelyn announced you were investigating the burglaries. But this is all theoretical. I would never do something like that."

Lila wanted to wipe that smug look off Ruth's face for scaring her and Bea, but there wasn't time for her to get angry. She glanced at her watch. She was scheduled to meet her lawyer at the police station in two hours. Lila needed to see what Ruth knew about the burglary and Sophia's death right now.

Jasper glared at Ruth. "The police are going to find this all very interesting."

"I'm not worried about the police," Ruth said. "I already told you that."

But Ruth was worried about Evelyn, that much was clear. Lila didn't blame her. Ruth looked at Evelyn, who nodded.

"Hypothetically, the burglar only stole those items from people she thought could afford to lose them. The burglar most likely knew it was wrong, but perhaps she didn't think she had a choice. Perhaps her husband had lost most of their money on bad investments and they were having trouble affording their daughter's law school tuition." Ruth looked down, hiding what appeared to be tears in her eyes. "This is a guess. I don't know for sure."

Despite everything, Lila felt a small pang of sympathy for Ruth. The things women were willing to do for their children.

"What about Sophia? She found out you were the burglar and confronted you, isn't that right?" Jasper asked.

Ruth looked genuinely confused now. "I don't know what you're talking about, hypothetically or otherwise. Sophia never confronted me. No one knew who the burglar was. I had nothing to do with what happened to her. I wasn't even in the building when she was killed."

"I read all the witness statements in Sophia's case," Jasper said. "You were at the cocktail party that evening. You easily could have slipped away, gone upstairs, and killed Sophia."

"I didn't do that!" Ruth exclaimed. "I'm telling you I was late to the cocktail party because I was meeting with Lionel Garrett in a parking garage. Hypothetically of course."

"Of course." Evelyn inclined her head.

"I couldn't tell the police where I really was at the time of the murder. Instead, I told them I was at the cocktail party the entire time. I arrived ten minutes before the police showed up. Sophia was already dead. The police had no idea where anyone was during the party. It was dark and crowded. They didn't really seem to care. I wasn't the only one who was late." Ruth stopped, realizing how much information she had given them. "This is all hypothetical obviously."

"What do you mean you weren't the only one who was late?" Lila asked.

Ruth shrugged. "I parked in the Primrose lot and walked down the side of the building. I was hoping to slip into the back of the party unnoticed. But I saw someone coming out of the side exit, the one in the stairwell out near the dumpsters. I hid in the bushes until she passed and then joined the party."

"Who was it?" Jasper asked.

"Helene Kent."

"Helene?" Lila asked, barely able to get out the word.

Ruth nodded, acknowledging their stunned expressions. "I know. It was really odd. She was right under that floodlight over the door so I could see her face clear as day. She was out of breath and holding her shoes, but then she put them on and straightened her long skirt and walked into the back of the party exactly like I did."

"You never told the police about seeing her?" Jasper asked.

"I never told the police about getting there late so no, I didn't tell them about seeing Helene. I did always wonder though what she was doing there," Ruth said.

Something was creeping over Lila, a memory, something important in the back of her mind was pushing its way to the front.

"Ruth, do you remember what shoes Helene put on?" Lila asked urgently.

Ruth raised her eyebrows, thinking for several seconds. "They were boots—thick, heavy things. I remember because I had never seen Helene wear boots before, only pumps or flats. It was one more odd thing about that night."

Lila froze, staring at Ruth. There was thunder in her ear. The voices next door died. Her vision narrowed to a sliver of wall across the room—chipped white molding. *The boots.*

Jasper grabbed Lila's shoulder. "What is it?"

"When I was looking at the photos of Sophia's body in the police file, I knew there was something off but I couldn't put my finger on it at the time. It was her *shoes*! They were all wrong! Alice told us Sophia always wore Dr. Marten boots. She was headed to a rock concert on the night she died. What sixteen-year-old girl wears CHANEL heels to a rock concert?"

"CHANEL pumps are appropriate for any occasion," Evelyn said, missing the point entirely.

"CHANEL is always good for resale," Ruth noted.

A chill went up Lila's spine. Invisible bits of ice nicked at her skin. *CHANEL pumps. Dr. Marten boots. Helene, Sophia.*

"Helene switched out their shoes before the police arrived and found Sophia," Lila said softly. "That means—"

"Helene was there when or right after Sophia died," Jasper finished.

"Good gracious. What are our good Richmond families coming to?" Evelyn sounded disgusted. "Murder is so tacky."

Chapter Forty

Helene had already left the jewelry party when Lila, Jasper, and Evelyn burst out of the Hydrangea Room. They were knocking on her door minutes later. Evelyn banged her walker on the floor to make it even louder. Helene opened the door calmly as if she was expecting them.

"Well, hello there. What brings you up here? I must say that was a lovely event. Thank you for helping to organize it," Helene said in her perfect, modulated voice.

Lila pushed her way through the door. She didn't have time for niceties at this point. She was due at the police station soon, and she had to prove someone else had killed Sophia Kent and Emily Canterbury or risk losing her daughter and her entire life.

"Is something wrong?" Helene asked as Jasper and Evelyn trailed behind Lila into the room. Evelyn settled herself onto the couch immediately.

Lila whirled around and pointed at Helene. "You killed Sophia."

Evelyn groaned. "We need to work on your subtlety, Lila. I can give you some tips later."

"I don't know what is going on here, but you should leave. I'm calling Stanley Ranger to complain about your behavior," Helene said.

Lila ignored the threat. She was on a roll.

"You also killed Emily because she found out about Sophia and was going to expose you," Lila said.

Helene looked to Evelyn and Jasper. "Are you going to do something about this? Remove her before I call the police," she demanded heatedly.

"Please call them. I dare you," Lila snapped.

Evelyn examined her nails. "Helene, dear, I really do think it's time for you to confess before things get more difficult. We've gathered a pile of evidence against you, mostly using my superior detective skills. Jasper and Lila helped a little too."

Jasper calmly moved beside Lila. "We know you weren't at the cocktail party when Sophia died. We have a witness who saw you coming out of the stairwell."

"I'm not sure what you're talking about." Helene didn't seem worried. She walked over to the small antique secretary desk in one corner.

"If they look into you, I'm sure the police can tie you to Emily's death too," Jasper said. "And they *will* look after we talk to them."

"That's ridiculous," Helene said calmly.

"What are you doing?" Lila asked.

Helene opened a drawer. "I'm checking on something."

She was checking on something? Right now? Lila didn't trust Helene. Evelyn rattled on about how she'd known it was Helene from the very beginning, while Lila craned her head to see what Helene was up to. Her view was blocked by the couch.

Helene finally turned. Her manicured fingers held a small black gun. Lila froze.

"Is that a real gun? It's not very impressive," Evelyn said, but her eyes were wide.

"Helene, put the gun down," Jasper said.

"Please. Don't," Lila managed to croak out. All she could think of was Bea finding out about her death. Lila had promised not to leave her. "We won't tell anyone."

Helene's face tightened. She moved around the side of the

couch, motioning for Lila and Jasper to sit by Evelyn. "I have to protect myself. You are threatening me in my own home."

"You can't kill all three of us. That would raise a lot of eyebrows at the club," Evelyn said. Her voice was steady, but Lila noticed Evelyn's gnarled fingers gripping the edge of the couch.

Lila sank down beside Evelyn, putting an arm around her shoulders. Jasper sat on her other side.

"I'll come up with a story," Helene said as if convincing herself. "I'll blame Lila. She broke into my apartment, shot Evelyn and Jasper, turned the gun on herself. The police already think she killed Emily."

"What's going on?" Alice asked, coming into the room from the foyer. She stood at the edge of the beautiful Persian rug, looking from the couch to Helene. Her face paled.

"Darling, you're not supposed to be here. You need to leave and let me handle this," Helene said. "These people are dangerous. They're threatening us."

"You're the one with a gun," Evelyn pointed out.

Helene's gaze locked on Alice. There was nothing else in the room for her. Lila suddenly knew Alice was the key to escape. Helene would never kill them in front of Alice. She cared about nothing other than her daughter.

Alice backed away toward the hallway, looking fearful.

Lila spoke up. "Helene was involved in your sister's death. It was her shoes that gave it away. Sophia was found wearing a pair of CHANEL pumps instead of her Dr. Marten boots." She turned to Helene. "You took the boots off Sophia's body. You were there when she died."

"I was not." Helene glared. "You can't prove anything by shoes. Lots of girls wear CHANEL pumps. Maybe not where you're from, but Sophia liked nice shoes."

Alice stopped backing up. "No. That's not right. Sophia hated high heels. She only wore her Dr. Marten boots. You used to yell at her to wear more appropriate shoes. I remember."

"Alice, don't say anything else," Helene snapped.

No one moved. Silence shrouded the room. Alice stared at Helene.

"Mama, what did you do?" Alice finally whispered.

Their faces were so alike, two pale ovals, mirrors of each other. Both with amber eyes, fighting tears. Helene's hand with the gun shook.

Lila spoke quietly. "She deserves to know."

Helene steadied her hand, pointing the gun straight at Lila. Lila's heart raced, her body trembling.

"What happened to Sophia?" Alice asked, stepping closer to Helene.

"I would never hurt your sister. I promise," Helene said.

"I believe you. But someone killed Sophia twenty-one years ago, and I think you know who it was," Alice said.

"Let this go," Helene begged. The gun lowered slightly but remained clutched in her hand.

"I need to know the truth. I wanted to move on. I *tried*, but I can't," Alice said.

Helene faltered. She gazed at Alice and her features sagged as she seemed to come to a decision. "You were young when Sophia died. All you saw was the funny, beautiful, charming older sister who doted on you. She was all those things, but she wasn't perfect. Sometimes she made terrible, impulsive decisions. She got herself into serious trouble when she was sixteen. Everything changed after that. She became difficult, always staying out past curfew, skipping class. We found evidence of drug use, alcohol use. She was withdrawn and unhappy. I thought it was a phase."

"I don't remember Sophia getting into serious trouble," Alice said, sounding confused.

"You didn't know. No one did," Helene said.

"What happened?" Evelyn asked sharply, unable to help herself.

Lila nudged Evelyn to quiet her. Helene still held the gun. They didn't want to draw her ire or attention.

"Please," Alice said. "I need to know the whole story."

Helene swallowed. "Sophia accidentally . . . she accidentally killed Melanie Livingston."

Lila inhaled sharply. She looked from Evelyn to Jasper. Their faces reflected her shock. She recalled Conrad telling her how they had fenced off the cliffs after someone fell, and Teddy describing Melanie's death.

"It *was* an accident," Helene said quickly. "I always believed her about that. Apparently there was a party at the cliffs behind the Primrose. Kids were drinking. Melanie went to leave, and Sophia followed her. They argued, something to do with Melanie starting a rumor about Susanna. Melanie pushed Sophia first, and Sophia pushed her back. It was dark, they were both drunk and too close to the edge, and Melanie lost her balance and fell."

"I remember Melanie. Her grandparents threw an elaborate memorial reception with a full bar. I thought it was a bit undignified, if you want to know the truth," Evelyn whispered.

"Sophia came straight home after Melanie's fall. She hadn't called for help. She was in shock. I wasn't going to let an accident ruin her life. I didn't even consider going to the police. We couldn't risk a murder investigation. If she'd gone to jail, her life would have been over. And even if she wasn't convicted, her reputation would never have recovered. I made her promise not to tell anyone what happened. It had to stay a secret. I was certain we'd made the right decision. I thought I understood what Sophia could handle. I thought I was saving her life." Helene stopped, seeming to escape into her own mind for a moment. "I didn't know what the guilt would do to her."

"That's why she wanted to see a psychiatrist," Lila said softly, putting the pieces together.

"I couldn't allow her to talk to a psychiatrist and risk the story coming out. I told her she needed to forget about it and move forward," Helene said.

"Mama," Alice said, a quiet rebuke.

Helene sagged under the weight of her daughter's judgment. "I know. I made a mistake. I should have helped Sophia deal with her remorse instead of pretending like Melanie never happened. I was certain she'd get over it eventually, but her destructive behavior only got worse as time went on. She convinced herself that God was coming to punish her." She closed her eyes. Tears dripped down her cheeks. "A couple days before her death, Sophia had gotten in trouble for trying to pass forged checks. Conrad found out about it."

"I had no idea," Alice murmured, looking distraught.

"The night of the cocktail party, Conrad arranged to meet Sophia beforehand. I was at my wit's end on how to handle her. I thought maybe he could talk some sense into her. But she came to his apartment after taking drugs. She cried and begged him for money to pay her drug dealer."

Evelyn inhaled. That drug dealer was her son.

Helene continued. "Conrad told Sophia he loved her and wanted to get her help. She said he wouldn't love her if he knew the truth. That's when she told him about Melanie. Conrad was understandably shocked and upset, and his reaction devastated Sophia. She grabbed the knife from the block on the counter and said she didn't deserve to live. He tried to take it away from her. They struggled, and the knife slashed both their arms. He stumbled and fell, hitting his head on the kitchen counter. I found them both on the kitchen floor." Helene's chin trembled, tears pouring down her face. "Sophia was already gone. The knife had cut the brachial artery in her arm, and she'd died from blood loss while Conrad lay unconscious."

"What!" Evelyn nearly shouted the word, echoing Lila's own sentiments of disbelief.

Alice covered her mouth with her hands, her eyes wide with shock.

"Why didn't you call the police?" Jasper asked.

"Conrad wanted to. He wanted to confess everything—the truth about Melanie, Sophia's drug habit, her cause of death. He was insistent on explaining every detail. I was horrified at the prospect. Why would we drag Sophia's name through the mud when she was already dead? I couldn't let that happen. Conrad only agreed to keep quiet because of his guilt; he wanted to honor my wishes. I made him promise he wouldn't tell," Helene said.

"You staged the burglary," Lila said.

Helene managed to nod. Her knuckles around the gun were white as she clutched it harder. "It was my idea. A way to explain Sophia's death where no one got hurt. I bandaged up Conrad's arm, helped him change his shirt. Luckily it was chilly that night. Some of his blood had gotten on Sophia's boots from when they were both lying on the floor. I wasn't sure if the police could run forensic tests on the leather, so I switched my heels with her boots. I was the one who screamed, knowing Emily's mother would hear me next door and assume the scream was Sophia's. At that point, Conrad was already at the cocktail party, so he had a solid alibi. I didn't trust him to hold up under questioning, but I knew that I would. I told the police I was at the cocktail party too. It was dark, and no one suspected me anyway."

A shocked silence had fallen over the room. No one even dared to breathe, absorbing the unbelievable truth of Sophia's death.

Evelyn finally cleared her throat. "I'm an expert at deductive reasoning but something doesn't make sense. Why would Conrad offer the reward if he was the one who killed Sophia? That seems rather counterintuitive, I'm sorry to say."

"Grandpa would never have broken a promise to Mama," Alice said softly.

"It's true. He was a man of his word, and he'd promised not to reveal how Sophia had died. But he wanted you to know. He came to me before his death and pleaded with me to tell you, but too much time had passed, and I knew it would do you more harm than good. And I—I worried you would never forgive me for lying." Helene stared at the floor, her voice trembling. "Conrad apparently disagreed and came up with his plan for the reward; I'm sure he thought if someone came forward with new information about Sophia's death, it would push me into admitting what really happened." She exhaled, lowering her gun.

"Someone did have information about Sophia's death—Emily Canterbury," Jasper said in his authoritative detective voice. "On the night Sophia died, you thought Emily's mother was alone in her apartment. Considering that she was ill and bedbound, you figured there was no chance she could make it to the door in time to see you escape down the hallway after you imitated Sophia's scream. You hadn't counted on Emily being there that night. My guess is Emily blackmailed you for years and that's the reason she never went to the police. But she decided to come clean and collect Conrad's reward. You killed her to keep her quiet."

Helene didn't deny Jasper's theory. Lila thought of Emily's wardrobe and fancy apartment. Helene must have paid for all those things. It was clear from Helene's silence and the resigned downturn to her mouth that Jasper had guessed correctly.

"How could you do this?" Alice spoke up. Her face was red and streaked with tears. "You should have told the truth from the beginning."

Helene looked straight at her daughter, her lip quivering. "I was protecting you. Conrad was like a father to you, and you loved Sophia so much. I didn't think you could handle knowing what either of them had done. I wanted to preserve their memories *for you*. And I didn't want a family scandal hanging over your head. You deserved more than that. You deserved a full and healthy life. You are all I have left, and I would do anything to keep you safe." Her voice was guttural, fierce.

Lila recognized that ferocity; the need to defend her child at all costs. Helene had thought she was doing the right thing by hiding a scandal and promulgating a false legacy for Sophia. She had covered up a difficult reality to protect Alice from a hard truth but that wasn't fair to her daughter. Alice deserved the chance to face what had happened and process her own emotions about Sophia's death. Helene's need to control the story had kept Alice from forming her own opinions and making sense of her sister's death. In the end, the lie had hurt Alice and Helene far more than the truth.

"I know you're angry with me, but this doesn't need to ruin our lives." Helene's face was drawn, her eyes desperate and wild. She held up the gun once more and pointed it toward the couch.

Lila huddled closer to Evelyn and Jasper. After everything they'd learned, was it possible this was really the end? Evelyn trembled on her right, and Jasper kneaded his legs nervously on her left. The air went still. Lila dropped her chin, closed her eyes. *Bea, Bea, Bea*—the name echoed through her head in a prayer.

There was a shuffle of movement. Lila's eyes flew open. Alice had stepped in front of the gun. She was openly crying. Tears streamed down Helene's face too.

"Alice, please," Helene said. "Let me fix this."

"No," Alice said. "No more."

Helene's arm shook, outstretched. Lila held her breath for one . . . two . . . three seconds. And then Alice took the gun from Helene's hand, placing it gently on the table.

"We have to tell the police," Alice said.

"I know." Helene bowed her head.

"I hate what you did, but I still love you." Alice's voice was clogged with tears.

"I will always love you more than anything," Helene said and reached out her arms for her daughter.

Chapter Forty-One

Helene was arrested for the murder of Emily Canterbury later that day. Jasper's colleagues indicated that they found a silencer in Helene's Hermès handbag and her tiny black gun was a match for the firearm used in Emily's murder. That, combined with her confession, made it clear the case was effectively closed. After a couple of hours at the police station, Detective Roberts reluctantly told Lila she was no longer a suspect. Jasper and Evelyn were at her side the entire time with Evelyn complaining loudly about the lack of proper tea, the chill in the waiting room, and the *most* unwelcoming decor.

Bea had gone straight to Nora's house after school and was furious when she got home and learned they had cracked the case without her. She made them tell her Helene's confession, word for word. Lila was standing in the kitchen, wiping down the counter when Bea rushed in and gave her a quick, hard hug. Before Lila could hug Bea back, she skipped into the living room. Lila suspected that was Bea's way of saying she was proud of her.

Lila had called Nate later that evening to tell him what happened. Nate broke the real story of Sophia Kent's death for the *Richmond Journal* the very next morning. He told Lila it was the most viewed article for the entire newspaper in the last ten years.

In the days after Helene's arrest, Lila called a divorce lawyer who came highly recommended by Edwin. She was ready to move on without Ryan. She didn't know if he would take a plea deal yet, but she planned to do everything she could to ensure he returned the money he'd stolen. She was already thinking about how Bea could visit Ryan in prison, assuming that was what Bea wanted. Bea would need a lot of support as they figured out how to navigate Ryan's incarceration, but Lila knew they would get through it together.

Zoe had said Lila could skip the grand opening at the club a few nights later, but there was no way Lila would miss it. She arrived at the club after the event started. Evelyn had gone earlier with Florence to ensure they arrived at the precise time the club opened. They'd decided to wear matching headdresses, which they said embodied the 1920s spirit of prohibition.

Bea stayed home with Jasper for a *Murder, She Wrote* marathon. Jasper had agreed to make snickerdoodle cookies in between watching the show and filling out his application for a business license. He'd decided to start a private investigation firm. Bea asked if he was looking for partners, and he'd looked straight at Lila when he answered, *Yes, I am*.

Music was pounding out of the club when Lila arrived. Nate had agreed to meet her outside. He was already there when she pulled up.

"You look amazing," Nate said immediately.

Lila turned to show him her dress. "If you can believe it, I borrowed it from Evelyn. She had this in the back of her closet."

The dress itself was navy silk that dipped low in the back with a high neck that showed off bare shoulders. It fit Lila perfectly, and she wasn't sure the dress had ever been worn. Now that she thought about it, she realized there was a chance Evelyn had bought the dress for her.

"You know, you're kind of famous now," Nate said.

"I do think describing me as a beautiful private investigator was a stretch. But I got calls from CNN, NBC, and CBS, all wanting interviews."

"Are you going to do it?"

Lila shook her head. "No way. I want my life to calm down, not get crazier. I'm just relieved I'm no longer a murder suspect."

They entered the club. The opening room was small with a dark curtain separating it from the main part of the club. A pretty, young hostess stood behind a podium. She winked at Lila, recognizing her from the setup earlier in the day. "Password please."

Lila leaned forward and whispered, "Primrose."

The girl grinned and pulled back the curtain. The other side was a revelation. Dark moody floral arrangements stood tall on the bar off to the right with a smattering of tables and chairs, all of them crowded with people. Lila and Nate moved farther back into the club past another room with bookshelves and more tables and chairs. Every space was filled with people chatting and laughing and drinking. In the very back, they came to the huge event space with the raised stage. Teddy's band was playing. Lila had to admit they sounded good.

The dance floor was full of men and women of all ages—mostly young adults in their twenties and thirties but a number of older people too. Some of them much older.

Evelyn stood in the back with Florence, Mary Dixon, and Edwin. They all held cocktails. June and Iris danced in the back. June wore a very low-cut blouse. Lila hoped her breasts remained covered, although frankly, it looked unlikely.

Lila sidled up to Evelyn. "Teddy sounds good."

Evelyn sighed. "Yes, he's a good singer. He's not a superstar by any means."

"He is talented," Florence said, offering up a compliment to her friend.

Evelyn eyed the crowd. "Do you think there are any acceptable young women here for Teddy to meet? I've made my peace with the fact he's never going to have a job, which is an embarrassment. I'm still hopeful he will get married, and I can get some grandchildren out of him. He's older, but for some men that's the right age to settle down."

Florence squinted into the crowd. "I think that is Miriam Vale's daughter over there. She's only twenty-five but that might appeal to Teddy. Her great-aunt was Catherine Lee so you know there's good genes in there."

Evelyn assessed the pretty girl who was dancing by the stage. "Shall we go talk to her?"

"Let's do," Florence said.

The two of them hobbled off in the direction of poor Miriam Vale's daughter. Who knew what they would say to her?

Zoe caught sight of Lila across the room and hurried over, stopping every few seconds to accept congratulations from various members of the crowd.

"Can you believe this?" Zoe asked Lila.

Lila looked admiringly at the scene—the crowd, the beautifully polished bar, the waitstaff in period costume, and the columns soaring above it all. "It's incredible. I'm so happy for you."

"For us," Zoe said. "You helped. If you hadn't stepped in when you did, this wouldn't even be happening. No one would have known about this place. Now it's a huge success. We're going to make a profit tonight and I can actually pay you something. You are really good at making things happen. I can't wait to see what you do next."

Lila smiled to cover up her discomfort. *What was she going to do next?* She still hadn't figured out a job but there were options. She could find a day job and finish her degree at night, pursuing marketing like she'd planned back in college. Or maybe she could capitalize on helping Zoe and the success of the club to convince an event-planning firm to let her start at the bottom and work her way up. There was a part of her that wondered if Jasper did want a partner in his new business. It turned out she *was* pretty good at getting people to tell her secrets. Whatever she ultimately decided to do, she'd find a way to make it successful.

Now that the apartment was clean and she was no longer a murder suspect, she could move anywhere. Bea would be out of school in two weeks, and Stanley wanted to put the apartment on the market right after. Lila's chest squeezed when she thought of leaving Gloria's place. It had begun as such a disaster, but she'd made it homey and comfortable. She would miss the mohair couch, the light through the living room windows, and the view of Grove Avenue. She could admit it. She didn't want to go, but she had no choice. There was no way she could afford a place like that, and she didn't meet the age requirement. She'd always known the Primrose was only temporary.

Zoe flitted off, immediately swallowed in the crowd. Nate came back to stand by Lila. "Mary Dixon told me they're calling an emergency meeting to vote Ruth off the board. She said something about not trusting Ruth's morals after the police came to talk to her this morning. I guess the news is all over the building."

"Interesting," Lila said.

She and Evelyn had agreed not to tell anyone about Ruth's hypothetical confession, but Jasper had not agreed to keep it from the police. Ruth getting arrested for the burglaries from twenty-one years ago was unlikely, but if a little police questioning ended her reign of terror as board president . . . well, that was an outcome Lila could live with.

"June keeps asking me to slow dance," Nate whispered.

"But this isn't a slow song," Lila said, her eyes twinkling.

"I know and I'm a little afraid," Nate said.

Lila laughed. She had no idea what was going to happen with

Nate. She needed to take things slow, finalize her divorce, talk with Bea about dating. There were a million hurdles to jump over before she could even think about settling down again. In the meantime, though, Nate was a fun distraction. Pulling him close, Lila linked her fingers through his.

* * *

THE CALL FROM Mama came early the next morning. Lila turned over in bed, briefly stretching and appreciating all the space around her. Pulling her phone toward her, she saw Mama's name on the caller ID and sighed. Mama had called six times, but Lila had avoided her. She hadn't wanted to hear that Stanley was upset about all the new publicity Lila was getting from solving Sophia Kent's murder.

Mama wasn't the only one who had called either. Several of her old acquaintances from Norfolk had reached out too, most of whom Lila ignored the same way that they had ignored her for the past eight months. She'd only picked up the phone to talk with Daphne, who was delighted by the news coverage and promised to drive up for a visit soon.

Patricia had also texted, demanding that Lila meet her for coffee in Norfolk to discuss Bea's education now that Ryan was in jail. Lila had sent back a quick response—*You deal with your son. I'll take care of my daughter.* She ignored Patricia's follow-up texts. She didn't owe her ex-mother-in-law a meeting about anything.

Lila turned back to the phone now. Mama's name pulsed on the screen. Lila couldn't avoid her forever. She pressed the answer button.

"Hi, Mama," Lila said.

"Honey, finally! Everyone is talking about you," Mama exclaimed.

"I'm sorry about that," Lila said.

"Why are you sorry? I think it's wonderful what you did," Mama said. "People are coming out of the woodwork telling Stanley how grateful they are for letting you live in the Primrose and getting a murderer out of the building. You're a hero."

"Oh," Lila said, sitting up and feeling more awake. "I'm glad to hear that."

"I can't believe you solved Sophia's murder, after all these years. Who would have thought you could do something like that?"

"Not you," Lila said without thinking.

Mama was silent for several seconds. "What does that mean?"

Lila bit her lip, thinking through how to smooth over her words. Although... why should she? Mama had told her there was no way Lila could solve the murder. Why should she pretend like that hadn't happened? "It means that you don't think I'm good at things like that."

"Things like what?" Mama asked quietly.

"Things like solving problems and using my brain."

Mama was quiet again, then followed a sharp gasp and then another. It was sobs. Mama was crying.

"Mama?" Lila asked tentatively.

"I'm sorry. But how—how could you think that?" Mama asked, her voice cracking.

"You told me I couldn't solve the murder."

"That's because you had no experience and I didn't want you putting yourself or Bea at risk. A murder investigation *is* potentially dangerous," Mama said.

Lila thought of Helene's gun and swallowed. Mama wasn't entirely wrong.

"It's more than the murder investigation, though. You never thought I could support myself. My whole life, you pushed me to get married and make Ryan love me," Lila said.

"I thought you loved him," Mama burst out. "All I wanted was for you to be happy."

"But I wasn't happy, not just after Ryan left but before," Lila said, and there was an unspoken blame in her words.

"I didn't know that. I wish you'd told me."

"Do you really? Because you never wanted me to complain in case I bothered whichever man was supporting us at the time," Lila said.

Mama stayed silent for several seconds. "You're right. I should have listened to you more." She didn't argue with Lila again. Her voice was defeated.

It was the unspoken defeat that did it. Something released inside Lila. There was no need for her to win this argument. She didn't agree with a lot of the things Mama had done or said to her over the years, but Lila had ultimately made her own choices about how to live as an adult. She'd hidden parts of herself away from everyone, Mama included. Lila should have spoken up a long time ago.

"I'm not mad at you," Lila said.

"Maybe you should be because I haven't done enough to convince you that I do think you're smart and I'm proud of you," Mama said, a hint of tears still in her voice. "I should tell you that more."

Those words were like sunshine on Lila's face. She would remember this lesson. She wasn't always going to get it right with Bea, but she could be proud of her daughter and she could tell her often. It could soothe a lot of heartache.

Mama continued in a soft voice. "I never wanted you to struggle like I did after your father died. You might not remember. You were little, but that was a bad time for us. My secretary job barely covered our rent and food. I was worried all the time about how I was going to support you. I thought someone like Ryan would take care of you so you wouldn't have to worry like I did. But I should have known you could take care of yourself."

"Thank you, Mama. This means a lot to me to hear. And please believe me when I tell you that my marriage wasn't your fault," Lila said.

"I don't know about that. It's my job to protect you," Mama said.

There it was. Mama had echoed Lila's very words to Bea. This was the same reason Helene had covered up Sophia's death and kept the truth from Alice, misguided as she was. Mothers protected . . . but that didn't mean they could fix everything. It didn't mean they could make every problem go away. It didn't mean they wouldn't make a million small and big mistakes. It meant they loved, and they loved, and they loved. In the end, that had to be enough.

Chapter Forty-Two

Later that morning, Lila got a call from Alice Kent, asking her to meet her at Rise Up Cafe. Lila didn't want to go. She couldn't imagine what Alice had to say to her. Lila had gotten Helene arrested and subjected her family to embarrassment and scrutiny. Alice must be resentful of Lila, but Lila was willing to let Alice yell at her if it gave her closure.

The national press was having a field day with the story and had camped out in front of the Primrose for over a week. Susanna refused to let any of them in the driveway, and they were all piled up on the sidewalk. Lila put on a baseball hat and went out the back to escape them.

Alice was seated at a table when Lila arrived. Lila made her way through the room and sank into the seat across from Alice.

"I got you a latte," Alice said. "I didn't know what you might like so I took a chance. You don't have to drink it if you don't want. I wanted to make it easier and I was hoping that you—" She stopped and took a breath. "Sorry. I know I'm babbling. I'm nervous."

Lila took the latte and sipped. "Thank you. This is perfect." She hesitated. "I'm nervous too."

"Why are you nervous? You did nothing wrong," Alice said.

Lila drew her brows together. "I got Helene arrested."

"Because of her own actions," Alice countered. "She hurt people, she lied to me and everyone else, and she planned to let you go to jail even though you have a daughter who depends on you. I still can't believe her." She sighed heavily. "I am sorry. That's what I wanted to say to you in person."

"Oh, Alice," Lila said, reaching over to squeeze her hand. "I don't blame you for anything. We are not our mothers."

Lila said it with fervor, with passion, because she *had* to believe this too. It was hard to be a single mother. Lila had experienced that firsthand. Mama had made her choices for how to get through life, but Lila would make different ones.

Alice nodded at Lila's statement. "It's going to take me a long time to come to terms with what she did. I still can't believe how much she covered up. I've always felt as though my life was on hold because of Sophia's death, and now . . ." She lifted her hands, looking bewildered. "I don't know what to feel. I'm mostly sad for Sophia and Grandpa. I wish I'd known what happened when he was alive so I could talk to him about it."

"You can't think like that," Lila said. "I wasted a lot of time regretting what I did or didn't know. But that doesn't do anything for you. It only makes you feel bad. I know you don't want to keep feeling bad."

"No, I don't. I'm going to get myself straight," Alice said, her lip quivering as she spoke. "Wyatt is helping. He's a good shoulder to cry on."

"I'm glad. You deserve a great life even if the people you love do something terrible," Lila said.

Alice smiled then. "You deserve a great life too, Lila. I've spoken with James Forrester. He plans to transfer the reward money to you by next week."

Lila stilled, her ears ringing with Alice's words. She hadn't even thought of the reward since she was cleared as a suspect. Once it became clear that the killer was Conrad Kent himself, and Sophia's death was covered up by his daughter-in-law, she'd assumed no one would get a reward for turning in the very people who were giving it to them. It made no sense to benefit from a tragedy of their own making.

"I can't accept that," Lila said automatically.

"Why? Grandpa wanted someone to tell the truth about what happened to Sophia, and Melanie too. Do you know I've tracked down her family? They live in South Carolina now. I told them how Melanie really died. They didn't say much to me. I'm sure they can't forgive my family, but I had to try." Alice was quiet, her head bent down toward the table. When she looked back up, her eyes were shining. "But as for you, I can do something for you. Something that you deserve."

"But Helene confessed. And even if I did deserve the reward, I didn't solve the murder on my own. Evelyn and Jasper did as much as me."

"They said you would say that. I already spoke to them. They don't want the money. They said it should all go to you. Evelyn said something like, *I'm much too rich to take charity from the Kents*, and Jasper said something like, *I already have everything I need.*" Alice nodded at her. "The money is yours."

"It feels wrong to take it with everything that happened," Lila said softly.

"It would feel more wrong to me if you didn't take it. Please. This was one of Grandpa's last requests. I think he would have been happy to know the truth finally came out. I can imagine this weighed on him until the day he died. As for me, you helped solve the biggest mystery of my life. It may not have turned out the way I wanted but I'm glad I know what really happened to Sophia. I can finally move on with my own life. Please, Lila. You earned this money."

Two million dollars. Alice was talking about a reward of two million dollars.

Lila's body flooded with something—a glow of happiness or... pride? She didn't know. All she knew was that she was free. She had enough money to do whatever she wanted. She had enough money to take care of Bea and herself. The money would change everything... or would it? Well, it didn't change the things that mattered—Bea, Mama, Evelyn, Jasper, Zoe, a new home, maybe someday Nate. Lila already had the things that were worth everything in the world. She had what she needed.

Although—and Lila could be honest with herself here—two million dollars never hurt anyone.

* * *

Lila walked slowly into the apartment, still dazed by the promise of the reward. Bea immediately burst through the door behind her. She'd waited in Evelyn's apartment while Lila met with Alice but was clearly listening out for Lila's footsteps in the hall.

"You will not believe this," Lila said and stooped down to Bea's level so she could see her face. "We got the reward."

"It's really happening? We got the two-million-dollar reward?" Bea's voice was high, incredulous.

"That's the one," Lila shouted.

They sprang into each other's arms. They spun around laughing. It was as if the very air in apartment 2B was infected with contagious laughter, and it felt amazing.

"Can we go to Paris?" Bea asked when she caught her breath. "Can I get a pony or a TV in my room? Can I have a phone? Can I get a fingerprint kit?"

Lila ticked off Bea's requests on her fingers. "You don't speak French, you don't ride horses, and you're definitely not getting a

TV or phone yet. I'll consider the fingerprint kit. You know what else we can definitely do? We can figure out a place to live. How about that for starters?"

Bea nodded, grinning. "That sounds good. I already know where I want to live."

"Where's that?" Lila asked, amused at Bea's sincerity regarding real estate.

"Here."

Lila frowned. "Here? As in right here in this apartment?"

"Yes, Mama. I love it here."

Lila looked around at the blue and white carpet and through to the kitchen with its old appliances and the broken furniture. There was no trash anymore, and you could see that, despite the outdated couches and scuffed walls, the bones of this place were good. The ceilings were high, the doors were solid wood, the moldings were intricate and beautiful beneath the chipped paint. The layout was perfect for two people, and she loved the view beyond the window. But still—the Primrose?

"Bea, I know you like it here. I do too. But there are lots of places we can live. Think about our house back in Norfolk—how much space we had," Lila said.

"I don't want to move back to Norfolk. I like it here in Richmond."

"We can stay in Richmond. I like it too. But how about a bigger house?"

"Why do we need a bigger house? I like living in a smaller place. In our old house, I had to go looking for you. But here, I always know where you are."

It was as if Bea had reached into her head and said the exact thing Lila thought too. She also liked knowing where Bea was, and she didn't need a big house or a lot of space. They each had their own room because everyone needs some privacy, even a ten-year-old. But she mostly wanted to be close to her daughter; watching her murder shows and drawing on the floor and listening to her complain and loving every second of it. But the Primrose still wouldn't work.

"The Primrose is for people over fifty-five. We don't fit the age requirement," Lila said.

"Evelyn already talked to the board and Susanna, and they'll vote to let us stay. Evelyn said that everyone always does what she wants eventually. They do make exceptions, Mama." Bea said it so seriously. Her little face was screwed up in an expression of solemnity.

"You already talked to Evelyn about this?"

"Duh, Mama," Bea said. "Evelyn told me about the reward after you left this morning, but I wasn't sure until you got home."

"What about moving to a neighborhood with kids your own age?" Lila asked.

"Why would I want to do that? I like the people here. But you don't have to worry that I only like old people now. I have friends at school too. I want to have Nora over so we can explore the gardens and figure out where Sophia met with Teddy before she was murdered. We're going to reenact the whole crime from start to finish. We might invite the entire Detective Club to come."

"That sounds like a lot of fun," Lila said, clearing her throat and wondering if Nora's mother would enjoy such a reenactment.

"I think Gloria would have wanted us to live here. We have some things in common. She was really observant and naturally suspicious like me, and she liked a lot of weird stuff, which I think is cool," Bea said.

For the first time since returning to the apartment, Lila registered that Bea was not wearing Ryan's old Braves T-shirt. Instead, she wore a Hawaiian shirt that she must have unearthed from Gloria's collection. It was a crisp, bright blue that matched Bea's eyes.

"So, what do you think?" Bea asked.

Lila looked around at the place that had terrified her not so long ago. She was sure Stanley would happily sell this place to her to avoid having to stage the apartment or pay a broker's fee. But it wasn't the safe choice. That was for sure. This was definitely the messy choice. The apartment still needed a lot of work, and the building was full of retired people who would keep track of their every move. They could easily find a small house on a quiet street where they waved hello to their neighbors from across a driveway but never had to deal with them on a personal level. They could keep their distance, literally and figuratively, which would mean they never had to worry about the problems or the pain caused by anyone else.

If they stayed here, there was no chance of keeping any distance from their neighbors. The residents of the Primrose would annoy Lila at times, she was certain of that. They'd insist on showing up at her apartment whenever they liked. They'd give her opinions she didn't ask for. They would probably do a million things to make her mad and upset. They might even hurt her.

It would be harder . . . but they would be happier.

"I'll call Mama today and tell her we want to buy the place," Lila said.

"I knew you would understand!" Bea beamed. She threw her arms around Lila before running to the door and calling into the hall, "She said we could stay!"

Then Jasper and Evelyn crowded into the apartment doorway. Jasper had brought cookies; Evelyn had brought the number of an interior decorator. There were more voices rising from the hallway—wasn't that Florence? And Mary Dixon and Edwin? And the Willoughby sisters? Wasn't that Susanna asking them to all calm down, please, and Zoe offering to get some champagne to celebrate? It was obvious they had planned this with Bea in advance, hoping Lila would say yes.

Lila closed her eyes for the last moment of peace she would have that day. Her heart lifted at the voices around her, already arguing and grumbling and driving her crazy. In the end, it turned out she didn't want to be alone. She wanted to be brave and take her chances on a real home, here with Bea, at the Primrose.

Acknowledgments

This is my first adult book, and to say I was nervous and intimidated to move into a new market is an understatement. I am fortunate to have so many people who encouraged my writing and supported me along this most recent publishing journey.

First, thank you to my amazing editor, Rachel Kahan. I still can't believe I am lucky enough to work with you. I am grateful for your insightful editing, unflagging enthusiasm, and reassuring expertise. And an enormous thank-you to everyone else at William Morrow, including Liate Stehlik, David Palmer, Hope Ellis, Alexandra Bessette, and Marie Rossi. I am so appreciative of your hard work and dedication to this book.

Thank you to my dear agent, Katie Grimm. Your absolute faith in my ability to write an adult book was the encouragement I needed to keep going. You have a way of pushing me to dig deeper while still applauding my efforts. Working with you is easily one of my best decisions; you're an exceptional champion and a cherished friend.

Thank you to everyone at Curtis Brown, particularly Karin Schulze and the foreign rights team. I'm grateful to have you in my corner.

Thank you to my readers. I appreciate every one of you. Your support means the world to me.

I am thankful for the friends who have cheered me on, especially my beloved Besties and my treasured Richmond crew who turned my adopted city into a true home and the inspiration for this book. I have an incredible extended family and could not ask for a more loving support system of in-laws, brothers-in-law, sisters-in-law, uncle, nieces, and nephews. Thank you to Grandma, my best bookseller and one of my favorite people on Earth. And thank you to Dad for instilling a love of mystery books in me and for being proud of anything I do.

Thank you to my sister, Sarah. You gave me the greatest pep talk over breakfast in NYC when I sorely needed it. You are my first reader, my best friend, my valued confidante. I don't think I could get through writing or life without you.

I am privileged to have the most wonderful sons in the world (this is a fact). I am genuinely delighted by all four of you, and I'm always happiest when we're together. You make me laugh and you make me proud. I love you, Gray, Colter, Bo, and West.

Finally, thank you to my husband, Roby. This book is dedicated to you because without you, it simply would not exist. There were many times over the past few years when I questioned myself and my writing. You insisted I keep going, you never wavered. You give me confidence and optimism and hope (and you really make me laugh). I love you beyond all measure.

About the Author

STACY HACKNEY lives in Richmond, Virginia, with her husband and four sons. She graduated from Wake Forest University and University of Virginia School of Law—after her legal briefs started bordering on a little too dramatic, she started writing fiction and never stopped. *The Primrose Murder Society* is her first book for adults.